# "The Sea Magician"
# and
# "The Living-Fire Menace"

## TWO CLASSIC ADVENTURES OF
# DOC SAVAGE

### by Lester Dent and
### Harold A. Davis writing as Kenneth Robeson

with new historical essays by Will Murray

Published by Sanctum Productions for
## NOSTALGIA VENTURES, INC.
P.O. Box 231183; Encinitas, CA 92023-1183

Copyright © 1934, 1937 by Street & Smith Publications, Inc. Copyright © renewed 1961, 1965 by The Condé Nast Publications, Inc. All rights reserved.

This edition copyright © 2007 by Sanctum Productions/Nostalgia Ventures, Inc.

Doc Savage copyright © 2007 Advance Magazine Publishers Inc./The Condé Nast Publications. "Doc Savage" is a registered trademark of Advance Magazine Publishers Inc. d/b/a The Condé Nast Publications.

"Intermission," "His Name was Savage" and Lester Dent photo © 2007 by Will Murray.

This Nostalgia Ventures edition is an unabridged republication of the text and illustrations of two stories from *Doc Savage Magazine,* as originally published by Street & Smith Publications, Inc., N.Y.: *The Sea Magician* from the November 1934 issue, and *The Living-Fire Menace* from the January 1938 issue. These two novels are works of their time. Consequently, the text is reprinted intact in its original historical form, including occasional out-of-date ethnic and cultural stereotyping. Typographical errors have been tacitly corrected in this edition.

ISBN 1-932806-75-X    13 DIGIT 978-1-932806-75-5

First printing: July 2007

Series editor: Anthony Tollin
P.O. Box 761474
San Antonio, TX 78245-1474
sanctumotr@earthlink.net

Contributing editor: Will Murray

Copy editor: Joseph Wrzos

Proofreader: Carl Gafford

Cover restoration: Michael Piper

The editor gratefully acknowledges the contributions of Tom Stephens, Scott Cranford and Kirk Kimball in the preparation of this volume, and William T. Stolz of the Western Historical Manuscript Collection of the University of Missouri at Columbia for research assistance with the Lester Dent Collection.

Nostalgia Ventures, Inc.
P.O. Box 231183; Encinitas, CA 92023-1183

Visit Doc Savage at www.nostalgiatown.com & www.shadowsanctum.com

## Thrilling Tales and Features

**THE SEA MAGICIAN by Lester Dent
(writing as "Kenneth Robeson")** ............... 4

**INTERMISSION** ............... 66

**THE LIVING-FIRE MENACE by Harold A. Davis and
Lester Dent (writing as "Kenneth Robeson")** ........ 68

**HAROLD DAVIS, PULP INVENTOR** ............... 121

**HIS NAME WAS SAVAGE by Will Murray** ............... 122

**THE MEN BEHIND DOC SAVAGE** ............... 128

**Cover art by Emery Clarke and Walter Baumhofer
Interior illustrations by Paul Orban**

*King John's ghost walked abroad in England and embroiled Doc Savage and his men with*

# THE SEA MAGICIAN

## A Complete Book-length Novel

### By KENNETH ROBESON

### Chapter I
### THE KILLING SPOOK

THE item which really got Doc Savage embroiled in the fantastic affair was one which came out in a London afternoon newspaper.

KING'S SPOOK KILLS

The good farmers in The Wash marshlands of Holland county are saying today that King John's ghost took another victim last night in the person of Joseph Shires, the peasant farmer who staggered into his home, mortally wounded.

Joseph Shires is reported to have gasped out that King John's ghost stabbed him; then he died.

The thing now puzzling the local police is that wounds in the dead man's body do look as if they had been made by an ancient broadsword such as King John, English ruler who reigned in the thirteenth century, might have carried.

Another puzzling thing is the tradepiece, or coin, dated 1216, which was found in Joseph Shires' pocket after he died. King John reigned in 1216.

Moreover, it is rumored that numerous persons in the vicinity of The Wash have recently seen a King John apparition—a towering ogre in armor, carrying a broadsword. King John is even said to have spoken to some, proclaiming his identity.

All in all, though, the police are inclined to believe the ghost stories are on a par with the sea serpent tales given such wide publicity some months ago. They are questioning Joseph Shires' neighbors, seeking to ascertain if one did not commit the crime with some farm implement, perhaps a scythe.

It was probable that quite a number of persons

read this article, but it created no great stir among most of those who perused it, for the bit was relegated to an inside page, since Joseph Shires was not an individual who had ranked highly.

William Harper Littlejohn was one exception. He first read the story casually, then went over it again with greatly accelerated interest.

WILLIAM HARPER LITTLEJOHN was a very tall man, and he was also thinner than it seemed any human being could be and still live. His intimates frequently described him as looking like the advance agent for a famine.

When William Harper Littlejohn stood before gatherings of geologists and archaeologists, no one smiled at the fact that he resembled an empty suit of clothes standing erect, nor commented on the monocle with which he always fumbled but never stuffed in an eye. William Harper Littlejohn was conceded to know more about archaeology and geology than almost any living man.

The item about the royal spook that killed caught William Harper Littlejohn's eye because he was hunting excitement. He had been lecturing for some weeks before the Fellowhood of Scientists, and he was getting tired of it.

One would never suspect it by looking at him, but William Harper Littlejohn's big love in life was excitement. He was happiest when in trouble.

That was why he was one of Doc Savage's group of five aides. Trouble was Doc Savage's business—other person's troubles. For Doc Savage was that amazing man of bronze, that combination of scientific genius and physical daring, who made a business of helping others out of serious trouble.

"Johnny"—he was called that by Doc Savage and his group of assistants—laid aside the newspaper which contained the spook story. He fished two radiograms from a pocket. The first was dated four days previously and read:

ARRIVING IN LONDON IN FIVE DAYS
DOC SAVAGE

The second radiogram, dated only a few hours later than the first, was evidently in answer to a message of inquiry which Johnny had dispatched, and read:

SORRY BUT WE HAVE NO ACTION TO PROMISE STOP AM COMING ONLY TO FILL SHORT LECTURE ENGAGEMENT BEFORE FELLOWHOOD OF SCIENTISTS
DOC

Johnny sighed gloomily. That second message had been a great disappointment, for he had held visions of Doc Savage coming to England for the purpose of helping someone who was in trouble. This would have been sure to mean plenty of action.

JOHNNY looked at the newspaper again and reached an abrupt decision. Doc Savage was not due in London until the following day; he would reach Southampton that night by liner. There was time, before his arrival, for a short trip up to The Wash to investigate this story of a kingly spook who slew with a broadsword. Johnny reached for the telephone.

"Connect me with the nearest aëronautical depot," he requested; then, having secured his connection, he stated, "Would it be feasible to charter an aërial conveyance for an immediate peregrination?"

"For a *what?*" the voice wanted to know.

"For an immediate noctambulation to the neighborhood of The Wash," said Johnny.

Johnny never used a small word when he had time to think of a big one. He was a walking dictionary of words of more than three syllables, and when he was really going good, an ordinary man could not even understand him.

"I'm not sure what you want, gov'nor," the voice at the airport told him. "But if you've got the money to pay for it, you can get it here "

"Expect me shortly," Johnny advised.

Hardly more than two hours later, his chartered plane deposited Johnny close to the village of Swineshead, which was on the edge of that great stretch of marshland surrounding the curious tidal bay known as The Wash. Johnny paid off his pilot and watched the plane take the air on its return trip to London. Johnny intended to charter another plane the next day, or motor back to the metropolis.

Despite the lateness of the hour, Johnny found that Swineshead pubs were still open, catering to various local citizens, not a few of whom were sufficiently inebriated to talk freely.

Johnny underwent a curious change. In engaging the plane and during the flight, he had scarcely spoken a sentence containing words small enough for the pilot to understand. But now he cocked his hat over an eye, tucked his monocle-magnifier where it would not be noticed, and began speaking a brand of English which would have shocked his learned colleagues of the Fellowhood of Scientists. Furthermore, his manner was certainly not that of an intellectual giant.

He asked questions about John Shires, whom King John's ghost was supposed to have stabbed to death with a broadsword. He learned several things.

For instance, the citizens of Swineshead—those abroad at this unearthly hour, at least—were fully convinced King John was really a spectral reality. Two men insisted absolutely that they had seen him.

"Hi talked to the bloomin' king not a fortnight ago!" asserted one man; then he paused to quaff the ale which Johnny thoughtfully provided. "'Twas while Hi was 'untin' 'ares in the rushes near the shore o' The Wash. King John walked right up an' gabbed to me, 'e did."

JOHNNY studied his informant, wondering just how intoxicated the fellow was; the speaker was pleasantly flushed, but certainly not entirely inebriated.

"How did you know he was King John's ghost?" Johnny asked quite seriously.

"'E told me so," said the other.

"Told you?"

"'E did, an' that's the truth, gov'nor. I'd 'av known it anyway, on account of the way 'e was dressed. 'Ad on a coat of mall, 'e did, and carried a bloomin' broadsword. It was King John, all right. I've seen 'is pictures in the school books."

Johnny paid for more ale. "What was this talk about?"

"Mostly about whether King John's ghost was to kill me or not," said the informant.

"Kill you?"

"'E claimed as 'ow I was the bloke who give 'im poison seven hundred years ago. 'E said 'e was 'untin' that bloke. Said 'e'd been 'untin' seven 'undred years, and that 'e'd finally find the bloke who poisoned 'im, an when that 'appened, 'e'd run the lad through with 'is broadsword."

"Very interesting," said Johnny.

"King John's ghost said as 'ow 'e killed people 'e met in 'is nightly wanderings, just on the chance 'e'd get the bloke who done the poisoning," the other went on. "Said 'e wasn't quite sure who did poison 'im, and that's why 'e did so much killin'."

"I see," said Johnny. "Was there anything else?"

"Only that Hi'd better stay away from The Wash," the other man muttered. "King John's ghost said as 'ow 'e might kill me next time we met. Said 'e was liable to kill anybody 'e met. I think that's 'ow poor Joseph Shires got 'is."

"Is this ghost usually seen in the same vicinity?" Johnny questioned.

"Mostly, yes, gov'nor," declared the other. "'E 'angs out near the mouth of the Wellstream."

Johnny retired to the quiet of the village street to consider what he had learned. King John, so history said, had been poisoned in this vicinity, and as a result of which, had died. King John had been a violent and intemperate ruler, Johnny recalled having read. It was King John who had signed the Magna Charta which formed the charter of English liberties and the inspiration of the "personal rights" portion of the United States constitution.

King John had a very violent temper, history said, and after being forced to sign the Magna Charta, had rolled on the floor, bit the oak legs of a table, and butted his head against a stone wall. Then he had raised an army and gone out to rob the barons who had forced him to sign. It was on this foray that he had died, either from overeating peaches and drinking new cider—or from poisoning.

Johnny fumbled out his monocle and twirled it idly, a habit he had when puzzled. He did not believe in ghosts abroad with armor and broadswords, but at the same time, the story of the apparition was a bit too prevalent to be dismissed.

"I'll be superamalgamated!" he murmured. "I think I shall investigate more comprehensively."

THE night was not much further along when Johnny turned up alone in the region of the junction of the river Wellstream and The Wash. Since it was night and the region one without population, the eminent archaeologist shed shoes, socks and trousers and moved about clad only in underwear shorts, vest, coat and shirt. His bony shanks presented a grotesque appearance.

Frequent stretches of water and bog holes made the dishabille necessary. There were also patches of quicksand, very treacherous, which could best be detected with bare feet.

At first, Johnny attempted to reach the beach and follow that, but he surrendered this idea upon discovering that there was actually no beach, but only salt water grass and mud flats. It was a grim and dreary region which presented an aspect similar to nothing so much as a storm-swept wheat field of vast expanse, spotted here and there with pools and stretches of slime.

He had been prowling the vicinity for perhaps an hour when he had a narrow escape. The tide came in. It was not like the advance of ordinary tide, this one, but it came in swiftly, rolling over the salt marsh a good deal faster than it was possible for a man to run. Johnny was soaked to the belt line before he reached higher ground.

He stood on a knoll, among gnarled bushes, and eyed the marshes surrounding The Wash with new respect. The moon was out, and the tidal waters creeping through the marsh grass caused the latter to undulate as if it were fur on the back of some fabulous monster.

Johnny jumped a full foot in the air when a hollowly ominous voice spoke behind him.

"Turnest thou around, that thine face may be seen!" commanded the sepulchral tones.

Johnny whirled, his first inclination being to laugh. The words were so foreign to the English of the present day that they were comical. But the bony geologist forgot to be mirthful as he looked at the figure before him.

## Chapter II
## KING JOHN'S CAPTIVE

THE individual who had spoken might have stepped from the pages of some historical tome, for his garb was that of a fighting man of the Thirteenth century. Chain mail of fine workmanship shod him from head to foot, and over that was worn a short gown affair of white silk which was gathered in by a belt that supported a dagger and a short sword, both in scabbards.

The features of the apparitional being were concealed behind a fierce bush of black beard. The eyes were dark, piercing, the nose a hooked beak.

Tilted back over a shoulder, rifle fashion, the figure carried one of the biggest broadswords Johnny had ever seen in a museum or outside of one.

"For the love of mud!" Johnny gulped, forgetting his big words for once.

"Ah," breathed the apparition. "Me thinks thou art the rascal who touched my wine goblet with poison."

The absurdity of the picture the other presented again seized Johnny, who was an extremely modern gentleman who did not believe in ghosts in any form. He burst into a snort of laughter.

"Listen, my friend," he chuckled. "Why the masquerading in that rig?"

The ghostly figure advanced two paces, the chain mail clinking and grinding softly, the moonlight shimmering on the metallic links.

"Fool, dost thou not know to whom thou speakest?" demanded the cavernous voice.

"To King John, I suppose," Johnny said dryly.

Then Johnny's facetiousness suddenly evaporated, for he caught sight of brownish stains upon the broadsword which certainly looked like remnants of dried blood.

"Down to thy knees!" rumbled the figure. "Dost thou not know how to come before royalty?"

Johnny stood his ground warily. He was now convinced that he faced a madman, some poor fellow who had gone insane and imagined himself to be the long-dead English ruler. The fellow was probably violent, and there was no telling what he would do.

"What are you doing here, King John?" Johnny queried.

"Somewhere in these fens dwells the person who didst cause me to die," boomed the one in mail. "I hunt him. Methinks thou art he."

Johnny was carrying his shoes, socks and trousers under an arm. They made a compact bundle which he shifted uncertainly.

"I thought you found the poisoner last night," he said.

"What meanest thou?"

"Didn't you chop a fellow up with that broadsword last night?" Johnny elaborated. "He was a farmer named Joseph Shires."

The black-bearded head shook slowly. "King John dost not trouble to remember the events which art in the past."

A hopeless lunatic, Johnny decided firmly. If the fellow was permitted to continue running loose, no telling how many persons he would slay or injure. It would be a service to the English countryside if he were seized and confined in an institution where he belonged.

Johnny knew insane persons could often be persuaded to do things, if one sympathized with them.

"I am not the man who poisoned you," he told the other solemnly. "But I know where he can be found, perhaps."

"Whence?" questioned the figure.

"In the village of Swineshead," Johnny said promptly. "Come with me and I will show you the way."

If Johnny could get the individual who claimed to be King John to the village, he could be seized easily. He could be seized here, too, if care was used, but there might be difficulty in getting him out of the marsh. If he could be persuaded to come out under his own power, so much the better.

But King John's ghost balked. "Nay, vassal. I knowest the one who poisoned me can be found here. I think *thou* art he!"

Lunging suddenly, the mailed figure slashed furiously at Johnny's head with his broadsword.

JOHNNY ducked. Simultaneously, he hurled the bundle composed of his shoes, socks and trousers. The lump of clothing hit the other in the face just as the broadsword missed Johnny's head.

The bony geologist leaped forward, feet-first. He landed squarely on the other's midriff. Air tore through the black beard with a swishing moan and the fellow went over backward.

Johnny pounced on the wide handle of the broadsword. It was intended for two-fisted operation anyway, and there was room enough for him to get a grip. He wrenched and wrestled, got the weapon, then threw it away.

A mailed fist bounced off Johnny's head, leaving a ringing and colored lights behind in his skull. He pumped two blows at his foe, but only barked his knuckles on the chain mail armor.

The fight was, Johnny perceived, going to be tough. The other was a big man, and strong; moreover, the fellow was encased in the protective linkage of metal.

Seizing his foe's arms, Johnny tried to hold the fellow. The other snapped like a dog at his throat.

Johnny retaliated by sticking a thumb in one of his opponent's eyes. They went over and over in the reeds and soft mud.

William Harper Littlejohn's eminent associates in the Fellowhood of Scientists would have been surprised to see him now, for the famous geologist and archaeologist was showing a knowledge of gutter fighting methods which would have been envied by the most brutal London dockwalloper. At that, he was barely holding his own.

The pseudo King John had lost the use of one eye temporarily, thanks to Johnny's probing thumb. But Johnny's lips were split, he had lost his coat, and his shirt hung to his person only by the sleeves.

Johnny managed to jam both hands inside the facial opening of the armor hood and got hold of his foe's throat. He squeezed; at the same time, he wrapped his bony legs around the other's torso, pinioning his arms.

King John began making squawking sounds. His dark face purpled. Foam shot past his teeth and his tongue came out. Finally his struggle weakened.

Johnny ceased his choking before the other was seriously damaged, and utilized stripes of his own torn garments for binding. Yanking the knots tight, he started to stand erect—and a firecracker seemed to go off in the back of his head.

He saw the black muck of the marsh rush up at his face; he seemed to plunge far down into the earth where it was infinitely black and silent, and to remain there for a long time.

WHEN Johnny came up out of the earth and opened his eyes, the pseudo King John was standing at his side, leaning on the broadsword.

"What—what happened?" Johnny gulped vaguely.

"Mine faithful horse came to mine rescue," rumbled the other. "Yea. With his hoofs, mine animal subdued thee."

"Hell," growled Johnny, and felt of the back of his head.

There was a knob on the rear of his cranium, and it did feel as if a horse had kicked him. But Johnny knew no horse could have approached without being seen or heard. A horse could not travel over this marshy ground, anyway, because quicksands were too plentiful.

Johnny sat up. He was promptly knocked back with a forcible blow from the flat of the heavy broadsword, but before that happened, he saw that there was no one else around them. The marsh was as empty of life as if no one dwelled within hundreds of miles.

The figure in chain mail was rubbing his throat where Johnny's fingers had tightened, this indicating the fight must not have occurred long ago. The moon had not changed its position perceptibly, so Johnny concluded he had not been unconscious for long.

Throat massaged to his satisfaction, Johnny's captor fumbled inside his white-silk doublet and produced a flint and tinder device for starting a fire. This surprised Johnny. He stared at the apparatus. Then he whistled softly in astonishment.

The fire-making mechanism was undoubtedly ancient, an historical piece. It was deeply pitted, as if it had lain in the weather for a long time, but was still serviceable. It struck sparks, the tinder ignited, and the flame was applied to a tallow candle which the ghostly figure also brought from under the white doublet. The figure bent over a pile of papers lying on the soft marsh muck.

Johnny, staring, perceived that the contents of his own pockets were being inspected. Among these was a weapon which resembled an overgrown automatic pistol, but which was in reality a machine pistol capable of firing shots with extreme rapidity.

The weapon was an invention of Doc Savage, and Doc's men all carried them, although they used them only on occasions of extreme necessity. Doc Savage and his five aides made it a practice never to take human life directly. They never killed an enemy, even when their lives were in the greatest danger.

The pseudo King John seemed unfamiliar with firearms, and fumbled the weapon in a manner which caused Johnny's thin hair to stand erect.

"Turn that thing the other way!" Johnny snapped. "You'll shoot somebody!"

The other seemed not to hear, but put the machine pistol down and picked up the papers.

"Verily, it is a strange writing which men use these days," he remarked.

Among the papers was the cablegram which Johnny had received from Doc Savage, advising of Doc's arrival in London. Its text was such to indicate that Johnny was one of Doc's five aides.

The weird individual who claimed to be King John seemed greatly interested in the cablegram. He scowled blackly at Johnny.

"Are you one of Doc Savage's men?" he growled.

JOHNNY did his best to keep from starting—for the other had spoken without using the weird English of other centuries.

"What difference does it make?" Johnny demanded.

"Are you?" the other snarled.

"Yes," said Johnny.

The figure in armor swore explosively, and they were violent Twentieth century oaths.

"Did Doc Savage send you up here?" he questioned harshly.

"No," Johnny denied.

"I think that's a damn lie, bloke!" snarled the other.

Johnny squirmed about, realizing fully for the first time that his arms and legs were loosely but effectively bound with stout cotton cords. He could move, but not enough to put up a fight.

"You seem to have abandoned your antiquated mannerisms of speech, King John," he suggested.

The other only glared.

Johnny, studying the man, abruptly decided the fellow was not insane after all, and that meant the individual had been playing the King John role for a deliberate purpose.

"What is the game?" Johnny asked sharply.

"Bloke, it'll be a long time before you know!" the other snarled.

He lunged over suddenly and struck Johnny with his broadsword. He used the flat of the blade, but the blow was heavy and sufficient to introduce Johnny to quick unconsciousness.

"Doc Savage must have sent you up here!" the pseudo King John told Johnny's insensible form. "And that'll bear lookin' into."

## Chapter III
### THE PRIVATE DETECTIVE

SOUTHAMPTON is one of the major ports for express passenger traffic across the Atlantic, and, as such, had seen the arrival and departure of more than one notable.

The chief London and Paris newspapers had ship reporters regularly assigned to the port, and it was a rare occasion when a personage arrived who was so important that the battery of regular journalists was amplified by the arrival of additional special writers.

But tonight, some of the leading newspapermen of England and the Continent were on hand as snorting tugs pushed a certain transatlantic liner into her berth. The journalists were augmented by a battery of cameramen and quite a number of curious citizens.

The mayor was down in his robes of office, and numerous Englishmen of high rank were present in full regalia. Had a foreign potentate been arriving, the reception would hardly have been more elaborate.

It was all in honor of Doc Savage, the man of mystery, the individual who was a symbol of scientific knowledge and physical daring, the man who was by way of being the supreme adventurer of all time.

The newspapermen were down there because Doc Savage never did things in the ordinary fashion. Almost any move he made was good for a headline. Furthermore, it was a fact that Doc Savage did not look with a permissive eye on newspaper publicity. He was that rare individual, a celebrity who did not care about seeing his name and picture in the newspaper. More particularly, he did not care about seeing his picture, because it gave his enemies a means of familiarizing themselves with his physical appearance.

The reluctance which Doc Savage displayed toward newspaper publicity had the effect of making the journalists more determined. Had Doc Savage hired a publicity agent and showed a desire for news space, the scribes would have ignored him to a degree; as it was, they fell over themselves to get a story about him.

The high-ranking Englishmen were present because Doc Savage had done great service for their country in the past. For instance, there were delicate procedures in surgery which the unusual man of mystery had instituted and which had saved numerous lives. Too, there were charities to which Doc Savage had contributed enormous sums of money—money which, incidentally, he had taken from villainous individuals who had no right to it.

Doc Savage had cabled specifically that there was to be no reception in his honor; but the Englishmen had ignored that. They stood at the gangplank with the journalists and scrutinized each passenger to alight, in search of their remarkable visitor.

Roustabouts unloaded baggage at the cargo

gangway, sweating and swearing. Several of these noted a tall figure which strode past them and went ashore.

The individual wore a turban and a flowing robe. His face was almost hidden by a ruffle of the robe, but that portion of it which showed to view was a nut-brown color.

The roustabouts, thinking the one who had disembarked was an oriental, of which several were aboard the liner, paid no great attention, especially after they saw the individual in the turban show the proper papers to an officer on the dock. They did note that officer bowed with marked deference after he had seen the name on the papers.

Observers would have been surprised had they seen the strange personage after he entered an unused shed on the shore end of the dock.

Indeed, one person was watching as the individual in the turban entered the shack, but this watcher kept out of sight behind a huge wooden bitt on the dock, being very careful not to show himself.

AS soon as he was concealed inside the shed, the man who had just come ashore removed the turban. A few strokes erased brown grease paint from his features. He had been walking with a stoop, but as he whipped off the white robe, he straightened.

The erstwhile wearer of oriental garb, when he left the shack, was a striking personality. He seemed enormously larger than he had before, but it was only by comparing his size to the proportions of the shack that his true Herculean build was evident.

The man's complexion was a metallic bronze, a hue that could only have come from exposure to a good many tropical suns. His hands and neck were notable for the unearthly size of the tendons and muscles which stood out under the bronze skin at each movement.

Most striking of all, however, were the eyes which caught stray light rays from a nearby street lamp. They were weird eyes, like pools of flake-gold which were being stirred continuously. There was a strange quality in them, a power to compel. They were hypnotic eyes.

The bronze man's features were regular, firm, and possessed an aspect of undeniable handsomeness. He swung along the gloomy street with a silent, athletic ease.

So outstanding was his appearance that a cab driver, glimpsing him by chance, stopped short and stared, mouth agape.

"Blimme!" breathed the hackman. "Wouldn't *that* bloke be a tough one in a fight!"

It was many hours before that hack driver ceased to see, in his mental eye, the astounding bronze man whom he had merely glimpsed.

The driver was so awestruck that he failed to note a furtive individual who passed him in the nearby gloom. This man was the one who had been watching from behind the dock bitt, and he was trailing the giant of bronze. He did his shadowing furtively, showing experience at the art, and he seemed confident that the bronze man had not observed him.

The bronze man seemed in no hurry, nor did he give evidence of having a definite destination. He walked to the north, then swung west, and came finally to a corner. He loitered there for a time, apparently waiting for someone. His hands rested behind him, as if to support his weight, as he lounged against the corner.

The man who was shadowing the bronze individual was not close enough to note that the bronze man was doing something with one of his hands—he was apparently writing on the glass of the show window against which he leaned.

After a while, the bronze man walked on, moving slowly, heading into streets which were dark and filled with smells none too appetizing.

The shadow fell in behind.

SLIGHTLY less than five minutes later, two men approached the corner where the bronze giant had loitered and written on the glass show window. These two newcomers carried bags, and came from the direction of the dock where the transatlantic liner had tied up.

The pair were quarreling. They seemed on the point of flying at each other's throats.

"You awful mistake of nature!" gritted the one who was slender and extremely dapper of dress, and who carried a thin, black cane. "I'm ashamed to be seen with you, and especially with that filthy hog you're leading!"

"A horse collar for you, you overdressed shyster!" growled the other.

The latter's head came scarcely to the shoulders of his companion, who was not tall. But the man lacked very little of being as wide as he was tall. His arms were some inches longer than his stubby, bowed legs, and hands and wrists were rusty monstrosities from which grew hairs as thick as small shingle nails.

The man had an incredibly homely face, garnished with a mouth so huge that it seemed his maker had had an accident. He could easily be mistaken for a gorilla on the gloomy street.

"Go on, take a taxi to your hotel," snapped the man with the black cane. "Otherwise, some of these bobbies are likely to throw you in the local zoo, you missing link!"

The homely one said with a small, almost childlike voice, "If you think I like going around with an overdressed snob, you're nuts, you pain in the neck!"

At the apish man's heels trailed a pig. The pig was a remarkable specimen of the porker family, obviously a runt who would never grow beyond his present size—that of a small dog. The pig had long, thin legs, a gaunt body, and ears so huge that they looked as if they might serve for wings in an emergency.

The dapperly dressed man glared at the pig and wrenched at his black cane, which came apart near the handle, disclosing that it was a sword cane with a blade of fine steel.

"I'm certainly going to turn that hog into breakfast bacon one of these days, Monk!" he promised fiercely.

"Any time you're ready, Ham," growled the apish "Monk."

They came within sight of the corner where the bronze man had loitered. They stopped, seeming surprised.

"Doc ain't there!" grunted the gorillalike Monk.

"Hm-m-m," said "Ham," and absently sheathed his sword cane. "I wonder what happened? Doc said he would meet us there after he gave those newspaper men the slip."

They advanced, looked the vicinity over, and found no trace of the individual whom they sought.

"Maybe Doc left a message," Monk said, small-voiced.

The hairy fellow opened one of the leather bags and withdrew what at first might have been mistaken for a folding camera. He touched a switch on the side of this and pointed the round lens at the corner. The lens, instead of being clear glass, was purple, almost black.

Eventually, the homely man passed his queer device over the glass window. A strange thing happened. Written words sprang out where none had been before. They glowed in an eerie, electric blue.

MONK AND HAM: A MAN IS FOLLOWING ME. I AM CONTINUING ALONG THIS STREET. FOLLOW AND GRAB THE FELLOW.
DOC

Monk switched off the cameralike device without comment. Both he and Ham had received such messages from Doc Savage on other occasions, and knew that Doc had written the missive with a chemical chalk which was normally invisible, even with a moderately strong microscope, but which fluoresced, or glowed, when exposed to the ultra-violet light exuded by the lantern device which resembled a folding camera, or possibly a small magic lantern.

It was by this method that Doc Savage habitually left messages for his associates—and Monk and Ham were two members of Doc's group of five unusual aides.

Monk—Lieutenant Colonel Andrew Blodgett Mayfair—despite his low forehead and apish appearance, was one of the most learned industrial chemists alive. Ham—Brigadier General Theodore Marley Brooks—the dapper dresser was a lawyer whose oratorical powers had swayed many a jury, and whose keen legal mind was capable of grasping the most intricate problem of law.

The two sought the shadows and glided up the street. They were working in harmony now, their late quarrel temporarily elapsed. As a matter of fact, they were the best of friends, although acquaintances could not recall having heard one speak a civil word to the other.

The homely pig—Monk had long ago named him Habeas Corpus to aggravate Ham—followed them silently at a word from Monk. The pig was well trained. Monk spent all his spare time—rather, that which was not expended in goading Ham—in training Habeas.

A FEW minutes after Monk and Ham merged themselves with the shadows of the Southampton Street, there was a sudden outburst of peculiar sounds. These came from a point some distance up the murky thoroughfare.

The sounds were such as might be made by two small dogs and a very big rat. The growling of the dogs was absent, but not so the noises of the rodent. Perhaps such burghers of Southampton as were aroused by the brief outburst did believe it to be made by prowling canines, and accordingly dismissed it, for no one came to investigate.

No one, that is, with the exception of Doc Savage. The giant of bronze was loitering along when he heard the small tumult. He promptly wheeled, retraced his steps and almost at once came upon Monk and Ham.

"Good work," said the bronze man, in a voice which was striking for its controlled power.

Monk and Ham had seized the individual who had been trailing Doc Savage. This man was a thin-faced fellow with the neck of a turkey and the round body of a stunted ostrich. There was an ostrich aspect about his eyes, as well, for they were large for his thin face. He was attired in dark clothing, and his black hat had fallen off in the scuffle as he was seized.

The pig, Habeas Corpus, was engaged in systematically pulling the hat to pieces.

Doc Savage produced a flashlight which got its current from a self-contained spring generator, gave it a wind, and then twisted the lens head so that the beam became very wide. Not only was the captive's scrawny face illuminated, but the bronze man's as well.

For several seconds, nothing was said or done. The remarkable bronze man merely studied the captive—and the latter stared at Doc, looking very uneasy, moistening his lips often. There was something grim and terrible about the bronze giant's features.

"Blimme!" the captive gulped. "I wasn't meaning no harm!"

"You were following me," Doc pointed out.

The other nodded. "Picked your trail up at the boat. I won't deny that."

The homely Monk put in, "Here's what he had in his pockets," and extended several articles in the palm of a hairy hand.

Doc turned the flashlight on the objects and saw cards bearing the inscription:

W. P. WALL-SAMUELS
PRIVATE INVESTIGATIONS

There was also a badge of the type issued to private detectives in England.

"That's right," the prisoner said earnestly. "I am W. P. Wall-Samuels, a private operative."

"Who hired you to trail me?" Doc questioned.

"No one," Wall-Samuels denied.

"Of course we will believe that!" the sword-cane carrying Ham clipped dryly.

"It's the truth," Wall-Samuels insisted. "I was following you on my own initiative. You see, I had a business proposition to put up to you. I had an idea you would avoid the newspapermen, so I watched the gangways where they were unloading baggage. Sure enough, I recognized you under your oriental disguise. I had seen your picture before."

Doc Savage asked, "What is your business proposition?"

"I hoped to persuade you to become my partner in a London detective agency," said Wall-Samuels. "With you as my partner, I could make a lot of money. You would not even have to do any of the work. Just lend your name to my firm, and take half the profits."

"Blazes!" snorted Monk. "The brass of this guy!"

Wall-Samuels looked injured. "Then you won't become my partner."

"No," Doc said.

"If you were Doc's partner, somebody would kill you within twenty-four hours," the homely Monk growled.

"I'll take that chance," said Wall-Samuels.

"No," Doc told him again.

Wall-Samuels scowled and snapped, "Then I'll thank you to let me go free!"

"Release him," Doc directed.

With reluctance, Monk and Ham took their hands off the person of the private detective, and the latter stood erect, glanced around, saw Habeas Corpus putting the final touches on the ruination of his hat, and fell to glaring.

"You owe me a new hat!" he grated.

"You'll get a swift kick where it'll do the most good, if you don't haul out of here," Monk promised.

Muttering under his breath, Wall-Samuels took a hasty departure.

WALL-SAMUELS walked in the middle of the sidewalk, making his footsteps heavy, until he rounded a corner and judged himself out of hearing of Doc Savage and his two companions. Then Wall-Samuels ducked into a doorway and waited for some minutes, eyeing the gloomy shadows along his back trail and listening. He became satisfied that he was not being followed.

Arising on tiptoe, Wall-Samuels began to run. He slackened his pace to a walk when he sighted a bobby, then ran again, keeping to the more gloomy side streets until at last he reached a corner which held a shop that was labeled, "Apothecary." In the United States, this establishment would have been called a drug store. It held telephone booths.

Wall-Samuels secured a number.

"Chief?" he asked.

"All right, what is it?" snapped an impatient voice. "Did you follow Doc Savage?"

"Not very far," Wall-Samuels admitted ruefully. "I picked up his trail when he left the liner by the cargo gangway which I was watching. But somehow he found out I was on his heels—or his two men, Monk and Ham, found it out. I don't know how they did it. But they grabbed me before I knew what was happening."

"You were warned to be very careful!" grated the other over the telephone wire.

"How in the bloody deuce was I to know this man Savage wasn't human?" Wall-Samuels snapped. "I was as careful as I could be."

"What happened?" queried the other impatiently.

"I fed Doc Savage and his two men a fast story," Wall-Samuels chuckled. "I always carry fake private detective credentials with me, and I told them I was a private sleuth who wanted to take Doc Savage on as a partner."

"Did you think they would swallow that silly yarn?" the distant man asked sarcastically.

"It was a good story," the false detective growled. "And they believed it."

"You sure?" asked the distant man.

"Positive!"

"All right—here is what you are to do," said the voice over the wire. "You are to go back and shadow Doc Savage again. Do it so that he will catch you once more. I don't think you will have any trouble with that part, after the flop you just made."

"Let him—catch me again!" Wall-Samuels wailed. "But I do not understand this."

"It has become necessary to get Doc Savage out of England," said the other. "When he catches you this second time, you are to tell him a story which will cause him to leave."

"But what can I tell him?" Wall-Samuels asked wildly.

"Tell him that William Harper Littlejohn, one of his men, sailed on a boat last night for South America," directed the other. "Tell him you are not sure what it is all about, except that William Harper Littlejohn was trailing somebody, and left a letter containing the particulars behind for Doc Savage."

"Tell Doc Savage you were hired by the man whom Littlejohn was trailing, and that you stole the letter and gave it to that man. Then tell Savage that you were hired to watch him and radio the man who hired you if Doc Savage made a move to go to South America."

"This is complicated," Wall-Samuels groaned.

"You are an expert liar," the distant speaker complimented. "You can put it over. The idea is to get Doc Savage to take a boat for South America, thinking he is following his helper, William Harper Littlejohn, or Johnny, as they call him."

"Where is Johnny?" the fake detective wanted to know.

"We have him," said the other. "The fool got to chasing King John's ghost up in The Wash region, and we had to seize him."

"This is bad," Wall-Samuels muttered.

"Do not fall down on this," growled the distant voice. "We have other troubles on our hands, too, I'm afraid."

"What do you mean?"

"Wehman Mills."

"What about him?"

"He has disappeared in Brest, France."

"What in the hell was he doing over there?" asked Wall-Samuels.

"He said he had to have certain machinery, and I sent him over with some of the men," replied the mastermind. "Now he's disappeared."

"Think he's wise to the set-up?"

"It looks as if he was. I have the men hunting for him."

"What about his niece? She's in Brest, isn't she?"

"Yes. But we'll take care of that end. You get Doc Savage out of England. We cannot have him hunting this Johnny."

"I'll do my best," promised Wall-Samuels.

Then he hung up, freed himself from the telephone booth and walked outside.

The instant he was through the door, two men stepped close to him from either side. It happened so swiftly that he did not even have time to try to escape. Muscular hands gripped his arms.

Wall-Samuels tried to assemble his shattered composure, and exploded, "What does this mean?"

His two captors were Monk and Ham.

## Chapter IV
## SOUTH AMERICA BOUND

"KEEP your shirt on, guy," Monk advised.

Wall-Samuels was walked forcibly toward the nearest corner. He dared not protest; the formidable expressions on the features of Monk and Ham promised violent handling if there was the slightest resistance. Around the corner, they halted.

"Doc will be here shortly," imparted Ham. The dapper lawyer had shoved his sword cane through his belt.

There was a brief wait, then Doc Savage approached. The bronze man seemed more Herculean than ever as he swung up out of the murk.

"What do you want with me?" Wall-Samuels demanded, trying to bristle. "I told you my story."

"You told us a string of lies," Monk informed him.

"I did not!"

"Then why did you run after you left us? And who did you just call?"

Wall-Samuels moistened his lips. "So you followed me?"

"Sure," said Monk. "What kind of saps did you think we were?"

The pretended detective neglected to reply to that; he was reflecting that if anyone had showed a lack of canniness, it was himself. These men, he was realizing, were considerably harder to deceive than he had thought.

Doc Savage inquired, "What about telling the truth, Wall-Samuels, or whatever your name is?"

Wall-Samuels swallowed rapidly. He looked scared. He tried to assume an appearance of even greater fright, which was unnecessary.

"Listen," he whined. "I can't talk. It'll get me into all kinds of trouble."

"Maybe you think you're at a tea social now?" Monk asked sourly. "Doc, how about me giving this guy a little osteopath treatment?"

Monk opened and closed his enormous furry hands, and Wall-Samuels stared at the hirsute digits as if they were ravenous animals. Then he peered at Doc's bronze-cabled hands, and his fright increased. He knew inhuman strength when he saw it, and was fully convinced either of these men could do him infinite damage.

"I was hired by a man who is being chased by William Harper Littlejohn," the man gulped, rolling his ostrich eyes.

"Hey!" Monk exploded. "What's Johnny got himself mixed in?"

Wall-Samuels told his false story slyly, letting a bit of it slip each time he was threatened. The whole fabrication came out as if it were being rendered by a man in mortal terror. Wall-Samuels, studying the faces of his three unusual captors, became convinced that the story was getting over.

The yarn was substantially the same one which the man on the telephone had outlined.

"Wait here," Doc Savage directed, at the end of the tale.

The bronze man departed with the silence of a metallic wraith, a silence which caused Wall-Samuels to shiver. He was becoming convinced that this giant of metal was not entirely human.

Early milk wagons and delivery trucks were beginning to rumble over the Southampton streets, and a few porters had started to work on show windows with sponges, wipers and suds buckets, cleaning up for the day which was soon to come.

DOC SAVAGE reappeared.

"A call to Johnny's London hotel discloses that he left last night," the bronze man imparted. "He has not come back."

"I told you he sailed for South America," Wall-Samuels stuttered.

"Pipe down!" Monk growled.

"Other calls reveal that a steamer did sail for South America last night," Doc continued.

"The vessel was fitted with ship-to-shore radio telephone, so it was a simple matter to establish communication."

Wall-Samuels began to tremble violently. He had not foreseen this contingency. He would have to try to make them believe that Johnny must have taken another ship.

"Was Johnny aboard the ship?" Ham questioned.

"His name is on the passenger list," Doc informed them. "But the authorities aboard the vessel were unable to locate him. A steward did report, however, that the bed in his stateroom had been slept in. The steward reported also that there were bloodstains on the bed clothing."

"Damn it!" Monk grated. "Something has happened to Johnny!"

Wall-Samuels tried not to look as relieved as he felt. At the same time, he experienced a rush of admiration for the chief of the sinister organization to which he belonged. Nothing had been overlooked; they must have put a man aboard the South American-bound vessel. The fellow was using the name of William Harper Littlejohn to mislead further Doc Savage.

"You can see," Wall-Samuels said happily, "that I have told you the truth."

"There any chance of our overhauling Johnny's ship?" Monk demanded.

"No," Doc advised. "But we can take passage on another craft which sails almost at once. It is a faster vessel, and arrives in Buenos Aires, South America, a day ahead of Johnny's ship."

"Then we'd better grab it," Monk grunted.

Wall-Samuels swallowed and asked, "What about me?"

"How about a nice English jail for him, Doc?" Monk questioned.

"That is as good a solution as any for the present," Doc decided.

HARDLY more than fifteen minutes after that, Wall-Samuels found himself behind bars, charged with nothing more serious than malicious mischief. He immediately demanded a lawyer—and got something of a shock. The lawyer was refused him. Furthermore, he was denied even the privilege of telephoning outside the jail.

The indignant pseudo detective failed to understand exactly what had happened. The charge against him was one which was ordinarily bailable, but he could not get bail without contacting someone to put it up for him, and he was being kept strictly incommunicado. This was not like the usual procedure of the police.

Wall-Samuels did not know that Doc Savage had once been tendered an honorary inspector's commission with Scotland Yard as an expression of gratitude for services rendered. A word from the bronze man had been sufficient to cause the fake detective to be held in the state which an American cop would have called "buried."

But Wall-Samuels had been in jails before, and he knew the ropes. There is scarcely a bastile existent where the inmates do not have secret methods of smuggling messages outside. Quite often this is done through the trusty who delivers the meals.

Wall-Samuels had an early breakfast, and, at his request, was served with milk. Fashioning a brush of a twist of cloth wrenched from the lining of his coat, he dipped into the milk and wrote on the bottom of the plate on which the breakfast was served. He was careful not to make too pronounced smears out of the milk.

The trusty was given the accepted signal; the cook, also a trusty, placed the plates on the stove, and when it became very hot, the milk stains came out in a readily decipherable brown.

Wall-Samuels had used one of the most primitive of invisible inks; but it had served its purpose, and before long, his message was relayed to the intended destination. It read:

Doc Savage on way to South America. Better check on him to see that he actually leaves. Savage clever. And get me out of this jail.
                                                WALL-SAMUELS.

In due course of time an answer came by the same obscure route.

Savage angle being taken care of. You will stay in jail and be paid for it. To release you might give a line on the organization.

The communication was unsigned—and Wall-Samuels, after swearing steadily for some minutes, carefully destroyed it. His position was not so bad. He could not imagine an easier way of earning money than reposing in jail—at least, no other method of earning the amount of money which he was being paid.

IN the meantime, Doc Savage and his two men arrived, amid a flurry of excitement, at the dock from which the South American bound boat was due to sail in a very few minutes. A small army of flunkies rushed their baggage aboard.

Doc and his men were ensconced in a suite. The bronze man retired at once to the radio room, where he attempted to get in touch with Johnny on the other South American boat. He was unsuccessful. The commander of the other boat transmitted that his stewards had been unable to find a trace of William Harper Littlejohn.

Mooring lines were cast off; the gangplanks hauled in, and a bevy of snorting and whistling tugs busied themselves at jockeying the liner out into the harbor.

It is the custom on passenger ships to put such visitors as are caught aboard at sailing time, off on the tugs or pilot boats. It now developed that there was one such individual who had failed to heed the warning gong that meant visitors down the gangplank.

This man was a fat fellow who kept his coat collar turned up so as not to show too much of his features, and he was put aboard a tug amid some mild excitement.

The South American liner nosed out into the Channel and set a course into the Atlantic.

The man who had been taken off on the tug showed extreme anxiety to reach shore, and the instant he set his foot on land, he sought a telephone and called a number.

"It worked," he reported. "Doc Savage and his two men are on the boat bound for South America."

"Excellent!" said the same gruff voice which had given Wall-Samuels his orders. "But something else has come up, and there is hell to pay."

"What?" gulped the informant.

"Old Wehman Mills," said the other.

"What about that old buzzard?"

"He's gotten away!"

The fat man swore in a low, uneasy voice. "How did it happen?"

"The old man said he had to get some machinery from France," replied the other. "In order to keep him from getting suspicious, we took him over. But he must have been wise. When we got him to Brest, he cut loose and skipped out."

The fat man swore again. "He'll try to see the girl," he said.

"Of course he will," said the voice over the wire. "And that has me worried."

"What are you going to do?"

"I'm going to Brest," said the distant mastermind. "I'll keep in the background there, but it's best for me to be on hand."

## Chapter V
### THE UNCLE IN INDIA

IT was a dark night in the French seaport town of Brest.

It was also dark inside the house, as dark as if there had never been light. A man stopped just inside the door and breathed with a rattling hoarseness which made it sound as if the lining of his throat had worked loose in flaps. His fingers dug at the cloth over his chest while he caught up with his breathing.

"Elaine!" he yelled shrilly.

In the infinitely thick blackness, a second and harsher voice said, "So here's where you headed for, Mills! You dumb old lug, you must have thought we were kidding when—"

"Do not tell him about it, monsieur," purred a third voice, calm, catlike, out of the sable interior. "Seize him! *Dépechez-vous!* Make haste!"

The sounds which followed might have been made by pieces of raw meat being thrown together in a pile, except that they were louder. Sliding feet made sharp hisses on the bare wooden floor, and twice men cursed because they had fallen down.

"Elaine!" cried the victim—and a bit later, he managed to get out the French cry for help, *"Au secours!"*

At least four men were striving to hold the victim and hit him at the same time. The victim had been fighting back and trying to escape; now he knew it was useless, so he devoted all efforts to getting a hand into the watch pocket of his trousers. The pocket was torn open; a small object fell out.

The victim caught the object, but instantly threw it away, over the heads of his assailants.

"Elaine!" he shrieked, to cover the sound as it fell somewhere down the hallway.

**Carrying their captive, the men moved away ... changed their course hastily to avoid a gendarme.**

Then a fist hit his jaw, causing his struggles to become aimless, so that he was easily seized and carried to the door which the fellow with the cat-like voice opened.

They all passed out into a night only slightly less dark than the hall interior. As they went down a cobbled street, it was evident that they all wore shoes with rubber soles, for they were very silent.

There was a slight breeze, salty, with a tang of petrol, from the warehouses on the commercial side of Brest, across the Cours d'Ajot. There were numerous harbor lights on the water, especially down where the castle with its donjon and seven towers commanded the entrance to the river.

Here, however, where things were happening, there were few lights, until one of the men darted a flashlight beam briefly at their victim. The light hunted over the half-conscious form like a small, hungry white animal.

The victim was a long linkage of bone and cartilage encased in a shiny black suit. He wore old-fashioned Congress gaiters, a wing collar of the type affected by United States senators of the last generation, and a black shoestring tie. His hair was white.

"Where is his *chapeau, m'sieu's?*" demanded the cat voice.

"His hat?" grunted a man. "I picked it up."

The hat, black and broad of brim, was shoved into the path of the flashlight. It was a picturesque headpiece.

"*Bon!*" said the feline voice. "Good! Take him on a short distance and wait for me."

"Where you going, Paquis?" asked the man with the hat.

"Back," said the other. "Back, to take care of a small detail."

THE house from which the victim had been taken was of stone, rambling and old, and it possessed the flattering designation, *l'auberge,* bestowed on it by the owner, who was also the proprietor. But it was more of a rooming house than an inn. An entirely respectable place, to be sure.

The house guests were awake. Some were up, others were getting up. The fray downstairs, just inside the street door, had been short for all of its violence, and no one in the house knew what it was all about.

They began venturing downstairs, one at a time, with the proprietor, a night-shirted gentleman notable for his skinny shanks and the size of his mustache, carrying the same *chau-chau* rifle which he had no doubt used in the Great War. The innkeeper's overweight wife brought an old-fashioned candle lantern, and they took note of the upset furniture and the scratches on the floor where straining shoes had slipped.

"It is very mysterious," said a guest in French. "I thought I heard a name yelled loudly. It was 'Elaine', or something like that."

The proprietor crooked his rifle with an arm, looked up the stairs and called through his mustache, "Mademoiselle Elaine Mills!"

"*Oui,*" replied a faint feminine voice. "*Que vou—vou—*" She gave it up and demanded in English, "What do you want?"

Her last words had the rolling freedom of American speech.

"Did someone mak' call to yo'?" asked the proprietor, struggling along in English.

Instead of answering, Elaine Mills appeared at the top of the stairs. Several male eyebrows shot skyward and the owners drew their stomachs in and shoved their chests out, at the same time putting very polite expressions on their faces, as men are wont to do in the presence of an entrancing member of the opposite sex.

And Elaine Mills was entrancing. She was tall, young, altogether luscious and feminine. Her hair was the color of sand, her eyes a dark blue which made them bright by contrast, and her lips were perfect. She had apparently dressed in a hurry, for she wore brown pumps, but no hose, and she was twisting her brown sports frock into its proper hang.

"What happened?" Elaine demanded, and came down the stairs.

Two Frenchmen bowed and tried to explain, but they did not speak English and the young woman, without smiling, said, "I am sorry, but I speak very little French. Who was it called my name? And what was the noise?"

Before she could get her answer, there was an interruption. A man reeled in from the street darkness. He was a tall man, with his hair down over his eyes his coat askew and a slack expression on his features. He brought with him the odor of strong cognac.

"Whoopee!" he yelled thickly. "I'm a ring-tailed wolf from Wyoming! Listen to me howl! *Ye-e-o-v-w!*"

He tried to wave an arm, lost his balance, teetered across the floor and tried to anchor himself to the proprietor; but that worthy stepped out of the way, and the newcomer slammed down on the floor. With much noisy difficulty with his feet, he heaved partially erect.

"Feels likesh shame floor I was on a whilesh ago," he mouthed. "Yesh shir! Shame floor!"

He endeavored to wave the arm again, and this time succeeded.

"Hurray!" he howled. "Hurray for France! Hurray for everybody!"

He made his "hurrays" sound very like "Elaines!"

"*Cochon!*" snarled the proprietor. "Pig! So it was *you* who caused all the uproar."

With that, the celebrant was seized and propelled into the street.

A FEW minutes later, the erstwhile inebriant joined his fellows, who were holding their prisoner down the street. The man had combed his hair, straightened his coat, and was smiling slyly.

"What'd you do, Paquis?" he was asked.

Paquis traded his sly smile for a chuckle. "You should have seen me work, *m'sieu's*. Not for nothing was I formerly an actor for a short time in the American Hollywood."

"What did you do?" the interrogator repeated.

"Made them think the noise of the fight as we seized Wehman Mills, here, was caused by the playfulness of a Yankee tourist celebrating," said Paquis.

Carrying their captive, the men moved away, one of their number, who seemed to know the streets of Brest, acting as guide. Once they changed their course hastily to avoid a gendarme, and again they swung wide to circle an omnibus station where there was light and activity.

Eventually they entered a neat dwelling, the windows of which were carefully curtained. Inside were several men, one or two apparently Americans, but the rest speaking with the more precise speech of the English. Only Paquis seemed to be French.

"We succeeded in stopping him, *mes enfants,*" chuckled Paquis, and ordered Wehman Mills dumped on the floor.

Wehman Mills was conscious now, and he got to his feet, trembling with anger. Mills had a high forehead and many wrinkles about the mouth. His eyes were the bright orbs of a dreamer. His age must have been well past sixty.

He glared at the men and his manner was not that of one looking at strangers.

"You cannot make a fool out of me!" he shouted.

"We would not try to improve the jolly job nature did," smiled one of the Englishmen. "And do not yell your bloody head off."

Old Wehman Mills moistened his lips. "What are you going to do about it?"

"Keep you under cover," said the other. "That is all we have to do. Everything else is running smoothly."

At this point a newcomer put in an appearance, coming in from the outer night. He greeted those present in a casual manner.

"I just came from the cable office," he said.

"Any word from the chief?" a man asked.

"Sure." The newcomer tossed a fold of paper on the table. "That."

Paquis and the others bent over the paper, which proved to be a cablegram in code, but the messenger had translated it already, writing the true text between the lines of typing. Address and signature had been torn off.

"I burned them," explained the messenger.

They all read the decoded missive:

ELAINE MILLS MAY GIVE TROUBLE IF SHE STARTS HUNTING FOR HER UNCLE WEHMAN MILLS STOP SUGGEST SHE BE LED TO THINK UNCLE WEHMAN HAS GONE TO INDIA STOP GOOD IDEA IF SHE COULD BE LED TO TAKE TRIP TO INDIA HERSELF STOP SPARE NO EXPENSE ON THIS

The suave Paquis teetered back on his heels and his catlike voice held much elation as he said, *"M'sieu's,* depend on Paquis!"

"Yeah?" growled one of the Yankees.

*"Que c'est beau!"* smirked Paquis. "How beautiful, this idea of mine!"

ELAINE MILLS had retired to her room in the *auberge,* as had the rest of the guests; but whereas the others had gone to sleep again, Elaine had not disrobed. She had even added sheer hose to her attire, as if she did not expect to sleep.

In Elaine Mills' slender, shapely hands was a sheaf of papers, through which she riffled repeatedly. The topmost was from the French equivalent of a private detective agency, and stated:

REGRET TO INFORM YOU WE HAVE BEEN UNABLE TO FIND A TRACE OF YOUR UNCLE WEHMAN MILLS STOP HE SEEMS TO HAVE DISAPPEARED COMPLETELY WHILE YOU AND HE WERE STAYING AT THE BREST HOTEL

There were others, all in the same vein. It was evident that Elaine Mills had employed private detectives to search for her uncle, and they had been unable to locate the elderly gentleman.

There came a gentle knock at the door and the mustached *auberge* proprietor said, "A Monsieur Smith to see you, mademoiselle."

A few seconds later, Elaine Mills was appraising her visitor, Monsieur Smith, with curious eyes. Smith was squat, had a thick neck, and looked like the popular conception of an overfed lawyer. He wore pince-nez spectacles and carried a briefcase.

"I have a message from your uncle, Wehman Mills," stated Smith. "I am his lawyer."

"I didn't know he had a lawyer," Elaine said shortly.

Smith, seeming not to have heard, continued, "Your uncle, Wehman Mills, has found it necessary to sail immediately for India—"

"Why?" Elaine demanded.

"He neglected to tell me," said Smith. "He only provided me with the means of sending you to join him at such a time as he should authorize me to do so by cable. Here is the card I received a few hours ago."

From his briefcase, Smith extracted a cablegram, which he extended. The young woman took it, and read:

THIS WILL COME TO YOU THROUGH MY LAWYER SMITH STOP AWFULLY SORRY YOU HAVE BEEN UNAWARE MY WHEREABOUTS STOP PRESSING AND VERY SPECIAL BUSINESS DEMANDED

MY PRESENCE IN INDIA STOP EVERYTHING ALL RIGHT STOP SMITH WILL GIVE YOU STEAM-SHIP TICKET AND EXPENSE MONEY TO INDIA STOP PLEASE JOIN ME

WEHMAN MILLS

Elaine Mills looked up from the cablegram and said, "This is not at all like Uncle Wehman."

Smith smiled and murmured, "I think everything is as it should be," as he extracted from his briefcase a small bundle of currency snapped around with a rubber band, and one of the tough brown envelopes in which steamship companies enclose their tickets. He extended these.

"A paid passage to India on a liner sailing tomorrow, together with some expense funds," he stated.

"But what about a passport?" Elaine gasped.

Smith bowed, said, "A lawyer's business is to think of everything," and produced from the case a passport folder.

Elaine opened the passport and stared in astonishment at her own picture.

"Why, this is a picture of me that Uncle Wehman had," she exclaimed.

"Your Uncle Wehman gave it to me before sailing," Smith smirked.

Elaine fumbled with passport, money and steamship tickets and said queerly, "This is all very strange. Uncle Wehman never acted like this before."

Smith patted her shoulder in a kindly fashion. "I wouldn't worry about it. Your uncle is rather an eccentric character and I presume he has his own very good reasons for what he did."

Elaine sighed. "That may be," she said.

"You intend to go to India, of course?" Smith queried casually.

Elaine hesitated; then: "Why, yes."

"Then I wish you a happy voyage."

With that platitude, Smith gathered up his briefcase and took his departure.

SOME five minutes later, Smith joined the cat-voiced Paquis, who was awaiting some blocks distant in a small French car.

Paquis laughed at sight of Smith.

"One would not think, m'sieu', that you are a man much wanted by Scotland Yard," he chuckled. "You look most respectable."

"Keep your bloomin' jokes under your 'at," growled Smith, lapsing into the gutter dialect of London.

"*Oui,*" Paquis agreed. "How did it go?"

"She swallowed it, 'ook, line an' sinker," said Smith.

"She is going to sail for India?"

"She said as 'ow she was."

Paquis sighed happily as he put the little car into motion over the none-too-smooth streets in that section of Brest.

"A great idea, m'sieu'," he chuckled. 'But then, all the ideas of Paquis are great, *non?*"

"You guff too much about yourself,' grunted the other.

Paquis ignored the sarcasm.

"Elaine Mills will soon be off for India," he said. "It is a long journey to India. The young lady will be out of our way for some time."

## Chapter VI
## THE MAN OF BRONZE

PAQUIS was too optimistic.

Elaine Mills stood still in the hallway of the French inn, her thoughts in a whirl, eyeing the papers given her by Smith. She counted the money and found it hardly sufficient to cover the tips the stewards would expect on an India voyage, but that did not arouse her suspicions, because Wehman Mills had never been exactly a prodigal.

"Poor Uncle Wehman," she murmured. "He has never made much money. I hope he has found something now that will make him rich."

Consulting a wrist watch, Elaine learned the night was well along.

"I had better start packing," she decided, and turned for the stairway.

In her hand she carried a small, flat flashlight. This inn, in common with many such establishments in France, was not fitted with electric lights, because a certain section of the population liked to live as their ancestors had.

The flashlight beam darted toward the stairs casually, missed them, went beyond and glinted on a small metal object which reposed under a rickety antique chair.

Curious, Elaine went over and picked the article up. It was a watch, a rather thick timepiece built for service.

Elaine turned the watch over and emitted a gasp. She had recognized it. She pried the back open and turned her flashlight on the inscription within:

TO UNCLE WEHMAN MILLS
FROM ELAINE

Elaine Mills was a quick-witted young woman, and the significance of the watch being where it was dawned on her.

"Uncle Wehman came here," she told herself grimly. "He called out my name, then something happened to him."

Elaine did not go upstairs; instead she hurried

out into the night and made her way to the nearest *poste de police*. A good-natured gendarme was on duty. He recognized his visitor.

"Ah, you are the mademoiselle who has lost her uncle," he said in fair English. "We are very sorry to report that we have no clue to his whereabouts."

"Well, I have a clue," Elaine told him.

Then she imparted a brief outline of what had happened at her lodgings.

"I am convinced something is wrong," she declared. "Uncle Wehman tried to come to me, and he must have been seized and carried away."

"This Monsieur Uncle Wehman—what is his business?" the gendarme asked curiously.

"He is a chemist and an inventor," Elaine replied.

The gendarme drew some papers from his desk. These were fastened together with a paper clip. He consulted them, then leaned back in his squeaking chair.

"Is it not a fact that the Monsieur Uncle Wehman was once in trouble in the United States because he sold some mining stock that was of no value?" he inquired politely.

Elaine flushed. "That was not Uncle Wehman's fault. He had a process for recovering metals which he thought would work. Some men put money behind him, and had it fixed up so they would hog the profits. The process was a failure and they turned around and tried to send Uncle Wehman to jail. They were not good sports. Uncle Wehman lost more than they did."

The gendarme nodded sagely. "Is it not true that Monsieur Uncle Wehman has invented a number of things which have been a failure?"

"What has that got to do with the fact that something has happened to him?" Elaine wanted to know.

The gendarme smiled and said, "You may rest assured, mademoiselle, that we shall investigate."

But Elaine left the *poste de police* with the feeling that the hunt for Wehman Mills had hit a snag. Not that the French police were sluggards; they were as efficient as the law enforcement agencies of other nations. But the discovery that Wehman Mills had once been in trouble with the law in the United States had dampened their ardor.

Elaine stood in the street and punished an attractive lower lip with her teeth.

"Darn it!" she said angrily, and stamped a foot.

THE young woman's wrathful ejaculation was destined to have far-reaching consequences. Simply because she stamped her foot and exclaimed aloud, many men were to come under a pall of horrible danger, and some were to die.

A news vendor had his sidewalk stand a few yards distant, and not understanding English and unable to see the young woman's facial expression because of the darkness, he thought she wanted a newspaper. He ran over with an armload of his wares and began to spout profusely in French.

Elaine had enough experience with French street hawkers to know that the easiest way of getting rid of the vendor was to spend a few pennies for one of his papers. She passed over the Paris and Brest editions and selected a London paper, one she could read because it was in English.

She glanced casually at the headlines.

DOC SAVAGE TO VISIT ENGLAND

Back in Elaine's memory something stirred. She read the subheads and the story below:

MAN OF MYSTERY DUE TO LAND
SOUTHAMPTON TONIGHT

Clark Savage, Jr., better known in the far corners of the world as Doc Savage, is due aboard a liner which arrives at Southampton from New York City tonight.

He is a man of mystery, this Doc Savage, probably one of the most amazing combinations of scientific genius and physical daring to be found in the world. He is a man of profound learning, a man whose knowledge is said to be unequaled in the fields of electricity, chemistry, geology, archaeology, engineering and other lines. He is reported to be a mental wizard.

Equal to his mental ability are Doc Savage's physical powers, according to those who know of his work. Scientific exercise routines, carried on unfailingly from childhood, have given him a muscular strength which borders on the supernatural.

Strangest thing of all about this man, perhaps, is his profession—that of aiding those in trouble and punishing wrongdoers. It is said that he never accepts financial remuneration for anything that he does.

Doc Savage is coming to England to aid one of his colleagues, William Harper Littlejohn, famous archaeologist and geologist, who is now delivering a series of lectures before the Fellowhood of Scientists.

William Harper Littlejohn is one of a group of five men closely associated with Doc Savage in his strange career. The other four men are lawyer, chemist, engineer and electrical expert, each famous in his profession. Yet it is reported that each of the five is exceeded in his own specialty by this superman, Doc Savage.

"GOOD night!" exclaimed Elaine Mills, and glanced up at the title of the paper, thinking she must have gotten hold of the London equivalent of a New York tabloid. But the newspaper was one of the more staid of Britain's journalistic sheets.

That such a paper should eulogize an individual, especially an American, in this fashion, was unusual. This paper happened to be one addicted to taking digs at Americans.

ELAINE re-read the portion of the highly-flattering—for that newspaper—story which dealt with Doc Savage's profession of helping those who were in trouble. Then she folded the paper slowly, her thoughts busy.

She was recalling what she had heard of this man of mystery, Doc Savage. Now that she concentrated, she could remember having heard a great deal of the man. The newspapers frequently carried stories about him. Just recently, there had been an affair in which some clever criminal had hit upon the idea of using a submarine in New York harbor as a get-away vehicle, and Doc Savage had put him out of business.

A bit earlier than that, Doc Savage had, it was rumored, put down a revolution in one of the Balkan countries. Doc Savage seemed always to be in the thick of trouble.

"Doc Savage must have something on the ball," Elaine Mills told herself. "Otherwise this old fogy London paper would not give him a write-up like that." She reached a decision. Tucking the paper under an arm, she swung rapidly along the narrow, dark streets of Brest until she found a cab. Twenty minutes later, she was at the ticket office of the line which had issued her passage to India.

There was a good deal of argument. The French clerk shouted and waved his arms; Elaine looked grim and determined. Probably the fact that she was a beauty helped.

Eventually, Elaine got the money back on her ticket. She bought another ticket, this one to Southampton—where Doc Savage had arrived, by this time.

Elaine had determined to call on this man of mystery for assistance in the matter of her uncle, Wehman Mills. That Uncle Wehman was in trouble, she was convinced. And Doc Savage had the reputation of helping people who were in trouble.

If Doc Savage should be hesitant about looking into the matter, Elaine Mills was confident that her own beauty, of which she was not unaware, would sway him. Not that Elaine depended entirely upon her beauty. But men usually showed great willingness to aid her.

Elaine was due for a surprise when she tried her wiles on Doc Savage. And she was also due for other and more unpleasant surprises much before that.

THE shipping company clerk was a bit concerned after the young woman departed. He did some thinking, the result of which was that he picked up the telephone and called the number of the stout gentleman, Monsieur Smith, who had purchased the ticket which Elaine had cashed in.

The clerk wanted to know if it was all right that he had given the money back.

Smith thanked him and said it was quite all right, then he asked where the young woman had gone after getting her money. He was advised that she had purchased a steamer passage to Southampton, England.

Smith inquired for and was given the name of the boat, a craft which made regular cross-Channel passages.

The clerk hung up, thinking Monsieur Smith a very kindly, benevolent gentleman. He would have put his fingers tightly in his ears if he had heard the blistering profanity which Smith exercised after he had hung up.

"What is it?" asked Paquis, who was present.

"There's 'ell to pay!" Smith said fervently, relapsing into Cockney. "The blarsted female 'as smelled the rat!"

Paquis purred blandly, "Ah, then I shall have to exercise my remarkable wits again."

*LA COLOMBE* is French for "The Dove." It was also the name of the Channel boat on which Elaine Mills had taken passage.

*La Colombe* looked more like a broken-down crow which had fallen victim to a shotgun firing rust specks, than it looked like a dove. Her bows were blunt, black, and the superstructure either needed a paint job or a good washing.

The one smokestack was very tall and seemed entirely too large for a boat of *La Colombe's* size; it spouted prodigious quantities of sparks and black smoke, which promptly settled down on deck to burn small holes in clothing and dirty the passenger's faces.

Elaine Mills stood in her cabin, peering through a grimy porthole and watching the last of Brest slip past. They were beyond the portion of the harbor which served as a naval base, and because of the darkness, the castle, with its donjon and seven towers, was not even discernible.

*La Colombe* kept up a great rumbling and thumping which sounded, here in the young woman's cabin, not unlike the cooing of a gigantic and extremely decrepit dove, this being about the only characteristic the good ship bore in keeping with her name.

The riding lights of vessels at anchor in Brest harbor were blotted from sight, and eventually the winking of the lighthouse receded until it was only a scared scud of light in the infinite blackness of the sea night.

Assured they were off, Elaine sought out the radio cabin, her intention being to send a message to Doc Savage on his liner, apprising the man of mystery of her coming.

She did not send the message. The skipper of *La Colombe* and two of his officers were in the radio cabin, and much head-scratching was going on. A vandal, it seemed, had given each transmitting tube a tap with a hammer during the absence of the operator from his key.

Elaine Mills shivered when she heard the news. She thought of a small automatic which she carried in her handbag. The gun was a target weapon, not built for knocking men down, but it would be a great consolation in case of trouble.

The young woman was hurrying down the corridor to her stateroom when she heard a sound behind her. She whirled, took one glance, and opened her mouth to shout for aid.

She had faced the same tall, darkhaired man who had pretended to be a drunken tourist in the *auberge* back in Brest. He lunged swiftly and clamped a hand over Elaine's mouth, halting her outcry.

The girl bit him. He growled profanely, whipped out a silk handkerchief and managed to jam it between her jaws. Then he picked her up and carried her into the nearest stateroom.

"Bite Paquis, would you!" he purred. "I ought to hand you a good American bust on the jaw, mademoiselle!"

Elaine ignored him. She was looking at the other occupants of the stateroom. These numbered more than half a dozen, and she had seen only one of them before. That one was the portly man who had played lawyer, giving the name of Smith.

The men assisted in tying Elaine to a chair, not at all abashed by the frosty stares which she bent upon them. One contributed his necktie so that it could be tied across her jaws to keep the gag in place.

Smith had departed, and his mission remained a mystery only until he came back bearing Elaine's handbag. This was opened and the contents dumped on the floor in full view. The target pistol came to light, as well as the folded newspaper.

The men read the newspaper, and Paquis, living up to his vaunted quick wit, was first to catch its significance.

"This Doc Savage!" he snapped. *"M'sieu's,* the young lady here must have been on her way to enlist his aid."

"'Ell's on fire!" Smith swore in a strangely shrill voice. He had become slightly pale. He walked over to the group's baggage, selected a yellow atrocity which must have been his own luggage, and started for the door.

*"Qu'y a-t-il?"* Paquis purred wonderingly. "What is the matter, m'sieu'?"

Smith scowled. "'Aven't you 'eard of this Doc Savage bloke?"

Paquis shrugged. *"Oui,* vaguely, m'sieu'."

"Vaguely!" Smith snorted. "That's 'ow you'll remember 'im, too, if you're in any shape to remember 'im at all."

"What do you mean, m'sieu'?" Paquis demanded.

"Hi means that fightin' all 'is Majesty's bloody navy would be safer'n tanglin' with this Savage bloke," Smith said grimly. "Count me out from now on. Count me out on everything."

"Do you mean you would give up your share of some millions of pounds in order to avoid fighting this Doc Savage?" Paquis queried sarcastically.

"Bloomin' right," Smith growled. "And hit wouldn't be no fight. That Doc Savage just comes along and before you know 'arf of what hits about, 'e's got you laid by the 'eels."

"You seem to have met this Monsieur Savage," Paquis purred.

Smith grunted. "A friend o' mine 'ired 'imself out once to croak Doc Savage."

Paquis looked interested. "What happened to the friend? Tell us that."

Smith shifted his yellow bag from one thick hand to the other while he considered. Not only was his face pale, but he was now perspiring freely.

"Somethin' deuced queer 'appened to me friend," he imparted at last. "Doc Savage caught 'im and 'e must've done somethin' to the poor bloke's head. I met me friend an' 'e didn't know me from Adam's left overshoe. 'E didn't know any of 'is old pals. The poor goose got 'imself a position in a box factory, an' 'e's workin' there now, 'onest as they come. 'E 'asn't never remembered a thing in 'is life before 'e went up against Doc Savage."

"Very interesting, *oui,"* Paquis said skeptically.

"This Doc Savage ain't 'arf an ordinary man," Smith said firmly. "'E's a bloomin' male witch, that's what 'e is!"

Paquis laughed loudly.

"I will tell you a secret which our chief imparted only to me," he smirked. "One of Doc Savage's men, this William Harper Littlejohn, was so foolish as to invade The Wash vicinity, looking for King John's ghost. Our men found it necessary to seize him, and they hold him now."

"Blimme!" Smith wailed. "We're the same as sunk! This Doc Savage bloke will—"

"Will do nothing, m'sieu'," smirked Paquis. "Doc Savage has been deceived by our estimable leader."

"What d'you mean?" Smith demanded.

"Doc Savage is now on his way to South America, chasing the wild goose," Paquis laughed.

## Chapter VII
## THE GOLD MAKER

DOC SAVAGE was not on his way to South America.

The bronze man was not even going in the direction of the continent which Columbus discovered on his third voyage. He was headed in a direction almost exactly opposite.

The bronze man had made careful arrangements, guessing that the South American boat would be watched by his mysterious foes. A tug had met the boat well beyond the mouth of the harbor, taken off Doc, Monk, Habeas Corpus and Ham, and put them ashore at a point where there was little chance of their being observed.

The whole affair of the false start for South America had been executed with such a pell-mell rush that Monk and Ham were a bit confused on certain major points.

"How in blazes did you know that whole story about Johnny being on his way to South America was a fake?" Monk demanded.

"Remember when the man who pretended to be a detective, Wall-Samuels, was talking over the drug store telephone just before you seized him?" Doc queried.

Monk nodded. "Sure."

"Remember I was with you until we saw Wall-Samuels go into the telephone, then I asked you fellows to watch him and seize him when he came out?"

Monk nodded again. "You turned around and went back while we watched him."

"Exactly," Doc agreed. "It was not a difficult task to find where those telephone wires passed through the rear wall of the drug store, then tap them."

Monk grinned. "Who did Wall-Samuels talk to?"

"An unnamed gentleman," Doc explained. "The latter carefully outlined the story which was to lead us off on the wild-goose chase to South America."

"But what was behind it?" Monk demanded.

"A rather mysterious affair having to do with a ghost of King John, a man named Wehman Mills and a young woman who is Wehman Mills' niece," Doc replied.

Monk muttered, "I still don't see why they mixed us up in it in the first place."

"Johnny was responsible for that," Doc answered.

"Johnny?"

"Johnny evidently went to investigate the King John ghost," Doc explained. "He was seized."

"He was *what?*" Monk howled. "When? Where?"

"In the vicinity of The Wash," Doc said. "And it must have happened earlier in the night."

The bronze man hailed a taxi. "To the nearest airport from which we can get a plane for London," he directed—and the cab got underway noisily.

Monk, showing puzzlement, queried, "Where are we heading for?"

"When Wall-Samuels telephoned from the drug store, and I tapped the wire, there was a chance to trace the call," Doc replied. "It came from an office in the name of Benjamin Giltstein, on Fleet Street in London."

"Benjamin Giltstein," Ham murmured. "Ever hear of him before, Doc?"

The bronze man shook his head in a negative.

The Southampton airport was astir at this early hour, since it was a focus for various airlines operating planes to the islands in the English Channel. Another line also ran to London, and the early plane was on the point of departing.

FLEET STREET, beginning at Ludgate Circus and leading to the Strand and the West End, is one of London's busiest streets. But the principal fame of Fleet Street comes from its multiplicity of newspaper plants. The leading journals of England have their headquarters there, together with book publishers, press associations, literary agents, clipping bureaus, and the other professions which gain their livelihood from the printed word.

The high-pressure methods of modern existence has come to demand many specialists in peculiar lines. Some men devote their working lives to nothing but making a particular type of motor casting. In the literary field, some writers turn out only detective yarns; in the newspaper business, some reporters specialize in writing about the stock exchange, to the exclusion of all else.

Benjamin Giltstein was a specialist. His forte was publicity. In the United States, he would have called himself a public relations counsel and the newspaper reporters would probably have dubbed him a press agent.

If an actor wanted his name in the newspapers, his best bet was to employ a man in Benjamin Giltstein's profession. The press agent would think up stunts that would pass as news, write them up, give them to the newspapers, and some would be printed.

Should an industrial magnate desire his concern publicized in a favorable light, he usually engaged one of these public relations counselors, who, being a specialist, knew the best way to inveigle the newspaper into printing the publicity matter under the impression that they were disseminating news.

Benjamin Giltstein was a portly fellow with a red face. He affected spats and eyeglasses on a ribbon. A newspaper reporter who got hard up could always borrow a few dollars from Giltstein. He stood in well with the Press, for that was his business. The news hawks for whom he did favors reciprocated by getting his publicity stuff printed.

At this early morning hour, sleepy-eyed reporters were gathering at Benjamin Giltstein's comfortably furnished offices in Fleet Street. The scribes grumbled about being robbed of their sleep, but Giltstein had telephoned them, saying he had a piece of news which was due to shake the world.

Great enthusiasm had been in Giltstein's voice. In the past, the press agent had always been frank, telling the reporters when he was trying to put out straight publicity. It did not pay to try to fool the gentlemen of the press, as Giltstein well knew.

Fearing Benjamin Giltstein really did have a big piece of news, the journalists had not dared stay away. But they arrived in a cloud of skepticism, sprawled themselves in the luxurious chairs, and demanded to know what was what.

"It is big, gentlemen," Giltstein insisted. "When you are all present, I shall talk."

The press agent knew most of the leading London reporters, but two scribes put in an appearance whom he could not recall. They did not come together.

One stranger was a broad man, smooth-shaven and very pale of face, who wore glasses with thick lenses and shell rims. This fellow had a tremendous stomach and walked with a pronounced limp. He also smoked a large and extremely evil-smelling cigar.

The second stranger, who arrived almost half an hour later, was a lean chap who had two large gold teeth in front and wore a perpetual scowl. His clothing was baggy and would have been the better for a visit to the cleaners. He spoke with a pronounced Latin accent.

"I worka for da Italian Newspaper Union," he explained. "I just geta da job."

The other scribe, the one with the big stomach and the limp, said that he was a new reporter on the *Crown Daily*.

BENJAMIN GILTSTIEN passed good cigars, then expanded his chest with a full breath.

"Gentlemen, I am about to break one of the greatest stories of the Twentieth century!" he said grandly. "What I am about to tell you is highly likely to alter the whole course of the world's economic existence. It is colossal, stupendous, as an American motion picture man would say."

"Cut the blarney and out with it," a journalist suggested. "We can tell whether it's worth a line or two on an inside page."

Giltstein looked patient. "You will put this on the front page. Every paper in the world will put it on the front page."

"What is it?" repeated the scribe.

"Do you gentlemen know what ingredients make up sea water?" Giltstein asked suddenly.

"Water," someone said.

"Salt water," said somebody else. "Whales, sharks, and assorted fishes."

"Please," suggested Giltstein. "Be serious about this. Sea water contains, in solution, some thirty-two of the eighty known elements. In sea water you will find, besides salt, magnesium chloride, gypsum, copper, zinc, nickel, lead, cobalt, manganese, bromide, chlorine—"

"We'll take your word for it," interjected the scribe. "What is this leading up to?"

"There are at present in existence plants which take bromine from the sea water in commercial quantities," said Giltstein.

"Are you trying to get publicity for one of them?" another newspaper man demanded.

"No!" snapped the press agent. "Keep still and listen. There is another substance present in sea water. It is gold!"

No one said anything.

"Gold!" Giltstein repeated dramatically.

"Is this where we all applaud?" asked a journalist sarcastically.

Benjamin Giltstein was beginning to perspire. It seemed that the scribes were unusually cold toward press agents this morning.

"The gold in its native state in the water is in colloidal suspension form," said the publicity man. "There is approximately ten million dollars worth of gold in a cubic mile of water. There are nearly three hundred million cubic miles of sea water on the earth. That gives us, as the total value of the gold in the sea—"

"Don't say it!" groaned a reporter. "Not with me flat broke. Say, just what are you trying to tell us?"

"Gentlemen, a feasible method has been discovered for taking gold from sea water," said Benjamin Giltstein.

THE journalists digested this information. Having had experience in the past with press agents, they took anything from such a source with several grains of salt. Their jobs depended a good deal on such precautions.

"Nothing doing on this," one snapped. "We print a story and somebody unloads stock in this gold-from-sea-water idea. Isn't that it?"

"On the contrary, you could not buy a share of stock in this project with a million dollars in cash," Giltstein said promptly.

"When is the plant for getting the gold to be built?" someone queried.

"It is already completed," said Giltstein.

There was a pronounced perking up of ears at this information. It removed the story from the category of a press agent's dream and made it strictly news.

"Where is the place?" the reporter with the big stomach and the limp questioned.

"Have you ever heard of Magna Island?" asked Giltstein.

"Sure," said the reporter whom Giltstein had not met before this conclave. "It is a tiny island near here. It holds the position of an independent monarchy, under our protectorate, but it pays no taxes to us, and we English have no voice in its government or anything that goes on there."

"There was talk that an American utilities king who was running away from the law intended to buy the island and set himself up as king, so he would be safe," put in another reporter.

"Magna Island was recently purchased," Giltstein said blandly. "And the plant for taking gold from sea water is now in operation there."

"Can you prove dis, meester?" inquired the lean reporter with the perpetual scowl.

"I am prepared to prove every word," Benjamin

Giltstein snapped. "If you gentlemen care to charter planes, I shall be glad to accompany you to Magna Island, where you will be shown over the plant which is taking gold from sea water. Furthermore, I can guarantee that each of you will receive a small sample of the sea gold as proof."

"Can we bringa da technical expert along?"

"You certainly can."

A reporter, who was still skeptical, demanded, "Listen here, Giltstein, are you sure this is not a high-powered stock-selling scheme?"

"It positively is nothing of the sort," the press agent asserted.

"Who is the scientist who is taking this gold out of the sea water?"

Benjamin Giltstein put the proper drama on this announcement of the identity.

"An American inventor named Wehman Mills," he said.

THE meeting now broke up, for the reporters wanted to telephone the story to their respective sheets, as well as get permission to visit Magna Island. Since there was only one telephone in Benjamin Giltstein's office, the scribes scattered.

Strangely enough, the reporter with the big stomach and the limp, and the scribe with the scowl and the Latin accent, made it a point to meet in a corner of the lobby downstairs.

"That pot belly certainly becomes you, Monk," chuckled the one who had used the Latin accent.

The other leered, "That's a nice suit you're wearing, Ham."

Ham retrieved his scowl, which he had temporarily wiped off his features. He hated the baggy suit which he had assumed for a disguise.

It was doubtful if intimate acquaintances would have recognized either Monk or Ham. Doc Savage had equipped them with their disguises and done an excellent job of it.

Monk abandoned personalities, and demanded, "What do you make of this gold-out-of-sea-water business?"

"Hokum?" said Ham.

"On the contrary," Monk told him. "It can be done. It *has* been done on a laboratory scale, in fact, but the cost of recovery has always exceeded the value of the gold taken."

Ham shrugged. "We'd better consult Doc."

They left the building, walked down the street and entered a small hotel. Doc Savage occupied a room there, and was seated before a telephone. Monk's pig, Habeas Corpus, was also in the room.

"I have been doing some calling," Doc told them. "Johnny seems to have chartered a plane which took him to Swineshead, a village in the vicinity of The Wash. Johnny made inquiries at the local pubs about King John's ghost, then he disappeared from the settlement and has not been heard from since."

"This whole blasted thing is mighty queer," Monk growled.

"What did you learn at Benjamin Giltstein's office?" Doc questioned.

Monk and Ham collaborated in reciting the story about the discovery of the process for taking the rare yellow metal from ocean brine, ending with the information that the gentlemen of the press had been invited to pay Magna Island a visit to inspect the new plant.

"What are we going to do about this gold angle?" Ham pondered aloud.

"In your assumed personality of newspaper men, you will go to the island and look things over," Doc suggested. "Monk, being one of the greatest living chemists, should be able to tell whether the thing is a fake."

"But suppose they learn we are not newspaper men?" Monk grunted.

"It is not likely," Doc replied. "I have made arrangements with the newspapers for which you are supposed to work. Your names are on the payrolls of those sheets, in case anyone calls up."

Neither Monk nor Ham commented on that, for they were accustomed to the manner in which Doc Savage cared for details, rarely overlooking anything.

"What's your end, Doc?" Monk asked.

"Johnny," said the bronze man; "we must find him."

"Maybe we'd better go with you," Ham suggested hopefully.

"No," Doc said. "You take care of the gold from the sea angle. And try to find out what you can about this Wehman Mills who is supposed to have discovered the process."

"We'll interview him," Monk grinned.

"I doubt it," Doc said.

"Huh? Why not?"

"From the telephone conversation I overheard between Wall-Samuels and the mysterious chief of the organization, it seems that Wehman Mills has escaped from the gang and they are trying to find him. This happened in Brest. Wehman Mills happens to have a niece in Brest."

"Maybe one of us had better look into the Brest angle," Monk suggested.

"We'll take care of that later," Doc said. "Johnny comes first. And I think you two will do more good investigating Benjamin Giltstein and his gold-from-sea-water-story."

"I wonder how Wehman Mills hooks into this," Monk pondered aloud. "And I wonder what it's all about, anyhow."

## Chapter VIII
### THE SAMARITAN

ELAINE MILLS, on the Channel boat *La Colombe,* was mentally echoing the same questions which Monk had put into words. Her attempts to raise an alarm had been futile and she was beginning to be badly scared. She was tightly bound and gagged.

So far, she had not the slightest idea of what was behind all of the trouble, although she had listened to all that was said by her captors.

Paquis, the suave gentleman with the voice of a cat, was absent. He had been gone some minutes, and putting in an appearance now, he winked broadly at his fellows.

"I have decided how we shall dispose of the girl," he said. "We are now doctors, *m'sieu's*. Be sure and act the part."

"'Ave you gone balmy?" Smith demanded.

Paquis exhibited a small bottle which he drew from a pocket. "This, m'sieu's, is a drug which will cause mademoiselle to go out of her head. It will cause her to become sleepy, and later go into a stupor."

"Hi don't get this, gov'nor," Smith muttered.

"We are *médicins,* doctors," Paquis repeated. "The unfortunate young mademoiselle in our charge is a victim of madness, and we have to keep her drugged. We are taking her to an English institution."

"You mean we put her in a bloomin' madhouse?"

"Exactly!" smiled Paquis.

"Hit won't work."

"On the contrary, it will be simple," Paquis assured Smith. "Our chief will arrange it. Mademoiselle will be thoroughly out of the way."

Smith snorted. "Hi'll give you blokes credit. You think of things!"

Paquis expanded under this praise, tucking thumbs in vest pockets and riding his heels.

"The English are not slow about releasing persons from their madhouses, m'sieu's," he smiled. "Elaine Mills will be confined for some months—and long before that, our present project will be completed."

ELAINE MILLS remained perfectly still in her chair, relaxed so that the cotton cords which secured her would not cause so much muscle ache.

The steamer whistle was moaning at intervals, an indication that they must have entered one of the Channel's frequent fogs; but Elaine Mills hardly heard the mournful blasts.

At first, the disposition these men intended to make of her had not seemed especially terrifying; but now that she thought it over, the prospect was not pleasant. A madhouse would be infinitely worse than a penitentiary, and it would carry a stigma. Moreover, she would be in a position where any opportunity to aid her uncle would be hopelessly impossible.

Attendants in institutions for the insane paid little attention of the talk of the patients therein. If she told the story of what had happened to her tonight, it would be ignored as the raving of an unbalanced individual.

Elaine Mills suddenly wrenched as bolt upright in her chair as the ropes would permit. Then she slumped; her head dropped forward.

"What's wrong with the blarsted wench?" Smith growled.

Paquis eyed the young woman doubtfully, then advanced and felt of her wrist. Then he watched for some sign of breathing. He heard none.

*"Dépechez-vous!"* he exploded. "Make haste! Untie the mademoiselle!"

Smith questioned, "What's 'appened?"

"Take the gag out!" rapped Paquis.

Smith snarled, "Listen, bloke, Hi arsked you—"

"Did you ever hear of a person with a bad case of adenoids smothering when they are gagged?" Paquis demanded. "They cannot breathe, except through their mouths, and the gag strangles them."

Smith sprang to aid in extracting the gag. He listened for a trace of breathing from the girl, heard none, and showed sudden worriment.

"If she's up an' died, we're in an 'ell of a kettle!" he groaned.

"She has only fainted, m'sieu'," replied Paquis. "But we must revive her or she may die."

Elaine Mills was a strikingly beautiful young woman, and it was doubtful if any male, however tough he might consider himself, could help showing concern over her life. Too, the death of the girl would certainly interest the English police, and those hounds of the law had a reputation of being very difficult to evade.

Not only was Elaine's gag removed, but she was untied and placed on a berth. Her wrists were massaged and her face slapped lightly; but nothing happened, except that her limbs seemed to become slightly stiff.

"Get water!" Paquis snapped. *"Non!* Never mind! I shall get it myself."

He sprang to the wash basin and roared the stream into the bowl. A startled shout behind him caused him to wheel. His eyes protruded.

He was just in time to see Elaine Mills dive through the stateroom door into the passage outside.

"The blarsted hussy tricked us!" Smith snarled.

ELAINE MILLS ran wildly down the corridor. She had no delusions about her escape or the dumbness of her captors. They were not dumb. They had fallen for one of the oldest ruses, simply because Elaine was exquisitely beautiful.

A man in the same circumstances could never have worked the trick. A pretty girl about to die on their hands, seemingly, had excited them greatly and caused them to relax their usual caution.

Elaine had slammed the door of the stateroom from which she had escaped. She heard it bang open. Without turning her head, she knew Paquis, Smith and the others were charging in pursuit.

A cross passage opened to one side and Elaine wheeled into that. The nap on the carpet was worn, making that covering slick, and she nearly slipped and fell.

"Help!" she shrieked.

No one was in sight, and the boat's engines were making considerable noise. The chances were that no one had heard her. She continued to run, shouting loudly.

She became convinced that she would not reach the end of the corridor and the deck before she was overhauled. Her limbs were stiff from the bonds, and did not function with full efficiency.

"Help!" she called shrilly.

Ahead, to the left, a stateroom door opened.

Elaine did not wait to see who had opened the door. Head down, she plunged inside. Her shoulder struck a figure forcibly.

The individual with whom she had collided gasped in a startled fashion. The voice was masculine, but gloom was too thick in the cabin to make out the man's features.

Seizing the door, Elaine slammed it shut. She found the lock—a bolt—clicked it, then leaped to one side. She did not put it above her late captors to drive a few bullets through the panel.

"Beauty in distress, eh?" murmured a rather pleasant voice.

The occupant of the room in which she had taken refuge was the speaker, and Elaine studied him curiously.

She saw a rather amply muscled young man with wide, amazed blue eyes, a mouth which was open and showing a firm set of white teeth, and a face which was healthily tanned. The young man was well under thirty, and he had a shock of curly brown hair. His shirt was off and he held a tube of patent shaving cream in one hand, a safety razor in the other.

"Just what does this mean?" he demanded.

"Sh-h-h!" warned Elaine.

She could hear her late hosts outside. They went past with a great tumult of footsteps, reached the deck and, judging by the sounds, turned back and began opening cabin doors. Elaine clenched her fists anxiously.

"Can't you hide me in here somewhere?" she demanded of the shirtless young man.

"I'll be darned if I see why I should," said that worthy.

"Those men are after me!" Elaine gasped.

The young man looked her up and down with an appreciative glance, then said: "If I don't miss my guess, almost any man would run after you. You're pretty enough."

"Darn it!" Elaine snapped. "They will probably kill me if they catch me."

"Oh!" said the young man. "That's different."

He tossed his shaving cream and razor on the berth, wrenched open a hand bag and produced an enormous black automatic pistol.

"We'll see about the killing," he said grimly. "Who are they?"

"I only know the names of two named Paquis and Smith," Elaine breathed. "There are others with them. They belong to a gang which has done something to my uncle, Wehman Mills."

Elaine and her new-found champion listened to the sounds in the corridor. These had changed in quality. There were many voices, some of which Elaine had not heard before. The explanation dawned upon her.

"The ships' officers had heard the noise and come to investigate," she said in a relieved voice.

She grasped the door and started to open it, intending to go outside.

The young man knocked her hand off the door fastening.

"Don't be a fool!" he growled quietly.

ELAINE MILLS stared at the young man wonderingly, and said, "I am going out there and accuse those fellows. Why is that foolish?"

"Are they armed?"

"Yes. Of course."

"Then don't be a fool," whispered the young man. "They would only shoot you and the ship officers. The latter are probably not armed. They might shoot me, too."

Considering, Elaine saw the possibilities of that. She retreated from the door.

"What am I going to do, then?" she asked wildly.

"Stay here, and in a little while I will go to the captain and tell him your story. You can stay here."

"I won't stay here," Elaine retorted. "They might find me while you are gone."

"I'll leave you my gun."

"You are very kind," Elaine told the young man.

"Trump is the name," he told her. "Henry Trump."

"Well, you certainly turned out to be my trump card," Elaine advised.

The young man scowled mildly and said, "I do not like for people to make puns about my name, ordinarily."

"Sorry," Elaine told him.

"Ordinarily, I said," he grinned. "When *you* do it, it sounds all right."

Outside, the voices were receding. The door was sufficient of a muffler that they could not understand what was being said, but the purring voice of Paquis was going at full speed, injecting *"ouis"* and *m'sieu's"* in every sentence.

"You're an American, aren't you?" Elaine asked Henry Trump.

He nodded. "Missourian, to be exact. An aunt kindly left me a few thousand dollars in hopes I would set myself up in business. I've been using the dough to see Europe."

"A tourist," Elaine murmured.

"Guilty," Henry Trump grinned.

Elaine listened at the door.

"I think those men are gone," she decided aloud.

"We'll wait a bit yet," Henry Trump suggested. "Say, are you married?"

"What?"

"Are you tied up in matrimonial bonds with some mug?"

"No," Elaine told him. "And I think that is a very impertinent question."

"Sure," Henry Trump grinned. "But it suddenly struck me as a very important thing to know."

"Anything else you are interested in learning?" Elaine asked him in as frosty a voice as she could manage.

"You bet!" he told her. "I'd like to hear your story."

Elaine could think of no reason why she should not tell him, so she immediately launched on the tale, starting with the excitement at the French *auberge* when, as she was now convinced, her uncle, Wehman Mills, had entered, called her name, then been carried off.

Henry Trump heard her through between low whistles of interest and sly glances at the young woman's attractive features. It was hard to tell which interested him the more.

"A whooping mystery, eh?" he smiled when Elaine had finished. "Elaine, I'm going to like this. Now it looks like things are sort of breaking out around me. That is, if you are going to permit me to help you."

"I don't want anyone to get hurt," Elaine told him.

"Don't worry about me," Trump chuckled. "Here's my gun. I'm going to talk to the captain."

Elaine received the big automatic, made sure she knew how to fire it, then Henry Trump let himself out of the stateroom.

"I'll be back in a jiff," he breathed, just before shutting the door.

## Chapter IX
## SEA SPAWN

HENRY TRUMP, returning to the stateroom, closed the door swiftly, shot the bolt and leaned against the panel. His boyish face had a worried expression.

"A dickens of a way for things to turn out!" he muttered.

Wide-eyed, Elaine Mills demanded, "What is wrong?"

Instead of answering, Henry Trump looked the young woman up and down, his manner one of solemn appraisal, his features still wearing their serious cast.

"Nope," he said to himself. "You can't be."

"Be what?" Elaine demanded.

"A nut," said Trump.

Elaine snapped, "Well, I like that!"

"Oh, don't get hot around the collar," Henry Trump advised her gloomily. "The captain of the ship has been sold on the idea that you are a goof on the way to an English nut house."

"So Paquis and Smith and the rest told him that!" Elaine snapped.

"They sure did. They did a swell job of it, too."

Elaine advanced on the door. "Let me out of here. I'll see about that."

"Nix," said Henry Trump. "This captain is a thick-headed dope. You couldn't tell him a thing. Paquis has him sold, I tell you. Say, I listened to this Paquis talk. He's some spieler. His purring voice almost got me to thinking he was really a doctor and you were his patient."

Elaine waved the heavy automatic. "After I get sight of Paquis, he won't tell anybody anything."

Henry Trump looked interested. "You'd shoot him?"

"No," said Elaine. "But I'd scare him until he lost that purring voice."

Henry Trump grinned, but shook his head. "It might be a pleasant diversion, but it would not get you anywhere. It would just convince the captain of the boat that you were really unbalanced. They'd throw you in the brig, probably."

The whistle moaned a long blast, and Elaine waited until the mournful orchestration of echoes had died.

"I've got to do something," she declared.

"Stay in here until we dock at Southampton," Henry Trump suggested. "I'll stay with you until the stewards come. They'll be around, because they're going to search the ship for you. You get in the clothes locker, and I'll convince them you're not here."

Elaine did not answer to that.

"Well, maybe you can think of something better," the young man suggested. "After the stewards go, I'll leave you alone if you wish. I'll put a deck chair outside, under this porthole, and you can yell if you want me."

"I don't know how I'll ever repay you for this," Elaine smiled.

"Am I kicking?" Henry Trump grinned. "Say, the nearest I ever got to playing hero to a girl as pretty as you are was watching a movie."

Elaine said hastily, "There is one thing more we can do."

"What's that?"

"Send Doc Savage a message telling him he has been tricked."

"Swell idea," Henry Trump agreed. "But I thought the radio apparatus on this ship had been put out of commission by Paquis and his gang."

"It may have been repaired by now."

"In that case, how will we know what boat Doc Savage is on?"

"We can find what boats sailed for South America last night and send a message to all of them." Elaine eyed the young man curiously.

"Say, I don't believe you're very enthusiastic about this."

Henry Trump grinned sheepishly. "To tell the truth, I'm afraid Paquis and his crowd will find us."

Elaine Mills, in a determined voice, said, "I am going to the radio room."

"I'll go along," Henry Trump told her. "But I think we're taking unnecessary chances."

They opened the stateroom door and reconnoitered cautiously. Seeing no one, they stepped outside, Elaine bundled in a spare topcoat which Henry Trump produced.

They rounded a corner and saw a deck hand in worn coveralls on hands and knees, polishing brass and washing down woodwork.

"Don't let the sailor see your face," Henry Trump breathed, as he and the young woman hurried forward.

They were abreast of the deck hand when he dipped his cleaning rag into his pail of suds. But instead of bringing it out, he wrenched a dripping revolver from the bucket.

"These cartridges are the kind which do not get wet!" he said grimly. "Stand still, you two!"

HENRY TRUMP had declared he craved action, and he now lived up to his word. He lunged with astonishing speed, kicked, and the fake deck hand's revolver spun down the passage.

Snarling, the other man scuttled backward. He tore buttons off his shirt getting a hand under it, and brought out a long knife.

Henry Trump picked up the bucket of suds and dashed it into the fellow's face. The man swore hoarsely and pawed at his eyes, which were blinded by the soapy spray.

"Come on!" Trump exploded, and grabbed Elaine's arm.

They whirled to flee—and froze to stillness. Cabin doors nearby had opened and Paquis, Smith and the others had appeared, guns in hand. Henry Trump started to reach for his gun.

"Non!" Paquis advised vehemently.

Henry Trump thought better of it and lifted his hands.

"We realized mademoiselle must have entered one of the cabins," Paquis chuckled. "By the judicious use of a few francs, we managed to put one of our men to scrubbing. He served as a lookout."

"You mugs seem to think you're slick," Henry Trump growled.

"Smarter than you, m'sieu'," Paquis murmured ominously. "You are going to wish you had never met the pretty mademoiselle."

"Rats!" Trump snapped. "Mark me, you lads will get yours for this."

Guns were held on Elaine Mills and Henry Trump while their wrists were bound. Then gags were forced between their jaws.

"Mademoiselle will not trick us again," Paquis assured the young woman.

Their ankles were not secured, and the reason for this became apparent when they were forced toward the door. One of the gang scuttled out and reconnoitered the corridor, came back and reported the coast clear.

Thanks to a wet drizzle and plenty of fog, the decks were virtually deserted. No one observed the prisoners being hurried toward the stern.

Paquis issued quiet orders. Ring lifebuoys were yanked loose from the rail, lengths of line were cut from around the edge of a lifeboat, and the buoys were bound to the prisoners.

Each of the buoys had a cannister device attached to it.

Elaine watched in wide-eyed horror as Henry Trump was seized, lifted and hurled, feet-first, over the rail. Then she herself received the same treatment.

The young woman hit the water with a terrific shock. She saw the rusty sides of the Channel boat racing past her, was spun around and around in the disturbed water, then all but drawn under by the churning of the propellers. Almost choking, breathing impeded by the gag, she came back to the surface.

There was a loud bubbling sound made by the steamer, the sight of a receding hump of darkness that was the stern, then both receded and there was only the watery loneliness of the Channel.

Elaine bobbed wildly, for the sea was still upset by the passage of the ship; but soon that subsided and there was only the rather ugly chop of the Channel itself. Waves broke over the buoy and splashed into her face.

It must have been near dawn, but the fog and the rain clouds above made thick gloom, thicker gloom than Elaine believed she had ever seen before.

Abruptly there was a hissing roar, and a blinding light sprang up almost beside her. The young woman squeezed her eyes shut and struggled to get free of the ring buoy; but the bindings were too secure. It was doubtful if she could have stayed afloat for long, anyway, with her hands bound.

Then she realized what was making the eye-hurting light. It was the cannister which had been attached to the buoy. It was a modern safety flare—a can of chemicals which ignited upon contact with the water and would burn for many minutes. They were intended to facilitate locating persons lost overboard at night.

The fog, however, would prevent anyone aboard *La Colombe* from sighting them.

Elaine was shuddering, and between shudders endeavoring to free herself, when she got a shock.

"Elaine!" called a masculine voice nearby.

A MOMENT later, Henry Trump appeared in the glare of the flare, rafting himself along on his ring buoy. His hands were free and he had ridded himself of the gag.

"I managed to get loose," Trump puffed. "Gosh, I'm glad you're safe! I was worried—afraid you had been pulled into the ship's propellers."

At that point, the chemical flare attached to Trump's life ring ignited itself and, fizzing and spitting, made such a terrific glare that they could not see each other. Overhead, thunder whooped and gobbled, and the rain fell more furiously, making a white cream on the green water around about.

"Danged if we aren't in a mess," Trump said grimly. "I wonder how far it is to shore?"

A series of grunts answered him—and Trump, remembering, removed the young woman's gag.

"Too far," Elaine shivered. "I'm no Channel swimmer."

Trump was working at Elaine's bonds now, and soon got them free. Then they worked together and joined their life preservers with ropes, in order that they might not drift apart.

"They picked a queer way of getting rid of us," Trump growled.

"That is what I cannot understand," Elaine murmured. "Why did they tie us to life preservers before they threw us overboard?"

"Listen!" Trump barked.

Elaine strained her ears. At first, there was only the burning noises made by their chemical flares, which seemed quite proof against extinguishing by water. Then the young woman caught a sound which might have been made by a distant doorbell from which the clapper had been removed. This grew louder, approaching.

"Plane," decided Trump.

Before long, the plane materialized in the being of two brilliant wingtip landing lights which were pale in comparison with the nearer brilliance of the flares. The ship settled to a landing, a feat which could only have been accomplished by a large and sturdy seaplane. It taxied close.

A man appeared on the seaplane, and with both legs and one arm wrapped around struts, fished for Trump and Elaine with a boat hook. He was proficient. A moment later they both were scrambling up into the seaplane cabin.

Three other men were inside the ship. Elaine looked them over and was quite sure she had never seen any of the trio previously.

"We had a bloody time findin' you," advised one of the rescuers. "We thought for a while we weren't going to be able to locate the flares in the fog."

"You were looking for us?" Elaine gulped.

"Sure!" the other told her.

"But why?"

The man produced a nickel-plated revolver, waved it idly and said, "Maybe you did not know it, but you have just been changing conveyances."

HENRY TRUMP yelled angrily, "So you are in with Paquis, Smith and that gang?"

"I'm not ashamed of it," their new captor grinned. "That Paquis is almost half as smart as he thinks he is, but that makes him a very clever gentleman indeed."

Elaine gasped, "But why the elaborate affair of dropping us overboard to be picked up by this plane?"

"To save trouble," the informant smirked. "You see, young lady, the captain of that ship got the bright idea of having the police at Southampton look into the story of the insane girl."

Elaine and Henry Trump exchanged glances.

"I wish I had known of that," Trump groaned.

A man produced thin but stout cords and prepared to bind Elaine and Trump.

"Where are we going?" Elaine demanded.

"To visit your esteemed uncle, Wehman Mills," the other growled. "But you won't like that. Not a bit!"

Another man chuckled. "Tell them about the other guest they'll have for company—an esteemed archaeologist and geologist known as William Harper Littlejohn."

"You blokes talk too much!" snarled the man who was doing the flying.

The plane now bounced across the water's surface, motors making a great deal of uproar, and finally went on step, skipping from one wave top to another. The result was a procession of terrific slams which threatened to jar the wings off the seaplane.

Apprehension overspread the features of pilot and passengers. It was a dangerous moment, alleviated only when the ship got into the fog-gorged halflight of early morning.

The man with the cords resumed the task of tying the prisoners. Then he produced handkerchiefs which were evidently to serve as gags.

"You birds are in for trouble!" Henry Trump threatened. "Doc Savage is tangled up in this."

"Doc Savage is on his way to South America," the man smirked.

## Chapter X
## THE KING JOHN TRAIL

FOG lay over The Wash. it was a particularly soupy fog, so very wet it deposited big globules of moisture on the rushes which composed most of the marsh vegetation. The sun was a weak red eye overhead.

An occasional flying water bird seemed about the only vestige of animate life, and even the feathered amphibians did not show much energy in the face of a day which, starting off with a clear sky, had turned dreary and moist.

There was movement in The Wash, however. But it was furtive action, carefully managed, to escape notice.

Doc Savage was following Johnny's trail. The Swineshead village stories about the ghost of King John had given him a clue as to where Johnny might have gone. Johnny's tracks had not been difficult to locate, because muck of The Wash was soft and retained footprints.

They were unusually long and slender, these tracks of Johnny's, indicating with accuracy the skeletonlike physical build of the man who made them.

The track showed where the bony archaeologist and geologist had prowled in search of the spectre of an ancient English monarch, or something less fantastic, which would explain the ghost stories. Then came the point where Johnny had encountered the nocturnal prowler.

With great interest Doc Savage scrutinized the prints of the individual Johnny had met. The peculiar pattern was easily identified as having been made by an ancient sandal. Doc found the mark made by the big broadsword when Johnny seized it and threw it away.

Then came the marks made during the fight in which Johnny had overpowered his strange foe. Reeds were crushed down and salt water grass uprooted, where the fight had occurred.

At this point, Doc Savage located a third set of tracks, also made by a man. It was this individual who had belted Johnny over the head, bringing the unconsciousness which had been so inexplicable to Johnny. There seemed to be two King John ghosts.

The third arrival, after striking Johnny down, seemed to have crept away and concealed himself in the marsh growth nearby while the pretended ghost of King John questioned Johnny, perhaps; then he had returned, and Johnny had been marched off through the muck and reeds by both the King John apparitions.

Doc followed. He kept close to the ground, although there hardly seemed necessity for that in view of the fog.

The great marsh, being partially inundated by the tide at times, was cut here and there by streams, rips which the violent tidal currents had opened. At the present moment the tide seemed to be high, and these rips were either full or overflowing.

Doc lost the trail at one of the rips. He swam across with a few strokes which showed a remarkable swimming ability, and examined the other bank. He became convinced that Johnny had been put aboard a boat of some type.

Doc proceeded to move along the bank of the watercourse. Since it was impossible to tell what direction the water craft had taken, the only thing he could do was trace the stream—first toward the sea, then inland.

POSSIBLY half a mile from where Doc Savage was working his way, a strange-looking figure crouched in the rushes. This individual had a bushy black beard, wore a close-fitting suit of chain mail and a white silk jerkin. An enormous broadsword was thrust point down into the soft earth beside him.

The individual himself presented an exotic picture, a touch of the thirteenth century. He looked very like pictures of King John.

But he had peeled back his helmet to permit the wearing of an extremely modern-looking telephonic headset. The cord of this connected to a box of electrical apparatus; from this in turn ran wires that terminated in devices buried in the ground, and other devices which dangled in the water of the stream which Doc Savage had crossed.

The contrivance over which the queer figure crouched was a listening device utilizing sensitive microphones, vacuum tube amplifiers and the headset. It caught the faintest sounds through earth or water and stepped them up to tremendous volume. The splash of a fish a quarter of a mile distant sounded as a great crackling and rushing.

The listener now unplugged his headset from the listening device and inserted the receivers into the circuit of a small portable radio. He spoke into the microphone.

"Someone is approaching," he advised.

"Know who it is?" asked a voice over the radio.

"No," said the informant. "But he seems to be heading this way."

"Pull your King John act on him," commanded the distant voice. "Scare him away from here."

The King John now picked up his broadsword, wiped mud off the point, examined the edge to make sure it was razor-sharp, then started forward. He moved in a crouching position, a posture which his mail armor made difficult, and he stopped frequently to rub his aching back and rest his muscles. But this method of travel was necessary, if his head was not to be seen above the rushes.

Frequently the man paused and jammed an ear

to the ground. He heard nothing. After he had repeated this procedure several times, he looked a bit worried. He began searching for tracks.

Eventually, he found where Doc Savage had crossed the stream. But there was no trace of Doc.

The prowler now tried to follow Doc's trail. He managed to accomplish this for perhaps a hundred yards. What he discovered caused his lips to pull thin over his teeth. He broke out in a thin film of perspiration.

For it was perfectly evident that Doc Savage had heard him approach, and was in turn shadowing him.

The man in chain mail and jerkin did not show a great deal of fright, but merely looked worried. He tucked his broadsword under an arm, fished a very modern pistol from under his jerkin and kept it in his hand. Then he devoted himself to hunting industriously for his quarry. He was able to locate no one.

Walking warily, keeping away from taller patches of reeds, the man returned to the spot where his listening device and radio apparatus were concealed. He used the listener. It brought him no sound which could be ascribed to other than natural causes.

The man shifted to the radio and got in touch with his associates.

"Something very strange about this," he advised. "I have not been able to find the fellow, but I did locate his tracks. I think he is following me."

"Only one man?" he was asked.

"One, according to the signs. What shall I do?"

"Look scared," advised the voice over the radio. "Gather up your apparatus and follow the stream inshore."

"But that will lead him toward—"

"Do not worry about that," directed the other. "We will take care of this person. You have not seen him? You have no idea what he looks like?"

"No idea at all."

The conversation terminated, and the King John gathered up the electrical apparatus, as he had been ordered, and moved along the bank of the stream.

THE air was becoming slightly warmer, and the fog correspondingly more oppressive. The vapor took on the quality of steam. Occasionally, a breath of a breeze wafted across The Wash lowlands, causing the fog to writhe and dance along in nebulous bundles. These, when seen unexpectedly, had an unnerving likeness to creeping figures, and the King John jutted his gun at more than one, thinking he was being attacked.

The man had not relaxed his vigilance. He was positive there was some stranger here in the marsh, but the other's uncanny ability in keeping himself from being seen was more than a little nerve-racking.

The ground became higher, more dry. The stream which he followed was hardly flowing, while the water it held was green, vile of hue. A water bird flew up with a noisy clattering of wings, dragging its legs for a time in the stream as it took to the air.

The King John stumbled on another hundred yards. Perspiration was oozing through the apertures in the chain mail, for the armor itself was heavy and the boxes of electrical apparatus had considerable weight.

Nervousness and physical exertion had the man nearly fagged. Tripping finally, he lowered the boxes and sat upon them, puffing.

Forty paces to his left, a bit behind, a gun whacked out thunder that bumped and rolled over the marsh in long resounding waves.

The King John popped erect. He thought at first that he had been attacked. But there was no bullet squeak nearby.

More shots crashed. A machine gun began a staccato gobbling. The shots came from both sides and the rear. Men were standing up in the marsh grass and reeds.

They all wore King John costumes, these men, and they were doing the shooting. As they fired, they charged along the back trail just traversed by the first King John.

The first King John abruptly comprehended what had happened. His companions had set a trap to catch the mysterious individual who was following him. They must have sighted the fellow.

Dropping his electrical apparatus, the first King John joined in the chase. Fatigue was forgotten. He overhauled a mailed figure with a submachine gun.

"Did you see the bloke?" he yelled.

"Not clear!" barked the other. "'E was in the bloomin' rushes. Just got a flash of 'im. But 'e ain't goin' to get away."

Yelling, using their guns steadily, the King Johns converged on the stream bank. They had their quarry hemmed in.

A man shouted suddenly. His gun muzzle guttered red flame; the ejector mechanism spouted emptied brass cartridges.

There was a loud splash.

"Got 'im!" howled the gunner.

They piled forward to the creek bank. The mud slope was scraped and indented as if a body had fallen down it. Up from the dark green water came a softly-bursting procession of bubbles.

"'E's under there," chuckled the King John who had done the last shooting.

## 34  THE SEA MAGICIAN

"DIVE in and get 'im," somebody suggested.

"With these bloomin' tin suits on?" another snorted. "You'd never come up!"

Two men strove hurriedly to undo their armor of chain mail, but it was a task requiring time. They grunted, cursed, tore their fingernails, but made little headway.

Another King John, more alert, fumbled in a knapsack which he wore and brought out what might have been paper-covered candles tied together with a string. The stuff was dynamite, already capped and fused. He used a patent lighter to set the fuse to sparking.

"Leg it away from 'ere," he warned.

Leaning over, he very carefully dropped the package of dynamite in the middle of the bubbles which were still arising from the water. The explosive sank slowly until it was out of sight, and only smoke crawling from the water denoted its presence.

**A great sheet of water climbed over the stream bank.**

The man whirled and ran. Because of the armor, he was forced to use a peculiar hopping gait. He tangled with rushes and fell down, cursing wildly.

A great sheet of water climbed over the stream bank, reached the fallen man and washed him head over heels. Flame, a gush of smoke leaped into the fog. The earth seemed to pull down several inches, then spring back into place.

The concussion bent reeds and saw-edged grass over a considerable area; and startled birds flew up. The stream was boiling mud, and the water which had been blown out made a gurgling as it ran back.

The man who had dropped the bomb got up, still swearing, his armor leaking water. He ran to the stream. His companions joined him. They stared, waiting.

"Some pieces of the body should come up," one muttered.

"Probably it was blowed right down into the

**Flame ... leaped into the fog.**

mud," the bomber grunted.

"Look!" said another.

The stream was riled, very muddy, but the mud was taking on a pronounced reddish tinge.

"Blood!" someone offered.

"What do you say we get the 'ell out of 'ere?" the first King John queried.

They turned away.

## Chapter XI
### THE PLANT IN THE MARSH

NOWHERE did the marsh growth around The Wash exceed six feet in height. But at some points there were tufts of high ground, and these promontories had a slightly greater altitude which made them distinguishable from a distance. There were enough of these, however, that no one of them stood out with particular distinctness.

Some half dozen of these tufts stood close to the bank of the stream in which the bomb had been dropped. The stream here was wider and more shallow, almost a lake.

The tufts were not natural, but it would have taken a close observer to discern this, even at a distance of only a few rods. The reeds and grass stuck up very naturally; they had been treated with green paint or perhaps dye. In other places, there was only paint over sheet tin, but the work had been expertly done. The camouflaging was perfect.

The sheds were low and rather extensive. The frames were of wood, covered with the tin, then the paint and the dyed reeds and grass on top.

One structure, abutting on the water, housed a seaplane. The craft was large, sturdy, a ship built for hard service rather than great speed or fancy looks.

What the other buildings housed was not apparent, but from one came a low mutter which could not be heard many yards, and which an expert could have identified as an excellently muffled engine.

The group of King Johns approached the camouflaged group of buildings. They walked swiftly, and all were perspiring.

Paquis came out of the secreted hut in which the engine was running. He was dapper, having changed to a tweed hunting jacket, knickers and rubber boots.

Smith also appeared, drawn by the noise of the approaching men, the clinking of their armor, the occasional clang of the broadswords. Muck smeared Smith from head to foot, and in one hand he carried a large rag. He dabbed at his face with this.

"*Bonjour, m'sieu's,*" Paquis said dryly. "What is it that brings you back looking so excited?"

"What the 'ell's wrong?" Smith echoed. "Did something go bad, you blokes?"

The King Johns dropped to the soft ground, puffing, and the man who had dropped the dynamite bomb told the story. He left out no details.

"Who was this *homme* whom you blew up?" Paquis demanded.

"We did not see 'is face," said the spokesman. "We did not even see enough of him to get an idea of what 'e looked like."

"But the body, *m'sieu's,*" Paquis murmured. "Surely, you examined that closely?"

"It was blown up."

"What about the fragments?" asked Paquis.

The spokesman shrugged. "We saw blood, gov'nor."

"*En verite!*" Paquis exploded. "Indeed! Did you not examine? Did you not search for the parts of the body?"

The other shrugged again. "The blood—"

"Have I the only brains here?" Paquis yelled. "You should have made sure, *m'sieu's*. The man might only have been wounded."

Paquis waved his arms and launched into choice expletives garnered from his native tongue. He was quite explicit about the ancestry of his colleagues.

"We will go back and make sure," he snapped. "*Dépechez-vous!* Quickly!"

RETURN to the bank of the creek required half an hour, because the King Johns were tired. They cursed the weight of their armor with each step, and some paused to remove the weighty costumes.

The stream was still riled, cloudy with mud. Water birds, circling overhead, had not returned to their feeding.

At Paquis' profane order, two King Johns stripped to their underwear and dived into the green water, which was not foul, but seemed so only because of its color.

They brought up fragments of glass. These were fitted together, and it became evident that they had once been parts of two tiny glass bottles.

Nothing else came to light.

"*Cella est impossible!*" Paquis murmured. "It is impossible. *Oui.* There should be at least some small part of a body."

"Probably washed away, gov'nor," grunted Smith.

"Maybe, m'sieu'," Paquis admitted. "But we cannot take the chance."

"What's the bloody difference?" snorted Smith. "We finish up 'ere today, anyhow."

Paquis nodded. "But no one, m'sieu', must suspect a connection between this and our delightful arrangement at Magna Island."

Smith emitted a snort. "If anybody suspects

Magna Island it'll be because that publicity bloke, Benjamin Giltstein, fell down on the bloomin' job."

"Giltstein is very wise," said Paquis. "He will handle his portion."

They argued a while longer, and because there seemed to be nothing else to do, they turned back.

All was quiet around the camouflaged buildings. The engine still ran exhaust into its silencers. A man crouched just under cover, watchful, a submachine gun on his knees.

"No action 'ere gov'nor," he reported.

Paquis entered another of the buildings. He was not inside long.

"We will push the work to completion," he directed upon reappearing. "I have consulted with our chief."

"The boss is goin' to a blarsted lot of trouble to keep 'imself undercover," a man snorted.

"The chief is taking no chances, m'sieu's," said Paquis. "He is clever."

And that, coming from Paquis, who was wont to brag about his own cunning, was high praise indeed.

Work got underway, the men entering the secreted hut. An occasional clang of tools could be heard. The men did not show themselves, for the buildings were connected by low thatched sheds. There was also activity in the shed which housed the seaplane. A man was working on the motor.

Once, all activity ceased while a plane passed overhead, bound northward. The marshes were quiet, with no movement and no sound to show that anything untoward was going on.

Solitary evidence of nearby civilization was that plane; except for its advent, the marsh remained as deserted as if it had been in some uninhabited nook of the world instead of within a few miles of fertile farms which stout Dutch emigrants had won from this swampy section of England with the same industry shown by their race in turning stretches of the Zuider Zee into tillable acreage.

Paquis seated himself before a radio transmitting-and-receiving apparatus and spoke softly. The outfit was one of small power, and it was doubtful if its etheric waves reached beyond the confines of The Wash.

Later, in compliance with Paquis' orders, King Johns came trooping in and shed their heavy armor with grateful grunts. It was evident that numerous men, all wearing the same disguise, had been posted about the marsh to keep away chance visitors, either by terrorism or violence.

About the only attraction the marshlands held was waterfowl shooting, and it was out of season for that.

The false beards, the armor, the broadswords, composing the King John masquerades were made into compact bundles and thrown into a convenient pool of quicksand, into the depths of which they were rapidly sucked.

"We had best post a guard with the listening devices, m'sieu'," Paquis decided, and dispatched a man with one of the intricate electrical contrivances.

The man penetrated alone through the rushes for a few yards, carrying his box, then knelt down to fit the connections.

Unexpectedly, there was a faint crunching sound at the man's side. He looked down. There were shiny particles on the ground; they might have been gossamery flakes of glass, and they reposed in a smear of liquid which seemed to evaporate with magical suddenness.

The man sighed deeply and lay down quite motionless beside his apparatus.

A STIRRING in the fog, and a giant man of bronze materialized among the rushes, came close and held the wrist of the fallen man briefly. There was strong pulse. The prone man's lower lip fluttered and outgoing breath made a sound faintly reminiscent of a snore.

The thing which had broken beside the unconscious victim was a glass ball, thin-walled, holding a chemical compound which vaporized instantly and produced senselessness, should anyone be breathing within a few feet of it.

Doc Savage wore a peculiar type of vest beneath his outer clothing. Its foundation was composed of light, bulletproof plates, lying scale fashion, and over the plates were pockets and numerous receptacles. Padding between these made the vest almost unnoticeable.

The contents of the vest pockets made up a remarkable assortment. There were delicate mechanical devices, strange scientific weapons, glass vials holding chemical concoctions calculated to accomplish the unusual.

It was two of these glass bottles which had enabled the bronze man to feign his death in the stream. One contained a chemical which, mixing with water, caused bubbles; the other held merely red dye, imitation blood.

The bronze giant, cornered, not wishing his identity to become known, had taken to the water, swimming beneath the surface until he was clear of pursuit. He had been out of the stream when the explosive was tossed in.

Doc Savage advanced, moving like a wraith through the fog. The strange marsh structure loomed ahead. He sank flat and seemed to vanish, only to reappear shortly, close against the wall of a structure.

The surface was of tin, daubed with streaks of green and pale brown to imitate rushes growing from mud. The paint had a fresh appearance, as if it had not been there long. Doc planted an ear to the gaudy metal.

Nearby, the muffled engine labored steadily. There was a faint sighing, as if pumps were at work, and occasionally a dull sizzling noise. Men moving about made some sound.

Doc Savage became convinced that the hut at which he listened was occupied. A time or two, someone shifted position.

A voice said, "This inaction comes under the nomenclature of an unmitigatedly irksome vocation."

Doc Savage remained very quiet, but there came into being a weird, tiny sound. This note was so vague that it might easily have been mistaken for some vagary of the fitful breezes which stirred the fog. It was a trilling, one which might have been made by a wind through a cold, denuded forest; or it might have been the note of some exotic tropical songster.

This was the sound of Doc Savage, a tiny and unconscious thing which he often made in moments of stress. But such a quality of ventriloquism did the trilling possess that a close bystander, looking at the bronze man, could not have told from whence it came. The metallic lips did not move; there was no undulation of throat sinews. It was doubtful that Doc himself was aware just how the sound came into being.

The trilling must have penetrated the hut. The voice which had spoken before, spoke again. It was not English, French or any language known to the so-called civilized world which was uttered. The dialect was the language of a lost race, that of the ancient Mayan civilization of Central America. It was a tongue known only to a few white men—and the inhabitants of a remote valley in Central America, which Doc Savage had once visited in successful quest of the immense treasure trove of ancient Maya.

"There is one guard in here, Doc," said the voice in Mayan.

It was Johnny's scholastic tone.

"WHAT in 'ades are you sayin'?" the guard snarled, glaring at the gaunt Johnny.

"That was an incantation calculated to engender a smile from good dame fortune," Johnny said dryly.

The guard scowled, mulling over Johnny's large words. He was a beetle of a fellow with overhanging brows and a vague forehead.

"Pipe down!" he advised.

"I am an individual with a superpreponderance of terminology," Johnny said. "I am a verbarian, a glossographer, abundantly interested in the intricacies of allocution."

"Whew!" gulped the guard. "Such a gab! Lay off, will you!"

The man fumbled his gun, but not too purposefully; he seemed to be intrigued by Johnny's flow of many-syllabled words.

Johnny went on speaking. He had heard Doc's trilling sound, and knew the bronze man was near. No hint of inner excitement appeared on his long, angular features, but he was greatly interested in fastening the watchman's attention until Doc completed whatever move he might have in mind.

"The art of harangue," Johnny advised, "is the essence of erudition, one of the acmes of menticulture. It is—"

A hard metallic cloud seemed to fill the hut entrance. It shifted with lightning speed, flashing for the guard who was entranced by the big words.

The guard was warned by some drifting shadow. He whirled. His mouth flew open, his gun came up. But his motions seemed infinitely slow in comparison to the speed of the bronze giant.

Metallic fingers clamped the guard's gun hand, twisted, and removed the weapon. Another hand found the fellow's mouth, gathering his lips together tightly so that he could not cry out.

Doc Savage dropped the gun and snapped the hand which had held it to the back of the prisoner's neck. The fingers tensed, exerting tremendous pressure upon certain nerve centers.

A peculiar thing happened. The guard gave one tremendous jerk, then became quite stiff. Doc lowered him to the ground. The guard was quite conscious, endeavoring to move, but gripped by a strange paralysis.

Johnny eyed the stricken man curiously. Johnny had seen Doc Savage do this thing before, but the feat still amazed him. It would be hours before the guard recovered the use of his limbs, unless Doc made a readjustment which would relieve the paralyzing pressure. The bronze man's remarkable knowledge of human anatomy made the feat possible.

Doc Savage swooped beside Johnny, grasped the handcuff links, and his tremendous sinews coiled and tensed. Bundles of thews the size of small footballs stood out on his vast shoulders.

Johnny's eyes widened as the links snapped. He knew just how much strength that performance really required. It was something few professional strong men could have performed.

"What is going on here?" Doc demanded.

"Blessed if I know," breathed Johnny. "They have been very careful not to tell me."

Doc moved an admonishing hand. "Listen!"

Johnny strained his ears. "Someone coming!"

Sh-h-h! We'll let you in on something. "Johnny" is not at heart the collegiate, dignified gentleman whom he pretends to be. Those four-dollar words are used by Johnny largely because they annoy his companions.

Johnny—he is William Harper Littlejohn to his learned college associates—was once the head of the natural-science research department of a famous university, hence he is no dumbbell. Few men know more about ancient peoples or their surroundings than Johnny, and he can tell you the exact formation of earth structure in nearly any portion of the globe. As an archæologist and geologist, he is second only to Doc Savage.

The big-worded Johnny loves a fight. He would rather be in a scrap than inspecting an ancient hieroglyphic with that monocle which he wears suspended by a ribbon from his lapel, and that is saying a great deal.

Johnny forgets his big words when the going gets tough.

## Chapter XII
## KING JOHN'S GOBLET

IT was Smith who was approaching. He had donned hip boots and there must have been a leak in one, because it made sobbing noises with each step. His coat was off, revealing the harness which held an automatic under each armpit.

He reached the hut which held the prisoner, stooped and peered inside.

Johnny sat on the floor, arms held together in front of him, so that it seemed as if he were still handcuffed. The faint light glinted on the manacle circlets.

Smith's jaw sagged as he saw the guard reposing motionless in the soft muck just inside.

"What the bloody 'ell?" he growled.

"Your custodian seems to have encountered an unpropitious eventuation," said Johnny.

"Damn you an' them big words!" grated Smith. "What'd you do to this bloke?"

"I did not molest him," Johnny advised truthfully.

Smith, unsuspicious and enraged at Johnny, lunged inside, driving a hand at his left armpit gun. At that point, he suffered a mild accident. He stumbled, turned half sidewise and put his free hand down to keep from falling.

This caused him to face Doc Savage, who was poised just inside the door.

Smith squalled. He still fought to get the gun out, and because the weapon was holstered on the side of Doc Savage, Smith flung up the arm which covered it and began to pull the trigger. That was a mistake. The slide jacked back the first time and stuck, empty cartridge jammed in the ejector.

With a revolver, the firing from the holster trick might have been accomplished.

Doc whipped forward. Smith whirled and ran. His face was a mask of terror, for he had recognized Doc Savage and all his earlier fear of the bronze man had returned manyfold.

Smith was not headed toward the door; the sheet-tin wall of the shack barred his way. He put his head down, bundled his round skull in his arms and hit the wall full speed. Construction was rickety. Thin metal plates caved off and let the scared man out.

Johnny clattered up from the floor, a lean scarecrow who looked angry.

"Of all the breaks!" he yelled. "Of all the unmitigated misfortunes!"

The vicinity was in an uproar. Men shouted, swore. Smith was screaming as might a man who was being mauled by a tiger. Terror tipped and guttered in his tone.

Inside the hut there was suddenly a sound as if some giant had a handful of oversize buckshot and was dropping them in quick succession on the roof. Rents opened. The pop and clank of lead made the more distant bawl of the machine gun almost indistinguishable.

The shooting interrupted itself. They could hear tufts of dyed reeds, cut loose from the roof by the bullets, sifting to the ground. They fell with a small, very dry noise.

"How many are here?" Doc asked.

"Dozen, anyway," said Johnny.

"Come," Doc directed. "We had best get out of here."

The bronze man approached one tin wall, turned sidewise when he was close, and went through as easily as if the sheet metal had been paper. Johnny followed.

ONE of the King Johns—without his costume now—had been close to the wall. The crash and roar as Doc came through caused him to leap backward. He lifted his gun.

What happened then smacked of the miraculous. The gun gushed noise and powder lightning. But the bullet missed, missed because the bronze giant had shifted with uncanny speed. With eyes trying to get out of their sockets like bugs out of holes, the King John tried for a second shot. He did not make it.

Metallic fingers clamped the nape of his neck, twisted. The King John jammed his arms down stiff at his sides and his whole body seemed to become rigid.

After Doc released him the man stood upright for a moment, as if he were a log standing on end, and when he fell, it was as a log would fall, rigidly unbending. After he lay on the ground he breathed and his eyes were open, but none of his limbs functioned.

Doc Savage dived a hand inside his clothing, brought out a tiny sphere of metal and threw it. The ball sailed over the hut roof, to land among the men beyond. It opened with a handclap report. Black smoke geysered and spread with uncanny speed.

Howling, Paquis and his men ran from the pall, fearing it had a gaseous content. Order was in their retreat, however. They piled into another of the huts, and, after the elapse of some ten seconds, began coming out again, wrenching gas mask hoods over their heads.

Johnny said dryly, "They are going to make a fight of it, Doc."

The bronze man gestured with his head, then flattened and crept back through the tall reeds.

Johnny, following, was very quiet, because their foes had fallen silent. The smoke, a sepia worm that still uncoiled from the metallic egg that Doc had thrown, concealed them for the moment. Paquis and his crew were trying to locate them by ear.

Doc was a silent ghost of bronze. Johnny picked each step with care. It was very possible that their lives depended on not being heard, for they were in the open now. The reeds and salt water grass would not turn bullets.

They covered perhaps a hundred yards. The fitful breezes that had been doing things with the fog moved the smoke cloud away from the cluster of camouflaged buildings. Paquis began barking angry orders.

"They are going to trail us," murmured Johnny, who had a habit of forgetting his big words when the going became tough.

Doc Savage's answer to that was to pause and employ one finger to make a small pit in the ground. In this he buried one of his thin-walled glass anaesthetic balls. He left it near the surface, where treading feet would break it. The gas, being odorless, would overcome the unwary.

"But they're wearing gas masks," Johnny pointed out.

"They may have them off by the time they reach here," Doc reminded. "This fog will smear the windows of the eyepieces and make the masks a nuisance."

The two men continued to crawl. They were soaked, fog having deposited on the marsh growth like rain. Doc left others of the anaesthetic bulbs buried.

After a while they heard surprised, horrified yells. As Doc had surmised, the gas masks must have been removed, and one of the glass balls had been broken unwittingly underfoot.

They did not see how many men were overcome. Pursuit, however, ended suddenly.

JOHNNY, listening intently, was unable to tell just what their foes were doing.

"They are going back," Doc said.

Johnny nodded, not at all surprised at the evidence of the bronze man's superior hearing. Doc had developed all his faculties to an almost incredible sensitivity. He did this by scientific exercises, two hours of them daily since childhood.

Johnny crouched and considered. He was scarcely breathing rapidly. There was an astonishing endurance in his bony frame, and he had been in tight places before.

"Think," Doc requested. "Didn't you overhear anything that might show what they are doing here in the marsh?"

"They blindfolded me when they brought me here," Johnny said slowly. "What I saw was insignificant."

"The engine seemed to be operating a compressor," Doc stated.

Johnny nodded. "Yes. A pump or kindred appurtenance. The specific category to which the appliance is affinitive defeats me for the moment."

The bony archaeologist and geologist was falling back upon his large words, now that danger had receded.

"Smell anything?" Doc questioned.

Johnny sniffed. "Only the rather unpleasant aroma of this inelegant terrain."

"Ammonia," Doc said.

Johnny tried again with his olfactory organs. Then he nodded soberly.

"Correct," he admitted. "I mistook it for one of the marsh smells. Do you attach significance to it?"

Doc said, "We must get a look at their plant."

There came a few scattered reports from the direction of their foes. An inexperienced ear might have mistaken the sounds for shots.

"Engine backfiring," Doc said.

An instant later, the engine started. It was an airplane motor, for there was the added quality of a propeller turning, a hollow whining note. Shouts reached them, voices lifted over the motor sound.

"Maybe they are going to hunt us from the air?" Johnny groaned.

"Don't worry," Doc told him. "I have enough smoke bombs to keep us hidden."

Doc and Johnny now worked toward the strange marsh establishment of their enemies. But before they came near, the plane took the air. The craft ran down the stream and was out of sight in the fog before it lifted. It had not taken the air easily.

Instead of circling back, the ship continued straight out over The Wash until its sound died completely.

"I'll be superamalgamated!" said Johnny. "I fail to understand this."

Doc leveled an arm. "Look."

The fog above the camouflaged shacks was turning black, as if it were being mixed with a vaporized ink or dye.

"Smoke!" gasped Johnny.

"Exactly!" Doc began to run. "They have set fire to their buildings."

Johnny set out, longlegged, after the bronze man. They covered ground swiftly until the shacks—they were bundled in red flames now—loomed out of the fog. The two men slackened their pace, even stopping to listen.

But they might as well have come on boldly, they found out a few moments later—for Paquis and the rest of their foes had departed, taking along the men whom Doc had made unconscious.

"WE scared them out!" Johnny shouted.

Doc Savage did not answer. The silenced engine no longer ran. He lunged to the shack which held it, but instead of going in the door, swerved around and kicked in a side slab of tin.

Johnny leaped for the door.

"Careful!" Doc warned. "Don't go in that way."

Johnny shifted from the door, came to Doc's side and peered into the shack. His eyes flew wide. The door was partially ajar, and wedged under it was a hand grenade, fastened in such a position that a movement of the door would have caused the key to be wrenched out with a resultant explosion.

"Their parting gift," Doc said quietly.

It was very hot inside the shed, for flames were all over the roof, consuming the camouflaging reeds and rushes. Gasoline seemed to have been doused on the wooden framework, too, as this was burning savagely.

Machinery occupied the center of the structure. In it was a large Diesel engine, silenced; there was also a compressing device. The odor of ammonia was very strong.

"Back," Doc advised. "One of the ammonia pipes has ruptured."

Johnny was puzzled enough that he forgot his exaggerated phraseology.

"I don't get it," he exploded. "That looks like a—"

"Refrigerating machine," Doc agreed. "It is."

"But why a refrigerating plant here in the marsh?"

"Let's see if some of these other shacks will answer that."

The next camouflaged building proved to be a crude barracks. The bunks and tables inside had been fired thoroughly. They tried another structure, which was by far the largest of the lot.

Roof and sides of this edifice were burning, but there was an infinitely hotter flame in the center of the floor. It poured up with a violent roar from a chimney-like aperture.

"A hole, a shaft of some kind," Doc stated.

"They poured down a barrel of gasoline and dropped in a match," added Johnny.

Pipes made a complex interlacing around the burning shaft mouth. Some of these ran off in the direction of the refrigerating plant. Others extended toward the nearby stream. Still more, smaller pipes stood up like pickets around the shaft maw. There was another engine and a large-capacity muck suction pump.

"Simple," Doc said.

"Sure," Johnny echoed. "So juvenile that I fail to make heads or tails of it."

"Ever hear of the method used in sinking ventilating shafts in the large vehicular tunnel at Antwerp, Belgium, when it was necessary to go through soft quicksand and muck such as this?"

"I'm not an engineer," Johnny replied.

"They simply installed a large refrigerating plant and froze the muck," Doc explained. "Then they could excavate without sinking caissons."

"You mean—"

"That our friends simply sank a shaft by using the most up-to-date engineering methods."

"But what were they after?"

IF Doc Savage had any ideas on that question, he did not voice them. It was furnace-hot in the hut; parts of the room were already falling in. They backed away.

Johnny said thoughtfully, "I believe the men completed whatever machination they had under way."

Doc Savage's strange flake-gold eyes were roving, searching. Without glancing at his aide, he queried, "What makes you think that?"

"Morsels of information which I overheard," said Johnny. "On several occasions, my captors mentioned that their work here was nearly completed. It was to be finished today, I gathered. Then they were going to take me to some island where I could be held until I could no longer endanger their plans."

"Get the name of the island?" Doc asked.

"Maggie, or something similar," Johnny murmured.

"Magna Island?"

"That was it." Johnny's nod was vehement. "What do you know about Magna Island?"

"Monk and Ham are investigating it now," Doc advised.

The bronze man now moved away. He seemed to have a definite objective, striding through the rushes and wading mud puddles. Johnny, trailing curiously, discovered that Doc was following a series of footprints.

"You think one of them did not flee—" Johnny began, then failed to finish when he saw that the footprints were double, going and coming.

"One man seems to have crept out of the camp just before they departed," Doc said. "The prints are fresh. And if you will notice closely, the man was taking pains not to be seen by his companions. It looks as if he had something hidden out here, and went to get it before they left."

Doc's surmise seemed to be accurate, for they soon came upon a spot where moist earth had been clawed up hastily.

"They must have trusted each other," Johnny snorted. "This fellow evidently incarcerated his valuables away from his friends, fearing he would be robbed."

Doc did not comment. He knelt and sifted through the soft loam, turning over lumps as if to ascertain if there were indentations which would show the nature of the thing that had been hidden. He found no such molds. But he did turn up an object which had been overlooked, possibly because of haste.

The bronze man scraped mud from the piece. He used a handkerchief to wipe it carefully. Then he held it up. It was of bright yellow metal.

The object was large, of almost quart capacity. Its lines were those of a rather grotesque cup. A rather elaborate design of enamel was done on one side.

Johnny peered closely.

"The coat of arms of King John," he murmured. "Is it brass?"

"Gold," Doc said. "Soft enough that it can be dented with a fingernail. That means very pure gold."

"Fake?" Johnny questioned.

"Genuine," Doc corrected. "A museum piece. You are an authority on ancient things. What would you say it was worth?"

"A thousand pounds," said Johnny.

"A bit more," Doc decided. "You remember the local peasant who was wounded by one of the King Johns last night?"

"Yes." Johnny nodded vehemently. "They said that he had a coin in his pocket. A coin dated during King John's reign. But how did you know that?"

"The newspapers," Doc told him.

"They must have robbed a museum," Johnny murmured. "Yes, they must have done that to get genuine relics to help out their King John ghost deception. But why?"

"The King John scheme was to keep the natives away, so this establishment would not be found."

"That wasn't what I meant," said Johnny. "Why all this rigamarole? What is behind it all?"

"The answer to that must be on Magna Island," Doc decided slowly. "Monk and Ham may turn it up."

## Chapter XIII
## THE ATTEMPT TO KILL

MONK and Ham jammed their faces to the windows of the big transport seaplane and got their first glimpse of Magna Island. Nearly a dozen other correspondents in the aircraft did the same thing. The plane was very large and had three motors.

"The thing looks like a big green frog spraddled out in the ocean," Monk decided.

"She is gooda way for describe da place," said Ham, who was still playing the part of a Latin who did not speak any too good English.

Out of the corner of his mouth, Monk said, "Blast you, get away from me! They'll get suspicious."

"If you think I want your company, you're crazy, you bug-eyed gorilla," Ham advised, also in an aside.

Ham then changed his position, ostensibly to see Magna Island better, and to take some pictures with the camera which he had thoughtfully brought. It was the first time since leaving London that he and Monk had been in close proximity.

Suave Benjamin Giltstein was forward, where he had been haranguing the newspaper correspondents vociferously up to the point when Magna Island had been sighted. The plane, which Giltstein had provided, had a cabin which was nearly soundproof, permitting conversation if voices were lifted slightly.

If Benjamin Giltstein suspected Monk and Ham, he had shown no sign of it. He had treated them with that glad-handed manner that a press agent always displays toward a newspaperman.

The plane circled Magna Island at an altitude of less than two hundred feet. The isle was low, slightly rocky, and in shape did resemble a sprawled frog of a particularly bilious green hue.

The open, spraddled legs faced in the direction of the prevailing ocean current, and might have been likened to dikes.

Benjamin Giltstein pointed at the crotch where the legs, had the island been a frog, would have joined.

"Look, gentlemen!" he said. "The plant which accomplishes what man has always dreamed of—taking gold from sea water."

The plant was a scattering of buildings of bright new brick and freshly painted roofing. The structures numbered four. One was a gate house, close to the water, and from this a canal ran to another building, which was very large. The other two structures were obviously a power house and tool shed.

From the building, a waste canal carried the water across the island and emptied it out of what would have been the frog's mouth.

"You see, the island is perfect," said Giltstein. "Prevailing ocean currents bring water in between two arms of land, and after the gold is extracted, the water is permitted to flow out at the other end of the island, where the currents carry it away. That way, we do not treat the same water twice."

Monk paid no particular attention. He was studying the rest of Magna Island. Along the west side, where the ground was a bit higher, there were several ancient-looking stone houses arrayed along a street.

"What's that?" Monk asked, nudging Giltstein.

"The small village which was formerly on the island," said the press agent. "It is now occupied by workmen who operate the gold-extracting plant."

The pilot of the seaplane executed a fair enough landing between the frog-leg peninsulas, then beached the craft.

THE journalists pulled off shoes and socks and waded ashore, those who had cameras carrying them above their heads. They were met by several grim-looking men who carried rifles and pistols.

Each of these armed men also wore a uniform comprised of boots, laced breeches, jacket and a rather picturesque beret.

"Why the bally regalia?" asked the representative of a London afternoon sheet.

"These are Royal Magna Guards," said Giltstein.

"Royal?" murmured the other questioningly.

Benjamin Giltatein smiled. "Have you forgotten that I told you this island is independent? It is not owned by any nation. The king of Magna Island is an absolute monarch."

"Who is king?" Monk put in.

Without batting an eye, Giltstein said, "Wehman Mills."

"The man who discovered the method of taking gold from sea water?"

"Correct."

"May we interview King Wehman Mills?" Monk requested promptly.

Giltstein smiled. "I am sorry. He is not receiving the press."

"Then will he pose for a picture?" persisted Monk.

"No," said Giltstein. "But later I shall give each of you gentlemen a picture of Wehman Mills."

They were working toward the cluster of buildings which housed the gold extraction plant.

Ham came to an abrupt stop. The dapper lawyer looked very unlike his usual self in the baggy suit. To his credit, he did wear the disguise excellently. No examination with the naked eye would show that the dark cast of his skin came from a dye. The large gold front teeth were merely shells which clipped in place.

"Me, I forgetta da plate for the cam'ra," Ham declared. "Gotta go back and get, or no da picture tak'."

He started back toward the plane.

"Wait!" Benjamin Giltstein said sharply. "One of the Royal Magna Guards will have to accompany you."

"Whatsa da idea?" demanded Ham.

"A rule of King Wehman Mills," the other said smugly.

Ham, hurrying toward the plane, found himself accompanied by a strapping, sour-faced man with a rifle. The lawyer was disgusted. He had hoped to get a chance to do some scouting, once he was clear of the others.

Just why the newspaper correspondents had been brought to the island, Ham was not sure, but he was certain they would only be shown the gold-from-sea-water plant. Monk, who had few equals in the realms of chemistry, could tell whether the plant would actually work. Ham had wanted to examine other parts of the island, the small village on the west side, for instance.

Ham and his escort were working through brush now. Sounds made by the other party were lost to their ears.

With great casualness, Ham drifted a hand inside his clothing. When he brought it out, he held one of the little glass anaesthetic bombs which were Doc Savage's invention.

The barrister halted suddenly.

"Whew!" he exclaimed. "Whatsa da smell?"

The guard sniffed, scowled and said, "I don't smell a thing."

Ham put a blank, wide-mouthed expression on his face, swayed violently, then sagged down on all fours. He slumped prone. As he did this, he held his breath and broke the anaesthetic bulb in his hand.

The escort stared. He sniffed again, thinking something had overcome Ham. Then he slouched down, toppling over on his back and went soundly asleep.

Ham bounded erect. The anaesthetic gas dissipated itself in less than a minute, and he had escaped its effects simply by holding his breath.

He chuckled as he eyed the sleeping escort. Ham intended to do a bit of investigating, then come back and lie down beside the guard, faking the same kind of unconsciousness. When the guard revived, he would think they had both lain senseless; he would be certain Ham had been overcome first.

THE village on the west side of the island had never been very pretentious, and it now showed signs of having received very little care for some weeks. Weeds were uncut, the grass untrimmed; windows needed washing, and wadded newspapers had been stuffed in where some panes had been broken.

The houses were of stone, some with tiled roofs, and others thatched. The one narrow street was unpaved, but the gravelly nature of the ground made that unimportant. Instead of sidewalks, there were trampled paths.

Ham silently blessed the height and profusion of the weeds, then got down on all fours and crawled ahead. He missed his sword cane; carrying the unique weapon had been out of the question, for it would have furnished too strong a clue to his identity.

The open rear door of a house invited. Ham approached it, only to stop abruptly as a voice came from within.

"There is no cause for alarm, *m'sieu's.*" The tone was remindful of the purr of a big cat. "What if Doc Savage did appear at The Wash? He learned nothing. We destroyed our plant there, so that he will have no idea of what we were doing."

"Hi wouldn't be too blarsted sure, Paquis," growled another voice. "That bronze bloke ain't human!"

"I must admit he is difficult to deceive," said Paquis. *"Oui.* It was a great shock when he turned up and rescued his friend, William Harper Littlejohn. *Quelle honte!* What a shame! But Doc Savage has no inkling of the connection of this island with The Wash."

Ham, digesting this, permitted himself a wide grin. Johnny, it seemed, was now safe.

Smith said in his strong Cockney, "Bringin' them bloomin' journalists 'ere was a bad move, if you'd arsk me."

"It was the idea of *le commandant-enchef,*" Paquis reminded.

"Hi know," Smith muttered. "The big boss 'as 'is own ideas."

*"Oui,* and excellent ones, too," said Paquis, his purr more pronounced. "The visit of the newspapermen was quite necessary."

"Hi fails to see why."

"Publicity," explained cat-voiced Paquis. "The more publicity we have, the less likelihood there is of anyone becoming suspicious."

Smith snorted. "If one of our prisoners 'ere was to get away an' talk to a journalist bloke, there'd be some publicity of the wrong bloomin' kind."

*"Oui,"* Paquis agreed. "And for that reason, I suggest that you assist the guard now watching our prisoners."

Smith, burly and uneasy of face, came out of the house and moved along one of the paths.

HAM trickled along through the weeds behind the Cockney. Ham was recovering from a surprise. He had not known there were other prisoners. He was highly curious to know who they could be.

Smith reached a stone house, paused under the overhang of the thatched roof and peered about intently. Ham lay perfectly motionless in the weeds.

Overhead, gulls circled and quarreled. A faint pounding of surf could be heard, and from the direction of the gold-extracting plant came the muted rumble of machinery.

Smith entered the house.

Ham drifted a hand to an armpit, where there was a holster so cleverly padded that its presence was hardly discernible. He withdrew one of Doc Savage's compact machine pistols. Fitted in a pocket at the side of the holster was a canisterlike device—a silencer for use on the weapons.

Ham fitted it in place, then examined the ammo drum to make sure it was charged with mercy bullets, slugs which would penetrate barely through the skin and produce unconsciousness. He latched the gun into single-fire position.

Changing his position, he managed to sight

Smith. The portly man stood just inside the door—and Ham, sighting carefully, shot him in one leg.

The report of the silenced gun could be heard—it fired only one bullet and that was launched with a tongue-click of a noise.

Smith jumped violently, clapped a hand to the spot where the metal chemical-bearing shell had bitten him. He bent backward and tried to examine the wound. He was still bending backward when he upset and hit the floor heavily. After that, he did not move.

A second man leaped to Smith's side. He was burly, and cradled a submachine gun under an arm.

Ham's silenced rapid-firer clicked again; the empty cartridge which jumped from the ejector hit a rock in falling and made a sound almost as loud as the gun report.

In the house, the burly man stood up stiffly and put a hand to his side. He reeled to the door, leaned over to look out, and seemed unable to stop himself from tilting. A sluggish bundle of arms and legs, he rolled through the door.

Ham ran for the door. If there was another man inside, he had little hopes of potting him; he could shoot on the run if he had to. Ham was an excellent shot.

But there was only one man in the room. He was an elderly chain of bone and sinew in a rumpled black suit that had once been shiny. His white hair was mussed and stood out like the wig of an elderly circus wild man.

The man was a prisoner by a simple device. A steel flywheel, which must have weighed five hundred pounds, was shackled to one of his ankles.

Ham tangled fingers in the hair of the last man to fall a victim to the mercy bullets and hauled him back into the room, where he would not be seen. Then he eyed the white-haired prisoner.

"Who," Ham demanded, "are you?"

The other got to his feet. He looked as if he had not been fed recently.

"Where is my niece?" he demanded. "Is she all right?"

Ham said, "I asked who in blazes you are?"

"Wehman Mills," muttered the old man.

HAM had no idea what name to expect, but he was surprised. Wehman Mills was the name of the man who was supposed to be king of the island, as well as the inventor of the process for taking gold from the ocean.

"My niece!" said Wehman Mills anxiously. "Find her! Never mind me. Look for Elaine."

"Where is she?" Ham demanded.

Wehman Mills kicked the leg which was shackled to the flywheel and the manacle links jingled.

"How do I know," he groaned. "Around here somewhere. In one of these houses, I suppose."

Ham clipped a fresh ammo drum into his machine pistol, then lifted the unusual weapon.

Wehman Mills recoiled, tried wildly to break his chain, then wailed, "Please, I haven't done anything!"

Ham pulled the trigger and got a sound as if someone in a speeding automobile had put out a stick as a picket fence was being passed. Lead boiled on the flywheel; Wehman's shackled chain whipped madly. Then the padlock which held it came apart, spewing its innards.

Wehman Mills snapped, "You might have told me what you were going to do! You scared me silly!"

"Where do you think this Elaine is?" Ham demanded.

"They talked like she was near here," said Mills. "Let's look around."

The elderly man would have rushed outside had Ham not stayed him with an arm. Ham made a survey through a window, and saw a man come to the door of the shack in which he had first heard voices. The fellow had heard the noise as the supermachine gun cut through the cuff padlock, and he was curious.

"Anything wrong, Monsieur Smith?" he called.

Ham lacked a great deal of being the expert voice mimic that Doc Savage was, but he did his best.

"Blimme, no!" he shouted.

He managed a faint resemblance to Smith's harsh voice, and the hollow reverberations within the room disguised the tone further, so that Paquis' suspicions were allayed. He turned back out of sight.

Ham selected a window on the other side, and worked at getting the hinged sash open.

"Will this island plant really take gold from sea water?" he asked.

"Yes," said Wehman Mills. "Emphatically!"

"Then what is this all about?"

"I am being robbed of my secret," snarled Mills. "Men came to me and financed the construction of the plant. Then I discovered they were holding up letters which I had written to my niece, Elaine. I pretended that I needed some materials which could only be purchased in the French town of Brest, where Elaine was staying. They took me there, and I managed to escape. But they seized me again. Then they seized Elaine when she became suspicious and started investigating."

Ham had the window open. He peered through, saw no one and eased outside.

"You escaped in Brest," repeated Ham. "And they caught you and brought you back. Then they caught Elaine, too."

"Elaine and some young man named Henry Trump." Mills showed his age by the difficulty with which he negotiated the passage through the open window. He grunted and winced as stiffened joints bothered him.

"Where does The Wash angle come in?" Ham asked.

"What?"

"The Wash. These men were doing something up there. You know, that's the marsh region on the east coast of England."

"I haven't the slightest idea why the men should have been at The Wash," declared Wehman Mills. "It is all quite simple. They are stealing my plan for taking gold from sea water. It amounts to nothing more than that."

"Let's find Elaine and Henry Trump," Ham suggested. "Then we'll argue."

THEY found Elaine in the first house into which they looked. Like Wehman Mills had been, she was manacled to a heavy piece of machinery.

There was one guard. Ham shot him through the window, after clipping mercy bullets into the rapid-firer, and the man weaved around for only a short time before he slammed himself down on the floor, unconscious.

"Uncle Wehman!" the young woman gasped.

Ham gazed at the young woman in astonishment, reflecting that she offered about as entrancing a picture as he had ever seen. The rigors of confinement had done little to detract from her charm.

The superfirer stuttered through its excellent muffler. The padlock did not give and Elaine Mills gasped as needlelike bits of splashing lead imbedded in her shapely ankle.

Ham shed his coat, folded it and used it as a pad, then tried again. This time, the lock was blasted open.

"Henry Trump," Elaine exclaimed. "We've got to free him, too."

Ham frowned. "Who's Henry Trump?"

"A young man who was very kind to me on the boat," said Elaine Mills. "They locked him up in the house next door, I think."

Ham nodded, and peered through a window to ascertain if the noise of the silenced gun—the impact of the lead bullets on the padlock had made considerable noise—had attracted attention; but the straggling village remained deserted.

"What become of the original inhabitants of this town?" Ham demanded.

"They were moved away when the village was purchased," Wehman Mills advised.

"Why was this island selected as the spot to take gold from sea water?" Ham asked curiously.

"Because it is independent," the elderly inventor told him. "Taxes do not have to be paid to anybody."

"Taxes?"

"Income taxes," Wehman Mills reminded, "are terrible. They are bad enough in America, but worse in England. We figured it all out. If you make a million dollars, the government takes more than half of it."

"It's hard for me to feel sorry for the poor fellow who worries about the taxes on a million," Ham snorted.

"The island cost only fifty thousand," said Wehman Mills. "That equals only a few days taxes on the profits from my process of taking gold from the sea."

"How fast do you think the plant will recover gold?"

"At the rate of at least half a million dollars a day," the other declared solemnly.

Ham was still watching for some sign that an alarm had been spread, although Magna Island seemed outwardly quiet.

"Can you show me the house where you think they are holding Henry Trump?" he asked.

Elaine Mills came to his side, selected a cottage and pointed. "There," she said.

"We can make it there all right, keeping under cover," Ham decided.

"We must rescue Henry Trump," Elaine said fervently.

Ham tried to keep it from showing on his face, but he did not care for the fervor with which the attractive young woman spoke of Henry Trump. Trump seemed to have made a hit.

THE house which was supposed to hold Henry Trump was closed up tightly, the windows being shuttered and the door locked.

Ham circled the place once, sheltered by a low stone wall and an arbor of untrimmed grapevines.

"Sure this is the place?" he asked Elaine Mills.

"I think so," said the young woman.

Ham recharged his gun with mercy bullets, concealed the weapon under his coat, and rapped on the door. Elaine Mills was close at Ham's elbow.

"Yes?" said a pleasant masculine voice from within the house.

"That's Henry Trump," Elaine breathed.

"Any guards over you, Trump?" Ham called.

"No!" exploded the voice from within. "Who the devil are you?"

"It's a rescue party," Elaine gasped. "We're coming in!"

It sounded as if Henry Trump swore softly and

in a highly surprised tone. Then Ham was shoving at the door. It was stuck rather than locked, and it came open briskly, spilling him inside.

The closed shutters made the place gloomy. The lawyer blinked about, gun ready.

A clinking of metal came from the corner.

"Over here," said Henry Trump's voice.

Ham made out the young man then. Trump was seated on the floor, wrists and ankles ornamented with handcuffs.

"Who are you?" he demanded.

"Brigadier General Theodore Marley Brooks, more often known as Ham," Ham told him. "One of Doc Savage's men."

"One of *whose* men?" Henry Trump demanded, and his mouth fell open.

"Doc Savage's."

"Is *he* here?" Trump asked, then let his mouth fall open again.

"No," said Ham. "Let me try to pick the lock on those bracelets."

"You won't have much luck," Trump grunted. "I've been trying to do it for hours."

"Got a hairpin?" Ham asked Elaine.

"A bobbie pin," she admitted, and fumbled at her hair.

Ham took the bobbie pin, which was superior to the ordinary wire type, being stiffer, and went to work on the locks. Ham had studied many things besides law, locks being one of them.

"What's going on here?" Henry Trump demanded. "What is behind all of this trouble?"

"Search me," said Ham.

"These men are trying to steal my system of taking gold from the sea!" snapped thin, white-haired Wehman Mills. "That is what is behind it."

The handcuff locks came open in quick succession.

"I'll be danged," Trump grinned. "And I worked my head off trying to open them."

He got to his feet.

There was a crash. Slats fell out of a window shutter. Glass broke and spilled in a jingling stream on the floor.

The rifle barrel which had broken shutter and pane became plainly visible. It was obvious from the shape of the magazine that the rifle was of the automatic variety.

*"Ne bougez pas,"* said Paquis' cat voice.

Pretty Elaine Mills, who did not speak French, breathed, "What did he say?"

"'Don't stir'," Ham translated. "Better take the advice."

PAQUIS kept his rifle perfectly steady, did not move his eye from the sights, and gave an order to someone behind him. There was fluttering outside in the weeds, the crunch of an occasional dry stick. Then the door slammed ajar and men walked in. They let Ham and the others look down the muzzles of submachine guns.

"Give up your gun, my dark-faced friend in the baggy clothes!" directed Paquis.

Stress of the moment had caused Ham to forget his disguise of dyed features and ill-fitting garb; at first, he did not realize he was being spoken to. A gritted oath from Paquis put him aright.

Ham surrendered his superfirer. Under other circumstances, he might have made a fight of it. One sweep of the machine pistol would throw bullets about the room as a hose would hurl water. But Elaine Mills and the others would be in deadly danger should gunplay occur.

The men examined the superfirer wonderingly, showing the admiration of men inspecting a superior tool of their trade.

"A beaut of a thing!" a man grunted. "Just like the one we took from that bony Johnny bloke at The Wash."

"Silence, *m'sieu's,*" growled Paquis. "Search him."

A man came over and put a hand in Ham's pocket. Ham made a face, lifted a foot and drove it down on the other's instep. Bones crunched in the man's foot.

The fellow howled, leaped back and with the same gesture whipped a fist at Ham's jaw.

Ham was boxer enough to have evaded the blow. He did shift, but just enough to take the smash high up on his head, where it would not stun him.

But Ham's actions after he had been hit were those of a man who had been knocked out. His arms flailed loosely; his eyes rolled. He slammed down heavily.

It was with great care that Ham managed to land on his left side, body bending so as to put his full weight on one coat pocket. In that pocket reposed the case which held the glass bulbs of anaesthetic gas. Ham knew if he hit hard enough, the case would be crushed.

He felt the container mash flat. He held his breath.

A moment later, men began to topple over. The gas had no color, no odor, hence they were without warning of its presence.

But Paquis lived up to the reputation for cleverness which he habitually gave himself. Up on his toes, he danced backward. He reached the door and bobbed outside.

*"Au secours!"* he bawled. "Help!"

Ham ran for the door, but the menace of Paquis' gun drove him back. Next, the lawyer broke open a shuttered window. When he tried to clamber through, he was met by the threatening muzzles of men who were running up in answer to Paquis' howl.

Ham began to breathe again, for the anaesthetic gas had by now become harmless.

Paquis' men had nerve. They rushed the house, pitching through the door, smashing in the shuttered windows. They were too many to hope to fight.

Ham did the wise thing. He surrendered.

## Chapter XIV
## GOLD FROM THE SEA

MONK heard the yell for assistance which Paquis voiced. The homely chemist halted. With his bleached close-shaven features, his thick spectacles, his padded stomach, his pronounced limp and the large and foul cigars which he smoked, Monk bore little resemblance to a gorillalike chemist. The spectacles had magnifying lenses which hampered his vision somewhat, but made his eyes look larger.

"What was that?" Monk growled.

"One of the workmen celebrating, no doubt," smiled suave Benjamin Giltstein. "Let us now enter the plant."

Monk hesitated. He was worried about Ham, although he kept his features from showing it. But to push an inquiry into that shout might stir up trouble, and Monk wanted to delay showing his true identity as long as possible. The fact that the yell had not been in Ham's voice was somewhat reassuring.

The quota of newspaper men had been shown the salt water intake. This was nothing more than a hastily excavated canal which carried a rushing stream of sea water to the plant.

Two armed men guarded the door of the plant, but at a word from Giltstein, they opened it. Giltstein made a little speech before escorting the journalists inside.

"When you return to London, gentlemen, you may want to refer to a similar process in handling sea water, in order to write your stories intelligently," the press agent stated. "In that case, you have merely to describe the ordinary method used in extracting bromine from sea water."

"What is bromine?" asked a scribe.

"It is a dark reddish-brown nonmetallic liquid used in synthetic chemistry, medicine and the color industry, and also in the making of what motorists know as 'ethyl'," explained Giltstein. "And it has nothing to do with this plant here, except that our plant resembles those used in extracting bromine."

There followed a somewhat dry technical discourse, during which the party was conducted to each piece of machinery as it was described. Benjamin Giltstein proved to have a complete vocabulary of technical phraseology.

After the sea water came from the canal, it was explained, the brine went into a chamber where it received an injection of sulphuric acid. This made the future processes feasible.

Next the water was conducted into a second tank, a long affair with valves and numerous electrodes. From this, a dense fog of vapor was arising, to be trapped overhead and conducted to other apparatus.

"In this tank," Giltstein announced, "the gold content of the sea water is ionized, or made electrically conductive. This is a very difficult process, since the gold in its native state in the water is in the form of a collodial suspension. Chlorine is pumped into this tank, which, as any chemist will tell you, joins with the sodium in the sea water and literally "kicks" the bromine out."

"Is this a scientific fact?" asked someone. "Or is it hocus pocus?"

"A fact!" insisted Giltstein.

Monk, looking on, nodded soberly to himself. So far, the process was perfectly feasible. Monk had not the slightest doubt of that.

"Where is the gold now?" asked the reporter.

Giltstein pointed to the vapor that arose like fog. "In there."

"Rats!" snorted the scribe. "Now I know this is a fake. Gold is a heavy yellow metal."

"Do you see the gold in the sea water?" Benjamin Giltstein countered.

The other was stumped there. "No."

"All right," snapped the press agent. "You still don't see it. But follow me and you will."

The party now moved to a room which held a long metal cylinder. The cylinder was replete with pipes and cables.

Giltstein gave an order, and valves were turned, shutting off the stream of vapor, after which the cylinder was unlocked and the scribes were permitted to look within. There was nothing inside.

"Here is the heart of the whole process," said Giltstein. "Chemicals are introduced, and the gold is filtered out because it adheres to these chemicals."

"What are the chemicals?" questioned the representative of an afternoon sheet.

"I cannot reveal that," said Giltstein. "It is the invention, the secret."

The vapor stream was now turned back into the tank; a bit later, a valve was opened, permitting a thick, creamy mass to ooze out.

"The gold," Giltstein exclaimed dramatically.

"It don't look like gold to me!" someone snorted.

The press agent ignored that, and followed the creamy stream to where it was introduced into a roaring furnace.

"The chemicals are now driven off by heat," he exclaimed. "That leaves the raw gold."

A man appeared with a ladle on a long handle. He opened a valve; there was a blaze of brilliant heat from the furnace. The man with the ladle ran to a mold. A few moments later he broke the mold, and there was disclosed a small yellow cube.

The workman dunked the cube in water to cool it, then gave it to Giltstein, who passed it to the most doubting of the reporters.

"Gold!" he said. "Approximately a thousand dollars' worth."

"Bless me!" gasped the reporter. "I believe it *is* gold."

"It is yours," said the press agent. "Have it tested when you get back to London."

"What?" yelled the scribbler. "This is mine?"

Giltstein smiled smugly. "There will be a cube for each of you gentlemen. We have plenty. The oceans of the world are large, and there are ten million dollars in each cubic mile of sea water."

Monk shoved forward. He took the gold cube from the reluctant reporter, scratched it, examined it closely, then handed it back, looking somewhat stunned.

It *was* gold!

FOR the next five minutes, there was uproar. The British minions of the press were no more highly paid than their fellows in the United States, and finding they were to be given a thousand-dollar gold brick was a shock comparable to being struck by lightning. Finally, they sobered.

"Listen," one demanded, "what is the catch in this?"

"No catch," Benjamin Giltstein insisted. "These samples are merely in the nature of proof, so that you can go back to London and write the truth."

One journalist fell to scratching his head. "But why are you taking such pains to get this in the newspapers?"

"I will explain, providing you do not publish the facts," said the press agent.

"Shoot!"

"Wehman Mills, the owner, king and sole ruler of Magna Island, is a man who does not believe in giving his money to a lot of government chair warmers in the form of taxes."

"Taxes have gotten terrible," admitted a reporter.

"Exactly! That is why the plant was built here. This is an independent island. Therefore, no taxes will be paid. That means a tremendous saving. If we took out ten million dollars' worth of gold, we would have to pay at least half of it in taxes. Well, we don't like the idea. Securing the island was a business proposition with us."

A scribe chuckled, "Pretty slick!"

"We are going to give a third of our gold to charity," said Benjamin Giltstein. "I wish you would publish that."

"Sure," the reporter agreed. "But why the wish to have that in the newspapers?"

"Partly a philanthropic spirit on Wehman Mills' part," said the press agent, "and partly business. You see, if we build up a favorable feeling with the public, there will be a big howl if the government of England tries to seize this island."

"Can they seize it legally?"

"No, sir! We had lawyers investigate thoroughly before we bought the place."

A man entered the plant. He seemed excited. Drawing Benjamin Giltstein aside, the fellow spoke in a rapid whisper which none of the scribes could hear.

Monk watched closely. His homely face became a bit paler than the bleached hue lent by the disguise. Doc Savage was a skilled lip reader, and Monk had been studying the art from the bronze man. He was not an expert, but he got part of what was said.

The messenger advised, "We just caught a man named Ham, who is one of Doc Savage's assistants."

Monk failed to get the rest.

MONK slapped a hand to his armpit. A guard standing nearby started and began to bring up his gun. He froze when he found himself eyeing the round snout of the supermachine pistol which Monk had produced.

"Grab a cloud!" Monk grated, and spat out his black cigar.

Benjamin Giltstein screamed, "What does this mean?"

"It means a big lead party if you guys don't do what I tell you!" Monk said, an angry grit in his childlike voice. "And it means I'm gonna find what is behind this if I have to bust your scatter wide open!"

Monk had one characteristic which occasionally got the best of him. He liked violent action. When he got in a tight place, he had a habit of cutting loose and blasting his way out. He had now decided to start blasting.

Benjamin Giltstein tried to speak, but he was so excited he could only stutter.

Monk took off the magnifying spectacles and threw them aside. They broke on the concrete floor.

**Monk drifted out a fist. ... The guard went around and around, senseless on his feet.**

A reporter surreptitiously drew back a hand holding a gold brick, evidently with the idea of lobbing the rich yellow cube at Monk.

"If you feel that you're bulletproof, go ahead and throw it," Monk advised him.

The scribe shuddered and let his gold brick fall.

Giltstein, pointing at Monk, managed to get words out. "This man is no newspaper reporter! I should have been suspicious of him from the first! Guards, shoot him!"

Monk's gun banged. Giltstein sprang high in the air and fell down when he came back to the floor. He rolled over and over, a hand clenched to his side.

The reporters saw crimson oozing through the press agent's fingers, and had no way of knowing that the wound was only a superficial one made by a mercy bullet. When Benjamin Giltstein relaxed motionless upon the floor, they thought he was dead.

"You murderer!" one howled at Monk.

Monk spied an outside guard working at one of the windows. He shot glass out of the window, but the guard ducked clear, then shoved his rifle inside and began to shoot wildly.

Newspaper reporters knocked each other down getting behind the bulky iron gold-extraction tank.

Another guard tried to take advantage of the confusion and shoot Monk. Monk drifted out a fist from which the usual adornment of shingle nail-sized bristles had been shaved. The guard went around and around, top fashion, senseless on his feet.

Monk could open a large horseshoe with the brute strength in his two bare hands, and he packed a comparative wallop.

The man was still shooting wildly through the window. Monk ran over, grasped the hot rifle barrel, jerked it out of the fellow's grasp, then leaned through the window and jabbed the man's head as if he were making a billiard shot with the rifle stock.

"Three!" Monk snorted.

Then he calmly ran the total up to seven by mowing four more guards down with a hooting blast of mercy bullets from the machine pistol. They were still jigging around and falling over senseless when the apish chemist charged out into the afternoon sunlight.

IT was doubtful if Monk stopped to debate the chances of whipping Magna Island single-handed, but he started out as if that were his intention.

Two guards who had been at the door took point-blank aim at Monk with submachine guns.

With the precision of a man who had looked into gun snouts before, Monk twisted aside. His superfirer hooted as he fell. It sounded as if someone had sawed violently on the base string of a huge bullfiddle.

Impact of mercy bullets kicked the two back. Guns fell from their torn hands; and before they could recover, the powerful chemical in the slugs was stupefying them.

"Nine!" said Monk, keeping count.

There seemed to be no one else in the immediate vicinity of the gold-extracting plant. Monk listened.

Inside the building, frightened reporters were talking in low voices, demanding of each other if anyone had been injured, commenting forcibly on Monk's bloodthirstiness. In the distance, the surf grumbled noisily on the rocky shore line, and the inevitable gulls spun and squeaked high overhead.

From the direction of the village, a yell came. "Why the shootin' over there?"

"Forget it!" Monk howled back. "The guards were putting on a show."

Then the homely chemist ran in the direction of the village. He kept his head up and the supermachine pistol alert. There was a path and he followed that, frightening up songbirds which lurked in the brush and low-hanging tree branches.

Brush fluttered behind Monk. A voice gritted, "You! Stop!"

Monk knew better than to attempt to dodge bullets from a gun which he could not see. He pulled up, wheeled slowly and eyed the individual who had halted him. This personage stepped from the brush beside the path. He was a short man, nondescript except for his eyes, which were ugly.

He jutted an automatic pistol and demanded, "Who are you, bloke? And what's goin' on 'ere?"

"I'm one of the newspaper gang," Monk said promptly. "I was coming for help."

"Why?" the other growled.

"One of the blasted journalists up and cut loose like a wild man," declared Monk. "He's shot four or five people. Maybe he's trying to grab what gold you've got on the island."

All of which was not exactly the truth, but also not entirely wide of the facts. To Monk's disgust, however, the man he had encountered did not seem to be particularly gullible.

"Go help them!" Monk rapped. "I'll secure more assistance."

The other scowled, and moved his automatic suggestively.

"This sounds thin, gov'nor," he growled. "Drop that funny-lookin' gun you're carryin'!"

Monk promptly dropped the gun. He held it directly in front of his stomach as he let it fall, then he put his hands up swiftly. The other advanced.

Monk kicked with his right foot. The supermachine pistol which he had dropped had landed on his foot, and it was propelled forward by the kick.

The other man tried to dodge, failed partially and reeled aside, stunned by the blow which the flying weapon delivered to the side of his head.

An instant later, Monk's hard-swinging fist dropped him.

"Ten!" Monk enumerated gleefully.

AS Monk ran on, he abandoned the path, not wishing to encounter other foes in such an unexpected fashion. He could hear some excited cries from the vicinity of the village, and these indicated his foes were becoming alarmed. Too, from the plant, newspaper reporters were howling at the tops of their voices, adding to the general confusion.

Monk grinned, loosened his belt and hauled out the padding which had given him the abdominal bulge. He pulled off his shirt, as well as coat and vest, and discarded them. Then he cinched his belt very tight.

Monk considered himself to be doing very nicely, and his nubbin of a head entertained not a doubt as to the future. In this respect, Monk had the psychology of the perfect fighting man. He never reckoned consequences, once conflict started. He took the most unearthly chances and, accordingly, had a habit of securing results.

A squad of his foes came down the path. They went swiftly, making much noise. Monk got behind a tree and let them go past. He looked them over. None of them were men he had seen before.

Monk continued, intent on finding Ham and releasing him. But he took no more than a dozen steps and then halted.

Feet were slapping rapidly on the path. Evidently a straggler was hurrying to join the group which had just passed.

Monk selected a bush close to the trail and crouched there.

The straggler had his mouth open wide for easier breathing, and this had the effect of making him seem chinless. He emitted a sheep bleat as Monk exploded from behind the shrub and crouched into him. They went over and over and when they came to a stop, Monk was astride his prize.

The captive had watery eyes, and Monk mashed the left one slightly with the muzzle of his supermachine pistol.

"Where's Ham?" he demanded.

"Blimme!" the other choked. "Don't shoot—"

"Where's Ham, you lug?" Monk gritted.

"Fourth house as yer goes into the bloomin' village!" gulped the captive.

Monk grasped the waggling chin, pushed it up so that the fellow's mouth was closed; then, before the other knew what was going to happen, Monk struck once, as if he were seeking to drive a large nail with a single blow.

The man made a blubbling noise and his eyeballs rolled as if trying to turn around and around in their sockets.

"Eleven!" Monk grinned.

The fourth house, as one went into the village, was a rambling edifice with unusually steep roofs and a large chimney at each end. Architecturally, it was possibly the most imposing structure in the village—with one exception, a stone school house which stood slightly apart on a small hill.

A fat man stood in front of the door, a rifle in one hand, the other hand cupped to an ear. Since all of his attention was concentrated on intercepting any sound which came from the direction of the plant, he did not hear Monk glide up behind him. On occasion, Monk could move with surprising lightness for one of his bulk.

Monk dashed one big hand, knocking the man's rifle to the ground. Then Monk seized the fellow by the throat, held him at arm's length, and used him as a club to knock the door open.

In the house, Monk had not expected to find more men. He had reasoned that they would all be out hunting him.

He got a surprise.

SEVERAL men were inside. There was a table in the center of the room and on this a box, around which they were gathered. They were engaged in opening the box, and passing out rifles which it contained.

The men whirled as Monk came in behind his squirming, bruised victim. They wore expressions of gap-mouthed surprise.

Monk lifted his machine pistol and tightened on the firing lever, his idea being to mow the gang down with the mercy bullets before they could go into action.

Monk's captive spoiled the plan. He grabbed the superfirer with both hands and held on as if he was a drowning man and the gun was the only life preserver in a large ocean.

A lump of bone and bone-hard gristle, Monk's free fist bounced off the fellow's head. The man screamed, but continued to hold on. Monk growled, then got down on his knees, endeavoring to twist the gun muzzle up at his foes.

One enemy took a running jump and came down feet-first on the small of Monk's back. The impact would have broken an ordinary spine. Monk only snorted, reached up and knocked the other head over heels with a lusty swing.

Then Monk hit the man holding the gun another blow, harder than those which had been struck before. The fellow began to tremble all over.

"Twelve!" Monk roared.

He tried to free his superfirer from the spasmodic clutch of the unconscious man, but could not do so before he was forced to rear up and meet the rush of two foes. The pair had nothing but their fists, which was unfortunate, because one sat down with an unutterably pained expression and wrapped both arms over his middle, where Monk's fist had rested momentarily.

The other man missed a swing. Then he danced back, wary, brushed into a chair, nearly fell over it, then picked the chair up. He threw it at Monk.

The homely chemist had plenty of time to dodge the chair, for he saw it coming. But he did not dodge; he reached up and, with a skill that made the feat seem easy, caught the chair. Holding it by one leg, he swung it club-fashion and charged.

Men faded before him. One got out a revolver,

only to lose it and get a broken wrist as Monk clubbed with his chair.

The outer door darkened as men came in. The party which had gone down the trail had heard the uproar and dashed back.

"Take the ape alive!" someone yelled. "We've got to make him tell how much Doc Savage knows about us!"

Two men picked up the table, spilling the box of rifles. They ran at Monk with the table held high enough that the gorillalike chemist could not wield his chair. They pinned him to the wall.

Monk dropped his chair and climbed, roaring, from between table and wall. His fists windmilled. Men leeched to his legs, his midriff, and finally to his arms. He was borne down.

The mêlée became like excited flies after a morsel of sugar. Several times Monk, squalling at the top of his voice, emerged from the top of the dogpile, only to be dragged down and submerged.

The more violent the combat became, the louder Monk howled. The amount of noise Monk made always gauged the violence of a fight. He would start off barely whispering in his childlike tone, and in a particularly hard fray would bellow himself hoarse.

Monk was now yelling so loudly that the loss of his voice threatened. He was far under the pile of men, and since there was no room for blows, he pinched, gouged and twisted, getting handfuls of cloth and, not infrequently, fragments of flesh. By a Herculean effort, he got his head out of the pile to breathe.

Someone began to kick his head. Monk tried to withdraw into the mound of bodies, turtle-fashion, but could not. Again and again the kicking foot impacted against Monk's temple The shocks were too much even for the homely chemist's vast endurance.

"Thirteen!" he moaned, and went to sleep.

WITHIN slightly less than an hour, the big seaplane took off, rising easily from the stretch of comparatively calm water between the headlands which had resembled, from the sky, the spraddled legs of a great green bullfrog.

Inside the plane cabin, the newspaper correspondents were cackling among themselves— those who were not already hunched over their portable typewriters battering out stories which would be rushed into print the instant they reached their home sheets.

They had been given a story which accounted for the trouble which had engulfed Monk and Ham, and they believed every word of it, a fact that was not entirely to their discredit, for it had been an exceedingly glib and plausible yarn.

Monk and Ham, it had been explained, were not journalists at all, but plotters out to steal the secret of the process of taking yellow gold from the green, briny sea.

Monk and Ham were not on the plane. They were prisoners, the scribes had been assured, and such they would remain, awaiting the judgment of the rulers of Magna Island.

The newspapermen had been asked not to forget that Magna Island was an independent power, as much a separate nation as England herself, or France, or the United States.

The gentlemen of the press were not likely to forget that. In fact, it would be a long time before they forgot anything about this remarkable island and the things which had occurred there. Nor would the newspapers of England, the Continent or America forget it for some time to come. This was a story fit to be spread on the front pages of even the most conservative London journal.

Benjamin Giltstein, suave purveyor of publicity, was not returning in the plane. The reporters still thought Giltstein was dead, as the latter worthy had not yet awakened from the effects of Monk's mercy bullet.

By way of a reminder, each reporter carried his small gold brick, worth approximately a thousand dollars.

## Chapter XV
### ATTACK IN LONDON

THE newspapers made a hullabaloo. Those sheets whose reporters had been so thoughtless as not to take cameras to Magna Island, reproduced sketches which their artists hastily drew.

Only two papers, the most conservative, did not put out extras, but one of these had not published an extra edition when the World War ended, so that did not mean that they failed to consider the business about Magna Island a good yarn.

A hotel flunky delivered the latest editions of the extras to Doc Savage in his London hotel. The remarkable bronze man was alone, and he went over the sheets without a change appearing on his unusual metallic features.

However the bronze man's weird trilling note, the strangely exotic sound which was a part of him, did come into being and trace its nebulous way up and down the musical scale, adhering to no definite tune, but nevertheless plainly musical in its undulating quality.

The newspaper stories told of the process for taking gold from sea water, the dream of mankind for many years. The more staid journalists made this the main point, with the attempt of two criminals to seize the secret subordinated to minor headlines. The more bombastic sheets played up the theft attempt.

One sheet published the opinion of an international lawyer that Magna Island was definitely an independency, free of taxation. This barrister also expressed the view that the authorities of Magna Island were entitled to do whatever they pleased with the two crooks who had been so unwise as to endeavor to steal the secret of taking gold from the ocean.

Doc Savage put the papers aside, picked up a telephone and called, long-distance, the jail in Southampton where Wall-Samuels, the man who had pretended to be a private detective, had been confined.

*Had been* was correct. A clever lawyer had succeeded in getting Wall-Samuels out on bail. This had occurred some hours previously, and Wall-Samuels had lost no time ridding his feet of the dust of Southampton. No one knew his present whereabouts.

Doc Savage turned out the lights, then went to the window and peered down into the London street. It was near dusk, and he was waiting for the return of Johnny. Turning off the lights was by way of precaution, one of the habitual safety-first touches which had kept this bronze man alive through years of infinite peril.

Down in the street a taxicab stopped, and a tall man who was so thin that he seemed merely a suit of clothes animated with life, alighted. Johnny's bony frame was striking, even from that distance.

Johnny paid off his hack and entered the hostelry.

Perhaps three minutes later a hand tried the doorknob, found it locked, and delivered a sharp rapping.

Doc went over and turned the key, then swung the panel open.

Powder sound roared in his ears and a stiff red lance lunged hungrily at his chest.

DOC SAVAGE, flexing his arms, got them up level with his massive shoulders so that they would be clear as he twisted aside. He wore a bulletproof vest, but his arms were unprotected.

The bullet, passing him by the grace of an inch or two, went on and ripped a spread on the table, jerking it awry, making a furrow of splinters in the table-top wood. Acrid powder smell followed the lead.

Doc had stepped to the side on which the door swung. He shoved the panel, starting it shut. A shoulder hit the wood, trying to keep the door from closing. The bronze man exerted force, got the panel shut; and the spring lock, clicking, fastened itself.

Big splinters began falling out of the door to the accompaniment of the smashing impact of bullets.

"Fools!" snarled the voice of Wall-Samuels. "Shoot at the lock!"

The firing became less random and *slam-slammed* with violent precision. The lock jumped, then exploded out of its bed, taking wood with it, and gyrated across the floor.

"Careful!" Wall-Samuels ordered.

He gave the door a kick and it flew ajar. With a revolver—an automatic revolver, practically the only weapon of its kind, manufactured by an English concern—he smashed bullets at various corners of the room. He swore because the chamber was dark. Then he felt for the switch, located it and thumbed it up.

"Hell!" said Wall-Samuels when the lights did not come on.

Another man struck a match, held himself behind the door and shoved the light within. At that point, a curious guest popped into the hallway, only to fly back into his room as a bullet chopped plaster off the wall near his head.

Wall-Samuels had nerve, or maybe he still smarted because of his earlier bad showing against Doc Savage. He walked into the hotel room, automatic revolver ready. He turned, holding the deadly weapon close to his chest.

His lips separated slightly. His expression became that of a man who has just seen a particularly baffling act of magic.

"Search the closet," he grated.

His men ran over—four men accompanied him, and they all wore the grim expressions of those who had set their minds on taking life. They opened the closet; they upended the bed.

"Where'd the bronze bloke go?" one demanded wonderingly.

Wall-Samuels peered around the room, which was undeniably empty. Finally his gaze found the window, and he swung over. The sash was down, but not locked.

"He went this way," grated Wall-Samuels.

But after looking out, he changed his mind, for the wall was of bricks closely fitted together, and no human fly, however skilled, could have gone up or down it. Of that, Wall-Samuels was positive.

"Damn me!" he muttered. "The more I see of the bronze devil the more I am convinced that he is not human."

"Where'd he go?" some one asked foolishly.

"How do I know?" Wall-Samuels snapped. "I thought we had him when we waited until we saw his man arrive downstairs, then we came up. I was reasonably sure he would think it was his man at the door, and that would give us our chance."

"We'd better get out of here," said the man.

"Yes," said Wall-Samuels, "we had."
They left in great haste.

DOWNSTAIRS somewhere, a woman began screaming.

The woman doing the shrieking was elderly, raw-boned and had a face that made one think of a jinn mule. She had her mouth open to its widest, and the howls which poured forth were raucous and startled. She was the perfect picture of a frightened old maid.

"There's a man in my room!" she screeched.

"Quiet, please, madam," Doc Savage requested mildly.

The bronze man had come in through the window, being deposited on the ledge outside by a thin silk cord down which he had slid from the room above. There was a grapple hook attached to the cord; this had engaged the ledge higher up, and a flip of the cord had freed it.

Doc was coiling the cord about the grapple, which was collapsible, and stowing it within his clothing.

"Help! Murder! Police!" squalled the mule-faced woman; then she got a better look at the bronze man's remarkable physique, stopped her yelling and demanded in a mollified voice, "What on earth are you doing in here?"

The key was on the inside of the door. The bronze man turned it and an instant later was outside in the corridor.

The mule-faced woman began yelling again.

Doc Savage listened at the elevator shafts and heard an uproar which told him there was a scuffle going on in one of the cages—evidently the operator being overpowered. He promptly ran down the stairs, his speed amazing. Shots banged below.

He found the lobby in confusion, the big central chandelier having been shot loose by Wall-Samuels and his gang by way of terrorizing those present. Cars waiting outside had wafted the gang away. Doc got a fleeting glimpse of the last machine.

An elevator came down and Johnny sloped out, slightly under seven feet of ungainly disgust.

"Of all the unmitigated caprices of mordacious adversity," he groaned. "I missed the excitement!"

"They apparently timed their attack to your arrival," Doc said. "They took it for granted I would let you in myself, and they would get a chance at me."

"Did they?"

"They did." Doc assured the bony archaeologist and geologist.

"Ultrareprehensible!" said Johnny. "And they got away?"

"So it seems," the bronze man admitted. "But I saw the last of their cars, and secured the license number."

Doc strode off, found a London policeman and gave the license numerals of the machine which he had seen. The bobbie promised to broadcast an immediate alarm for the vehicle.

Johnny was reading extra editions of the afternoon newspapers when Doc rejoined him. The archaeologist's nodular features were a study as he digested the story. Names of Monk and Ham were not mentioned, they being designated merely as mercenary crooks by the authorities of Magna Island; but Johnny knew who was meant.

Johnny looked up at Doc. He did not use big words.

"This is a devil of a note," he said slowly.

DOC SAVAGE led the way to an untenanted corner of the hotel lobby.

"What did you learn?" he asked.

Johnny tapped the newspaper: "From this story, it is hard to tell—"

"I do not mean about that," Doc interpolated. "Before you returned to the hotel, you were getting historical data on the events during the reign of King John."

"Oh, that!" The bony man fumbled inside his slack coat and brought out a sheaf of documents. "Here is a brief synopsis of King John's reign. Say, King John was some tough lad, probably one of the worst kings England ever had!"

At this point, a police officer approached with

---

**WHERE DOES DOC SAVAGE GET HIS MONEY?**

Doc possesses a fabulous hoard of gold. The treasure trove lies in a lost valley in the remote mountain vastness of a Central American republic. Descendants of the ancient Mayan race live in this valley and mine the treasure.

When Doc Savage is in need of funds, he has merely to step into a powerful radio station at a certain hour on a certain day of each week and broadcast a few words in the Mayan language. This is picked up by a sensitive receiver in the lost valley. A few days later, a burro train laden with gold will appear in the capitol of the Central American republic. These gold cargoes are always deposited to Doc's credit in a bank. It is a slim trip when one of the burro trains does not bring out a treasure of four or five million dollars.

Only Doc and his men know the location of the lost valley of the golden trove and the Mayans.

word that Wall-Samuels' car had been sighted near Kentish Town. Wall-Samuels and all four of his men now occupied the one machine. Bobbies had sought to stop them and had been fired upon, the car roaring on northward.

Doc Savage heard that through in silence. Then he riffled over the documents concerning King John, which Johnny had given him. He pocketed them without comment, and it was impossible to tell from his features whether or not he had secured anything of value from them.

"Come on," he directed Johnny.

They went to Doc's room and got a number of metal cases fitted with carrying straps. These containers held the bronze man's numerous scientific devices. They were, figuratively speaking, his bag of tricks, and he took them wherever he went.

A fast taxicab carried them from the hotel, worked through the early evening London traffic jams, and eventually reached an airport. The field was not Croydon, where the commercial lines came in, but another 'drome patronized by sportsmen and smaller concerns which made a business of selling planes.

The bronze man bought a plane, one of the latest and fastest types of ships, a job which sold for slightly in excess of two thousand pounds.

Doc Savage paid the sum in cash, without comment or perceptible concern. Two thousand pounds, in fact, was not an excessive amount of money in his life, for the bronze man possessed access to a treasure trove, the value of which would stagger some imaginations.

Before taking off in the newly purchased plane, and while the craft was being loaded with fuel and oil, Doc made a telephone call to the police.

Wall-Samuels' car had been found—at another airport. And Wall-Samuels and his four men had taken off in a plane and lost themselves in the night.

"My hypothesis is that they have departed for Magna Island," Johnny hazarded.

Doc tested the single powerful motor of the new plane. It ran perfectly.

"Magna Island is a good bet," he admitted.

Johnny began loading duffle into the cabin of the fast craft.

"I gather that we are going to direct a scrutiny at the mystery which is Magna Island," he said.

"Exactly!" Doc agreed.

## Chapter XVI
## FLAME THREADS

THE moon was bright; the stars, like iridescent sparks, glittered permanently in the sky; but some seven or eight thousand feet above the earth clouds were massed—first, in gray and bulging masses which were given the aspect of silver foam by the moonlight, then, below these, ranged darker, thicker phalanxes of vapor which threatened momentarily to leak rain. On the sea, and for two thousand feet above, it was very dark.

Doc Savage sent the new plane toward Magna Island at an altitude of fourteen thousand, where it was clear and cold. From time to time he consulted instruments, then shifted a position pin in the chart which was clamped to the sliding map board under the instrument panel. His idea of their position was uncannily accurate.

Johnny was going over supermachine pistols, springing cartridges from the ammo drums and running each through a chambering device which made sure there were no microscopic flaws that might cause one of the weapons to jam.

"This is still a profound enigma," he murmured. "The fact remains unalterably clear that we can conjure up no hypothesis that will clarify the connection of The Wash with Magna Island."

"Guns in good shape?" Doc asked.

"Yes."

"We are going down now," Doc advised. "Magna Island is a few miles directly ahead."

The bronze man cut the ignition switch and the propeller, unable to turn over against the compression in the new motor, became a rigid blade of aluminum alloy which glittered in the moonlight. The ship tilted in a glide and went down like a whining, stiff-winged ghost.

The cloud mass bulged up at them. Vapor streamers whipped past like foam, and darker spires and chasms appeared as if they were hungry mouths and stained fangs.

"Entrancing place," offered Johnny.

As if they had been swallowed completely, blackness took them in. The plane interior became damp. Once rain shotted against the windows.

"The infra-ray searchlight," Doc directed.

Johnny sprang to one of the metal equipment cases, opened it and brought out a bulky apparatus. A cable from this he connected to another case which held a generator that operated from a powerful spring motor. He grunted and perspired winding the motor.

A third case yielded box-shaped eyepieces, which both Johnny and Doc donned. Then Johnny opened a window, shoved the infra-ray lantern through and clicked a switch.

There had been only dense blackness ahead and below, a blackness that was infinitely forbidding. But the beam from the infra-ray lantern wrought a startling change. The clouds and fog were pierced to a much greater degree than would have been possible with an ordinary searchlight.

The infra rays, being outside the visible spectrum, were unnoticeable to the unaided eye. Only with the intricate eyepieces which Doc and Johnny had strapped to their orbs could the beam be utilized for a survey.

They were not below the clouds. Doc flattened the plane a bit more, not wishing the howl of wind past flying wires to become loud enough to reveal their approach.

With a suddenness which caused Johnny to start slightly, they dropped under the clouds. He peered through his eyepiece.

"There!" he breathed.

MAGNA ISLAND was below. It looked strangely unnatural, for there were no impressions of color through the infra-ray device, only varying shades of light and darkness.

Doc Savage did not fly directly over the island, but circled widely, keeping clear of the shoreline. They could make out the village, the plant for taking gold from sea water. The latter was dark.

There was a beach along the inside of the two arms of land on which they could land. Other than this, no other suitable landing place presented.

Doc sent the plane in a bit closer.

Down on the island, there was a small flash, and from it a string of sparks stretched upward. This passed the plane and became a sudden, blinding ball of light which hung almost motionless in the night sky.

"Parachute flare," Doc said grimly. "They were not asleep."

The plane began to vibrate slightly. It was an all-metal job, and out on the left wingtip the skin was getting ragged, while down on the ground, a machine gun fluttered an ugly red eye.

"The beginning of a hectic night," Johnny prophesied quietly.

DOC banked the plane right, left, right, and got away from the stream of machine gun slugs. The flare, suspended from its swaying parachute, sank until they were above it and in darkness

On the most westerly of the frog-leg peninsulas, two planes were being urged into the water. They had been almost hidden in the trees which covered that end of the island.

A second flare climbed up and ripened whitely; machine guns opened again. They were using tracer this time, and Doc's best maneuvering did not escape an occasional hit.

"I have a remedy for such obstreperous conduct," Johnny commented.

He replaced a drum of mercy bullets in his machine pistol with a drum marked by a different identifying numeral, then leaned out, took a deliberate aim and fired a single shot.

On the ground there was a great gush of flame, and a tree toppled over, uprooted. This happened near one of the machine guns.

Johnny fired again. That slug dug a great pock in the earth. The explosive in the pellets was tremendously powerful.

Johnny continued to fire, and the men manning the machine gun—it was a regulation anti-aircraft type—lost their nerve and ran. Johnny had to shoot five more times before he destroyed the gun itself.

The two planes were now in the water, scudding along at the heads of long wake streamers. Doc stood his ship on a wingtip and went spinning down over one. Johnny took his time, then launched a brief burst of explosive bullets.

Water was kicked up in a boiling turmoil ahead of one of the planes. The craft heaved, bucked. For a moment, it seemed that the ship would go on safely. Then it tilted until a wingtip knifed the surface, and the resultant drag spun it around so violently that it turned completely over. As it began sinking, men clambered wildly through the cabin windows.

The second plane got on step and vaulted off. The pilot banked steeply, then gave his craft all of the climbing angle it would handle. In a few moments it was pointing in the direction of Doc's ship. Two faint red sparks danced atop the engine cowling.

There was a violent vibration, then Doc battled the controls and skidded his new craft aside. He snapped open the cockpit window and looked out and down.

The landing gear was dangling from mutilated struts.

"Synchronized guns," he told Johnny. "This second ship is not going to be an easy nut to crack. It seems to be as fast or faster than our own bus."

A third flare had crawled up against the clouds and was spreading its calcium whiteness. Johnny, squinting narrowly, saw that the flares were being secured from the tool shed near the large building which he reasoned was the gold extraction plant.

The gaunt geologist took a careful aim at the tool house and launched an explosive bullet. He missed, and had to fire three times more before the shed jumped apart in a puff of timbers, tin and dust.

"That stops the business of the flares," he grunted.

IF the occupants of the plane with the synchronized machine guns expected Doc Savage to stay aloft and make a bat battle of the affair, they got a surprise. The instant the last flare sank, sizzling, into the sea, Doc banked sharply and put the nose of his craft down.

"We came to help Monk and Ham," the bronze man told Johnny, "and not to fight for the fun of it."

The thunder of the other plane throbbed across the island and swallowed completely such small sounds as were made by Doc's ship after he cut the motors. He hoped to land without the engines, but if they were needed, there was an electro-inertia starter for setting them off again while still in the air.

Once more the infra-red projector and the strange eyepieces were employed. Doc sent the plane for the beach, swung around into the wind— he had previously noted its direction from the drift of the parachute flares—and flattened out.

Johnny flattened himself against the instrument board and padded his face with his coat. They had no landing gear, and there was no telling what would happen.

Doc Savage picked a spot in the mild surf, a few yards offshore, killed all the headway possible by trampling the rudder violently, then put the plane down. There was a smash, a bounce, then a terrific jarring as the surf mauled them. With a whining of metal as one wing collapsed, the plane finally stood on its nose.

Then there was silence, except for the gurgle of sea water and the excited shouts of their enemies above the distant buzz of the other plane.

"Hurt?" Doc asked.

"No," said Johnny.

The bronze man climbed out, found the water waist-deep, and waded for shore. Johnny made splashings coming after him.

They found it most convenient to run in the direction of the gold-extracting plant. Behind them, men shouted anxiously to each other. Flashlights and hand searchlights raced hungry plumes of luminosity.

A volley of profanity indicated the finding of the plane in the surf. Lights were turned upon the wreck to indicate to those overhead in the other plane that they might as well land.

Ahead of Doc, a square building showed up. Nearby, wreckage was smoking and burning redly—the remnants of the tool shed which Johnny had destroyed.

"Wait!" Doc directed.

Johnny opened his mouth to ask what Doc intended doing, but the bronze man left him too quickly, and the bony geologist stood rigid, his breath rapid and uneasily hoarse, listening.

Doc Savage went to the door of the gold extraction plant. There was a massive padlock on it, but that surrendered to the probing of the metal pick which he removed from a pocket of his unusual vest.

Passing inside, Doc produced a flashlight from the vest. This operated from a spring generator, and the head could be focused until it threw a beam no larger than an ordinary lead pencil.

The beam traveled rapidly over the ponderous tanks and arrays of piping. A time or two, the light widened briefly; it remained wide for some seconds when Doc came to the long tank from which came the final concentration of stuff that the newspaper correspondents had seen retorted into a small gold brick.

Outside, Johnny shifted from one bony leg to the other. He was getting anxious, for he could hear their enemies coming closer. The men were following the tracks which Doc and himself had made in the soft beach sand.

Johnny latched his machine pistol into rapid-fire position, and made sure there was an ammo drum of mercy bullets in place.

When Doc appeared at his side, Johnny started and all but began shooting.

"What did you find?" Johnny gulped.

"They'll hear us," Doc breathed. "Let's head toward the village."

They crept away, and in the intense darkness, it was necessary to ferret out a course by the sense of touch alone. Doc went ahead. Often his hands guided Johnny over or around obstructions which the latter failed to distinguish.

"They won't hear us now," Johnny whispered after a time. "What did you find?"

"Plenty!" Doc told him. "The gold-from-sea-water plant is a fake!"

"What?"

"A fake!" Doc repeated. "They are not taking gold from the ocean."

## Chapter XVII
## TROUBLE IN THE NIGHT

JOHNNY followed Doc Savage in silence for some little distance, digesting what he had just been told.

He began, "But the newspapermen said—"

"Were deceived," Doc interposed. "The whole idea of taking gold from sea water is not impossible. It has actually been done on a laboratory scale. But these men are not doing it with the apparatus they have back there."

Johnny grumbled his disgust. "Then what is behind this? They've spent a lot of money building this plant and buying the island."

"Considerably less than a hundred thousand, all told," Doc reminded. "If you deal in millions, that is not a great deal of money."

"Then suppose you tell me why they built the plant?" Johnny requested dryly.

"That may come out before we're through," Doc replied. "Quiet! The village is close ahead."

Lights burned in some of the cottages. Fast-moving figures darted past windows. A man appeared in a door, his shoulders draped with serpentine ammo belts for full-size machine guns.

"They were certainly prepared for a siege," Johnny breathed.

Doc Savage said nothing, but stared intently ahead. Another man strode through the lighted door, his hands filled with metallic eggs which were undoubtedly grenades. That particular house, Doc concluded, was the armory.

"Wait here," he advised Johnny.

He glided forward, making few sounds. Because of the intense darkness, it was unnecessary to use much care against being seen, except to be ready to drop should some one turn on a flashlight. He reached a window of the cottage from which the men had carried weapons.

Inside, there was one large room, the floor littered with packing cases containing guns and ammunition. Doc worked at the window, got it open and eased inside. He found a small hammer which had been used in opening the cases.

Sharp blows with the hammer rendered gun after gun useless.

There was a case of ammo belts for the machine guns, already plugged full of cartridges. With a pocket knife, Doc rendered the belts useless.

There was a box of grenades. Putting them out of commission would take too long. He would have to conceal them.

Another item which held his interest was a case of dynamite, high-percentage stuff which must have been used in blasting for the gold extraction plant. Only a few sticks were missing.

Near by was a large coil of insulated wire and a detonating generator of the old-fashioned type which had an upright handle. The shoving down of the handle spun the generator and hurled current to the electrical detonating caps attached to the device.

Doc Savage made two trips outside, taking first the grenades, then the dynamite, the wire and the generator. They might come in useful. He hid them all in the shrubbery, covering them with soft dirt. A few of the grenades he kept in a pocket.

If the blows as he broke the guns had been heard—and no doubt they had—the sound had been dismissed as being made by one of the men themselves.

Johnny was waiting anxiously.

"What now?" he questioned.

"Find Monk and Ham," Doc breathed. "But first, this gang will have to think we are near the other end of the island. You wait here."

SOME five minutes later, Paquis was holding a profane conference with his men on the opposite side of Magna Island. Paquis had recovered fully from his encounter with the anaesthetic gas bulbs which had been broken in Ham's pocket.

*"Non, non!"* Paquis snapped insistently. "They would not dare go toward the village."

"This Doc Savage bloke would do anything, gov'nor," the pursy Smith insisted.

Paquis shrugged. "Anyway, we have him cornered here on the island. Our one plane is the only way he can get off. And I have ordered the craft to take the air and stay there, where he cannot get it, until we have this thing settled."

A moment later, the plane motor began to roar. The sound receded, changed note as the ship took the air, then the wingtip searchlights appeared, racing like two big eyes over the treetops. The craft started cruising in slow circles around the island.

Paquis swore thickly. "The fools! They are so close that the roar of the motor will prevent us hearing this Doc Savage."

He began to yell and wave a flashlight, trying to signal the pilot of the plane to put more distance between himself and the island.

Almost beside Paquis, there was a terrific report and a flash. Paquis' hair all but stood on end and he lost his hat diving for cover.

*"Prenez garde!"* he shrieked. "Take care! A grenade!"

A second grenade exploded, closer than the first. Men scattered. Some had presence of mind enough to use flashlights. The white funnels, spiking through the darkness and the vegetation, picked up a gigantic man-figure.

"Doc Savage!" Paquis roared. "I told you he was at this side of the island!"

Leaping backward, Doc Savage lost himself to the flashlight beam. A solitary pistol whacked, then an ear-splitting salvo of gunfire crashed out. Bark, small limbs, leaves showered down. A sapling, cut completely by the blast of lead, toppled over noisily.

But Doc Savage was some yards away, and moving swiftly. Before throwing the two grenades to attract attention, he had gone over the terrain. He made no noise that was perceptible over the moan of the plane motor.

*"Ecoutez!"* Paquis was yelling. "Listen. Maybe we can hear him! Damn that infernal plane!"

Paquis was still yelling and swearing in the distance when Doc Savage appeared beside Johnny, as soundless in his coming as a phantom of the night.

"I was worried," Johnny gulped. "The grenades—"

"The grenades were some from their own armory," Doc explained. "The rest are hidden. Did anyone leave the village during the excitement?"

"Three men," said Johnny, and pointed. "I think one of the prisoners is in that house yonder. At least there is a man at the door, obviously on guard."

THE house—the lights of a house, rather—which Johnny indicated, lay on the south side of the street. He and Doc went toward it cautiously. Before they had gone far the door opened, spilling reddish light which must come from a lantern, and an armed man stood in the aperture for a moment, listening.

"Look! There's the guard!" Johnny breathed.

With hand pressure, Doc indicated that Johnny was to wait. Then the bronze man glided ahead. There was little chance of his being discovered, thanks to the night and the noisy plane overhead.

The guard cupped a hand back of his ear. Then he removed it and scowled up at the boisterous plane. There was a distinctly fleshy smack of a sound. The guard's scowl faded to utter blankness and he took two rubber-knead steps, then folded down atop his gun.

The grenade which Doc had thrown bounced off the partially open door, whence it had glanced from the man's head, and sailed into the house, where it rattled about.

A hoarse scream in a man's voice came out of the house, a stifled shriek full of the fear of death.

Doc Savage ran to the door. A thin old man with white hair sat on the floor. He wore Congress gaiters and a soiled, sweated-down wing collar. He was handcuffed to an iron flywheel too heavy for him possibly to move, and he stared with an awful expression at the grenade, which had stopped barely a yard distant from him.

"The pin has not been pulled," Doc told him. "It will not explode."

Surprise shook the old man as if he had received a violent electrical shock. He spoke, but his words were at first unintelligible. Taking a full breath, he tried again.

"D-Doc Savage!" he floundered. "You c-couldn't be anyone else."

The bronze giant sank beside the old man and took the handcuff chain in cabled fingers. His arms, straining apart, became great, corded bars.

The white-haired man made a choking sound of wonder as the links snapped.

"I'm Wehman Mills," he mumbled, and got to his feet as rapidly as age-stiffened joints would permit. "My niece! She's next door."

"Who?" Doc questioned.

"Elaine!"

It was the first the bronze man had heard of Elaine, but full explanations would have to wait.

"Where are Monk and Ham?" he asked.

"I don't know," Wehman Mills gulped. "But Elaine—"

"We'll get Elaine." Because the old man was slow on his feet, Doc grasped him bodily and ran him through the door. The bronze man paused briefly to examine the guard. That worthy would be fortunate if he awakened some time the following day.

Elaine was in the next dwelling. There was no guard over her. Doc used a flashlight to illuminate her handcuff links as he performed the amazing feat of breaking them with his bare hands.

PRETTY Elaine Mills looked the bronze man over, and seemed eminently satisfied with what she saw.

"I don't believe this rescue attempt will turn out like the other one," she said, and there was no perceptible tremble in her pleasant voice.

"What other one?" Doc asked.

"Your man, Ham, tried it once."

Doc said, "Ham usually manages to do fairly well."

"He did excellently," said Elaine Mills. "I think he would have gotten away with it, except that Paquis and his men found out where Ham was. They turned up at just the wrong moment. How they managed to do that was very mysterious."

"Where is Ham now?" Doc demanded. "And Monk?"

"Up the street," said Elaine Mills. "I think they are together."

Doc and his party left the house hurriedly. Johnny was helping elderly Wehman Mills. Elaine managed by herself, although she limped a little, being stiff from the handcuff confinement.

The first house they tried was empty. So was the second, and a third. Before they reached the fourth, they heard voices.

"Listen, you blasted shyster!" complained Monk's childlike voice. "You're gouging me purposely with that pin!"

"Shut up!" Ham snapped. "I've still got a notion to try that window glass idea."

Monk and Ham were handcuffed to heavy pieces of machinery, and they had managed to drag these until they sat close together. Ham was employing a tie pin in an endeavor to pick the lock on Monk's manacles.

They greeted Doc with wide grins. The bronze man took the tie pin and went to work on the locks.

"You should have heard the bright idea this shyster had for getting us loose," Monk said indignantly. "He wanted to break a window and use the glass to cut one of my thumbs off so the handcuff ring would slide over my hand."

"I am sure it would have worked," Ham declared, and kept his features serious.

Monk snorted, then asked, "Where's the other guy—Henry Trump?"

The bronze man shook his head. "I'm behind on the story, Monk. Who is Henry Trump?"

Elaine Mills supplied, "A very nice young man who tried to help me and got involved in this awful mess for his pains."

"We'll look for him," Doc said. "And we'll look for a house which is probably under heavy guard."

Monk registered surprise. "What's that last?"

"A house under guard," Doc repeated. "Or it may not be in a house. It may be somewhere else on the island."

"What?" Monk demanded.

"The thing which will explain all of this," Doc told him.

Old Wehman Mills hobbled to the door, glanced out, choked, "Oh, my goodness!" and fell backward just before a bullet made a neat round hole in the door jamb.

## Chapter XVIII
### THE SCHOOL HOUSE

"OUR sinecure has terminated precipitously," big-worded Johnny offered dryly.

Without obvious haste, Johnny sloped to a window, smashed through with a shower of glass and galloped for the house corner.

The man who had fired on Wehman Mills heard the window breaking and ran to get in a shot. He had a strong hand searchlight and he turned this on.

Johnny glimpsed the light, surmised the fellow would be holding it out to one side, and latched his superfirer into continuous discharge position. He triggered slugs over an area extending a dozen feet on either side of the light.

The light fell; the man who had held it yelled, and a moment later he staggered into view, clutching at his chest where mercy bullets had hit him, and probably wondering just exactly what was wrong. He weakened and sat down, then laid his full length on the ground.

"We had best retreat through the village," Doc advised. "Search the houses as we go."

"Yes," gasped Elaine Mills. "We must find Henry Trump!"

"And something these men will be guarding," Doc added.

The houses were smaller now, little more than hovels. Beyond them, but invisible in the night, was the big stone school house which stood on the hill.

Paquis was yelling, not on the other side now, but nearer; his shouts were directed at his men, summoning them to the attack. He took time out at frequent intervals to curse the airplane which still made noise overhead.

Monk and Ham had taken the left side of the street, growing uncomplimentary things at each other while they searched houses.

"Listen, stupid," Ham requested of Monk, "just what does Doc think we're going to find around here?"

Monk kicked down a door which was locked. "I suppose all things were clear to that great brain of yours," he told Ham sourly.

Ham found a flashlight on a table in the shack which they were investigating. He thumbed it on, and the beam illuminated Monk briefly. Ham extinguished it with great haste.

Monk squalled and dived for the nearest cover, just ahead of a shower of bullets directed at Ham's light.

"You turned that on me a-purpose!" Monk grated. "You tried to get me shot!"

"No such luck," Ham gritted back. "The light came on pointed toward you by accident."

"If I was to throw a rock and it bashed your head in, that'd be an accident, too," Monk said fiercely.

"Any time you feel ambitious," Ham invited.

Elaine Mills, overhearing the exchange, and detecting nothing but utter hate and rage in the tones of the two men, moved over and grasped Doc Savage's elbow apprehensively.

"I am afraid your two men are going to fight," she said. "Can't you do something?"

"Don't worry," Doc told her. "They're like that all the time."

From a spot ahead, a voice called, "Doc Savage! Help!"

"That's Henry Trump!" gasped Elaine Mills, and ran forward.

THEY found Henry Trump seated in an open shed, a none-too-clean place where the original inhabitants of the island must have kept cows. Trump's legs were manacled around a post which supported the shed roof.

"I could tell you were hunting me," he gasped.

Doc went to work on the handcuffs. Henry Trump swore wonderingly when the links parted under Doc's incredible hands.

"Good night!" he exploded. "I've read about you, Savage, and didn't believe half of the stuff. But I don't think it was exaggerated."

Doc hauled the young man to his feet.

"Have you noticed any particular spot on the island that the men were guarding?" he asked.

"No," said Trump in a puzzled tone. "Why?"

"We're trying to find such a place."

Monk put in, "There's the school house. It's on the hill ahead."

"And it is the only building of any size left," added Ham.

Doc said swiftly, "We'll try the school house."

Old Wehman Mills interjected anxiously, "Now, look here, I think we should try to escape from this—"

"The plane is the only route of escape," Doc told him. "And that is in the air. We'll have to make a fight of it."

Paquis and his men were closing in, but not recklessly. They fired an occasional shot, and were evidently keeping in groups for the sake of safety.

Doc distinguished the voice of Smith, and then the squealing tone of Wall-Samuels, the fake detective.

Henry Trump came close to Doc Savage. "Are you heading for the school house?"

"Right!" Doc told him.

"Why?"

"They may have their cache there."

"Cache?" Trump murmured. "You mean—the gold they have taken from the ocean?"

"They have not taken any gold from the sea," Doc advised Trump. "Their plant is a fake."

"For the love of mud!" Trump gulped. "Then what is behind all of this?"

"I'll explain as soon as we are under cover," Doc replied. "The school house is of stone. We can barricade ourselves there."

Trump muttered, "I don't think it's a good idea to pen ourselves up."

Doc did not reply, but moved on in the darkness. He found Johnny, Monk, Ham and the others, breathed a low command, and they strung out in single file, so that they could travel with more stealth.

Behind them, Paquis was expressing profane opinions about the intellect of the pilot who was still circling the big plane so close to the island that its noise interfered with the search.

PAQUIS was worried. He was a little frightened too, and part of his profanity was intended to bolster his own nerve. He did not like the idea of hunting for Doc Savage in the darkness.

*"Prenez garde!"* he warned his men. "Take care! There is no great hurry."

"I been tellin' you that bronze bloke is bad medicine," Smith mumbled.

"Shut up!" advised Benjamin Giltstein. "We still have a hole card which the bronze man does not know about."

*"Oui,"* Paquis agreed. "But he must not suspect. Therefore it is up to us to make a great pretense of hunting him."

At that point, Paquis gave a violent lunge and fell flat on the earth: a voice out of the adjacent darkness had given him one of the big starts of his checkered career.

"Fool!" snarled the voice. "Do not make a noise that will cause Savage to suspect that I am near."

"The chief!" someone breathed.

*"Oui,"* said Paquis. "What is it?"

"Doc Savage is taking his party to the school house," said the voice.

*"Comment!"* exploded Paquis. "What? But how did he guess—"

"He searched the village," said the voice of the leader who had kept himself in the background throughout. "He is now going to try the school house."

"Then he must suspect the truth, *m'sieu'*," Paquis groaned.

"He does," agreed the other. "The incident at The Wash must have given him a clue."

Paquis demanded, "What shall we do?"

"Take all of your men to the school house," directed the other. "Get them inside. When Doc Savage appears, try to get him and some of his men. But keep them out of the school house, at all costs."

*"Oui,"* Paquis agreed.

"Later, we will corner Savage," stated the other "I will arrange that. He does not suspect me."

"You are going to join him again?" Paquis questioned.

"Of course," chuckled the man who had given orders.

The mysterious speaker stood only a few feet from Paquis and the others. Now he stepped backward, parted the shrubbery and eased himself off in the direction of Doc Savage and his party. The man traveled with all the speed consistent with silence, and, glancing upward where the plane moaned in the darkness, he grinned fiercely, thankful for the noise the craft was making.

Scarcely four minutes later, he had made himself one of Doc Savage's group. Apparently, his absence had not been missed. Not once had a light shone on his features.

Paquis was busy mustering his men. When he had them assembled they set off, running, in a roundabout way for the school house. It did not take them long to reach the structure.

Playing children had worn grass and vegetation off the ground adjacent to the school house, so that it was bare, a dome of rocky clay atop which the building towered.

Nearing the door, Paquis called softly. There was no answer. Paquis muttered uneasily, took a chance, and dabbed his flashlight beam. Then he swore.

The door was ajar, and a man sprawled beside it. His eyes were wide open and he breathed regularly, but his limbs were weirdly stiff, incapable of movement.

"The work of that devil, Savage!" Paquis breathed.

"Righto," muttered Smith. "That same thing 'appened to one of our men in The Wash. Doc Savage squeezes the back of 'is neck some bloomin' way."

"Inside!" Paquis grated. "We must rush them, *m'sieu's!*"

The order had to be issued twice again before men got up nerve enough to dive inside the school house. They had their guns ready.

But to their unbounded astonishment, nothing happened. There was no one in the building.

"*Bon!*" Paquis exploded. "Doc Savage came ahead and cleared the way, then went back for the others. We have beaten them!"

With all of the men inside, the door was slammed and bolted. The windows had been fitted with large sheet shields of bulletproof steel. Loopholes perforated these.

Smith chuckled. "Hit looks like we're sittin' hon top o' the bloomin' world."

His satisfaction had a short life.

From outside, Doc Savage's powerful voice called, "You gentlemen have walked into a trap!"

THE men in the school house received the words with varied mien.

Smith groaned. Benjamin Giltstein said a tight-lipped nothing. Paquis was frankly skeptical.

"Use your guns, *mon hommes!*" he barked. "Shoot at his voice!"

"Wait!" Doc Savage called, and there was an unconcerned grimness in his powerful tone which compelled attention. "I was inside before you came."

"He ain't lyin'," Smith mumbled. "Remember the bloke we found at the door!"

"In the basement," Doc Savage continued, "is a packing box. It contains the dynamite which was removed from your armory. Attached to it are the wires of the blasting generator."

Paquis rapped, "Look and see if he is lying!"

"The light is on in the basement," Doc called. "We can see the container of explosive, and can set it off before one of you can move it."

The basement door was torn open, and Smith peered down into the brilliantly lighted interior.

"Blimme!" he exploded, and drew back.

The case of explosives was suspended by a length of wire from the ceiling, perhaps six feet inside the open window. Other wires, insulated, extended from it through the window.

"Out with the lights," Benjamin Giltstein suggested. "Then the wires can be cut without him seeing.'

"*Non!*" gulped Paquis. "He would set the stuff off the instant the lights went out."

Doc Savage's voice reached them faintly. "Think it over, you fellows. Then get rid of your guns and come out."

Outside, Doc Savage and his party waited. They had planted flashlights so that the beams illuminated the four sides of the school house.

The backglow from the flashes bathed Doc's group faintly, so that they kept behind rocks and trees. Johnny, gaunt and bony as death itself, hunched over the electrical generator which was attached to the explosive.

Henry Trump was very tense, very pale. He wet his lips repeatedly and looked at Doc Savage, who had been continually near him during the last few moments.

"You pretended to help Elaine Mills so as to make sure she was captured, did you not?" Doc asked him abruptly.

Henry Trump did not start. Possibly his features grew a bit more pallid.

"What gave me away?" he asked thickly.

"Your going back to talk to Paquis after we started for the school house," Doc told him. "You thought I was in front, but I was behind, making sure that none of the enemy overhauled us. I heard you slip away."

Trump bowed slightly, then put both arms down stiffly at his sides.

"I am not going to be fool enough to deny it," he said. "Yes, I did throw in with the girl to make sure she was seized. I also was responsible for the capture of Ham. When Ham came for me, I had time to signal my men before putting on handcuffs and pretending to be a prisoner."

"You were rather clever," Doc admitted.

"Yes, rather," Trump grated, and shook his right arm violently.

A small automatic—it must have been on a hook inside his sleeve—dropped into view. Trump, cupping his right hand, managed to catch it.

But he never used the weapon. Doc Savage, lunging at the first shake of the right arm, lashed with a fist and reached Trump's jaw. The young man's head flew back, then forward; he coughed and the explosion blew loosened teeth past his lips. Then he went down.

The noise as he fell got Elaine Mills' attention. She ran up.

"Why, what happened to him?" she gasped. "He was such a nice young man."

The door of the school house opened and Paquis came out. He had no gun and his hands were stiffly above his head. The rest of his men trailed after him, looking back nervously, as if fearing the explosive would detonate before they got out.

## Chapter XIX
## KING JOHN'S LOOT

THE room had once been the office of the principal of the little school. An empty desk and bookcase still remained.

On the floor were many packages done in burlap, and numerous stout boxes, none of the latter very large, but stoutly built. Some of the packages and boxes had been opened.

The contents, strewn on the floor, looked at first glance like junk. There were vases, goblets, eating utensils. There were shapeless lumps which had once been bowls, and there were bulky statues, plaques, chains.

Monk threw down the hammer with which he had been opening the containers.

"Gold, all of it!" he said. "There's no need of making chemical tests."

Old Wehman Mills drew himself up to his trembling height and wailed, "Gentlemen, I tell you there is a mistake. You are wrong! The plant for taking gold from sea water will actually work!"

"Uncle!" admonished Elaine Mills.

"I'm sorry," Doc told him, "but it will not work. I made a further examination this morning."

Johnny, his disheveled clothing making him look slightly more bony than usual, finished reading the sheaf of papers which contained the data he had assembled in London on King John.

"It all hooks up," he said absently, forgetting to use big words. "When King John was forced to sign the Magna Charta in the year of 1215, he was enraged at the barons who made him sign. He got together an army of ruffians and set out to loot the castles of his barons by way of revenge. He was very successful, and got a great deal of swag."

"Where'd you get that stuff?" Monk demanded.

"Out of the official history of England," Johnny retorted. "Quiet, please, while I finish. The outraged barons got together and pursued King John. To escape them, he took a shortcut across The Wash. The tide trapped his treasure train, and it was lost, King John barely escaping with his life. The shock of losing the loot is believed to have been a cause contributing to his death shortly afterward."

Monk indicated the stuff in the packages and boxes. "This is King John's treasure?"

"It is," Doc Savage put in. "Henry Trump, Paquis, Smith, Benjamin Giltstein and the rest found it. They removed it from the quicksands by sinking shafts, using the modern expedient of freezing the muck so that it could be excavated."

"That explains the refrigerating apparatus which we found in the marshes near The Wash," added Johnny.

Wehman Mills groaned. "I tell you, my process for taking gold from the sea is feasible," he cried.

"Maybe," Doc agreed quietly. "But it will require more work before it is practical on a commercial scale. These men simply duped you. They used your plant as a cover for producing the King John gold and marketing it."

"It was an elaborate tax-evasion scheme, uncle," said Elaine.

Outside, Ham yelled, "Say, have I got to watch these prisoners all day? How about a little help?"

FROM a window, Doc glanced over the captives. They were all there—from Henry Trump, the ringleader, down to the most disgruntled of the lot, the pilot of the plane, which had run out of gasoline near dawn. Forced down, the pilot had been captured easily.

The pilot was the butt of considerable sarcasm from his fellows, they insisting that had he not made so much noise overhead, Doc Savage might have been seized.

Doc Savage listened to the wrangling without interest. It was not important.

Nor was the bronze man greatly excited over the treasure behind him, although it would undoubtedly total into the millions. Doc held no possessive interest in the trove. Like all of the moneys which he recovered in the course of his strange career of helping others out of trouble, this King John wealth would go to worthy charities, to the construction of hospitals, to the establishment of trust funds for the school of ambitious students.

Old Wehman Mills wanted to stay on the island and work with his dream of extracting gold from the sea. That could be arranged. And old Wehman Mills might succeed. Some day, someone would accomplish the feat. The ideas of Wehman Mills were not crackbrained, by any means.

Elaine, of course, would stay with her uncle. No doubt she would be a prominent figure in the flurry of newspaper publicity which was sure to come. Her features would photograph excellently.

Elaine had said little, so far. She was bitter toward Henry Trump, and with cause. True, she had shown a marked liking for the company of Doc Savage through the morning, a fact that had embarrassed the bronze man somewhat. There was no place for feminine entanglements in the perilous existence which he led.

Doc Savage glanced upward. The clouds had cleared away, except for the west, where they lay thick still.

They might have been an omen, those clouds in the west, for it was there that peril was to again find the bronze man. In New York, even now, there brewed a profound mystery, and soon a man was to drop dead, with no mark upon his body, but with his eyes protruding horribly; others would die, men of high and low station, until the greatest metropolis of the world would go mad with terror.

*The Annihilist*, men came to call the power. And in fighting the sinister thing, Doc Savage was to uncover untold danger and a plot utterly fiendish in conception.

Battling *The Annihilist*, Doc Savage and his men were to encounter opposition such as they had never before experienced. It was as if they fought the eerie, the supernatural, the impossible.

Monk, standing in the middle of the treasure of King John, grinned widely and started a yawn. His big mouth froze suddenly in midstretch.

"Blazes!" he exploded. "I just thought of something funny."

Doc eyed him questioningly.

"Since this thing started," Monk explained, "there ain't been a dang soul killed. Boy, are we getting efficient!"

THE END

# INTERMISSION by Will Murray

*The Sea Magician* was written during one of the most hectic periods of Lester Dent's tenure on *Doc Savage Magazine*. It was spring 1934, and Dent was juggling the series' monthly demands, as well as turning out episodes of the half-forgotten *Doc Savage* radio series for Don Lee's Golden West Network.

It was hard, hard work. The radio people were resisting Lester's pleas to let him inject more continuity into the show, which would have made it easier to write. And he appeared to be having problems with the magazine version of his hero, or perhaps with his editor, John L. Nanovic, whom he sometimes grumblingly called "John God." Dent hoped to inject more continuity into his Doc novels as well.

Dent had prevailed on Street & Smith to allow him to sometimes leave out some of Doc's five assistants, as storylines permitted, beginning with *Death in Silver*. The device he used to set up this new approach was to scatter Renny, Long Tom and Johnny to the far corners of the earth, informing readers that they were busy with their civilian professions. Dent's plan was to write a trilogy of Docs, each concentrating on one of the missing trio.

After turning in *Death in Silver*, Dent submitted two outlines, "Python Isle" and "The Scottish Spook," which were planned as Doc Savages #21 and #22 respectively. The former storyline was kicked off by Renny Renwick running into trouble in Africa, while Johnny Littlejohn's brush with danger in London was the springboard for "The Scottish Spook."

Dent hit a snag when Nanovic rejected "Python Isle" outright. Lester must have been stunned. He was even more startled to learn the reason.

Nanovic had been buying short stories from a budding young writer fresh out of Washington & Lee University named Richard Sale. An amateur herpetologist, Sale liked to write suspense stories involving venomous snakes and reptiles. Nanovic purchased "The White Cobra" for *The Shadow*.

"It was a good story and I asked for more," Nanovic recalled. "He sent three more, which I purchased. Then the first story appeared in print. We got more mail on that story than anything else. It was a snake story and everyone objected to it. I printed one more story of his, then stopped. Those other stories are probably still in a safe somewhere."

Evidently, Nanovic had signed off on the next Doc plot under its working title, "Lost Island." When he saw the new title, he may not have bothered to read the rest. Snake stories were out at Street & Smith.

The remarkable thing about this was that Dent had hired Sale himself to ghost "Python Isle." The germ of the plot was something Sale pitched to Dent under the title, "The Serpent Empire." The young author had managed to accidentally torpedo his first chance to ghost a Doc Savage!

Having no means of appeal, Dent filed "Python Isle" away, moving on to "The Scottish Spook," which he retitled *The Sea Magician*. He wrote it himself, as he had probably planned all along. But the idea was not entirely his. At a meeting of the American Fiction Guild, Dent met a writer named Ryerson Johnson. Dent liked to pick the brains of other authors. When "Johnny" told the story of a pair of Florida confidence men who were promoting stock in a new technological wrinkle in gold mining by exploiting the gold particles suspended in sea water, Dent smelled the germ of an exciting Doc Savage novel.

"Les was impressed by that story," Johnson remembered. "I used it myself since then."

Coincidentally, Dent's favorite magazine *Popular Mechanics* ran an article on the potential of extracting gold from the sea in its June, 1934 issue. No doubt this provided technical details.

The disgraced American utilities king mentioned in Chapter VII is a topical reference to Chicago electrical and transportation magnate, Samuel Insull. He was one of the most powerful businessmen in the U.S. until the Depression wiped him out, landing him in serious legal trouble. Fleeing a 1932 indictment for embezzlement and mail fraud, Insull settled in Greece. When his Visa expired in 1934, he became a man without a country. Attempting to enter Romania, but was refused. Ultimately extradited from Turkey, Insull returned to the U.S. in May, 1934, the most famous international fugitive of his day.

Insull's business practices were blamed for triggering the Great Depression, and his country-hopping attempts to evade U.S. justice were making wild headlines at this time.

Acquitted of all charges, Insull went into exile, dying in Paris in 1938.

Another topical reference in Chapter I is one that still makes headlines today. The sea serpent Dent mentions is none other than the Loch Ness monster, which first made world headlines in 1933 and 1934 when several persons claimed to have observed it both on sea and land. Public awareness of spooky doings in Loch Ness might have prompted Dent to chose Great Britain for this novel's locale.

Magna Island off the coast of England is of course fictitious. It's based on one of the smaller

Channel Islands in the Guernsey or Jersey group Samuel Insull was rumored to be interested in buying. Doc Savage later returned to this unusual locality in *The Submarine Mystery.*\*

Dent's problems did not end when he submitted *The Sea Magician*. The exact details are unclear, but evidently Nanovic sent the manuscript back for a restructuring.

Dent hated to rewrite. Sometimes when he got stuck on a Doc, he simply put it aside and went on to the next outline until he unknotted the plot problem. But with his other plots shot down, Dent had no choice but to rework the storyline.

Originally *The Sea Magician* opened with the chapter entitled "The Uncle in India." This was moved deeper into the story to become Chapter V. Chapter III, "The Tidal Flat Ghost," was revised to create the new beginning. One chapter was thrown out entirely. Virtually all of the revisions were confined to the first seven chapters. It appears Nanovic wanted Dent to jump into the heart of the mystery in The Wash right away. And he was correct.

Despite all this travail—or perhaps due to it—*The Sea Magician* is a corking great yarn and Monk Mayfair's memorable final line demonstrates how Lester Dent continually strove to surprise his readers.

When Dent completed the last chapter, he teased Nanovic with a blurb for a Doc set out West called "The Veil of Silence." Perhaps this was going to be the Long Tom Roberts exploit. But another snag forced Dent to lay the idea aside, and so he finally abandoned his plans to follow up on the adventures of the absent Doc Savage aides.

THE LIVING-FIRE MENACE was the work of one of Dent's most reliable ghosts, journalist Harold A. Davis. It's among the fastest-paced episodes in the career of the Man of Bronze, and perhaps one of the most influential. Hence its inclusion here.

Published in 1938, it showcased on its cover and in most interior illustrations Doc's new "emergency kit." For the first few years of the series, Doc Savage carried his handy crimefighting gadgets around in a many-pocketed bulletproof vest. Harold Davis introduced the belt kit in 1935's *Dust of Death,* but it did not survive Dent's rewrite of that story. It finally debuted in *The South Pole Terror*. Davis picked it up again in *The Land of Fear,* and it came into prominence in *The Living-Fire Menace*.

\**The Submarine Mystery,* paired with *The Spook Legion,* was reprinted in Volume Five of Nostalgia Ventures' *Doc Savage* reprints.

**Lester Dent circa 1938**

Davis never described it in detail, but Lester Dent did. The belt's pockets opened and closed with zippers and was padded so the pockets would not bulge when worn under street clothes. Doc seemed to prefer to wear the belt when stripped down to swim trunks, and it was here that he carried his favorite tool—the silk line and folding grappling hook.

Before too many months had passed, the gadget belt turned up in the pages of *Detective Comics,* in the form of Batman's utility belt. Writer Bill Finger was not shy about crediting his inspiration. He freely admitted that he had borrowed Batman's yellow utility belt from Doc Savage. Like Batman, Doc varied the contents of his emergency kit as circumstances required. Both heroes preferred to rely on non-lethal devices, like pellets of knockout gas, as well as an assortment of lock picks and other handy tools of the crimefighting trade.

But the impact of this wild adventure was not limited to Batman. Read this 1938 yarn and consider whether or not it might have influenced artist Carl Burgos to create for *Marvel Mystery Comics* in 1939 the Human Torch, a popular comic-book conception who survives to this day as a member of the Fantastic Four—another cultural comic-book icon which was also inspired by Doc Savage.

Finally, the early Harold Davis Doc Savage novels show unmistakable signs of Lester Dent's rewriting skills. Not so *The Living-Fire Menace*. By this time the red-headed reporter from Colorado had learned to be Kenneth Robeson all by himself.

*Living dead men carried the secret of a hideous death within their bodies—a death that Doc Savage risked when he took up the trail of*

# The Living-fire Menace

## By KENNETH ROBESON

### Complete Book-length Novel

### Chapter I
### A STRANGE WARNING

THE man reeled as he tried to run. His breath came in short gasps. Time after time his head twisted to dart quick, fearful looks behind him.

Perspiration was streaming from his body. His face was a queer cherry-red, the lips puffed and scarlet bright. His feet kicked up small clouds of sand.

Overhead, the sun was beating down relentlessly. On either side were cactus and sage. And ahead, not far now, were the scattered buildings of the desert town of Sandrit.

Mumbled words came from between the puffed lips.

"I've got to make it! I've got to make it! I've got to get word out—get word to Doc Savage!"

At Palm Springs, only a few short miles away, beautiful movie stars were lounging around in shorts. Cooling drinks were near at hand. The thermometer was well over a hundred.

But the running man was dressed as if for a zero winter day.

Strange wrappings on his feet accounted for part of his reeling gait. Strips from an old inner tube had been bound about those feet. The strips had cut into the flesh until blood drops marked the trail, but the man did not pause.

His body seemed sheathed in many clothes. And about those clothes other strips of rubber had been bound. On his hands were heavy rubber gloves.

But it was the man's eyes that held attention. Fear blazed from sunken orbs—deadly, unhealthy fear.

Some might have doubted that the reeling man was sane. And the words he babbled sounded like those of a man in the grip of a nightmare:

"The living fire! The death that cannot be avoided! The fire that spurts from within, that burns and destroys! A hell-fire! And it'll get me! I cannot escape!"

The man's heart pounded as he thought of the secret he carried—a secret he must reveal at once if he were to prevent untold calamity.

Once again his head twisted so that he looked behind him. A faint cloud of dust showed on the road over which he had just come. A big car came into view.

Frantically the man tried to run faster, his cherry-red face twisting with renewed anguish, his eyes popping.

"I've got to go on!" he gritted. "I've got to get word to Doc Savage!"

THE girl in the big car did not look dangerous. She looked as if she might be one of the movie stars visiting at Palm Springs.

Long black curls framed a face that was almost perfection. Only a stub nose broke the faultless symmetry of her features. Her eyes were dark pools of bewitching enchantry. Shorts and a halter did little to hide the seductiveness of her form.

But as the girl caught sight of the reeling man ahead, her face changed subtly. An expression almost of craftiness flashed in her dark eyes; her soft lips tightened.

The man had almost reached the filling station. The girl braked the big car, slowing it instantly until it was barely moving.

The girl glanced behind her. Something like a sigh escaped her lips as she saw the road was clear.

She reached into a side pocket of the car, even as she brought the machine to a stop at the edge of the road.

Then she had opened the door, had slid to the ground, was moving rapidly toward the filling station where the reeling man had vanished. The sunlight flickered wickedly on the small, deadly automatic she carried in her hand.

The filling-station attendant did not see her. He was gazing open-mouthed at the strange apparition that had materialized before him.

The queerly dressed man seemed oblivious of the attendant. With glazed eyes, he rushed toward the old-fashioned-type telephone in one corner of the room.

"I've got to tell them! There she is! I've got to get word to Doc Savage—"

Hands awkward in their heavy gloves, the man spun desperately on the crank to signal the telephone operator.

"Number, please," came a cool, crisp voice.

The frightened man's words tore from his swollen lips.

"Get me Doc Savage's office, in New York!" he half screamed. "Tell him this is Z-2 calling. Get Doc Savage! Get him!"

THE filling-station attendant's mouth dropped open even farther. His eyes tried to jump from his head.

"Doc Savage!" he repeated, and his voice held a note of awe.

There was frenzied fear in the stranger's face, in the queer pinched lines about his eyes as he waited for his call.

"Hurry!" he yelled impotently. "Hurry! I've got to reach Doc Savage before it's too late!"

The telephone operator was hurrying. The name Doc Savage had done something to her, also. Her voice had an unusually excited timbre as she implored intervening stations for speed.

"Doc Savage's office. William Harper Littlejohn speaking," came calm, measured tones from the other end of the wire.

The telephone operator's heart sank. "A call for Mr. Doc Savage," she said hopefully.

"Clark Savage, Jr., is absent for the nonce. I will hear the communication."

"Johnny! Johnny! Listen! This is Z-2!" the queerly dressed man shouted frantically into the telephone. "You've got to get word to Doc at once!"

He paused, subconsciously stripped one heavy glove from a hand to wipe the perspiration from his face.

"I've found something that's unbelievable! The fate of the world is at stake. And there's a plot aimed at Doc, at all of you! Listen. I'll give you the low-down fast. I haven't got long to live. There's a living fire. It's terrible! It's—"

A pretty face pressed close to a half-opened window of the filling station. Dark eyes gleamed with sudden anticipation.

*Blam!*

There was a noise like two boards smacking together sharply. A queer, burned odor filled the air.

At the other end of the wire, more than two thousand miles away, that sharp crack came clearly.

But no more words came over that wire.

## Chapter II
### ATTACKERS STRIKE

WILLIAM HARPER LITTLEJOHN, better known as "Johnny," seldom showed excitement. Lean, with a half-starved look, with glasses hiding his eyes, he appeared like just what he was a studious scientist, one of the world's greatest geologists and archaeologists.

But he was excited now. With almost unseemly haste, for him, he signaled for the long-distance operator, barked with unaccustomed harshness:

"Get that number back, operator. Get it back at once. This is Doc Savage's office speaking!"

Across the room a thin, lean man with yellow, unhealthy-appearing skin, lounged indolently in an easy chair. He was pulling absently at an oversized ear.

Major Thomas J. Roberts appeared a physical weakling. Appearances were deceitful, even as his slouching pose was now. He tried to seem nonchalant; actually, he was afire with curiosity.

"What is it, Johnny, some nut?" he asked.

"Nut, nothing!" Johnny rapped.

Major Thomas J. Roberts, familiarly called "Long Tom," sat up abruptly in his chair. The very fact that Johnny had failed to use his usual quota of big words was sufficient to tell him that something was in the air.

"That was Z-2," Johnny explained rapidly. "He's an undercover agent for the Department of Justice. I once knew him well, was in the army with him. He's tripped across something big."

Swiftly Johnny repeated the message the man known as Z-2 had given him.

"I wish Doc were here," Long Tom muttered.

But Doc Savage was not near by. He was not even in the city, but was miles away, possibly thousands of miles away.

The telephone rang sharply. Johnny grabbed for it.

"I have your party back for you," the operator said sweetly.

"Z-2?" Johnny demanded breathlessly. "What happened? What was that noise—"

"Naw," came a half-frightened, choking voice. "T-this ain't that guy who called himself Z-2. H-he ain't here no more. H-he's dead. T-this is Paul Smith, the filling-station attendant."

PAUL SMITH'S pimply face was still white. He'd witnessed something he knew he'd remember until he died—something that had horrified, yet fascinated him.

"This guy, see," he explained, as Johnny demanded details swiftly. "This guy he came in here all funny dressed. Hot as it is, he even had gloves on and had inner tire tubing wrapped around his feet for shoes."

"Go on," Johnny ordered crisply.

"His face was a funny red color, and his hand, too, when he took one glove off. I didn't think of it at the time, but I know now he was awful scared."

"I'll take that for granted. What happened?" Johnny interrupted impatiently.

"W-why, this guy, he called for Doc Savage," Paul Smith explained. "Somebody answered. He started to talk."

"Yes. Yes."

"He was awfully hot. He was wiping sweat off his face as he talked. And he really was shouting. He seemed awful worked up."

"I know." Johnny's voice became very resigned. "But tell me in words of one syllable, *what happened?*"

Paul Smith wet dry lips with the tip of his tongue.

"He—he blew up!" he shouted. "H-he just became a sheet of fire!"

There was silence for a moment.

"How did it happen?" Johnny asked softly.

"I—I don't know." Paul Smith was frankly sobbing now. "It—it was just as if a sheet of lightning hit him, or something. He—he just became one big flash of fire, like I said. He—he shriveled and burned, and the odor of his flesh, it—ah—"

"And there was nothing near him, no one close but you?"

"N-no one," Paul Smith whimpered. "It—it just happened. I—I couldn't'a done it. No one could. I-it seemed as if the flame came from within, not from outside him anywhere. No one but I was near him, anyway."

Paul Smith thought he told the truth. He never had seen the beautiful face of the girl that had been near the half-opened window.

Long Tom was an electrical genius. He shook his head when Johnny suggested there might have been something about the telephone that caused a short circuit or electrical discharge that could have killed Z-2.

"Impossible," he said flatly. "That could not have happened under any circumstances."

"But something did," Johnny reflected softly.

"What could a government man have been doing in a small desert town like Sandrit?" Long Tom puzzled aloud. "It had to be something big, but whoever heard of a living fire? And what was he trying to warn us about? How could we be in danger?"

Johnny shook his head. He was equally puzzled.

LONG TOM and Johnny would have been even more puzzled just then if they could have heard and seen what was going on in a lavish suite at a big hotel not many blocks away.

Three men were there. One was pacing nervously up and down the room. He was a tall man, and very thin. He looked almost like a scarecrow. His face was a peculiar cherry-red. Petrod Yardoff was not well known in the United States. In some European countries he was too well known. Many strange stories had been linked with his name.

Lounging across from Yardoff was a long, husky man, with the steely, unblinking eyes of a snake. Those eyes and the gun he always carried had earned him the nickname "Stinger." Stinger Salvatore *was* well known in the United States. Many strange tales had been linked with his name, too, but none had ever been proved in court.

The third of the group watched his companions with cynical amusement. Clement Hoskins was known to very few. He intended to remain that way. Huge, with a barrel-shaped body that was as big around as he was tall, Hoskins nevertheless gave the impression of rough, vicious strength.

"You have done good work so far, Stinger," Petrod Yardoff said softly. "But one job remains. A tough job."

Stinger shrugged slightly. He pulled a handkerchief from one sleeve, wiped his hands. "Spill it," he said laconically.

"Would you like to cut in on a game that will pay off in millions?" Clement Hoskins queried sardonically.

Stinger Salvatore's lounging frame came erect suddenly. "Millions?" he repeated slowly. "The job you've got for me *must* be a tough one!"

"A tough job, but worth it—if you consider the millions," Hoskins grated. "But I wonder—I wonder if you've got nerve enough to tackle it?"

Stinger's face reddened. "Spill it!" he snapped.

"We want six men—just six," Clement Hoskins breathed.

The gangleader snorted contemptuously. "And I thought it was a tough job. How do you want 'em? Alive or—"

"Those six men," Petrod Yardoff said gently, "are Doc Savage and his five aides."

THERE was sudden silence in the room. Stinger's face turned the shade of paste. "Doc Savage," he muttered.

Stinger's features became sober. "Friends of mine have tried to buck that bronze devil," he said. "They've never been seen again. He's poison."

"Are you afraid?" Yardoff sneered.

The gangster looked at him with unwinking eyes. "Afraid? No," he said softly. "Just careful."

"Yet we will cut you in on a deal that's going to pay off in millions," Hoskins reminded.

Stinger took a deep breath. "Perhaps I'll try it. If I really thought you guys had anything—"

"You have a bodyguard outside, haven't you?" Yardoff interrupted.

"Why, yes. But what—" Stinger frankly showed his surprise.

"Call him in!"

Stinger hesitated for a moment. Something in Yardoff's face decided him. He called, "Rudolph!"

A typical gunman shuffled into the room. In one hand was a short-barreled .38. "Trouble, boss?" he croaked.

"No trouble, no trouble at all," Petrod Yardoff said. His lips split thinly as he walked forward, tall frame swaying. "We were merely talking about making a million dollars, and Stinger here seems a little reluctant. You wouldn't be, now would you?"

"What?" The other's pig eyes opened wide.

Stinger's jaw dropped. He started to shout. Yardoff was stripping a glove from one hand. The glove was of transparent rubber. It had been practically invisible.

The words never came from the gangleader's mouth.

Yardoff, still smiling, dropped his hand casually on Rudolph's shoulder.

There was a sudden sheet of fire. The bodyguard jerked; his mouth opened, but he made no sound. The gun dropped from seared hand. He was dead before he hit the floor.

The odor of burned flesh filled the room.

"The living fire!" gasped Stinger.

STINGER'S features no longer were smooth and unruffled. They were drawn and taut. His fingers played nervously with the handkerchief in his sleeve.

Stinger had seen many men die. He wasn't afraid of death—as long as it was someone else who was checking out.

Petrod Yardoff apparently had had nothing in his hand when he had placed it on the bodyguard's shoulder. No one else in the room had made a move.

Yet the bodyguard showed every evidence of having died from a tremendous bolt of electricity—a bolt that had covered his entire body with flame. And Petrod Yardoff, touching him, had been unharmed!

Then the gangleader saw something that had escaped his attention before. There was a thin, transparent, practically invisible rubber mask covering Yardoff's peculiar cherry-red features. His shoes were of rubber. Even the gray suit he wore was made of rubber.

Stinger had heard of the living-fire death, had heard it spoken of in awe-stricken tones in the underworld. It had been tied with whispers of a mysterious secret—a secret worth millions.

Petrod Yardoff opened a big trunk. Then he picked up the shriveled, burned form of the bodyguard, placed it in the trunk and locked the lid.

"Was the exhibition satisfactory?" he asked.

Stinger gulped. "Y-yes," he agreed reluctantly.

"We're waiting for your answer!" the barrel-shaped Clement Hoskins reminded sharply.

"Doc Savage is s-still tough medicine," Stinger protested weakly.

Petrod Yardoff turned. Once again he started to strip a rubber glove from his hand. A merciless smile split his narrow face. He started to move forward, catlike.

"No! No!" Stinger shrilled. His hand shot for a telephone. Still breathing swiftly, he made several calls in rapid succession.

"Doc Savage is out of town," he reported at last, and there was no mistaking the relief in his voice. "The two they call Johnny and Long Tom are the only ones at his office, although I understand the other three aides are around."

"Get them," the thin man said. "They'll do to start with."

"Here are your instructions," Clement Hoskins rasped. The barrel-shaped man spoke rapidly.

Stinger nodded, the color gradually returning to his face. Then he lifted the telephone receiver again, barked quick orders when he was connected with his number.

"Johnny and Long Tom first," he concluded.

JOHNNY and Long Tom were unaware of their danger, but they were worried.

Long Tom turned away from the compact, short-wave set in one room of Doc's suite of offices, a frown smearing his forehead.

"Can't raise him," he said shortly.

The tall geologist nodded, glanced at his watch. "I know he implicitly instructed us to make no effort to interfere with his meditations until after eight o'clock at night, but I agree with you, I wish he would reply."

Long Tom rose to his feet, shrugged. Outside it was becoming dark.

"Let's go," he said shortly. "We're due to meet Monk and Ham for dinner. Perhaps they can help us dope out what this is all about."

A high-speed elevator dropped the two aides abruptly to the basement of the big building.

In the basement they moved without words to a big, closed car. A few moments later and they were out in traffic, heading rapidly downtown.

Both of Doc's men were thinking of Z-2's queer death, of the strange warning he had imparted. Long Tom drove automatically. Johnny sat hunched in the seat, eyes half closed behind his glasses.

Even had they been alert, it is doubtful that they would have known they were being followed. Traffic was heavy, and those trailing them knew their jobs.

The shadowers were in two cars. There were five in each automobile. Each of the men had a significant bulge under the left armpit. The drivers weaved in and out of traffic with the skill of cabmen.

Doc's big car was always kept in sight.

Near Brooklyn Bridge, Long Tom swung toward the East River, angling back to strike South Street.

A little while later, Long Tom swung off the smooth pavement of South Street onto the cobblestone street that led to a sea-food tavern called Reefer's. He noticed several cars parked nearby, but that meant nothing at the time. Reefer's was a popular place.

As Long Tom swung the big machine to the curb, he noticed several men alight from a car nearby. One glance was all the electrical expert needed to recognize the type.

For just a moment Long Tom hesitated, his unhealthy-appearing face doubtful. Johnny was already getting out of the machine. Then Long Tom shut off the motor and opened the car door.

In that moment, the attackers struck.

MEN seemed to erupt from dark doorways, from behind cars. A surging mass crashed into Long Tom and Johnny in the same instant, arms swinging, deadly blackjacks in hand.

Doc's men should have gone down under that first rush.

They didn't. Their attackers had been too anxious. They had massed too closely for their charge, got in each other's way.

A bellowed shout came from Johnny. Long Tom tried to dive back into the car. Hands grabbed him, yanked him back into the street.

Then the fight was on.

Johnny, fists swinging, head low, plunged into the men bearing down on him like a long, lean dreadnought. Speed and the very unexpectedness of his hammer-like blows, carried him across the sidewalk to a wall. He whirled, back firm against boards, clenched knuckles cracking with dazzling speed.

Long Tom sprawled forward, almost went to his knees. Still doubled up, he hit like a charging football guard. Small, weakly as he appeared, he spun men in all directions, got clear for a moment.

A swinging blackjack caught the electrical wizard across one arm, almost paralyzed it. He did not hesitate, did not pause. Lifting one big thug from his feet with a right that came from his shoe-tops, he made a second dive for the car.

This time Long Tom got as far as the car door before a terrific blow caught him across the head. A shower of sparks seemed to flash before his eyes, but even as he fell he yanked a queer-shaped weapon from the car door pocket. He whirled, his finger tightening on the trigger.

There was a sound like a bullfiddle's roar. Attackers tumbled limply.

The weapon was one of Doc's own inventions. The "mercy" bullets it shot produced unconsciousness, not death; but it was as effective as a machine gun.

LONG TOM was still dazed from the blow on top of his head. He could hear Johnny battling desperately. He thought only of that. He should have jumped inside the car. It had bullet-proof glass, was as impregnable as a tank. From there he could have rescued Johnny easily.

Instead, he darted around the rear of the car, weapon in hand.

A small man, a wicked grin on scarred features, reared up behind him, swung a blackjack coldly and efficiently.

Long Tom went down, sprawled awkwardly on the cobblestones.

Something resembling a moan came from Johnny's tight lips. He went berserk. For a moment, his flaying fists beat back the men who crowded upon him. But he saw there was no hope. There were too many assailants.

"Help, Doc!" he bellowed instinctively.

A second later he, also, went down. A billy caught him squarely behind an ear.

Then the attackers suddenly froze.

Clear and cold came a voice. It was low, but it had a peculiar timbre, one that made it carry plain and distinctly. It was the voice of Doc Savage.

"I'll soon be there," Doc said.

## Chapter III
## A GIRL CALLS

BUT Doc Savage was far from the waterfront battle scene.

His bronze skin gleaming in the reflected glow from an instrument board, his flake-gold eyes intent on the story those instruments told, he was far even from civilization.

Seated in the inclosed cockpit of a speedy plane that was the type pilots call a "flying motor," Doc Savage did not appear big. But that was due to the remarkable symmetry of his body. His hair was straight, and bronze like his skin. Corded muscles showed on the backs of the hands that held the controls. His features were classic and calm. Seldom did he smile or show emotion.

The roar of the powerful motor came but faintly inside the cockpit. For that cockpit was heavily

**DOC SAVAGE**

insulated. It had to be. The plane was flying thousands of feet up in the air, far up in the substratosphere. It was winging forward at nearly five hundred miles an hour.

The sound of Doc's strange, impelling voice had shocked the thugs in New York. They would have been more shocked if they had known just how far away he was when he had spoken. They would have thought it magic.

There was no magic about it. On the panel directly before the bronze man was a small television set. Above it was the speaker of a shortwave radio. A mike was near at hand.

The car Long Tom and Johnny had used was similarly equipped. Doc had seen part of the fight in New York; he had heard Johnny's cry for help. The bronze man's reply had merely come from the loudspeaker in the car his aides had occupied.

Now the bronze man was speeding toward New York. He had missed Long Tom's earlier calls. At that time he had not been in his plane.

Casual acquaintances had often wondered where Doc Savage ever found time to maintain his amazing grasp on every development of science, to study and keep ahead of a majority of those developments.

The secret was quite simple. Far in the north he had a hidden retreat—his "Fortress of Solitude." Here, when things were quiet, the bronze man would seek solitude for the tremendous concentration of which he was capable, would try new experiments, perfect new advances in medicine that would save thousands of lives, would solve some problem that had long puzzled chemists.

He was returning from such a trip now. For six months he had been apart from the world. And it was plain that he was returning just in time.

In a surprisingly short time, Doc's plane dived down from the heavens to circle the lights of Manhattan. Minutes more, and it was dropping gently to the waters of the Hudson River, gliding smoothly toward the dingy warehouse that bore the sign, "Hidalgo Trading Co." Doc was the Hidalgo Trading Co. He owned the pier and warehouse.

From an adjoining pier, a small man slipped away unobtrusively. His close-set eyes gleamed wickedly in the darkness. At a corner cigar store he slipped into a phone booth, dialed a number.

"He's here, chief," he said curtly. "The bronze boy himself ... O.K. ... Yeah, I'll keep him covered."

DOC SAVAGE had no way of knowing that his movements were being watched. Yet he moved inconspicuously as he made his way to the skyscraper where he had his offices. His private elevator shot him to the eighty-sixth floor.

In the hallway, he moved soundlessly. Just outside the door he paused, his flake-gold eyes narrowing slightly.

A faint whisper of sound came through the hallway. It was so low that the normal ear would have missed it.

Seeming almost to float, so swiftly, yet so silently did he move, the bronze man drifted down the hallway. He stopped before an apparently solid section of wall.

A low-pitched whisper came from his lips—a whisper that could not have been heard two feet away.

Instantly a section of the wall melted away and an opening appeared. Doc vanished within. The opening closed.

The bronze man was standing in one of the rear rooms of his suite of offices. It was dark, but he moved without hesitation, opened a small panel, flicked a switch.

Light glowed on a tiny screen. A desk and several chairs came into view. On the screen appeared a picture of the front office.

And in one corner, barely visible, was a crouching figure!

For several moments the bronze man studied the scene intently. Then he flicked off the small television set.

A second later, Doc opened another panel. A queer set of assorted switches came into view. Above them were two huge, oval, mercury tubes. A dull light glowed in the tubes as the bronze man pushed the switches home. A faint hum sounded for an instant, rose to a high pitch, then died out.

Doc walked over, opened the door, and entered calmly into the room where the crouching figure lurked.

A girl glanced up. In her hand she held a small, deadly automatic. Long black curls framed an almost flawless face.

She saw the opening door. She shrieked, raised her gun and fired. In the same instant she hurled two black cylinders she had in her other hand to the floor. The cylinders shattered into many pieces.

"To what am I indebted for your call?" came the low, peculiarly carrying voice of Doc Savage.

For an instant it appeared the girl was going to faint. The gun dropped from her nerveless fingers. Her dark eyes were strained wide, terror showing in their depths.

Frantically, those eyes probed every hidden recess of the room, every dark corner.

They could see nothing.

"A—a trick!" she breathed.

Strong hands caught her wrists, lifted her easily from her feet.

And if the girl had been frightened before, now she was panic-stricken. She could feel the grip of those hands, knew there must be someone there before her, someone who had grabbed her.

Her tongue stuck to the top of her mouth. She tried to scream, but emitted only a faint moan. Her eyes dropped down—and her heart seemed to stop.

She could not see her own body either. She, also, had become invisible.

She slumped, inert.

HAD the girl retained consciousness, she would have understood much. She was carried to a small sofa, laid there gently. Then a *click* sounded from the adjoining room as Doc released the switches he had pressed a few moments before.

Almost immediately he became visible again.

There was nothing supernatural about any of it. The faint sound the bronze man had heard in the hallway had told him some one had broken into his office. The low whisper he had given had merely been the proper tone to operate a familiar robot, a mechanical device that opened a sliding panel in a wall that looked solid.

And while becoming invisible was not commonplace, it was something that had been done before.

The switches he had operated had released a series of short high-powered light waves, known as invisible rays. As those rays struck a human being, that human gradually vanished simply because the eye could not distinguish it when penetrated by the speeding beams. Doc had not invented the process; that had been done by Stephan Pribil, a Hungarian scientist. But the bronze man had improved it, so that invisibility came almost immediately.

The bronze man knelt beside the girl, held smelling salts under her nose. She stirred restlessly, half opened her eyes, only to close them.

"Who sent you here?"

Doc's voice dropped even lower than usual. It held a queer, hypnotic quality.

"I—I came because I wished to."

The words came from the girl's lips dully, the voice that of a person speaking in his sleep.

"What did you wish?"

"I came to destroy a record I knew you must have. I came to keep—"

With startling suddenness the girl pulled erect on the sofa. Fear, tinged with horror, flamed in her dark eyes. One hand pressed against her lips.

"You are in no danger," Doc Savage said quietly.

The girl's eyes sought the bronze man's face.

"Doc Savage," she breathed.

The bronze man nodded. "Now if you will explain who you are, and what you desired here?" he suggested.

Fear returned to her eyes. "I—I can't! I can't!"

"But you must. It is necessary that I know. Someone has seized two of my men. I must know—"

Doc broke off suddenly. A hideous uproar had burst loose in the hallway just outside the door.

THE sounds were almost indescribable. First came the lordly roar of a bull ape, a fearsome sound. It was followed instantly by the shrill grunt of an angered pig.

As the girl's lips parted and her hands clenched, there was a furious burst of fighting. The pig seemed to be going wild as it squealed in rage. The bull ape's roars increased in violence.

There was a sudden, desperate squeal from the ape, then a ripping sound, as if that ape had been torn in two.

The door burst open. A gangling figure with long, apelike arms appeared. It had a titanic chest, with practically no hips, and the small eyes were almost lost in pits of gristle. Coarse, reddish hair covered the skin.

Behind that figure came a lean, dapper man who could have passed as a fashion plate at any time, so well was he dressed. He was waving a cane furiously, his face red with anger.

"That blasted pig can't win all the time!" he roared.

"Meet Lieutenant Colonel Andrew Blodgett Mayfair, known as Monk for quite obvious reasons," Doc said, with just a suspicion of a smile. "Pursuing him, dressed in the latest mode as usual, is Brigadier General Theodore Marley Brooks, more often called Ham."

There was sudden silence. The girl's glance went from one to the other of the newcomers with quick comprehension.

"Monk" stopped as if he had run into a ten-ton truck. A slow flush crept over his homely face.

"Ham" grinned openly, his anger disappearing as quickly as it had come. It always amused him to see Monk get flustered in the presence of a pretty girl.

"It was this ape here making all the noise," he explained maliciously. "Somewhere he found an out-of-work radio imitator who taught him to make those hideous sounds. He's been making them ever since, always pretending he's a pig licking an ape."

"At least he hasn't been able to figure out any way for the ape to lick the pig," Monk put in. His thin, childlike voice always came as a shock to those who first heard it. It sounded so out of place compared with his hulking frame.

Doc said nothing for the moment. Monk and Ham were always fighting each other when there was no one else to fight. Their quarreling dated far back to War days.

Yet despite the fact that they never seemed to work, Ham was known as Harvard's gift to the legal profession, an outstanding attorney; and Monk was a gifted chemist.

"What happened to Johnny and Long Tom?" Doc asked quietly.

LEVITY faded from the faces of the other two.

"That's what we really came up here to see if we could learn," Ham said seriously. "For some reason, they seem to have been kidnaped. I don't think it's anything serious, although I don't know.

"We were to meet them for dinner at Reefer's. We got there just after they'd been seized. Was quite a fight, from what witnesses told us. They were taken off toward the piers at the lower end of South Street, and probably put in a boat. We searched without finding a clue."

"Unless one remark we heard means something," Monk piped up. "I talked to a kid who was close to the car that carried Long Tom and Johnny away. He told me something that he said he'd overheard that sounded as if he was having a pipe dream."

"What was that?" Doc asked swiftly.

"He said he heard one of the crew say 'I wouldn't want to be these guys. They're gonna see the menace of the living fire.'"

A gasp came from the girl. The three whirled toward her.

Her eyes were wide and staring. Her lips moved, but no sound came. Once again she fainted.

## Chapter IV
## STINGER STRIKES

TWO men stood just outside the door of the office. One was Petrod Yardoff. He took a small, cup-shaped instrument away from the door, took headphones from his ears.

"We are just in time," he whispered.

His companion shuddered slightly. He was also dressed in rubber clothes, but so well were those clothes made that few would have guessed their composition. Thin, flesh-colored gloves covered his hands; tennis shoes were on his feet.

"This will be all that is asked of me?" he quavered.

"This will be all, Meeker," Yardoff said. His thin lips twisted sardonically. "After this, you will be—free."

The other's shoulders bunched; a shrewd gleam flashed for a moment in deep-set eyes.

"I am ready," he said.

"Good." One of Yardoff's hands slipped unnoticed into a pocket. It came out holding a small vial. As he talked swiftly, his fingers loosened the cork. A white liquid poured out, seeped under the feet of his companion.

"Be sure you make the argument strong enough," Yardoff concluded. "Tell just enough of the truth to arouse Doc Savage's interest. That is all that is—"

His companion waited for no more. His lips came together firmly. He opened the door, walked into the bronze man's office.

Ham spun; the end of his cane slipped off to reveal a long, deadly sword. Monk, leaning over the girl, whipped erect, jerked to his feet, long arms swinging.

"Watch the girl, Monk," Doc said quietly.

The newcomer closed the door carefully behind him. His face was working with some strange emotion.

Then fear flashed over the rubber-clad man's face; his features changed from a queer cherry-red to the color of chalk. He danced wildly from one foot to the other.

"Watch out, Doc!" he screamed. "I was sent here to try to lure you to California, to Sandrit. I was told I'd be free if I did that. I've been tricked! I'm going to die!"

Saliva trickled weirdly from the corners of his mouth.

"Don't go to Sandrit! Stay far away from there. The menace of the living fire protects it, kills all—"

The words broke off in a scream.

There was a sudden flash of fire—fire that came from inside the man's rubber suit. The man's body jerked violently; his eyes almost popped from his head. The odor of burned rubber and burned flesh filled the room.

The man fell. He was quite dead.

A peculiar, trilling sound filled the room. It seemed to come from no particular place, yet from everywhere. It was the sound Doc Savage unconsciously made when he was surprised.

With Monk and Ham at his heels, he darted to the side of the fallen man.

Outside, Petrod Yardoff smiled thinly as once more he replaced his listening device in his pocket. He had expected his companion to try to double-cross him, to try and give a warning.

That had been just what he wanted. From what he had heard of Doc Savage, the bronze man now would leave no stone unturned until he had tried to solve the mystery.

"BUT what caused it?" Monk's childlike voice was filled with wonderment.

"A bolt of lightning!" Ham snapped impatiently.

"The results are about the same at any rate," Doc agreed quietly. "Do you notice that the rubber suit he is wearing is untouched on the outside? The fire that destroyed him came from within."

"And he mentioned the menace of the living fire," Monk breathed. "Say. That's what that kid said Johnny and Long Tom was gonna have to face."

The bronze man nodded soberly. "I am afraid they are in great danger," he said slowly.

Monk jumped up, fairly danced about. "Then let's get going! What are we waiting for?"

"Do you recognize this guy?" Ham asked suddenly.

Doc inclined his head. "He was Darren Meeker, once a very great scientist," he said. "Meeker killed a man some years ago, and was committed to an asylum."

"And escaped about four months ago, very mysteriously. It happened while you were away," Ham added.

"Holy cow!"

The expression came in an awed tone of voice. Doc glanced up.

A huge man stood in the doorway—a man a good six feet four inches tall, who must have weighed over two hundred and fifty pounds. His face was severe, the mouth thin and grim. That mouth was set tightly now, the features puritanical. Bony monstrosities of fists hung at the end of enormous arms.

"You're just in time, Renny!" Monk howled.

"But what—"

Swiftly, Ham sketched what had occurred. The

"Monk" is the chemist of Doc Savage's little band of fighters. You couldn't tell from looking at him, for he looks more like the missing link, as his companion, Ham, would put it, than anything else.

But Monk is a chemist, and a good one. He is also a fighter—and if anything, a better fighter than a chemist.

Moreover, he's one of Doc's companions—and that's enough to stamp any man as the best in manhood!

MONK

puritanical look grew even more severe on the face of Colonel John Renwick. One huge fist smacked into an equally big palm, as if he were trying to batter down a door—one of his favorite pastimes.

"You say this fellow just walked in, bellowed a warning, then went up in fire?" he asked wonderingly.

"Right!" snapped Ham.

"Hmm." The corners of "Renny's" mouth drew down disapprovingly. "I wonder. Don't seem likely. But I wonder if that girl I saw going down the stairway could have had anything to do with this. She sure was a beauty, but beauty doesn't always—"

A howl came from Monk. His piglike eyes were staring with complete disillusionment at the sofa where the girl had been.

That sofa was empty now. The girl was gone.

DOC turned, looked at Monk. The hairy chemist's eyes dropped.

"Yeah, I—I know," he apologized weakly. "I was supposed to watch her. But I got excited—"

"The girl may not hold the key to this mystery, but I am sure she has information that we need," the bronze man said slowly.

"And this ape let her get away," Ham jeered.

Doc walked over to a small, square box on the desk. He opened the back, took out half a dozen slips of paper, handed one each to Monk, Ham and Renny.

"But—but these are pictures of the girl," Renny said.

"Right." Doc's voice was matter of fact. "I tried out this new camera while she was here. Complete prints are made in the matter of seconds and dropped through a slot into the rear of the camera to dry."

Renny's mouth dropped open, but he said nothing. He had seen too many of Doc's inventions to be greatly surprised.

"That girl was from the West. Her accent showed that," the bronze man went on. "She must be stopping at some hotel. Check each one, find out where she is, and find out what she knows."

As the door closed behind the three, Doc went to a bookcase near the far wall. That bookcase had been pulled out, disclosing a niche that held a machine.

The machine was a telephonic monitor, and recorded all telephone conversations. No disks were on the monitor now, however. The girl had found them. They were shattered on the floor.

The bronze man worked swiftly. Soon the disks had been put together again.

Doc played them over. He heard Z-2's conversation with Johnny. He heard Johnny's conversation with the filling-station attendant.

For a moment the bronze man's flake-gold eyes were half closed. He went to the telephone, placed a call. A few minutes later and he was talking to the youth at the Sandrit filling station. He asked only one question. His queer, trilling sound filled the room at the answer he received.

Soon afterward Doc left the building.

DOC SAVAGE had friends in many places. Thus it was that he had no difficulty in gaining access to the morgue of the city's largest newspaper.

A newspaper morgue contains clippings from scores of papers on everything that is printed.

The editor looked at the bronze man queerly when he heard the type of clippings Doc wanted to see, but he asked no questions. Soon several folders were laid on the editor's desk.

Doc Savage ran through them swiftly. He was interested only in those dated during the last six months.

The small mountain of clippings gradually faded. At last only five remained of the many he had read.

These five the bronze man reread carefully. The stories they told came from widely separated points. One said:

SAN QUENTIN, CAL.—Ten prisoners escaped mysteriously from San Quentin Penitentiary today. The men, all trustees, were tending flowers in the outer yard. In some manner they overcame and killed Herbert Yokes, thirty-two, the guard. His body, badly burned, was found shortly after the men must have escaped.

A strange feature of the case is the fact that the iron gate at the entrance to the yard seemed to have been melted as if an acetylene torch had been used, although prison officials say this was impossible.

Among those who escaped was Frederick Scone, a former university professor in chemistry, serving a life term for the murder of his wife. The others were—

Another clipping read:

ALBUQUERQUE, N.M.—A man, later identified as "Slug" Bremer, an escaped convict, was killed instantly here today when struck by a train. Bremer evidently had fallen from a freight train on the main tracks only a mile from town, and was run over by the *California Limited*. His body was badly mangled. Strange burns that seemed to cover the entire body could not be explained by Coroner Smith.

Of the three other items, two told of more escapes, one from a prison, in which more than twenty trusties had gotten away at the same time. The second told of a break at a Missouri asylum. The third reported the mysterious death of another of those who had gained freedom.

The editor was studying Doc's face curiously. "If there is anything more I can do," he began hopefully, "or if I can get you any more information—"

"This is satisfactory, thank you," Doc said.

The editor watched him leave with a long face.

In a telephone booth in the lobby, Doc called his office. The telephonic monitor had been put back in working order. At Doc's voice, another mechanical robot put the record into operation. It repeated the last call received.

"Renny calling in to report," came the recorded voice. "I have located the girl. She is staying at the Midtown Hotel, has just come in and gone to Room 1412. I'll keep watch."

Doc hung up, started for his car in front of the building.

THERE was a small, private alleyway only a hundred yards from the front of the newspaper building. In this alleyway, two men were crouching.

One rubbed his hands nervously on a handkerchief, flicked that handkerchief back into one sleeve.

He spoke out of one corner of his mouth. "You're sure everything is fixed? There must be no slip-ups. I was told to get this bronze devil alive, but that's too dangerous. I want him dead."

His companion squirmed uneasily. He wore greasy overalls, and his face was smeared with dirt. He held an odd-shaped object in his hands.

"It'd take more than a miracle to save that mug," he growled sourly, "even if he is—"

He broke off as Stinger's hand came down on his arm.

Doc Savage had emerged from the building.

The bronze man glanced up and down the street rapidly.

The car at the curb was a big, enclosed job, similar to the one Long Tom and Johnny had used. The door was locked. Doc took out a key, reached toward the lock.

AT the alleyway, Stinger drew a long sigh of relief. "I still wish we had the real thing to work on this guy," he muttered, "but the plaything you've got rigged up should work."

Doc inserted the key in the car door, started to open it.

Beside Stinger, his overalls-clad companion worked on the odd-shaped object he held in his hands. There was a faint, humming noise.

Doc's big figure seemed to jerk erect. Fire danced about the car. Flames crackled and jumped. Women screamed. The editor stood frozen, face vacant.

For a moment the bronze man appeared absolutely rigid. A peculiar odor filled the air.

Stinger's companion worked again on the odd-shaped object he held.

The bronze man's fingers fell nervelessly from the car door. His big frame crumpled to the sidewalk.

Stinger laughed, lips drawn back from his teeth.

"Let's go, punk!" he grated. "Things are goin' to be even hotter than that around here as soon as they learn that bronze devil is really dead."

## Chapter V
### A CALL TO THE MORGUE

RENNY had expected Doc to receive his message. He waited for a time in the lobby of the Midtown Hotel. Waiting became tiresome.

Towering high above others in the lobby, he approached the desk. "Who's in 1412?" he rumbled.

The clerk glanced up haughtily, inspected his fingernails with elaborate unconcern. "And your business?" he asked snippily.

Renny placed one huge, bony monstrosity of a fist on the desk. He closed that fist until it looked like a rough chunk of iron.

"Did you ever hear of Doc Savage?" he asked softly. "Or"—his fist rose and fell expressively—"does this look like a better argument?"

The clerk gulped. "D-Doc Savage. Why didn't you say so? Glad to do anything for a friend of Mr. Savage. It—ah—Miss Virginia Hoskins, of Sandrit, California, is in 1412. A very beautiful girl."

Renny's mouth drew down disapprovingly. "Anyone with her?"

"Yes. Ah—a Mr. Clement Hoskins, also of Sandrit, is registered in an adjoining room with a Mr. Petrod Yardoff."

"Know anything about them?"

"Ah—why, yes. Mr. H-Hoskins, I understand, owns a factory of some kind in Sandrit. He is a stout, very jolly sort of fellow. Mr. Yardoff, I believe, is connected with him in a business way. He—ah—does not seem so jolly. A very slender, tall sort of chap."

Renny nodded.

Across the lobby, concealed by a pillar, a very tall, slender man jerked his head to two companions. His eyes were narrow slits. Swiftly, the three made their way to an elevator. They disappeared just as Renny turned away from the desk.

The big engineer rode the elevator to the fifteenth floor, walked down one flight, and approached 1412 with silent tread. An ear to the door, he listened carefully, but heard nothing.

He knocked softly. A faint stir sounded inside the room, then ceased. There was a buzz, which might have been a whispered conversation.

Once more Renny knocked.

A lock turned. The door opened an inch. The dark eyes of Virginia Hoskins, fright showing in their depths, appeared fleetingly.

"What did you run away for?" Renny demanded primly. "Doc wanted to talk to you."

"I—I never saw you before," Virginia stammered. She tried to push the door closed. Renny put one big foot in the opening. It was as if a small-sized gunboat had moved in.

"P-please, please go," the girl whispered.

Renny snorted. "Monk might fall for that, but not me," he announced—and pushed the door wide as he stepped inside.

A blackjack caught him expertly, squarely at the base of the brain, with force enough to crush an ordinary skull.

Renny kept on going forward—right on his face. All six foot four of the big engineer sprawled, immense arms outstretched.

Strong hands grabbed him under the armpits, yanked him inside. The door closed softly.

HAM also thought Monk might fall prey again to those dark pools of enchantry if he should encounter the girl.

The dapper lawyer was glad when he reached the Midtown Hotel that he did not see the hairy form of his friend around. Monk was good in a fight, none better; but when it came to the fair sex he quite often seemed to park his brains at home.

Ham's face showed no sign of concentration as he walked across the lobby, but he was thinking swiftly. He also had received the robot message from Renny, and he knew the big engineer should be waiting; but Renny wasn't in sight.

Ham didn't go near the desk. If anything was wrong, someone would be sure to be watching there. He drifted back through the dining room, through a side door, and raced upstairs.

The dapper lawyer was breathing a little heavily as he reached the fourteenth floor. The climb was a long one, even for a man in perfect condition.

Then his eyes narrowed, his hand tightened on the sword cane he carried.

Lights were out in the hallway. Somewhere, close at hand, he could hear faint breathing.

Ham held his breath as long as he could.

Doubled over, he reached the top of the stairs in a silent leap—and jumped to one side.

Something swished by one ear. A heavy form lunged toward him. Ham spun, fast as a dancer, jerked the long blade of his sword free from the cane.

**A bronze thunderbolt, Doc Savage dived through the door in a flying tackle.**

Big arms wrapped around him. The sword was knocked from his hand to fall on the thick carpet of the hallway. Ham's elbow shot back, landed with satisfying solidness just below the ribs.

His assailant said *"Whoof!"* and put one big paw over Ham's face, almost cutting off his wind. The man made small, animal-like noises as he spun the dapper lawyer around, slugged him hard on the side of the head.

Ham's head rang. His right fist shot up, caught the other under the chin, staggering him. The hand came away from his face.

"Stop it, you overgrown ape!" Ham yelled.

The other sighed deeply. "Dang it," came Monk's piping voice, "and I really thought I'd caught something! But it turns out to be a clothing-store shyster!"

"WHAT'S happened?" Ham asked, still struggling to get his wind.

"I was watching to see when you came blundering along," Monk complained. "I doused the lights, so if that girl did come by I couldn't see her face. Then I could talk to her. But nobody's been in or out of that room."

"Let's go. Something's wrong!" Ham rapped swiftly.

A muffled murmur of voices came from Room 1412.

"Doesn't seem like a girl's room to me," Monk muttered.

"Unless she's entertaining," Ham agreed.

He knocked loudly on the door. There was a roar of laughter from inside the room. No one answered the summons.

Monk's piglike eyes sank deeper back in his head; a scowl crossed his homely face. His fist shook the door panel.

"Beat it!" a rough voice advised.

Monk's face assumed a hurt expression. "I don't like to do this," he said, his childlike voice annoyed. "It's really Renny's job, but he ain't here. So—"

His huge fists smashed into the door panel with all his apelike strength behind the blow. The panel split. Calmly he put one hand through the opening, turned the lock and opened the door.

With Ham at his heels, Monk pushed into the room. Then they froze.

"Did Renny make a mistake in the room number?" Ham wondered aloud.

It seemed that way. Certainly no girl was in the room now. Instead, four men were there. They were seated about a card table. Chips were before them. The room was full of cigarette smoke.

The green-shirted dealer was rising from his chair. His hand started for a gun that hung in a shoulder holster.

"What is this, a raid?" he snapped.

Monk lumbered forward, long arms swinging, half crooked. One of those arms shot out. "Greenshirt's" hand was knocked from the butt of his gun; he was spun halfway around.

"You boys been playing here long?" Monk inquired mildly.

"Not that it's any of your business," sneered one of the players, "but we've been here for the last two hours."

"Yeah?" Monk's voice was deceivingly bland. "Funny. Lots of smoke in here, sure enough. But there are no cigarette butts in the ash trays—and the scent of a woman's perfume is still strong in the air."

GREENSHIRT'S hand was lightning fast as it went for his gun. Monk hardly seemed to move.

Then Monk held the gun in one huge paw, while with the other, he caught Greenshirt by the collar, lifted him up, then smashed him down so hard the chair buckled under him.

"I really would like to play games," the hairy chemist invited plaintively.

Ham was grinning tightly. Light glittered on the bright blade of his sword cane. The other three card players had been caught flat-footed. They sat, hands partly raised, mouths open.

"I suggest we start by playing the game called Truth," Ham proposed. "We want some information as to what has happened to some friends of ours."

"Go to hell! We don't know nothing about any friends of yours," Greenshirt sneered.

Monk looked very hurt. He put his head forward, invitingly.

Without warning, Greenshirt kicked him viciously on a shin. "Dang it!" Monk howled. He danced around, one foot in the air.

Greenshirt thought he saw his chance. He ducked his head, butted Monk hard in the belly. Another of the card players grabbed a gun.

Monk, his piglike eyes blazing, caught Greenshirt by the middle, threw him across the table into the gunman. The two went down.

Without hesitation, the hairy chemist leaped after them. In the same instant, some one upset the table. It caught Ham off guard, knocked the sword cane out of his hand.

*"Hold everything, folks!"* a voice blared loudly.

THE fighting ceased. Six figures halted in varied and assorted attitudes. It was an instant before they realized the words had come from a radio loudspeaker in the room.

Before they could resume the struggle, the voice went on—and six pair of ears strained to catch every word.

*"I've got hot news, folks, a flash right off the griddle that involves two of the trusted aides of the famous Doc Savage."*

The voice hesitated a moment, then went on with machine-gun rapidity.

"You all know Doc Savage, folks, that famous adventurer, who, with his five aides, is always fighting against injustice. Two of those aides will never fight again."

The news announcer halted dramatically.

"A flash has just reached me from the harbor police, folks. There was an explosion on a speed-boat an hour ago. How many were killed has not been definitely ascertained, as yet. But two bodies were recovered. Those bodies were badly burned. But they were identified from water-soaked papers in their pockets.

"They were: Major Thomas J. Roberts, known to his friends as Long Tom, and William Harper Littlejohn, called Johnny. Long Tom, as you know, was a wizard with electricity. Johnny was a famous archaeologist and geologist.

"Just what caused the explosion has not as yet been learned. A passing tugboat—"

The voice went on. Monk and Ham were no longer listening.

Ham's face was white. "That was no accident!" he grated. "They were killed!"

"And I think maybe these mugs can tell us something." Monk's voice was hardly recognizable.

The gunmen were huddled together. Three had their guns. Those weapons were in their hands, but they looked fearful just the same.

"We'll shoot," quavered one.

Monk spun, started to advance.

"*A super-flash, folks! A super-flash!*" The excitement in the news announcer's voice penetrated even the red haze that seemed to float before Monk's eyes.

"*Doc Savage himself has met with a mishap, a serious one. Something big must be breaking, folks. This flash just came in. As Doc Savage started to get in his car in front of the Globe office, just fifteen minutes ago, there was a terrific flash. It must have been electrical. Doc Savage went down—*

"*Wait a minute, folks! Here it is: Doc Savage, the famous adventurer, was instantly killed tonight when he was electrocuted in some manner as he started to enter his car! His body is being taken to the morgue—*"

"The Morgue! I'm going there!" Monk moaned. He turned, raced from the room. Ham was close behind, stopping only to pick up his sword cane.

## Chapter VI
### A CHALLENGE ACCEPTED

GREENSHIRT grinned sheepishly and got to his feet.

"We coulda got 'em in the long run, but just the same, I'm glad those babies left," he said. "Let's play cards a while. The job is over with."

Cards were dealt. Chips clinked.

"What's it all about, anyway?" asked the small man with close-set eyes.

Greenshirt glanced about nervously. "Not even Stinger knows. But it's tied up with the living-fire death we heard about."

"The living-fire death!" The small man shivered. "I don't want nothing to—"

"Quiet!"

Greenshirt was tense. Perspiration appeared on his face. His head turned, an inch at a time, toward the windows that looked out over a side street. One of those windows was raised.

"You're hearing things," jeered the dealer. He riffled the cards rapidly.

"I—I thought I heard something out there," Greenshirt said shakily. He glanced at his hole card.

"Ace high, bets a dollar," said the dealer.

"I'm staying—" started Greenshirt. He glanced at the window again.

He shrieked. A high-pitched shriek of fear that froze in the roof of his mouth.

A face had appeared at the open window. It was looking in calmly, without expression. It was a bronze face. The face of Doc Savage!

The card players whirled, sat frozen as they looked at the face in the window.

Behind them, the shattered door swung wide. Stinger Salvatore walked in, two gunmen behind him.

Stinger's face went blank. He looked as if he were seeing a ghost.

"It can't be! He's dead!" Stinger gasped.

Sound of his voice seemed to break the spell. The small man with close-set eyes cursed with violent rapidity. His gun appeared in his hand, belched flame three times in swift succession.

The face at the window did not move, did not change expression.

THE small man prided himself as a marksman. It did not seem possible that he could have missed at such a close distance. He was sure his bullets had struck squarely in the center of that bronze forehead.

A whimpering sound came from the gunman's lips. Once more he fingered the trigger of his gun, sent lead screaming through the window, directly at the plainly seen target.

The bronze face wavered, but did not disappear.

Stinger tried to cry out. He found he had lost his voice. His legs wanted to run but his muscles would not obey his mind.

Then a bronze thunderbolt hit!

The thunderbolt did not come through the open window. It appeared through the door that led to an adjoining room.

That thunderbolt was Doc Savage. He dived through the door in a flying tackle. He was headed directly for Stinger Salvatore.

The small gunman rose suddenly from his chair. He was directly in front of Doc's flying figure. The bronze man struck him, crashed into the table. The table collapsed.

The room became filled with struggling, surging figures. Some were trying to fight. Some were trying to escape.

A gun spoke sharply and a gunman collapsed as the bullet intended for the bronze man found another victim.

The shots had attracted attention. The hotel was in an uproar. Outside, in the hallway, women were screaming. In the distance could be heard the approaching sirens of police cars.

Doc caught two of the thugs, smashed their heads together. A third dropped as strong fingers caught the back of his neck, bringing quick unconsciousness.

Stinger went away from there. He went swiftly. He went in as close to a panic as he had ever been. The hallways were filled with frightened, milling people. It was easy for the gangleader to dart into the crowd and disappear.

The house detective burst into the room. Behind him came an avalanche of blue-clad figures, carrying riot guns.

Doc looked at them calmly. Six prone figures were scattered about the room.

"But—but, Mr. Savage. I thought you were dead! The radio said so!" gulped the house detective.

Doc ignored the question in the other's voice. In calm, brief sentences, he explained that he had been looking for Renny, had been fired on by a room filled with thugs. He said nothing about Stinger.

The police were curious. They asked some questions. But they did not ask too many. They knew Doc rated high with the commissioner.

The unconscious gunmen were carted off to jail. The police restored order in the hotel.

When Doc had the room to himself, he examined it closely. Then he walked to a closet door. The door was locked. With a small instrument, the bronze man released the lock in a matter of seconds. He opened the door.

Renny was hanging inside!

THE huge engineer's feet were tied. His hands were bound behind him. A gag had been thrust in his mouth, puffing out his cheeks.

Doc reached in, freed the back of Renny's coat from the hook that was holding him in the air. He took the gag from Renny's mouth.

"Holy cow!" the engineer gasped. "I thought you were dead and I was sure I was."

Renny's legs were weak. They buckled up when he tried to stand. Doc carried him easily to a bed, made him comfortable while he freed him from his bonds.

"What happened?" Renny gulped.

"I wanted people to think I was dead for the time being," Doc explained briefly. "I had the newspaper editor instruct the ambulance driver to proceed toward the morgue."

"Yeah, I know," Renny argued. "But that radio guy said you had been electrocuted. It sounded as if you had been killed just like that fellow at your office."

"No." Doc shook his head. "There was nothing mysterious about the attack on me. A high-powered electric line had been attached to my car, and the juice was stepped up through a transformer as I touched it, but I was wearing rubber gloves. I was unhurt."

Renny wiped his head weakly, sat up. He still had but little strength.

"That girl tricked me, too," he confessed. "She acted frightened, and I pushed in. Somebody slugged me from behind. I came to in the closet and heard them talking."

Doc's face did not change. "And they said they were going to leave New York at once and go to Sandrit," he contributed.

Renny's eyes bulged, his puritanical features showed astonishment. "But how—how did you know?"

"Someone wants us to go there very much," Doc said slowly. "That is self-evident. By pretending to try and keep us away, they expect to decoy us there."

"But—but that fellow who died in the office, was that his purpose?"

Doc shook his head. "No. He sincerely meant his warning. But whoever was behind him anticipated what he would say, and wanted him to say it."

"I guess we are up against clever opponents," Renny agreed.

He then told Doc what the clerk had revealed about a Petrod Yardoff and Clement Hoskins.

"I'll tear them limb from limb!" a childlike voice promised with undeniable ferocity.

"You'll do nothing of the sort. You'll leave them alive until we can find out who is behind them," a second voice objected.

Monk and Ham burst into the room.

AN incredulous look of delight crossed the homely chemist's features as he saw the bronze man and Renny. Ham grinned delightedly.

"I told this hairy monstrosity from the antediluvian age it would take more than a gang of punks to get you!" the lawyer shouted.

Monk was making small noises. He walked to

the window, reached out and pulled in the bronze face that floated there.

"Ectoplasm!" he snorted. "Nothing but bronze tissue cloth in many folds, cut in the form of a mask, with small gas cylinders at the top to hold it in the air."

**RENNY**

Colonel John Renwick is a towering, bony giant who has a face which always looks as if its owner were enroute to the funeral of a friend. That expression, contrarily enough, means pleasure. If "Renny" were handed a million dollars, he would probably look gloomy.

And if Renny were presented with a roaring fight, he would probably burst into tears, for Renny likes a scrap above all else. In that, he is like Doc's other aides.

Renny's training is that of a civil engineer, and in that profession he has won fame and money. His name is known in all modern countries for work he has done, and he has a bank account of a size which does away with any fear of the poorhouse, to say the least.

Renny has one amusement, and that is the habit of smashing his tremendous fists through wooden door panels. Renny's boast is there is no wooden door built with a panel strong enough to resist the crashing impact of his knuckles. So far, his boast has not been contradicted. And woe unto the enemy head that gets in front of Renny's fist.

Renny has never been known to laugh.

Doc ignored the interruption. "At the start all this might have seemed a revenge plot. It does not now. Too many efforts are being made to decoy us to Sandrit."

"Will there be action?" Monk dropped the ectoplasm mask.

"We still don't know what has happened to Long Tom and Johnny," Renny reminded quietly.

Monk sobered in an instant. "We saw the two bodies at the morgue that were taken from the harbor."

"And they were those of escaped convicts," Doc put in quietly.

Ham's eyes grew large. "They were badly burned. I am sure they weren't those of Long Tom and Johnny, although identification is almost impossible. But escaped convicts—"

The bronze man nodded. "I believe that is what an investigation will show."

"And Long Tom and Johnny?"

"I am sure they are alive—at least so far. I am just as sure that it is intended they never shall be seen alive."

"I guess we'll be moving soon," Monk said, "so I'll get Habeas and—"

"I'm afraid not," Doc warned. "This fire menace is too dangerous to bring your pets along. They'll have to remain behind."

"Are we going to Sandrit then?" Renny demanded.

Doc nodded. "At once. We will accept the challenge that has been hurled at us."

## Chapter VII
### A WILD DRIVER

LONG TOM and Johnny were alive. That was the only thing they were absolutely sure about.

They did not know where they were. They did not know who their captors were. They did not know what had happened to them. They were fairly certain, however, that they were a long way from New York.

Long Tom twisted awkwardly until he could see Johnny's bound body. The archaeologist's eyes were open behind his glasses, but they held a dazed look. Long Tom seemed even more yellow and unhealthy-appearing than before.

There was only a faint hum of noise around them. They were lying in small, smelly bunks. The walls of the room were of steel.

"We got licked," Long Tom admitted.

"I dimly recall regaining consciousness only to be anaesthetized," Johnny said weakly.

"Chloroformed," the thin electrician agreed.

"But at some time we were transported by airplane."

"I remember coming to several times in the air, but each time I got another shot of chloroform," Long Tom conceded.

"But what transpired then? All that must have been hours, possibly aeons ago."

"I think I know where we are."

"On a submarine," Johnny nodded glumly.

Long Tom turned on his side, tried to hook the ropes that bound him over the edge of the bunk.

There was no sound of Diesels. That meant the sub was running on batteries, probably submerged. The sticky heat and heavy feeling of the air bore that out.

A small door opened. Several men filed in. They were dressed in greasy dungarees. There was a military bearing about them despite their attire.

The leader had a small beard that bobbed when he talked. His lips split in a grin. He spoke with a faint accent.

"You will not try to escape, please. It is useless."

"Yeah?" Long Tom asked belligerently.

"Yes." The small beard made a short dip. "We will now assist you remove the ropes you seem to dislike."

Johnny's mouth dropped, his eyes became wide behind his glasses. Two of the seamen stepped forward, stripped off the ropes.

The small beard came up firmly.

"You will come with me, please."

The leader turned, led the way. Johnny looked at Long Tom, shrugged. He followed. The seamen brought up the rear.

Their guide led them to the control compartment. He bowed deeply, and his short beard seemed just the least bit unsteady.

"Here they are, sir," he reported.

A tall, very thin man, with piercing eyes, dressed entirely in rubber, turned slowly.

"Welcome, gentlemen," Petrod Yardoff said with a sardonic twist to his sharp lips.

LONG TOM'S eyes traveled over the other shrewdly. He thought of Z-2 and the way the filling-station attendant had said the F.B.I. man had been dressed.

Yardoff divined his thoughts. "Yes," the thin man murmured with mock politeness, "your unfortunate friend wore a makeshift costume for much the same reason I wear this."

A long crease appeared in Long Tom's forehead. Yardoff was perspiring freely under the nearly air-tight costume he wore. His face was a peculiar cherry-red color.

"Strange," Long Tom muttered.

Johnny hunched forward, a strange look in his eyes. Others had left the control room. They were alone with Yardoff.

The thin man did not appear to be watching him. Johnny glanced at the controls. They were of a familiar type. His fist knotted behind him. He set himself for a haymaker swing.

"Don't!" Long Tom rapped swiftly.

Yardoff turned slowly, an enigmatic smile spreading his sharp lips. "I thought you might guess part of the truth, Long Tom," he complimented.

Johnny's eyes made saucers behind his glasses. He looked angrily at his comrade. "If you had only retained silence, I would have whiffed our repellent host to a land of unutterable oblivion."

Yardoff mocked him with his eyes. "Your friend saved your life," he said without interest.

Johnny looked a question at Long Tom. The electrical genius pulled the lobe of one oversized ear reflectively.

"It—it don't seem possible, Johnny," he said. "But I'm afraid this guy is right."

"Naturally you are asking yourself questions," Yardoff bowed. "I have no particular reason for not satisfying some of your curiosity. Look here."

Long Tom stepped forward gingerly. He glued his eye to the twin of the periscope through which Yardoff had been looking. His breath came in sharply.

Powerful lights were illuminating the course the submarine was following. That course was a weird one.

They were in a winding, stone passageway. The top of the submarine was barely awash. The submarine was moving slowly, twisting and turning on an erratic course.

As Long Tom watched, the channel widened. For a few moments they were in a huge, underground stream. The water appeared dark and malevolent.

Stalactites hung from the ceiling of the cavern. There was an oppressive air about the scene; the searchlight appeared unable to penetrate dark crevices.

With an effort, Long Tom brought his mind back to normal. Petrod Yardoff was surveying them with a leering, sardonic look. The electrical genius was glad when the cavern passed behind, when the submarine moved on into another dark, winding passageway.

Johnny stepped forward, took his place at the periscope. The geologist forgot all about danger. He exclaimed with sudden interest.

"This proves my theorem!" he shouted loudly. "Scrutinize those stratifications, those near the roof. Why, they are the oldest known type, and that directly beneath—why, it proves that—"

Petrod Yardoff chuckled. There was something evil, something dangerous about that chuckle.

"You will see more than that, my friend, where

we are going. You will see things you will wish never existed. You are going to a strange land, my friends."

Long Tom looked unconcerned. "Doc will show up sooner or later," he scoffed. "We have nothing to fear."

A thin cackle broke from Petrod Yardoff's sharp lips. "The bronze man! He cannot even take care of himself. Even now he is walking into a trap. He and the rest of his men."

The submarine moved on, slowly, through the dark, treacherous passageway.

IF Doc, Monk, Ham and Renny were running into a trap they gave no sign that they realized that fact. They were soaring westward in Doc's speedy transport plane. No words were exchanged during the trip. All were filled with a premonition of unusual danger.

In a short time the landing field at Palm Springs appeared below. Several cars were parked there, and as the crowd caught a glimpse of the bronze man descending from his ship as it rolled to a stop, they made a concerted rush toward Doc.

Doc's aides were pushed to the outskirts of the crowd in the mêlée that followed.

Monk's face had become a mile long. There were many beautiful girls surrounding Doc. "It's tough what Doc has to put up with," he growled.

"Yeah," chuckled Ham. "Just about what the fox said when he couldn't get the grapes."

DOC made a path through the crowd and rejoined Monk, Ham and Renny. They looked over the cars at the landing field. Several had "to hire" signs on the windshields.

Renny moved forward deliberately, glanced at each of the cars in turn. At an open car he paused.

The driver was short and chubby, with an amiable face and carefree smile. "Car, buddy?" he invited.

The four got into the car. "Where to?" asked the driver.

"Do you know a Clement or a Virginia Hoskins, at Sandrit?" Renny asked.

The driver nodded. "Sure. I know everybody in this neck of the woods. That Virginia sure is a good-looker."

He threw the car in gear, the motor roared. At the first corner, the car was doing better than forty.

Ham threw a quizzical look at Doc.

"I think this was the car we were expected to take," the bronze man said. His voice, with its peculiar carrying quality, reached the ears of his aides, but the driver did not hear.

Renny was startled. "Holy cow! How could it be?" he asked. "Nothing could happen to us in this machine."

Doc said nothing.

The fat driver, his face still cloaked in a friendly, reassuring grin, really put on the speed as they reached the open road. His passengers bounced around in the rear seat.

"I hope this mug leads us into a gang," Monk rumbled. "I'd like a fight."

Monk's childlike voice carried better than he knew. The driver heard. His ears wiggled, but he did not turn around.

They came to a road that left the main highway. The long touring car skidded as it made the bend.

Instinctively, those in the rear seat reached for something to hold onto.

The car hit sand. It skidded wildly. An observer might even have believed the driver was making it skid on purpose.

"Ouch!" Monk squealed.

He yanked his hand from the rod he had been holding, looking curiously at a finger. There was a tiny puncture near the first joint. A drop of blood appeared.

The car bucked, skidded, all but overturned. It was impossible to stay in the rear seat without holding on.

Renny tried to cry out, but his voice was lost in the wind. Ham's shoulders jerked.

Doc could have braced himself with his powerful legs, but the others crashed into him. He also was holding to a rod.

Something was happening to Monk. His head dropped. His mouth went slack. He slumped.

"Poison," Ham muttered weakly. "Poison on tiny barbs on those rods we grabbed."

Renny's huge frame sagged over on Doc. The bronze man's flake-gold eyes were flickering.

The fat, amiable driver glanced over a shoulder with a grin. He straightened the car out, slowed its pace to a more reasonable speed.

Behind him, his four passengers were sprawled in awkward, unconscious attitudes.

## Chapter VIII
### A GUNMAN SPEAKS

"SO that's the famous Doc Savage, the guy everybody is afraid of," the driver sneered. He drove on a short distance, then turned off on a road that was barely a trail.

He followed the trail until it dropped into a small arroyo. He shut off the motor, lighted a cigarette.

The hum of a second engine sounded, faintly at first, then more loudly. A big car appeared. The fat driver did not seem surprised. He motioned toward his unconscious passengers and drew a deep puff on his cigarette.

"Easy as falling off a log," he grinned.

Eight men poured out of the second car. Even

though Doc and his aides were unconscious, the men approached warily. Three were carrying Tommy guns. The others had automatics.

The bronze man's eyes flickered. The fingers of one of his powerful hands were pressed tight against the arteries in his other wrist. The pressure was as effective as a tourniquet. His lips, hidden as he bent over, sucked the powerful, quick-acting anaesthetic from his veins. That anaesthetic had been injected by the point of one of the many small pin-points hidden on the hand-holds.

Doc's frame was inert, apparently lifeless.

The gunmen opened both rear doors of the touring car. Doc and his men were yanked to the ground. They fell limply.

Doc was thrown into the rear of the second car. As the attackers were lifting Monk and Ham, Doc's hand rose, loosened the top of the gas tank. A moment more and the top was replaced.

Monk was pulled up first. He was tied firmly; then, still unconscious, he was tossed into the back of the second car. Renny was bound next. More men came toward Ham and Doc, ropes in their hands.

Two of the gunmen reached over, pulled the bronze man half up. One started to loop a rope about his wrists.

That was the last that gunman knew for a long time.

Doc galvanized into action. The palm of one hand caught the gunman in the back of the neck. The man never knew what hit him. The second thug opened his mouth to yell. He was lifted from his feet, hurled bodily into the gunmen tying Ham.

The others went for their guns. An automatic spoke. A Tommy gun went into action.

The gunners had to be careful not to hit their own men. Their first shots went wide.

The arroyo where the cars were was not particularly deep, but the walls rose sheer for nearly a dozen feet. It seemed impossible for anyone to escape that way.

The gunmen were not even expecting Doc to try it. The bronze man caught them unprepared.

With one leap, he was on top of the touring car. A second surge of his mighty muscles and his fingers reached the top of the canyon wall.

Hot lead tore only inches behind him as he flashed over the rim of that wall, sprawled on the ground at the top.

The Tommy guns kept up a deadly barrage. One gunman issued swift orders. A look, almost of awe, was in his eyes.

The driver of the second car, with Renny, Ham and Monk tied tightly in the rear seat, roared away.

The others made a thorough search for Doc Savage.

They did not find him.

A MILE away, a girl watched the scene through powerful binoculars.

She saw the gunmen hunt through sage and cactus, explore small ravines. Finally she saw them return to the touring car, drive away.

Still she watched. Her breath came in sharply as she saw a faint movement almost at the edge of the arroyo. Then Doc appeared, coming from a tiny depression. He had drawn sage over him until he was completely hidden.

The girl's hand reached for the rifle at her side. Her dark eyes held a strange expression, her lips were half parted.

She was clad in a riding habit. The trim-fitting pants emphasized her soft curves. A pulse beat rapidly in her throat, just over the collar of her flannel shirt.

For a moment Virginia Hoskins hesitated. She glanced behind her, where a groom was standing near two grazing horses. Then she pushed the rifle aside and raised the binoculars again.

She saw Doc Savage seat himself on a rock, reach inside his shirt and bring out the belt he always wore about his body. He worked swiftly. In a few minutes he no longer looked like Doc Savage.

A faint glow of admiration came to the girl's face. The bronze man placed a cap on his head, he reversed his coat. Glasses covered his flake-gold eyes.

Rising, he made for the main highway at a lope that was deceiving as to its speed. Apparently tirelessly he moved on, reached the point where the cars had turned.

There the bronze man slowed, but only for an instant. Unerringly, he turned in the direction taken by the gunmen's cars.

The girl hesitated no longer. She grabbed her rifle, ran toward the waiting groom and horses. She spoke to the groom briefly. They leaped into the saddles, cut off across the desert. The girl used her spurs hard, sending her roan recklessly onward.

Doc Savage did not see the girl. His eyes were on the road.

The glasses he wore were tinted. Through them he could see all that could be seen with normal eyes, and something more as well.

He could see a faint, irregular design, almost as if the road was marked for him.

In a way it was. When his hand had been at the gasoline tank, Doc had dropped a small powder into the fuel. This powder dissolved in the gasoline, but would not burn. It was thrown out by the exhaust.

**A brilliant, blinding light enveloped the watchman's shack.**

The normal eye could see nothing, but through the glasses a clear trail was left.

The trail finally turned off onto a hard, well-packed gravel road. Sandrit had been circled. Unknown danger lay ahead.

IN the space of a comparatively few hours, all five of Doc's men had been abducted. Those behind the dread events had shown cunning and cleverness. But if Doc Savage was concerned, he did not show it.

**The flame sizzled, white-hot, dazzling as a lightning flash.**

Doc might have been able to rescue his men in the arroyo. That he did not attempt to do so, was merely in line with the policy he always followed.

The attackers had been heavily armed. In a general fight, Monk, Ham or Renny might have been killed. Doc always was willing to face death himself, but when it could be avoided he never risked the lives of his men.

His aides undoubtedly were safe, at least for the present. Had the object been to kill them, there would have been no reason for delaying the execution.

The trail left by the car's exhaust thinned, then expanded to the size of a large smudge. It was as if the car had halted there briefly.

Doc did not pause. He moved past at a steady walk, eyes still downcast.

Behind him, two men rose suddenly from clumps of sagebrush that had hidden them at the sides of the road. Submachine guns were cradled under their arms.

Slowly they raised their guns, trained them on Doc's moving figure. The muzzles were held low, aimed at the legs, as if the purpose were to disable, but not kill.

"Sherlock, hell!" one of them sneered. "Let's see that wise mug deduce this!" His finger squeezed the trigger.

*Br-r-r-r-r-r-r-r!*

Lead rained down the road. It hit nothing.

Even as the gunmen fired, Doc Savage vanished. He vanished with a sidewise leap that carried him clear of the road, into the surrounding brush.

The gunners rushed forward.

A small, brittle, egg-shaped object caught the first squarely on the chin. His arms went up. The Tommy gun fell to the ground. Then the gunman followed it, curling up, as if asleep.

His companion paused, startled. Strong fingers suddenly caught the gunner around the neck; thumbs pressed down hard on the back of his skull. The machine gunner became limp.

The bronze man's expression was sober. The killers had expected him. Only tiny extensions on the glasses he wore had saved him. Those extensions protruded on either side of his face; they were mirrors. Even facing straight ahead, he could see behind him.

When Doc moved on, five minutes later, the glasses had disappeared. His features seemed covered by a two days' growth of beard. His face was putty-like, with weak lines about his mouth. He carried a Tommy gun under his arm and walked as if very weary.

Tire marks were plain in the road now. They led over a small hill. On the other side of that hill, looming starkly in the open desert, was a big building. A sign at the gate read:

HOSKINS GLASS FACTORY

The tire marks of the gunmen's car turned in there.

CLEMENT HOSKINS was peering from one of the big windows of the factory building. A cold grin was on his round face. His big, barrel-shaped figure was tense.

An angry expression flashed over his features as he saw a stooped, wavering figure approach down the road.

"The fool! What is he coming back for?" he muttered.

Hard-eyed killers were grouped about him. One shifted nervously. "Looks like Sam is suffering from a sunstroke, boss," he suggested uneasily.

The wavering figure on the road appeared to find it more and more difficult to walk. The submachine gun was trailing, held by limp fingers.

Once the man lifted his head, weakly, then dropped it again. The factory building was almost before him. High wire fences surrounded the sprawling building. Every other strand of the fence was barbed wire. "Stay out" and "No Trespassing" signs were posted at the top.

A grim, ominous silence pervaded the scene.

The only entry to the factory was through a large gate in front. At one side of the gate, built half inside, half outside the fence, was a watchman's shack.

The wavering figure headed toward the gate.

"Sam Belough! Come in here! Did you kill him?"

The voice came from within the shack. It was a girl's voice. There was a note of urgency in it—a note of almost hysterical fear.

The man with the machine-gun turned slowly toward the door of the shack. Virginia Hoskins stood there, black curls framing features that were almost perfect.

A gun was in her hand. It was aimed directly at the man before her.

"Come in here! Quick! If you've killed Doc Savage—"

Without hesitation, the wavering man entered the shack.

## Chapter IX
### THE TRAP CLOSES

ONLY a few miles away, movie stars were enjoying late afternoon siestas or dressing for dinner. Ice clinked in tall glasses. A subdued hum of conversation, of polite, well-bred phrases mingled with cheerful laughter.

There was none of this in the watchman's shack. But fear was there! Stark, horrible, fear!

It showed in the set of Virginia Hoskins' lips. Her finger tightened on the trigger.

"I wouldn't shoot, Miss Hoskins," Doc Savage said quietly.

A gasp came from the girl. The gun dropped as her hands twisted frenziedly.

"Doc Savage?" she breathed.

"Perhaps it is time now for you to tell me your story," the bronze man said.

His flake-gold eyes glanced about the shack

swiftly. It was comfortably furnished. The walls were thick, apparently of metal, strong enough to withstand rifle bullets. At the rear, looking toward the factory, was a window. The glass appeared bulletproof. Through the window, faint activity could be seen inside the factory.

The girl took a long breath. "Perhaps I *had* better explain."

Doc nodded. He glanced through the rear window again, and began to work swiftly with his hands.

Virginia Hoskins swallowed hard. She sank limply into a chair. "Clement Hoskins is my uncle. He is a crook," she started.

The bronze man said nothing.

"My money is invested in this factory. I have become rich, but my uncle has become even more wealthy. That aroused my suspicions. I investigated."

Doc remained silent

"He is involved in something crooked, something so big I am almost afraid even to guess what it means. But it's linked with the living-fire death!"

Doc glanced at her politely. "Yes?"

"I heard my uncle and Petrod Yardoff plotting. They wanted to capture you and your men. I was afraid for my uncle, for such lawless acts could have only one end. I was afraid for you, for if he succeeded, you eventually would have to die."

"So that is why you attempted to destroy the record of Z-2's conversation? You wanted to keep me from becoming interested?"

The girl nodded, dumbly. "I—I saw Z-2 die. It—it was terrible! I had followed him, trying to learn what he had discovered, hoping to learn what my uncle really was doing. Then Z-2 died. My uncle and Yardoff had flown to New York. I flew after them. They—"

"Quiet!" The bronze man raised his hand suddenly.

There was a faint noise just outside the shack. A man, listening there, turned swiftly and raced toward the factory.

The bronze man's deception had been discovered.

DOC spun, face emotionless. "Speak swiftly," he said. "Our time is short."

His tone brought the girl's head up. She flushed.

"Other men were in the plane with uncle, and Petrod, horrible men." She shuddered.

Doc nodded. That explained the man who had died in his office, the two whose bodies had been found in the harbor.

"I—I didn't intend to trick your friend, Renny. He—he wouldn't listen to my warning. And I wanted to warn you, earlier today. I couldn't. One of uncle's men was with me. Now if you go on, you are doomed. All your men are doomed."

"Why?" Doc's single word snapped like a pistol crack.

The girl paled. Fear returned to her dark eyes, her lips trembled.

"They—they've been taken in there, taken down to that horrible place—" She broke off, fought visibly for control.

Her eyes turned to the window at the rear of the shack. A scream burst from her lips.

A score of men were pouring from the factory, heavily armed men. In the lead was the big, barrel-shaped figure of Clement Hoskins.

"Surround that shack! Take no chances, but get Doc Savage!" Hoskins bellowed.

The big man glanced about anxiously. The sun was dropping. Already it was dusk. Soon the swift night of the desert would arrive. But Hoskins was confident. His men had circled the shack. Nothing, no one, could get out of there unseen.

"Virginia," Hoskins rapped, "come out of there before you get killed!"

For long seconds there was no answer to that command. Then the door to the shack opened. Virginia Hoskins came out. Her face was tear-stained.

Her uncle grinned without mirth.

"Now, Doc Savage," he bellowed, "you are surrounded! You cannot escape. Surrender, and your life will be spared. Attempt to fight, and you will die!"

Silence was his only answer.

Clement Hoskins swore bitterly. He motioned to one of the killers standing at his side.

The man stepped toward the gate. A small switch was just inside. He pulled that switch down.

A brilliant, blinding light enveloped the watchman's shack. The flame sizzled, white-hot, dazzling as a lightning flash.

A second time the switch was drawn back, shot home. A second time hell-fire danced about the shack.

Clement Hoskins closed his eyes, temporarily blinded by the flash. Then he opened them.

"Go get his body, boys," he said wearily. "I'm sorry we had to do that. I could have used that guy alive, but now—"

Cautiously, the gunmen crept to the shack. Guns were ready in their hands. Flashlights were turned on. The door was thrown open. A shrill yell of surprise broke from the first man to enter.

The shack was empty!

CLEMENT HOSKINS' jaw dropped. A look of utter bewilderment spread over his flabby countenance.

"He—he couldn'ta got away!" he bellowed.

"But he did. And I'm glad." Virginia Hoskins brushed tears from her eyes, smiled wanly.

Hoskins motioned to a gunman. "Take her!" he rapped. "Lock her up. She's getting too dangerous."

Virginia paled. She fought. She screamed. It was useless. She was carried away.

Hoskins, breathing hard, rushed into the shack. The gunman had been correct. No one was there.

"The floor is metal. The walls are lined with metal," the barrel-shaped man muttered incredulously. "Even the chairs are of metal, and connected with the floor. Enough juice went through here to fry a dozen men, but that devil escaped—"

"Could he 'a' ducked out when we was all blinded by the light?" one of the men asked, nervously.

Hoskins nodded. That had to be it. There was no other answer.

The big man jerked erect with sudden decision.

"He couldn't have gone far. He'll stay around here, trying to rescue his men. Spread out. Hunt for him."

"But—but that guy's poison. It's dark. We'll—"

Hoskins spun on the speaker. One huge paw shot out. The man soared through the air, fell sprawling, his face a crimson mass.

"Treat 'em rather rough, don't you, Hoskins?" a voice drawled mockingly.

The barrel-shaped man swung around, his hand held a gun suddenly. Then he relaxed.

Facing him was a tall, well-dressed man with the hard face of a killer. The man drew a handkerchief from one sleeve, wiped his hands casually.

"Stinger!" Hoskins exclaimed. "How did you get here?"

The other waved one arm negligently. "Easy enough. Came by plane. Walked up while you were all busy. But where did Savage go?"

The barrel-shaped man looked at Stinger with eyes that were tight slits. A dim suspicion had flared in his brain. Doc Savage was known to be an artist at disguises. He had reached the watchman's shack in the garb of Sam Belough. This man looked like Stinger, but was it Stinger? Could it be the bronze man in a new dis—

*Br-r-r-r-r-r-r!*

A Tommy gun spoke viciously. It came from the desert, across the road from the factory. Lead whistled overhead.

Clement Hoskins' face cleared; he smiled. Doc Savage was good, no question about that; but he couldn't be in two places at once. And the bronze man had carried Sam Belough's Tommy gun.

"Glad to see you, Stinger," Hoskins said.

HOSKINS' gunmen, twenty strong, spread out in a thin line. They vanished across the road, weapons ready.

Hoskins' big shoulders lifted and fell in a deep sigh. "They'll get him now," he said. "Come on in the factory."

His companion was looking about him curiously.

"You've got light, lots of light, and you must have power," he said wonderingly. "But I don't see any power lines. Where do you get your juice?"

The barrel-shaped man grinned thinly. "You'll wonder about lots of things if you stick around here. And, by the way, what did you come here for?"

The other shrugged, impatiently. "You mentioned millions, didn't you?" he drawled.

A peculiar light flashed for an instant in Clement Hoskins' eyes, and was as quickly veiled. He led the way to the factory.

In the distance, the Tommy gun spoke again.

Inside the doors, Hoskins waved his hand with ill-concealed pride.

In the rear of the rambling structure were huge electrical furnaces. Closer at hand were shelves stacked with glassware. The tall man's eyes narrowed slightly as he noticed some of that glassware. The handkerchief flicked from his sleeve.

"Making some rather queer things, aren't you?" he asked.

Hoskins chuckled. "We can make anything out of glass. Clothes, rope, instruments, or what have you."

He led the way to a small office. "We've got all Doc's men," he said. "When we get the bronze devil himself, we'll all be—"

Hoskins stopped, frowning. Running feet sounded outside. An excited summons came from the other side of the door.

SCOWLING, the big man went to the door, closing it behind him. He was gone only a few seconds.

Hoskins was smiling when he returned.

"You spoke of the glassware we make," he said. "I'm going to let you in on a secret: I'm going to show you one of our experiments."

The big man pushed the other ahead of him, toward the rear of the factory. A huge furnace was in a big room. Waves of heat swirled about them. The heat was pulsing from the furnace.

"This is where we do our testing," Hoskins said. There was an excited tremor in his voice. "Right now, molten sand is in that furnace. But in a few minutes—"

Sound of a scuffle came from outside the room. The door opened. Monk, Ham and Renny were pushed inside. Their hands were bound behind them. Gags were in their mouths.

Men pulled them along roughly. Ham kicked

THE LIVING-FIRE MENACE 93

"LONG TOM"

Major Thomas J. Roberts—"Long Tom"—is a thin young man who does not look any too healthy, but under his sallow hide are some very ropy and powerful muscles. Long Tom can probably whip ninety-nine out of every hundred men he would meet on a city street.

The "wizard of the juice," electrical men call Long Tom, for he is among the greatest in that field. He has a laboratory in an underground room where he experiments incessantly, and that possibly accounts for his pale complexion. Electrical engineers mention Long Tom's name in the same breath with Edison and Steinmetz.

Long Tom did not get his name because he is "long," but from an incident in the past, when he tried to repel an enemy attack by loading a "long tom" cannon, such as the ancient privateers used, with nails, tacks and pebbles. The "long tom" blew up. That fiasco earned Long Tom his name, and he wears a gold tooth in front, where a piece of the demolished cannon struck on that ill-fated occasion.

out; Monk struggled; Renny strained at his bonds. But they were helpless.

They were hauled to the top of a platform overlooking the furnace. An enclosed slide led from that platform into the vat where molten sand bubbled.

"Doc Savage really is a clever man," Clement Hoskins said. He spoke as if to himself. "He wasn't near that Tommy gun at all. My men found it, quite by chance. A clockwork arrangement had been attached to it, so it would fire at regular intervals."

"Yes?" His companion's features did not change, he remained relaxed.

"Yes." Hoskins' voice suddenly was harsh. Armed men were pushing into the room. Their weapons were ready in their hands.

"Yes," Hoskins repeated, "so I'm going to show you this experiment. The three men up there, the three aides of Doc Savage, are going to be thrown into that furnace. I've often wondered what the result would be, how it would affect the glass, I mean, to mix human bodies with the sand. So they are going to die, unless—"

"I see your point." The other spoke with the peculiar, low, yet carrying voice of Doc Savage. His flake-gold eyes looked full into Hoskins' fat face. "You want me to help you. If I refuse, then Monk, Ham and Renny die. I understand."

"And your answer?"

The flake-gold eyes swept unemotionally about the ring of armed men.

"Tell me your problem," Doc Savage said. "I will see if I can solve it for you."

### Chapter X
### MEN OF FIRE

CLEMENT HOSKINS' eyes narrowed slightly; his mouth tightened. For a moment he hesitated, then waved his hand. Monk, Ham and Renny, still struggling, were carried from the room.

Other armed guards stood close about Doc. They were alert, with nervous fingers on triggers.

Hoskins turned to the guards, motioned to the bronze man. "Take him to the escape room," he ordered harshly.

Doc turned obediently as muzzles of Tommy guns were thrust in his sides. Silently he permitted himself to be herded along.

He was taken down a short flight of stairs into a small room. The floor of the room was of glass. Light glowed eerily beneath it, revealing a narrow-walled passageway.

The bronze man was thrust inside roughly. Hoskins joined him. The guards stood in the doorway, weapons raised.

"You are a clever man, very clever," Hoskins said silkily. "I am afraid you are as clever with words as with deeds."

The bronze man did not move, did not speak.

"Your men have been taken to a place from which none may escape," Hoskins said grimly. "Should they attempt it, a terrible fate awaits them. None who go where they are may return and live—unless I will it. And now, whether they live or die, whether those aides of yours burn and suffer or survive unharmed, depends entirely on you."

Time seemed to stop. The guards held their breath. Hoskins' eyes were riveted on the emotionless features of the bronze man.

"Do you wish to speak in front of all your men, or would you rather tell me what you want me to do after we are alone?" Doc asked indifferently.

The tension went out of the barrel-shaped man suddenly. He wiped drops of perspiration from his forehead. With a faint smirk, he turned to the guards.

"Go outside, close the door, but guard it well," he ordered.

The gunmen obeyed.

"I'm glad you are showing sense, Savage," Hoskins said. There was no mistaking the relief in his voice. "I would rather have you with me than against me. You are a miracle man, if ever I saw one. No one but you could ever have escaped from that watchman's shack, as far as that is concerned."

Doc's face did not change. "That was simple," he said briefly. "I knew the shack was wired. Since I am wearing rubber-soled shoes and took care to stand where my body would not form a completed circuit, I was unharmed."

The fat man nodded. "Clever. But you will need more than that to solve what I want done."

He closed his lips quickly, went to the door. It was partly ajar. He slammed it.

"Now," he began, "we'll get down to business. To begin with, have you any idea what you are up against?"

"A faint idea," Doc said frankly.

"I thought you would have," Hoskins grinned. "And that gives you some idea of the peril, also. The stuff works fast. As fast—"

"—as this," Doc finished calmly. One big fist flashed through the air. It caught the barrel-shaped man just under the jaw. Big as he was, Clement Hoskins went out as if mowed down by a cannon ball. Doc caught him under the armpits, lowered him to the floor.

In the matter of seconds, the bronze man changed to Hoskins' garb. He padded himself with clothes, made up his face until he resembled Hoskins. He stepped to the door, quickly.

"He got rough," he said harshly as he moved from the room, closed the door behind him. "Keep him there for a time. Take no chances. I'm going below."

The guards looked startled, but said nothing. They did not penetrate Doc's disguise.

The bronze man walked on swiftly. Somewhere, near at hand, there must be a way of descent to that place of horror where his men had been taken.

THREE of Doc's men actually were not far away. But to Monk, Ham and Renny, it seemed that they were in a different world.

They were in an elevator cage. And that cage was made entirely of glass. Even the cables that held it were finely spun and woven glass.

The cage was dropping slowly, very slowly. A strange, peculiar hum came to their ears.

Armed guards were crowded about them. They carried weapons made of glass. That should have held the attention of their prisoners. It didn't. They were more interested in what they could see passing on either side as they dropped downward.

The rock formation changed steadily. Streaks of copper, yellow veins of gold were passed. Tunnels showed where those veins had once been worked.

The gags had been removed. Renny exclaimed in astonishment as he saw the store of mineral wealth as yet untouched.

"Holy cow! It don't seem possible! If all this is being passed up, what can be farther down?"

Monk and Ham shook their heads. They wondered, also.

A faint smell of sulphur drifted in the air. With it was another smell, a far more unusual one. It was the odor of ozone, such as sometimes is smelled in a severe electrical storm, after a bolt of lightning, or near a powerful dynamo.

Renny looked wordlessly at the others.

The glass elevator stopped. Long shafts led back on either side. A hundred yards away one shaft led into a big, roomlike cavern. There was a thunderous, stamping noise. Blast furnaces glowed. Queer instruments and utensils were nearby.

"An underground glass factory!" Monk breathed unbelievingly.

The guards who had accompanied them so far were leaving the elevator. Other men were taking their places. It was sight of these other men that brought the short hairs up on the back of the hairy chemist's neck.

With the queer newcomers at the controls, the elevator cage again began to sink.

Down, down it went, into the bowels of the earth. And for once, not even Monk had a word to say.

There were no lights visible. Rock pressed close on either side of the shaft. Yet the elevator cage glowed with a strange cherry-red glow.

It came from the bodies of the new guards.

OTHER strange things were taking place far down in the depths. A long, sleek, cigar-shaped monster was rising slowly in a huge, underground stream. Slowly the big submarine eased toward the tiny dock.

Men poured from the submarine, made it fast.

Petrod Yardoff appeared, his thin, scarecrow figure still clad in its rubber garments.

Long Tom and Johnny were boosted out of the tower hatch. Their hands had been tied, blindfolds were about their heads.

Guided by sailors, they were brought to the tiny dock.

"One false move, and you both will die," Petrod Yardoff warned in a strangely subdued voice. "I shall not be able to help you. We do not want you to die—yet. So please be careful."

The pair were pushed ahead. They walked up a long corridor of uncertain footing and were told to stop. Then the sound of machinery came to them. A change of air pressure told them that a great door had opened.

As the door closed behind them, Yardoff spoke: "Step ahead, carefully, then pause."

Without hesitation, Long Tom and Johnny obeyed. For minutes, it seemed, they stood motionless. There was no sound. Then their blindfolds were removed.

Above them walls glowed dully. They seemed translucent, to be admitting light from behind. But a closer examination showed the light came from the walls themselves in some unexplained manner.

Johnny's mouth opened and closed. "Most extraordinary manifestation of inspired luminescence," he muttered.

"Come on!' Yardoff snapped.

They struggled upward in a cavernous passageway. The weird light from the walls grew brighter. They wound through twisting, confusing tunnels, then passed through another great door. The portal apparently was made of lead. The men who opened it handled it carefully. They used rubber gloves of great thickness. Long Tom and Johnny were thrust inside. Both gasped.

The light was blinding. The tunnel was wider here. There were dozens of strange-appearing men in breechcloths. Light glowed from their reddened skins.

They were men of living fire!

"Well, I'll be—" Long Tom started.

A high-pitched voice came from around the corner. "I don't give a dang if we are in a spot!"

---

No one would take "Johnny," whose real name is William Harper Littlejohn, for a man of adventurous spirit. An archæologist of worldwide reputation, he seems immersed in his work, and his physical appearance belies any great activity on his part.

But as part of Doc Savage's little group of scrappers, he's a man entirely different. His gaunt frame can go without nourishment for days, at the same time sending forth energy and strength that is almost unbelievable. Even those glasses, which serve to make him more puny-looking, are useful, for one lens, covering an eye, is a high-powered magnifying glass.

Throw in your lot with Doc Savage and his pals. Thrill to their adventures in this exciting yarn.

JOHNNY

sounded the squealing tones of Monk. "You tinhorn shyster, you just mention again that you'd like to roast a pig down here, and I'll grind you to pieces on one of these rocks!"

Monk came around the corner. He was followed by Ham and Renny.

"Howling calamities!" the chemist shrilled. "How did you birds get here?"

"We were just out for a boat ride," Long Tom said dryly. "They let us off here."

"Holy cow, but I'm glad you two are alive!" Renny boomed.

"And I'll be glad when Doc gets us out of this place," Ham muttered.

"Quite an incongruous spot for a reunion," Johnny put in. "I don't like it."

The others glanced around. They were ringed by those strange cherry-red figures. There was something ominous about their silence.

## Chapter XI
### A MIRACLE NEEDED

THERE was a steady hum in the big cavern. It did not seem particularly noticeable after a time, but at first it was deafening. Doc's aides had been shouting, much as they would do in a subway. Now they, too, became silent.

The steady hum rasped on nerves. In the ring of cherry-red men about them were those whose hands and faces twitched in sympathy with that hum.

A faint look of uneasiness was on Petrod Yardoff's face, but he tried to look unconcerned. He was pulling rubber garments from his scarecrow body, he took the gloves from his hands, the thin, transparent rubber mask from his face.

"Move on. We'll go to the laboratory," he said.

The cherry-red men opened a path for them. They made no sound, but their eyes were full of hate. A glass weapon appeared in Yardoff's hand.

Then the party rounded a turn in the corridor. The ominous silence of the men behind them was forgotten.

"Jumping catfish!" Monk squealed. "I don't believe it!"

The tunnel-like corridor fanned out into a cavern of horrible magnificence. Pointed stalagmites of strange rock formation reached weird fingers up from the floor.

Johnny's eyes were staring. The geologist was looking at rock formations such as had never been known to science before.

Everywhere there were the strange, cherry-red men in breechcloths. Light glowed from their skins. The queer figures labored at strange tasks. Glass work benches were everywhere. At one side was a glass anvil, of steel-like hardness. A piece of glowing, blue-white rock lay on the anvil. One man held it with long glass tongs. The other swung a great sledge, also made of glass.

The piece of stone was small. The sledge undoubtedly was heavy. The sledge crashed down. The man grunted. The sledge did not break, but neither did the small piece of rock.

Then Ham's breath came in swiftly. For the first time he noticed the faces of the workers. He knew some of those faces, had seen them pictured in the newspaper. And every one was a criminal!

Yardoff leaned close to the lawyer, raised his voice above that constant hum of sound.

"That noise," he said. "It makes some of them crazy. We've got to be careful how we handle them."

Then Yardoff jerked erect. A piercing shriek rose above the humming sound.

"I can't stand it! I can't stand it!" the voice screamed.

That scream might have been a signal. All work stopped. For an instant everything hung motionless. Then there was a concerted movement.

From all sides men streamed toward Petrod Yardoff and Doc's aides!

YARDOFF whipped up the glass pistol. In the lead of the advancing men was the one who had screamed. His eyes were wild, protruding from his face.

The glass pistol spoke. The man curled up.

The sharp bark of the weapon brought a momentary halt in the ranks of the attackers. Yardoff's voice rang out.

"Halt, fools! You know you cannot escape!" he shouted.

The cherry-red men started to move ahead again. They moved slowly, cautiously.

Yardoff retreated, step by step. "Get behind me, head for the near wall," he gritted at Doc's men. They obeyed.

The advancing men suddenly abandoned caution. They started to run.

Yardoff turned, sprinted toward the wall. Monk, Ham, Johnny, Long Tom and Renny followed him. They did not know what it was all about, but they did know they stood no chance if they fell into the hands of the mob.

The tall, scarecrow figure of Yardoff reached a small niche. He grabbed open a small door, yanked out a coil of hose.

Liquid shot from the hose as he turned it toward the approaching mob. The liquid fell short. It landed on the hard, orelike floor of the cavern.

But it was enough. The mob halted. A long, disappointed wail burst from a hundred lips.

With hardly a pause, the cherry-red men

turned, raced back toward their work benches. Strain showed on Petrod Yardoff's features.

But blank astonishment was on the faces of Doc's aides. For the liquid spouting from the hose was common, ordinary, everyday water!

Yardoff replaced the hose. Where the water had struck the floor little eddies of steam arose. Shortly all sign of the water had disappeared.

"I—I don't understand!" gasped Renny.

"In time you will," Yardoff said. There was a thin, merciless grin on his features. "Now we will go on to the laboratory. There will be no further trouble, not for a time at any rate. These men are like children. A slight thing will set them off. Once stopped, they forget almost as quickly."

Confidently, Petrod Yardoff started forward, the others trailing.

A man approached at a half run. He spoke to Yardoff in a low tone. The message seemed to bring joy to the scarecrow figure. He was grinning widely as he turned.

"Wait here for a moment," he ordered. "I will return soon."

He started away with the messenger.

Johnny had eyes only for the strange rock formations. Ham was studying the features of the workers. One after another, he identified wanted criminals. Many were those who had been listed as escaped convicts in recent months. Long Tom and Renny were talking together in low tones.

A childlike grin overspread Monk's features. The chemist's little eyes glittered in their pits of gristle. He saw Yardoff and the messenger enter the corridor through which they had originally come.

Monk backed into that corridor. If he could grab Yardoff, perhaps a way out could be found. He looked ahead cautiously.

Scarcely fifty feet ahead Yardoff and the messenger had paused. Yardoff was putting his rubber clothes into a glass cabinet. Monk knew Yardoff had a glass gun. It was possible the messenger did, also. But that didn't bother him. He picked up a piece of loose rock. It was the only weapon he could find.

Cautiously he slipped along. Yardoff's back was toward him. The chemist was almost upon him when the messenger shouted a warning. And in the same instant the messenger drew a gun.

Monk hurled the rock. The messenger fell on his face. With a bellow of glee, the hairy chemist leaped forward.

Yardoff whirled. He seemed to be trying to say something, to give some warning. Monk paid no heed. He dived.

Yardoff tried to dodge. He tripped, went down.

A shout went up behind Monk. He heard other feet pounding into the corridor. The voice sounded like that of Long Tom. That voice also was crying a warning.

Monk paid no heed. With a roar, he sprang again. His huge hands closed around Yardoff's neck.

A crackling like that of high-powered static electricity burst into the air. Monk was hurled through the corridor. His hands were seared and burning. He landed flat, lay still.

WHEN Monk regained consciousness, Johnny, Renny, Long Tom and Ham were standing beside him. Close by was Yardoff, a thin grin on his thin lips.

"This is a good object lesson, my friend," he purred. "Fortunately you chose me for the victim and not the guard. Had you touched him you would now be a charred stump of flesh. The living fire is practically exhausted from my body."

Monk struggled to his feet weakly. "How'd you do it?" he demanded. "What happened?"

Yardoff's thin smile grew larger. "You might ask your friend, Long Tom. I think he has a glimmer of the truth, although he cannot bring himself to believe it."

"It—it can't be so," Long Tom muttered

"But it is so," Yardoff said grimly. "Now come with me."

The five men walked through the corridor with sober faces. They passed the men at the work benches, went on through another corridor until they approached a second cavern.

A blue, uneven light flashed at the far end. It was a strange, unreal light.

"Holy cow!" Renny muttered skeptically. "That looks like a nightmare."

A great pulsing, like the beating of some all-encompassing mechanical heart, came from a half-concealed chamber in the distance. A huge ball of the blue light seemed to be revolving around the walls. It danced unevenly.

Yardoff laughed. "That comes from another cavern, even deeper than this," he said. "My men do not like to go in there. They fear they will never come back. I call it the Pit of Horror."

"What is it?" Johnny demanded eagerly.

Yardoff's thin face wrinkled strangely, his eyes narrowed.

"It is the problem you have been brought here to solve," he snarled. Greed was in his voice, lust for power. "It is a problem that has defeated the best scientific brains I've been able to get so far. But you men, and Doc Savage, are supposed to be even better.

"That Pit of Horror holds a force and a material that will control the world. Some details I know. Some parts I can control; some I can't. You must solve the mystery that so far has baffled all of us, must learn how we can control what we have found."

A strange, unreal look was on Yardoff's face. It was as if a mask had dropped. A fiendish, driving lust for power was there, a merciless, satanic desire.

A breechclothed guard with a particularly brutal face appeared. Between Chicago and New York he had committed at least a hundred murders.

"Take these men to the laboratory, put them to work," Yardoff said.

The guard's mouth twisted into a snarling grin as he surveyed the new arrivals.

"Before I came here I woulda been afraid of Doc Savage," he gloated. "Not now!"

Ham apparently didn't hear him. He was looking with amazement at his companions. Their faces, also, were beginning to turn a faint cherry-red.

"Doc Savage was supposed to be a miracle man," the guard went on. "I want to see him pull one."

"He'll soon be here," Yardoff smiled. "He's a prisoner up above. He will be brought down soon."

"I want to see him pull a miracle, too," Ham whispered. "I hope he can do it."

## Chapter XII
### SANDS OF DEATH

DOC was doing pretty well. And Yardoff had been mistaken. The message to Yardoff that the bronze man was a prisoner had been relayed below before it had been learned that Doc, not Clement Hoskins, had left the escape room.

The bronze man, clad as Hoskins, was striding through the underground glass factory, the first stop made by the glass elevator toward the inferno beneath.

Machinery pounded and thumped around him. Blast furnaces threw a lurid red glare over the place. The bronze man hesitated now and then, let his eyes absorb every detail of the place.

The workers there paid no attention. They were accustomed to inspection trips by Hoskins.

There was one peculiar aspect to the cavern. Great motors whirred to run heavy machinery, the furnaces glowed; but nowhere was there any sign of a power line, just as there had been no such sign in the factory above. The machines seemed to draw their tremendous forces from the thin air itself.

Perhaps Doc delayed longer than he should have. Or perhaps Hoskins' jaw had been more solid than it seemed. Hoskins should have been out for more than an hour. He wasn't.

Before the bronze man was halfway through the great workshop, a shrill alarm bell sounded. Red lights flickered in a signal board up above the main doorway.

Shouts of surprise came from the workers. One seized a telephone. His face was pallid as he dropped the receiver.

"Grab that guy!" he shouted. "The one who looks like Hoskins. That ain't Hoskins. That's Doc Savage!"

Mingled howls of rage and panic resounded in the cavern. The men dropped their work, seized heavy tools as weapons. They rushed toward Doc.

One huge fellow was faster than the rest. He showed no caution as he rushed in, swinging a heavy wrench.

The bronze man dodged easily. His powerful hands shot out, seized the huge attacker. The man hurtled through the air like some long-legged medicine ball. His soaring figure bowled over leaders of the horde rushing behind him. They fell in a heap, arms and legs tangling.

A second man leaped out. He held a glass revolver. The next instant and he, too, lost consciousness. Doc's fingers had seemed barely to flick his neck. The gun was in Doc's hand.

Doc didn't shoot. The gun was loaded with deadly bullets. The bronze man had no desire to kill. He sped swiftly toward the elevator, dodging and twisting.

A group formed near the doorway. Doc turned to evade them. There was a sudden rush from behind him. The bronze man appeared hemmed in, trapped from in front and behind.

His flake-gold eyes sparkled. A route was open to one side. Without hesitation he turned that way, running lightly but with the speed of a deer.

Doc started to cross what seemed a bed of sand. Too late he saw what it really was. He twisted in mid-air, spun, tried to turn back.

He was too late. The sand gave beneath his feet like powder. Fierce heat surged up below him. The sand sucked him down as if it had been quicksand.

Doc had stepped into a sand conveyer. It led directly into a huge blast furnace in an adjoining room, a blast furnace filled with molten glass.

THE bronze man's pursuers gathered about. One raised a glass revolver.

"Don't shoot, fool!" the voice of Hoskins screamed. "We need that bronze devil!"

The barrel-shaped man shouldered his way through the mob.

"You're really caught this time, Savage," he gloated.

Doc relaxed, lay flat on his back, with only his

legs buried in the sand. The edge of the pit was almost within reach above his head. But that was of little good. Even if he could reach that edge, he still would have to face the pack of killers that lined the pit.

The bronze man's hands appeared relaxed. One was at his side, half hidden under the sand. Suddenly that arm shot up. It made two motions in the air.

A blinding flash filled the cavern. A second blast followed instantly. Concussion knocked men to the floor. Heavy, sulphurous smoke rolled through the cavern. Men choked, gasped for breath and ran in circles. They knocked against each other, blinded.

Hoskins realized what must have happened. He had seen Doc throw two small objects. Those objects, the barrel-shaped man knew, must have been small, concentrated thermite bombs. When the bombs struck the pyrite wall, the terrific heat of the thermite burned into the sulphur, flooded the cavern with the dense, choking smoke.

But although the fat man was not deceived, he, like the others, was blinded.

Doc alone was not.

The bronze man's eyes were closed. He popped an oxygen lozenge into his mouth. Then his long arms stretched out, he jerked forward. His steel-strong fingers caught the edge of the pit. A moment more and his feet were on firm rock.

DOC could not open his eyes because of the sulphur fumes. But that did not stop him. He moved forward swiftly, his remarkable sense of direction guiding him straight to the corridor that led to the elevator.

Two guards still stood at the elevator. They had heard sounds of the chase and of the explosion, but had not moved. Hoskins had ordered them to remain where they were. They looked surprised when they saw Doc approach, but made no move. They thought Hoskins had returned.

Doc jumped into the glass elevator, pressed the starting button and hung on. The elevator had two speeds, one very slow, one very fast. The bronze man used the fast one.

The glass car pitched downward. For a time the shaft appeared to have been hewn from solid rock. Then the rock took on a different quality. A weird, glowing surface lighted the shaft with bluish luminance. Here were other evidences of attempts at mining.

Efforts had been made to carve corridors in the rock. They had been unsuccessful. The surface appeared little more than scratched. Doc halted the car for a moment, inspected one of the mining efforts.

A faint, trilling sound came from his lips. The ore was different from any he had ever seen before. That very difference might explain why Hoskins was so eager to obtain the bronze man's services.

The bronze man started the elevator again. For several seconds it dropped swiftly. Then that drop was halted. It was halted so suddenly one of the glass-woven cables snapped; the cage bounced for an instant like some huge toy on the end of a rubber band.

The elevator had not reached the bottom of the shaft. It had been stopped by some other control, some switch operated from above. The next instant it began to ascend with dizzy speed.

The car jerked to a stop and the door grated open. It was at the mine level of the foundry cavern. Hoskins, armed men with him, rushed into the cage. The cage was empty.

"He isn't here!" Hoskins roared somewhat needlessly "He either got all the way down or got off at one of the experimental levels below."

The brutal-appearing guard whom Doc had hurled at his fellows in the cavern fight stepped in behind his leader.

"That mug won't get far, chief," he muttered. "We got him covered here. And if he did get through the lead door, why—"

"Yes, yes," Hoskins agreed. He seemed to think swiftly. "You come with me, I'll take care of you. The others can remain here."

The brutal-appearing guard quailed. Before he could object, Hoskins slammed the door of the cage. The lift shot again into the depths of the earth.

It stopped with a sickening jolt. The mine shaft terminated in a small cavern. At one side was a massive door, made of some leadlike metal.

Hoskins eyed the door for a long moment and a slow grin split his fat face. "It does not appear that he has passed through this door, although he is so damned tricky he may have figured out how to do so without leaving a sign. Go back up, keep guard."

AS the elevator shot upward once more, a shadow seemed to drift into a hidden corner of the cavern. That was all. But Doc was on the scene.

He had leaped into one of the mine shafts when the cage had been yanked up. As the cage returned, bearing Hoskins to the bottom, the bronze man had ridden with it. He had ridden on top.

Hoskins turned toward the great leadlike door. A smile was on his lips. He was sure Doc couldn't get away, even if he wanted to. And he was more than certain the bronze man could not run until his men were at least safe.

The barrel-shaped one reached beside the door, pressed a hidden lever. The big portal swung open suddenly. Hoskins stepped inside.

A sudden rush of feet swept him back. A thin, rat-faced man clad in a breechcloth, his skin a cherry-red, led a dozen others similarly appearing in a rush toward Hoskins.

"We know you, Doc Savage!" he cried. "We was telephoned you was comin' down dressed as Hoskins."

Hoskins opened his mouth to speak. But the words that apparently issued from his lips brought an expression of amazement over his fat face.

"What are you going to do about it?" he seemed to say.

"I didn't say that!" he screamed in the next breath.

"I said what are you going to do about it?" Hoskins' voice repeated.

Hoskins' expression was that of a man stunned, a man who couldn't believe his own ears, and seemingly not his own voice. But it was nothing to the consternation on the ratty pan of the breechclothed thug. Someone had told him once that when Doc Savage acted mysterious, he was doubly dangerous. And this was certainly mysterious. It didn't even make sense. "Rat-face" gulped.

"I ain't enjoying doing this, Savage," he shouted, "but it's the living fire if I don't!"

Hoskins' face became almost purple with apoplectic rage.

"What do you mean, you rat?" he screamed. He gulped.

"Well, get it over with, start something," he seemed to continue. "I can take all you guys!"

That was too much for Rat-face. He shouted to his fellows. Long strands, ropes of rubber and woven glass, swished through the air. They encircled Hoskins, caught him around the arms and the legs. In the end the barrel-shaped man was bound thoroughly.

The jolting brought Hoskins to his senses. He recalled then that Doc was known as an expert ventriloquist, realized the bronze man must have been close by and had thrown his voice to make it appear Hoskins was speaking when the barrel-shaped man really was not.

Hoskins looked directly at the rat-faced man. His lips moved soundlessly. Rat-face started; he looked incredulous.

Hoskins shook his head savagely. Again the lips formed words without sound.

Slowly, cautiously, almost fearfully, Rat-face moved forward. He leaned over, put a hand against Hoskins' face.

There was a faint snap. That was all.

"You—you're really Hoskins," Rat-face muttered.

"Of course." Hoskins sighed deeply. "I've been down here so often, I've taken the living fire from my body so much, that it takes only a few minutes for me to be safe here. Had you touched Doc Savage then, you know what would have happened: he would have been dead."

RAT-FACE was apologetic. He loosened the bonds about Hoskins with trembling fingers. "But Doc Savage is smart enough—" he began.

"No man is that smart!" Hoskins snarled. He got to his feet, whipped a glass gun from his pocket He spoke almost in a whisper:

"Savage had to be close, or he could not have made it appear I was speaking. Search the elevator cavern closely. Doc Savage must be there. Find him!"

The cherry-red men swarmed into the room where the elevator had descended.

Hoskins watched with narrow eyes. The men were finding nothing, but a strange thought had occurred to him.

"Come here!" he rasped.

The men obeyed, returned through the lead door. Hoskins closed and secured it. When he turned, his features were hard, a glass gun was ready in his hand.

"You know that those who first enter this cavern cannot touch one of you without immediate death," he said harshly. "It is only after they have remained here a while, until their bodies have become as yours, that they are safe. Now, stand in line. Join hands!"

There was one big cherry-red man in the group. He had been the last to come from the elevator cavern. He walked to one end of the fast-forming line.

Hoskins' eyes centered on that man. He couldn't be sure, but he didn't remember any of his attackers being that big. But he hadn't counted them. If this was Doc, then he would know soon.

"All right! Join hands!" Hoskins repeated impatiently.

The big man joined hands with the cherry-red figure closest him. It happened to be Rat-face.

Nothing happened.

Hoskins' face fell. He had been mistaken.

"O.K.—" he began.

"Chief! Chief! This guy's a fake!" Rat-face was screaming the words. He was trying to free his hand from the grasp of the big man who held him.

"This guy ain't one of us," Rat-face bellowed. "He—he's wearing rubber gloves!"

## Chapter XIII
## THE LIVING FIRE STRIKES

THE big man at the end of the line gave a tremendous surge. Mighty muscles rippled and tightened under smooth skin. The entire line of cherry-red men were snapped through the air like a group of skaters cracking the whip on slick ice. They smashed into Clement Hoskins, knocked him from his feet.

Then the big man let go. Flake-gold eyes flashed as he turned and raced down the corridor.

Doc Savage was on his way to the Pit of Horror!

Clement Hoskins was running almost before he got to his feet. Doc Savage on the loose in the underground labyrinth that surrounded the Pit of Horror did not suit him at all.

Hoskins was worried. He didn't know what the bronze man would do next.

Frantically he raced in pursuit. He stood no chance. His barrel-shaped figure was not built for running.

Hoskins soon realized that. He was panting as he reached that great cave of the workshop.

Yardoff took one look at his barrel-shaped partner. The scarecrow-shaped man halted.

"You let him get away?" he said.

Hoskins nodded. His shoulders slumped. "But—but he's down here," he said.

"Tell me what happened."

Hoskins did. "I'm afraid," he concluded simply. His breathing had returned to normal.

Yardoff's thin face narrowed in concentration. "He is smart," he said at last. "That was why we wanted him. But he is up against something he can't escape—unless we help him. We have no intention of doing that. You and I can get out of this place alive. No one else can. Sooner or later, since he is down here, we will find him."

"But—but suppose he catches us, holds us as hostages?"

"A checkmate," Yardoff agreed. He grinned venomously. "Or would be—if it wasn't for Virginia."

"Virginia?" Hoskins repeated vacantly.

"Certainly." Yardoff's face became malevolent. "She tried to save him. She has fallen for him. He knows this, and while I know he never falls for women himself, he would go to any length to save her from harm."

"So?"

"I want her." Yardoff spoke calmly, but his eyes were not nice to see. "Have her brought down. Put her on the submarine. If that bronze devil tries to disrupt our plans, we'll tell him she will die. She must be put out of the way anyway, sooner or later, because she knows too much; but we won't tell him that."

Hoskins' mouth opened and closed. He became old suddenly. But he did not argue. He turned to leave. Instructions must be given.

"No one can beat you," he said.

HOSKINS might not have been so sure had his eyes been equipped with television. Two scenes might have disturbed him:

One was the figure of a great, breechclothed man gliding silently through the queerly glowing recesses of the corridors and caverns of the underground labyrinth.

Doc Savage was heading directly for the Pit of Horror!

The other scene would have shaken Hoskins even more. It was taking place at Palm Springs.

Three silver-gray transport airships had landed. It was night now. A lean, hard-appearing man was the first to descend. Unconsciously he pulled a handkerchief from one sleeve and wiped the palms of his hands.

The men who poured out of the three planes did not look appealing. They were as choice a gang of murderers as ever gathered in a single spot.

They headed toward an open touring car at Stinger Salvatore's command.

The driver of the touring car was staring at Stinger with fear-stricken countenance. Like a hypnotized chicken, he could not move his gaze from the unblinking eyes of the gangleader.

"I—I'm lost," he breathed. "Stinger is going to kill me."

The driver tried to make himself small as Stinger Salvatore halted in front of the car.

"Double-crosser!" spat the gangleader.

"I—I ain't done nothin', boss," the moon-faced driver whimpered.

Stinger's eyes glittered. "You let me get tricked," he rasped softly.

"I—I don't understand."

"Get in, boys," Stinger ordered. The gangsters poured into the machine. There were so many, some had to stand on the running boards.

"Get going!" Stinger snarled.

So nervous his hands would not hold still, the fat driver put the car into motion.

"What is it, boss?" he quavered. "What is wrong; what have I done?"

"You let Hoskins and Yardoff pull a fast one on me!" Stinger cracked.

"But—but—"

"Yardoff and Hoskins came to me and talked of millions," Stinger explained softly. "They wanted me to get Doc and his men for them. I got two of them. And what happens?"

"I—I don't know."

"That was what they wanted to happen. As soon as they get the two guys, Yardoff and Hoskins go on their own. They never intended to cut me in, to begin with. They're giving me the run-around. And I had you here to keep me posted. You didn't. You let them make a sap out of me."

The fat driver wet dry lips. Stinger was right. Hoskins had paid him more than Stinger, had told him not to say anything about Doc Savage arriving. He tried, now, to clear himself.

"Doc and three of his men got here this afternoon," he muttered. "They were overpowered and captured."

"Good!" snapped Stinger. "Now I'll get the whole crowd."

If the driver hadn't given reports to Stinger before, he tried to make up for it now. The crooks on the running boards grinned. It always amused them to see someone else trying to talk his way out of being murdered.

The factory soon came into view. "Stop here!" rapped Stinger.

The crooks got out of the car. It was strange how many musicians there appeared to be. Nearly all were carrying violin cases.

"I—I can go now?" trembled the driver.

"Sure," said Stinger. As calmly as if he were butchering a chicken, the gangleader pulled out a silenced revolver and shot the driver. A round hole showed in the driver's forehead. He fell on his face.

"Okay, boys," Stinger said. "You know what to do. Let's go!"

"I wonder what we're going to find here," said one killer to his companion. "This whole set-up is a screwy one!"

THE gunman would have thought things were more screwy than ever if he could have seen Doc Savage just then.

The humming drone of disembodied power roared in his ears. In addition, now, there was a queer pulsing in the air.

Doc was proceeding slowly. The manner in which the bronze man stopped, examined every inch of queer rock formation around him, indicated he was trying to find the answer to some vital problem.

The bronze man stopped, looked at his hands and arms. His skin tingled with an odd, galvanizing sensation, was turning an actual cherry-red under the cherry-red dye he had used to hide his distinctive bronze coloring.

In the long, twisting passageway behind him a face showed for an instant. It disappeared when Doc stopped. As the bronze man went on, a stealthy figure crept slowly in pursuit.

Doc's ears were keen. But the constant humming drone was sufficient to drown out any other noise. He did not know he was being followed.

The figure behind him was neither the barrel-shaped one of Hoskins, nor the scarecrow figure that was Yardoff. Indeed, this one looked furtively behind him as often as he looked ahead. Whatever was his purpose, it seemed it was entirely his own.

Doc went on. He turned a corner. His bronze skin seemed to turn a livid blue. A large cavern lay before him. The air that filled it seemed to be a burning, livid blue. It was as if the cavern were a great mercury arc lamp. In the midst of this danced a great ball of even more brilliant blueness. It rocked about unevenly like a weird will-o'-the-wisp of hell.

The bronze man stood still for a moment. Then cautiously, he crept forward. He stopped, peered over a high ridge in the floor of the cavern.

Then he saw the wall of living fire!

A great, jagged wall of rock seemed to blaze with smokeless flame. The will-o'-the-wisp ball seemed to draw its strength from there. The humming noise was almost deafening. The pulsating vibration was strong enough to make the flesh quiver.

And at the bottom of that wall of living flame was the Pit of Horror.

Doc did not need to be told. The evidence was there. A heap of skulls lay suggestively at one side. But that was not what made the scene so loathsome. It was the pile of bodies that had not yet become skeletons that appeared fearsome.

The men were dead. They had been dead for some time. Flame played over their bodies, flame that sparkled and shot out tiny streams of sparks.

Doc's strong hands grasped the top of the ledge before him. He raised himself slightly for a better look as a faint, trilling sound came from his lips, sounded even over the pulsating roar.

Then it happened.

Strong, ghostly hands seemed to grasp the bronze man. His fingers, steel strong, grabbed at the ledge of rock.

Those fingers were not strong enough. So fast that his body itself seemed a streak of light, Doc was picked up from the ledge. He was jerked through space.

With a loud, smacking impact the bronze man was literally sucked hard against that wall of living flame.

He hung there, midway up a smooth, perpendicular surface. There were no obstructions near him. His arms were outflung, but they were limp.

Like a fly impaled on a pin, he was suspended. Flame flickered over his body. His eyes were glazed and unseeing.

Back in the corridor, soft footsteps drew closer. A figure dodged furtively behind a rock. A mirthless chuckle drifted through the air.

## Chapter XIV
## A PROFESSOR PLAYS TRICKS

DOC'S five aides were in the laboratory cavern. For a long time they had nothing to do. They could only look, while guards lounged near by.

The laboratory was worth inspecting. It was different from any they had ever seen before, but only in one respect: Everything was made of glass. In addition, however, it was as well equipped as even the best scientist could ask.

But just looking grew palling. And Doc's aides were not the kind to remain worried for any length of time. Even the guards grinned as Monk and Ham bickered.

"Enter, the scarecrow," grinned Ham. The others looked up. Yardoff was approaching.

"I see you couldn't catch Doc," Monk gibed.

Yardoff's eyes grew hard, but he ignored the remark. He held out his hand to Long Tom. In his palm was a small piece of queerly glowing rock. He said:

"Your job is to discover the atomic structure of this substance. Do not waste time. Your lives and the life of Doc Savage depend upon your success."

Yardoff dropped the small piece of rock in Long Tom's hand. Long Tom jerked in surprise. The rock was heavy—heavy beyond all proportion to its size.

His exclamation caught Monk's interest. Johnny moved forward, eyes lighting.

Yardoff grinned slightly. "I'll leave you in charge of my very able assistant, Professor Torgle," he said.

"Holy cow!" said Renny.

There was reason for his astonishment. The man who came from behind Yardoff would have attracted attention anywhere.

His feet headed one direction, his body another, as if some giant had at one time twisted him halfway around. His head was unbelievably flat on the top. Little eyes that had no color of their own, glowed like tiny red coals. The mouth looked like a ragged slit cut by a knife into a dull piece of red leather.

"I hope you boys are as smart as you're supposed to be," he said. The voice was a mirthless cackle.

Yardoff disappeared.

"In this laboratory," continued Professor Torgle, "you are all at my mercy. I have not been able to solve the secret of the power rock, so I have amused myself making death traps, that never fail. Make yourselves at home, gentlemen."

Ham was studying Professor Torgle with particular interest. Torgle had been one of the most dangerous criminals the world had ever encountered. He had been particularly dangerous because he was a scientist of more than ordinary ability, with a sharp, keen brain.

Torgle supposedly was in an asylum, but he wasn't. He was here.

Renny moved toward the queer-shaped professor.

Ham barked gutturally in a tongue that made Torgle's head snap around. It was the language of ancient Maya.

Professor Torgle's small eyes flamed with quick anger. "Plotting against me, are you?" he cackled. He gestured toward one side of the cavern.

Almost behind Ham was an enormous electric chair. It looked not unlike the one in Sing Sing's death house, save that it was larger and made of glass. There were metal contact plates in the seat, on the arms and on the high back.

"Watch" screamed Torgle.

Whipped about by an invisible force, Ham found himself suddenly seated in that chair.

AN expression of amazement came over the dapper lawyer's face. Clamps of glasslike substance snapped around his legs and arms.

"Now get to work, do what you were told to do!" Torgle screamed. "The lawyer is of no use down here anyway. So I will keep him here until you have finished."

Ham had not been plotting against Torgle when he spoke in Mayan. He had been warning them to be careful, not to arouse the queerly shaped man, that it might be dangerous.

"Let's get to work," Long Tom urged. "It looks like that is the best we could do for all concerned."

Ham did not appear to be in particular danger. And since he wasn't, the expression on the dapper lawyer's face was almost laughable.

The hairy Monk was scowling, however, as he followed the others to a work bench. He'd like to get the scrawny neck of Professor Torgle between his fists.

Monk spread an array of test tubes out before him, began to tinker with chemicals. Johnny and Long Tom pressed close by.

Renny wandered about. He was an engineer. The others were much better equipped for this job than he was.

Monk applied various chemicals to the piece of glowing rock. Nothing happened. It seemed insoluble in anything. He used a diamond drill on it. The diamond point wore flat. The rock was harder than the diamond.

Then with Johnny, he put the chunk in a small electric furnace. Long Tom turned the power on full. The indicator needle shot up. It went far beyond the melting point of any rock or metal they had ever heard of. Then they cooled it, took out the crucible holding the glowing chunk.

The piece of ore was as unscathed as if no heat had been turned on it at all!

"HOWLIN' calamities!" Monk shrilled. "I can't believe it!"

"A phenomenon of extraordinary possibilities," the geologist murmured. "If it could be smelted or milled, it would be an impregnable metallic substance."

"You boys ain't doin' so good," cackled Professor Torgle.

Monk growled to himself. Long Tom was bending over another bench. He had pulled about him a complicated array of indicator dials, induction coils, high-voltage batteries and transformers.

Renny was idling in the direction of the electric chair. He looked over a shoulder. Torgle's attention seemed centered on the experiments the others were making.

The big engineer dived toward Ham. If he could only get those big hands on the fastenings that held the lawyer down, he was sure he could free him.

A startled shout broke from the engineer. His severe-appearing features contorted with pain. He halted as if he had smashed into a wall in mid-air.

Torgle turned around, chuckled hideously. Monk looked up just as Renny went to the floor.

Monk bellowed like an enraged bull. He plunged toward Torgle. The queer-shaped man scuttled backward with unexpected speed. He reached a lever, pulled it.

Monk also stopped as if he had slammed flat against an invisible wall. He struck it with such force that he knocked over a large glass work bench.

The work bench did not go all the way to the floor. It stopped, tilted far over, as if held up by invisible hands.

Renny got to his feet, an incredulous expression on his disapproving face. Monk's arms were crooked, his piglike eyes flaring.

Torgle laughed.

"That is a high-frequency ray of greater voltage than man has ever known," he chortled. "Another one surrounds your friend in the electric chair. You are helpless."

Monk's face was grim. He understood how high-frequency rays worked. They set up an invisible wall, and this one had been as strong as steel.

Long Tom alone had gone on with his work. He labored with a feverish intensity. He hauled one huge step-up transformer before him, adjusted a complex array of coils and dials.

Experimentally, he pulled a lever. There was a sharp, whirring sound, and crackling sparks shot from the step-up transformer. The electrical wizard shut it off, adjusted another dial. Then he pulled the lever down again. A tight smile spread over his face.

The whirring was louder this time. The crackling sparks shot many feet into the air. Then the whirring became a hum.

A sharp crash came from behind them. The crazily leaning work bench had fallen to the floor. Ham leaped from the electric chair.

The high-frequency rays which had formed the invisible wall had been broken.

TORGLE howled in surprise. He hadn't thought these aides of Doc Savage could penetrate the mystery of his devices.

Renny started for him. The queer-shaped professor shuffled rapidly backward. Long Tom spoke swiftly in Mayan. Renny stopped.

"We've still got to figure out what this is," Long Tom reminded.

"Yeah, and Ham is no use to us, you shoulda left him where he was," Monk grumbled.

"You didn't do so hot yourself," Ham gibed.

Monk leaped toward him. Ham danced out of the way, seized a glass knife and brandished it in front of him.

"I'll carve slices off that hairy hide of yours!" he yelled.

Professor Torgle looked on with open mouth. "Get to work!" he screamed.

A faint grin was on Long Tom's face. As Torgle's attention was centered on the struggling pair in the center of the laboratory, the electrical genius moved toward the panel of levers the professor had been operating.

"Okay, boys," he yelled suddenly, "get him! I've got his control board. He's helpless!"

Torgle yelled with rage. The mock fight in the center of the room stopped. The four aides all raced toward the professor.

"Stop! Stop!" howled Torgle.

"Stop nothing!" said Ham. "I'm going—"

Professor Torgle pressed a concealed button. The effect was amazing.

Doc's aides stopped as if they had been

suddenly frozen. They seemed to hang grotesquely in the air. They looked like motion-picture films of runners suddenly halted in the projector. Long Tom's hands hung motionless over the levers on the panel board.

The five might have been living statues. They could not move; they could not speak.

A STRANGE light flickered in Professor Torgle's sunken red eyes.

"Fools!" he cackled. "If you had used brains, if you had solved the secret of the strange stone, we all would have been free men. Now you will remain here and die. But not me."

With his queer, sidling walk, Torgle slipped from the laboratory cavern. He went toward the Pit of Horror.

At the ledge, he peered over Doc Savage's body still hung, suspended against the wall of living fire. The professor laughed horribly. It had been he who had trailed the bronze man to this place.

"The others fear, and rightly," he chortled, "but not me. And now I have the famous Doc Savage at my mercy."

Carefully, his strange method of walking making his task more difficult, Torgle descended directly into the Pit of Horror. He paid no attention to the fearsome heap of bodies

Without hesitation, he walked to the wall of living fire. His fingers sought tiny projections. He pulled himself up, an inch at a time.

As he hung beside Doc's suspended body, he took a glass knife from his breechcloth. He lifted the knife, held it back of Doc's neck, the arm poised for a thrust.

His tiny eyes danced with wild glee.

## Chapter XV
### KILLERS CLASH

CLEMENT HOSKINS would have been worried if he could have seen Doc then. Not that he cared about the bronze man's health, but he needed him alive, needed Doc's brains.

But just then Hoskins wasn't even thinking of Doc. He had other worries.

Yardoff, his thin face venomous, was listening to a telephone description of things happening above ground. His eyes glittered dangerously. Armed gangsters were creeping upon the glass factory. One of the thugs on guard above thought he had recognized Stinger Salvatore.

Rapidly Yardoff told Hoskins what he had heard. Hoskins' moon face hardened savagely.

"It is time," he said, "that we eliminated Salvatore anyway. He has outlived his usefulness."

Yardoff nodded. "The fact that he is attacking without warning shows he realizes we intended to do that."

Hoskins rolled his barrel-shaped body toward one of the queerly glowing walls of the cavern in which they stood. There, above a rubber plate on the floor, protruded two short handles.

Hoskins seized the handles, kicked a lever with his feet. The ruddy complexion of his face turned a bright crimson. Sweat poured from his fat pores. He stood there, silent, for more than a minute. Then he released his grip and turned to Yardoff.

"Just a precaution," he rapped. "I have a plan."

The two strode toward the leaden door that opened onto the elevator shaft. As they passed it, Hoskins pressed a button and the whine of machinery announced the descent of the glass cage.

From a small locker, Hoskins took out rubber shoes, rubber gloves and outer clothing. Yardoff did the same. The cage jolted to a stop. The two got in.

"Perhaps," Yardoff grinned thinly, "we can talk suitable terms with this ambitious gangster."

The lift shot upward.

THE thugs in the glass factory did not know how many attackers there were. One of them, a huge, broken-nosed individual, had seen a dozen or more slinking figures. Suddenly he brought a machine gun to his shoulder, pressed the trigger.

*Br-r-r-r-r-r-r!*

Stinger had one less cohort. The broken-faced killer grinned. This was going to be simple. Only an artillery attack could take the glass factory

The killer looked out the window again. He saw a queer-looking weapon poke out from behind a pile of sand. It wasn't a machine-gun. It had a heavy gauge and a queer, pineapple-like protuberance.

There was a loud *bang!* and the protuberance disappeared. It hurtled through the window, scarcely an inch from the skull of "Broken-nose."

*Boom!*

The glass factory rocked as the bomb exploded. Broken-nose lost all interest in proceedings. Parts of his body splashed on the walls. Two other thugs dropped, dying.

Fear gripped the survivors. Machine guns were one thing. Fighting against virtual trench mortars was something else again. The factory walls were not built to withstand an attack of that kind.

"These guys are tough," whined one. "Maybe we'd better—"

He didn't finish his sentence. He saw Hoskins and Yardoff emerge from the elevator. Their appearance was more terrifying to him than the weapons in the hands of the attackers outside. He changed his mind about suggesting that perhaps they should join forces with Stinger Salvatore.

Hoskins conferred briefly with Yardoff and barked quick orders. Men lined the windows with deadly Tommy guns. Their death roar filled the air. Bursts of sand kicked up in front of the factory. Occasionally a scream announced a bullet had found its mark.

Powerful searchlights, sheltered by bulletproof glass, made the scene outside as light as day.

Hoskins drew in his breath sharply. The attackers had come prepared.

**Professor Torgle prepared for a thrust that would drive the glass knife into the bronze man's heart.**

A dozen armed thugs were creeping across an open space. Lead beat about them. But they were unharmed. They were pushing ahead of them prow-shaped shields of metal. The shields were so constructed that they deflected machine-gun slugs without injury to the men behind them.

The boom of grenades grew louder, like the bass notes to the higher whine of the Tommy guns in the symphony of death. Lethal bombs crashed through factory windows. One entered the open mouth of a blast furnace.

The explosion spewed molten glass out into the room. Men screamed in agony, covered with burning torment. The stench of singeing flesh filled the room.

Three blasts came in rapid succession. They were not inside the factory. They were just outside. Barbed wire leaped into the air.

A path through the death-charged strands had been cut by the exploding grenades.

The defending thugs cast frantic, desperate looks at Yardoff and Hoskins. Yardoff glanced at his barrel-shaped companion, nodded

Without a word, Hoskins pulled a great white sheet of cloth from a locker, hung it from a window.

"Cease firing!" Yardoff rapped.

STINGER SALVATORE grinned evilly as he saw that flag.

"They couldn't take it," he chuckled. A wizened-faced lieutenant, beside him, shook his head.

"It's too easy, boss," he cautioned "Watch out for a trick."

"Right!" agreed Stinger, and his unblinking eyes narrowed to deadly slits. "They plan to double-cross me again, probably. This time I'm going to do the double-crossing."

Hoskins' voice blared from a loudspeaker.

"There is no need for this killing, Stinger!" Hoskins bellowed. "There will be more millions than any of us will know what to do with. Together we can accomplish much. Will you talk business?"

Stinger's grin grew larger. "Sure, Hoskins, but not inside the factory. I've got to be careful."

"I will put myself at your mercy I'll come out to talk with you," Hoskins declared.

The barrel-shaped figure of Hoskins appeared in the factory door. He walked out into the square. He was an excellent target in the strong searchlights.

From behind the queer shields, half a dozen Tommy guns were aimed directly at his body.

"Now," Stinger whispered to his lieutenant, "you go talk to him."

"Me?" Fear showed on the wizened one's face.

"You." Stinger's voice was harsh. A heavy automatic was in his hand. "And when you get near him, this is what you do." He talked rapidly.

"I'm sending my chief lieutenant," Stinger's voice rolled out. "He can talk for me."

An expression of disappointment flickered for a moment over Hoskins' fat face, and was gone.

The wizened criminal slipped from behind a shield and stepped forward. He licked his lips, darted furtive eyes to each side of him. It was apparent he did not like his assignment.

Ten feet from the barrel-shaped man, the killer whipped out a gun. Without warning he leveled it, squeezed the trigger.

Hoskins dropped. He waved one hand toward the window of the factory.

THE ground shook as from a tremendous clap of thunder. Lightning seemed to play about the big yard. Sparks of terrific voltage leaped from one antenna post to another. The entire yard became a field of electricity, of voltage greater than a thundercloud.

The wizened thug died like an insect before a blowtorch. Those behind shields who had reached the outer limits of the yard withered and died, and turned into black, scorched things that had once been men.

A curse ripped from Stinger's tight lips.

Hoskins leaped up, ran unscathed from the scene of terror to reach the comparative safety of the factory

"A double double-cross!" Stinger swore. "The blasted fiend has no honor!"

Stinger could not understand Hoskins' escape, either from the bullet or the terrible lightning that rained in the yard. Hoskins hadn't entirely escaped the bullet. But the little killer who had shot at him had been nervous; the lead had merely nicked the big man.

Had Stinger witnessed the scene in the cavern far beneath the earth, before Hoskins came to the surface, he might have understood why the barrel-shaped one could run through lightning unscathed. Then again, he might not have understood.

But one thing the flashily dressed gangster did know, and that was that the blasts of electricity which were barring his advance, were flashing from the antennalike posts.

Grenades rained about those posts. The posts went down. The deadly lightning ceased.

Clement Hoskins' face was as nearly gray as it could be under the cherry-red complexion he now had.

Yardoff's sharp lips were tightly closed. His scarecrow figure was tense.

"A tight spot," he conceded.

Hoskins nodded. "Those damn grenades. And

108   THE LIVING-FIRE MENACE

he was too smart to come near me himself in the yard."

The defenders were quailing, ashen-faced. Frantically Hoskins and Yardoff drove them to the windows, forced them to keep up a rain of machine-gun bullets.

Both Yardoff and his barrel-shaped companion had removed a glove. Sight of the waving, cherry-red hands alone kept the thugs at their posts.

A second blast furnace erupted, spraying molten glass, as an explosive bomb hit it.

"Let them have the factory," Yardoff ordered suddenly. "We can get them easier if they do."

Hoskins rasped a brisk command.

Thugs wasted no time. They raced frantically toward the elevator that ran beneath. There weren't so many left now. One load could take them all.

As Stinger's men rushed in above, the glass cage of the elevator rocketed downward. It stopped at the furnace level.

Yardoff leaped out, pressed a button.

There was a dull boom from above. Sand and rock rained down. The upper part of the tunnel collapsed.

"Let them dig through that," Yardoff sneered. "If they do, they'll find some nice surprises for them."

Hoskins nodded, soberly. "Right, but we've got to work fast at that. We've got to find Doc Savage at once, put the pressure on him."

PROFESSOR TORGLE also was planning to put pressure on Doc Savage.

He had been amusing himself. Time after time he had swung his knife, to halt its razor-sharp point a hair's distance from the back of the bronze man's neck.

He wearied finally of the sport.

"Now," he cackled—and prepared for a thrust that would drive the glass knife into the bronze man's heart.

It was then that Doc Savage moved slightly.

Professor Torgle's knife hand froze. The bronze man's body had not moved much, but it was enough.

"Alive," breathed Torgle. "Alive. The key to safety and freedom. And I—I thinking him dead, was about to destroy that key!"

Torgle scampered down the sheer face of the wall of fire as if pursued by demons. A twisting, grotesque grin was on his face; his flat head bobbed up and down.

He was drooling as he reached the Pit of Horror. He kicked one of the bodies contemptuously, and climbed up the ledge until he could reach the corridor that led to the big caverns.

Torgle reached the first group of workers. He whispered to them excitedly.

Incredulous looks were his answer. He argued.

"But—but the Pit of Horror!" gasped one. "We—we dare not go there. That is death!"

Professor Torgle spat. "Fools!" he cackled contemptuously, "you carry your death with you in your own body. The wall of living fire in the Pit of Horror cannot hurt you, because you are already living fire. The pit of death has merely been used as a bogy to frighten such fools as you. Those who have gone there have been shot down, not mysteriously killed. But you will die, die horribly, like a sheet of fire, unless you take the chance I'm offering you."

His words carried conviction.

The cherry-red men dropped their tools; they began to pick up pieces of glass that could be used for weapons.

Others carried the message through the cavern. A mob formed swiftly.

"We will get this Doc Savage, we will hold him for a hostage!" Torgle shouted. "We will demand that we be given the secret which will bring us freedom or we will kill the bronze man. If Hoskins and Yardoff don't agree, we will kill them, also!"

The mob started racing for the Pit of Horror.

"But why is the bronze man helpless there?" one convict asked, not unreasonably.

"I do not know, fool!" Torgle shouted. "We will learn. And I need help to bring him out."

"I can't stand it! I can't stand it!" a voice screamed suddenly. The shriek was high and despairing.

"Kill! Kill!" another shouted.

An insane spirit gripped the mob. In a moment they were changed to a mob of maddened, kill-crazy convicts.

They raced on ahead of Torgle. The queer-shaped professor tried vainly to halt them. He saw his plans evaporating under the kill-crazy frenzy of the mob.

Then something happened to him, too. He also was affected by the steady, never-ending hum. He screamed, scampered forward with the rest. He forced his way to the front.

Professor Torgle had become just another murder-determined man, racing at the head of the pack.

"Kill! Kill!" the men screamed. "Kill Hoskins! Kill Yardoff! Kill Doc Savage!"

## Chapter XVI
### A MOB AMUCK

DOC SAVAGE heard the mob approaching. The bronze man stirred; his flake-gold eyes opened.

He had been slammed so hard against the wall that the blow had knocked him unconscious. His head had taken a terrific shock, his entire body had been subjected to terrific punishment.

But his powers of recuperation were far beyond those of an ordinary man. Almost in the same instant his eyes opened, his brain cleared, became alert.

Instantly Doc acted. His hands went to his waist. About that waist was the emergency kit he always carried with him. In it were compact instruments of all kinds.

Some of those instruments were of metal. And it was the metal that had caused his predicament.

The wall of living flame had acted as a gigantic, tremendously powerful electromagnet.

Electromagnets such as are used in handling of huge quantities of scrap iron are so powerful that they will lift a man from the ground merely by attraction to the nails in the bottom of his shoes.

The wall of living flame was even more powerful. It had literally jerked Doc through space in pulling toward it the metal that was in his emergency kit. As long as the bronze man had that belt around him, he was held suspended in the air.

There had been nothing of metal about Professor Torgle. He had escaped the action of the electromagnet.

Doc's fingers worked swiftly. They explored several pockets of the emergency kit.

The weird will-o'-the-wisp ball of fire, which had been dancing overhead, dropped lower, passed over the bronze man. He paid no heed.

The mob streamed over the ledge, dropped down in the Pit of Horror. Professor Torgle was in the lead. He had his glass knife.

Several of the more agile of the killers started up the wall.

Doc loosened the strap on the emergency kit. His body floated down—dropped to land squarely in the center of the pack of murder-mad convicts!

THERE were more than fifty armed killers in the pit. More were dropping down every moment. It appeared sure death for one man to oppose that mob. No one person—not even Doc Savage—could hope to overcome all of them.

Doc Savage had no intention of trying.

His arms smashed out. Those nearest him were thrown back. They crashed into others, kill-crazy.

That was all the bronze man intended. It was enough.

In an instant the pit was a snarling, whirling mass of fighting men. Men fighting each other.

Doc had correctly interpreted the temper of the mob. Knew that they had to fight, would fight any one, even each other.

Glass knives rose and fell; blood spurted. The screams of dead and dying made the Pit of Horror live up to its name.

Torgle's crafty, maddened brain alone saw what was happening.

"It's Doc Savage!" he screamed. "Don't let him get away! Kill him! Kill him!"

Doc twisted through the screaming, fighting throng. Occasionally his fist shot out and some killer dropped, unconscious. It was impossible for Torgle to keep him in sight.

Suddenly one of the convicts on the edge of the crowd screamed. He pointed at the pile of skulls at the bottom of the wall of living fire.

The pile of skulls began moving. No one was near.

Then one of the skulls seemed to mount, unaided, into the air. The vacant eye sockets appeared to be grinning in the ghastly, weird blue light.

The skull began to speak

"Those who have died here resent your presence," came the words. The jaw bone clicked. "Leave while you yet have time."

Fear of the supernatural swept over the crowd. Mob spirit is infectious. It sweeps with amazing speed. The men scrambled, tried to climb up the ledge to get out of the cavern.

But just as quickly, they stopped, turned around.

Perhaps if they had not been maddened, the trick would have worked. Killers fear what they cannot understand. But this mob of murderers was past that fear. They returned to their one idea: Kill! Regardless of the cost, kill!

The mob swept toward the skull hanging in mid-air. That one they would even kill again. Professor Torgle's flat head was in the lead. His slit of a mouth was working strangely.

Then Doc Savage stepped into view.

THE bronze man was dangling the skull from a black, invisible silken cord. A second thread was attached to the bony jaw. The supernatural was explained.

A yell of hate rose from the mob.

Doc Savage dropped the skull. He ran directly toward the mob.

Death seemed certain. Two score knives were ready. Some were thrown, to whistle dangerously close as the bronze man dived directly toward his foes.

Then one cabled arm shot out. The knife in Professor Torgle's hand clattered to the floor. Those near him were swept back by powerful blows.

The next moment Doc had picked up the queer-shaped scientist and had tucked him under an arm like some light bundle. As Professor Torgle kicked and twisted vainly, Doc whirled, raced away. The baying pack was in hot pursuit.

A wall of flame was in front. The bronze man dived through it. There was a thin, narrow trail. The trail skirted the edge of a mighty underground precipice. The pit stretched down from there many hundred feet.

Even the narrow trail did not go far. It ended in a thin line that not even a mountain goat could follow.

But Doc did not get that far. He took three quick steps. Then he seemed to lose his balance. Torgle cried out in horror.

Doc's feet faltered. Then he fell, taking Torgle with him, straight into the yawning pit below the precipice!

A howl of frustrated rage came from the pursuers. The more venturesome crowded to the lip of the clifflike rock. They peered down, muttered.

Nothing was to be seen. The bottom of the precipice was so far below that it was hidden in the veil of blue.

"Doc Savage is dead!" howled one.

The cry was taken up by others. From disappointment they turned to glee. They danced, raved, swung arms aloft.

"Now for the others!" screamed a convict who had once been Public Enemy No. 1. "Let's get them, get them all, Hoskins and Yardoff!"

The tide turned. The convicts rushed backward, scrambling over each other in their haste to leave the pit.

"Doc Savage is dead. Doc Savage is dead! Kill Hoskins! Kill Yardoff!" they shrieked.

Up the long corridor they rushed, toward the great cavern and the lead doors they knew opened to the outer world.

## Chapter XVII
### BETWEEN TWO FIRES

LONG TOM stared straight ahead. He could not even move his eyeballs. His lips had been caught half opened. He spoke through those lips, his voice strangled. One by one, he called out the names of the other four men in the room.

Johnny could only grunt. Ham's reply was smothered. Monk gave a faint squeal. Only one voice seemed freer than the others: that was Renny's.

"We are being held in an electrical field," said Long Tom. He articulated with difficulty. "You, Renny, seem nearer the outer edge than any of the rest. Try hard to move."

As Long Tom spoke, maddened shouts drifted through the closed door of the laboratory. The electrical wizard did not know what was happening.

But the tenor of the shouting of the convicts was not encouraging. The men were obviously out to escape—and to kill whatever lay in their path.

Renny's huge frame strained. Every ounce of muscle in his six feet four of solid strength strained in mighty surges to break the invisible bonds that held him.

"I can move a little, not much, though," he gasped. Perspiration was streaming down his severe, puritanical face.

Renny's huge fists clenched. He gave an exclamation of delight at the sign. It showed he was breathing through the invisible electrical field.

"Touch the wall, Renny!" Long Tom urged desperately.

The huge engineer worked like a man trying to swim in some heavy, clinging substance. Inch by inch, he worked one arm out. His outstretching fingers touched the glittering, luminescent wall.

There was a crackling noise. Sparks flew from the ends of Renny's fingers and the wall where he had touched it. The bonds that held him seemed to slacken.

Instantly, the big engineer threw himself hard against the rock where the luminescence was brightest.

His already cherry-red face became more and more livid.

"Feel anything, Renny?" Long Tom asked.

Renny's lips moved spasmodically. He swallowed hard. The words seemed to choke from his throat.

"Feels like some one tickling me all over," he muttered. "Sort of a queer tingling."

"Good!" Long Tom snapped. Then he was silent for a moment. Outside, the shouting was louder. The convicts were almost at the door of the laboratory.

Long Tom was sure the convicts would be as little affected by the electrical field as Torgle had been. He was sure they could come in and slash the five men with glass knives while they were helpless.

Sweat trickled down his face. His jaw was contorted, his own muscles strained to the utmost in a futile effort to escape.

"The button—the button Torgle pushed!" he gasped.

Renny lunged forward. He fought as though swimming against a strong tide.

"Kill them! Kill them!" came the roar of the mob. The roar came from just outside the laboratory door.

The big engineer gave a final, desperate lunge. He reached the button, pressed it.

THE roar of the mob swept by outside. The convicts were surging down the corridor, on toward the main workshop cavern. Evidently they had not known Doc's aides were in the laboratory, or if they had known, they had forgotten.

Monk and Ham stretched strained muscles. Johnny slumped as the electrical field was shut off and they were freed from their living-statue poses.

Long Tom leaped up. "We've got to get to work, and work fast!" he bellowed. "Something has gone wrong, or Doc would have been here."

"Right," said Ham.

"What do you know about it?" Monk protested in mock anger. "You can't do anything but talk. But perhaps you'd better practice up on a good speech, for if that gang comes back here after us, it may take some good talking to save our lives."

"If that Torgle comes back here, I'm going to wring his blasted neck!" Renny said solemnly.

"And me—" started Johnny.

The door of the laboratory opened slowly. A misshapen figure with a twisted head showed in the doorway.

The twisted figure started to speak. His words were drowned in a roar of animal rage from Monk. The homely chemist, his hairy arms outstretched menacingly, darted forward.

Renny was step to step with him. They reached the figure simultaneously.

Then a peculiar thing happened.

Monk was lifted into the air as lightly as if he had been a feather duster. Renny's big fist shot out, but whizzed through empty space. The two men charged again, slammed into each other with a force that almost knocked them both out.

"We should not fight against ourselves," Doc's voice said dryly. "That would impede our progress."

The amazement in Monk's eyes at the treatment he had received changed to wild delight.

"Howlin' calamities, Doc!" he squealed. "We didn't suspect it was you!"

Long Tom's shoulders lifted and fell. A smile of relief crossed features ordinarily pallid and unhealthy-appearing, now a bright cherry-red.

"I'm glad you're here, Doc," he said simply. "I think I know what this thing is all about, but what to do about it has got me licked."

"Doc's a spirit again," Ham jeered at Monk. "See, this time he returns to us as the spirit of Torgle."

"Shut up, you big-talking shyster!" the hairy chemist squealed. He danced about excitedly.

The tension was gone. Doc's aides didn't ask questions. It was enough for them that the bronze man was finally with them.

"What are our chances, Doc?" Renny asked.

The bronze man did not answer for a moment. He was busy assembling various pieces of equipment. He moved rapidly and without hesitation.

Long Tom watched him with the delight of a star pupil watching a master at work.

"What chance did you say we had, Doc?" Renny repeated.

"Many things are happening," the bronze man said slowly. "As to our chances—that I will know in a very few minutes. I am going to try an experiment. If it works, we have a chance. If it doesn't—"

THERE was silence for a moment in the laboratory. Doc's aides glanced at each other briefly. It was seldom they had heard the bronze man admit that they might not be able to get out of any jam in which they found themselves.

But they did not know all that Doc did.

The bronze man did not explain how he had escaped from the Pit of Horror. None of his men knew of his peril there, and he did not think it worthy of mention.

The escape really had been quite simple. Doc had seen a ledge beneath the precipice. The ledge was hidden so that only sharp eyes could see it at all.

When Doc had seized Torgle, he had leaped to that ledge and hidden. The convicts, peering down, did not know the ledge existed and missed it entirely. Doc had brought Torgle back to safety after the convicts had fled, donned his disguise and came to the laboratory.

The bronze man was working with startling swiftness. His aides stood silent, watching intently. From what Doc had said, and his actions now, they realized that their situation was indeed perilous.

The bronze man found zinc and copper plates carefully wrapped in pliant folds of malleable glass. He was careful not to touch the metal plates. He held them in glass tongs, suspended them in vats of acid.

Then he hooked them up in an intricate series of wiring. He pulled Long Tom's experiment apart, used much of the apparatus that was in it. He found half a dozen storage batteries with glass cases and from one corner pulled a huge electric motor. Its case was of glass. All metal parts were carefully covered.

The bronze man's muscles strained as he brought it into the center of the room. It was then that his men noticed his strange complexion.

They were cherry-red, but they appeared pallid compared with Doc. The bronze hue of his skin had been replaced with a fiery red glow more startling than that of any of the breechclothed men.

Doc hooked up the large motor. Then he walked silently to the other end of the complex circuit running through the zinc and copper plates in the acid vats. He paused for a moment before two large contact points of copper. He stood on a rubber mat.

Then it was that Doc Savage did a strange thing. He was pressed for time, he had been working with the utmost swiftness. But now he paused. Carefully he removed every bit of make-up, stood forth as Doc Savage, recognizable by all.

"If this experiment is not a success, do not try to leave the caverns," he said, and there was unexpected feeling in his voice. "You must barricade the door of this laboratory. Long Tom will continue to experiment until success has been achieved."

Long Tom leaped forward. Horror was on his face. He understood why Doc had removed his make-up, why he had spoken as he did.

Doc Savage was going to try a dangerous experiment. If he failed, he wanted Long Tom to know he was to carry on, wanted to look as his friend had always known him.

If the experiment did not succeed, Doc Savage would be dead!

LONG TOM'S tongue seemed to stick to the roof of his mouth. He dampened parched lips as he tried to speak. His voice came as if from a distance.

"Stop, Doc!" he cried. "Let me try it. You could carry on—"

Doc pushed him aside. Looks of understanding crossed over the faces of the bonze man's other aides. Monk would have stepped forward, would have tried to dissuade Doc by force, even though he knew it was useless.

Renny held him back. Sorrow was on the big engineer's thin, severe features. "He—he would do it anyway, Monk," he objected. "It's hard, hard for all of us, but there is nothing we could do."

Long Tom's figure was tense. He, more than any of the others, realized the chance Doc Savage was going to take.

The death of Z-2, the death of the escaped scientist in Doc's office, the fear the cherry-red men had shown for an ordinary stream of water, all pointed to one thing:

Each of them was carrying a lethal jolt of electricity in his body!

Long Tom did not pretend to know how to explain it. He only knew it was so. The human body always has a certain amount of electricity in it, and the cherry-red men in the cavern seemed charged so that they were almost walking dynamos. If they touched metal that was grounded, if they touched water so that it grounded their body, it brought their death.

They were doomed to die if they escaped. Only in this cavern, for some reason, were they safe.

And Doc Savage and all his aides were now cherry-red. It would seem logical that they would also face death unless they found something to counteract that peril.

The bronze man was going to try and experiment to see if he had solved the secret. If he failed, he would die. He would die as Z-2 had died, as others had died. He would die horribly, his body burned and scorched, his powerful muscles, his keen brain wiped out as a fuse is wiped out.

Doc's lips were set firmly. He reached out, seized the two contact points.

The smell of ozone filled the air. Acid in the vats began to boil.

The bronze man's muscles contorted in a mighty effort. An ammeter needle on a dial began to jump crazily. Wires glowed red-hot with the sudden burdening of terrific current.

Then the big electric motor began to turn!

It moved slowly at first, then began to whine with a sudden, mighty surge of power.

"Another extraordinary manifestation of electric phenomenon," Johnny muttered amazed, and gazed at Doc's face in sudden awe.

The ruddy hue of the bronze man began to pale, the natural bronze color of his skin appeared.

Doc's flake-gold eyes were flashing. He watched another ammeter needle slowly drop toward the zero marks.

"Success!" Long Tom breathed, and it appeared to be the first time he had taken a breath since Doc had seized hold of the contact points. "Now if we only have time—"

Sudden shots sounded from the corridor outside. A Tommy gun roared in the distance.

It did not appear there was going to be time.

THINGS were happening in the big workshop cavern. It was an uproar, a surging mass of fighting, savage men.

Hoskins' fat face was worried, his sunken eyes frantic. Yardoff was fighting with grim, bitter enjoyment, his scarecrow figure relaxed, as if, now that a show-down had arrived, he really enjoyed a battle.

And a showdown was near.

The blast in the upper tunnel had failed in its work. It had not completely blocked the shaft. Stinger Salvatore's men had found an opening, had worked their way down.

And Yardoff and Hoskins, with the few loyal thugs they had left, were between two fires.

Salvatore's men, armed and deadly, were attacking from one direction. The maddened convicts, with glass knives for weapons, were attacking from the other.

"A tough spot," Hoskins panted.

"The convicts complicate things," Yardoff agreed. A smile that was scarcely human split his thin face. "If they were with us, if they would attack Stinger's men, it would soon be over. As it is—"

He lifted the Tommy gun he held in rubber-clad hands, brutally mowed down a group of cherry-red men who had started to rush forward.

*Br-r-r-r-r-r-r!*

Lead hammered the corridor wall. One of Stinger's gunmen had turned a bend in the corridor, almost had the range.

"We've got you, Yardoff! You and Hoskins better give up. Maybe if you do we'll let you live, even if I do take the millions you expected to get."

Stinger Salvatore's voice was triumphant and jeering. It seemed to the flashily clad gangster that he held all the cards.

One of Yardoff's eyebrows lifted mockingly. He moved to a lever beside the wall, pulled it.

The passageway behind became a solid sheet of flame. The gunner who had fired a moment before became a burned chunk of flesh.

Stinger bellowed in frustrated rage. The roar of a grenade sounded.

Yardoff shrugged. "It will only take them a few moments to blast down the electrical connections," he conceded. "We had better retreat."

Hoskins nodded. Sweat was running from him in long streams under the hot rubber suit he wore.

Cautiously they backed up. More of the cherry-red men appeared.

The thugs with Hoskins and Yardoff appeared as frightened of the cherry-red men as they had been of Stinger's killers. Their guns popped ceaselessly.

But the convicts were canny. The first burst from Yardoff's Tommy gun had brought some measure of sanity back to them. They lurked in passageways leading off the main corridor.

As the thugs passed, a cherry-red hand would dart out. That hand would touch one of the thugs.

The thug would yell once. Then he became very dead. Half-insane shrieks of glee from the kill-crazy convicts would follow.

"Kill! Kill! Kill!" they chanted.

"The end?" Hoskins asked. His lips trembled.

Yardoff surveyed him scornfully. "Of course not!" he rapped. "Stinger and his men will destroy themselves. They do not understand what they are up against here."

"Then what are we to do?" Hoskins was almost sobbing.

Yardoff lifted his Tommy gun, blasted a path through an approaching horde of cherry-red men. Behind them another grenade exploded. Exultant yells followed.

"We will simply get Doc Savage and his men, take them to the submarine, and return when the fighting is over," Yardoff said.

His Tommy gun blared its song of death.

## Chapter XVIII
### A FLIGHT FOR LIFE

THE roar of the Tommy gun was warning enough to Doc and his men that things had gone wrong outside. And it told them enemies were approaching.

"If I only had my sword cane!" Ham moaned.

"Or if we had some super-firers!" Renny shouted.

"I'll take 'em! I'll take 'em all!" Monk howled. He jumped up and down, beat his chest in perfect imitation of a bull ape.

"Shut up, you guys!" Long Tom put in swiftly. "Help Doc. He can't save us all if you don't work."

"We'll stand guard," Renny said, motioning at Ham. "We're no good on the type of stuff you're doing, anyway."

The bronze man said nothing. The situation was one of the toughest of many tough spots he and his men had ever been in, but work, not idling, was the only thing that would save them.

Monk, with Long Tom, grabbed more plates, more glass boxes, worked rapidly to put together additional batteries of the type Doc had made.

Johnny was pulling out additional electric motors, working swiftly to splice connections to them, careful to use rubber and glass only when he came in contact with the wires.

Doc was mixing chemicals in several glass retorts. He poured the resulting liquid into glass balls, plugged the openings.

Swiftly he handed half a dozen each to Renny and Ham.

A wide smile overspread the dapper lawyer's face. He opened the door, tossed one of the glass balls down the corridor.

It landed not a score of feet in front of Yardoff and Hoskins.

There was a most satisfying explosion.

The barrel-shaped man and the scarecrow one almost went on their noses, so quickly did they stop.

Yardoff snarled, loosed a blast from his Tommy gun that played on the door.

Renny waited until the drum of the gun clicked empty. Then he jumped out, looped two of the glass balls down the corridor as if he had been a baseball pitcher.

Hoskins had raised a glass pistol. He shot, but he was so anxious to get away from there that he almost tripped over his own feet.

The two crooks raced back, until they could stand in the comparative safety of a small niche in the wall while they reloaded the Tommy gun.

Two more apparatus such as Doc had erected were ready for use now.

Monk seized the handles of one. Long Tom grabbed onto the other. Slowly the cherry-red color died from their faces; the queer, tingling sensation their skin had experienced faded. They felt more keen, more mentally alert than they had for some time.

"Hurry, Doc, hurry!" The cry came from Renny. The big engineer had left his post at the laboratory door, was rushing toward the back.

A cherry-red face had appeared around a bend. A hideous face, with lips drawn back over dirty teeth, with glass dagger held in one hand, only the glass dagger did not show its real color. It was dripping crimson.

"Give me those glass bombs!" Monk squealed. "You've got to get deloused!"

He reached out, almost touched Renny's hand. Doc shouted. Monk froze.

"Lay the bombs down, Renny, then let Monk pick them up," the bronze man said. "Had he touched you, he would have been killed."

Yardoff's submachine gun roared.

"Kill! Kill!" came cries from the cherry-red men. Doc and his aides were surrounded.

LONG TOM replaced Ham at the laboratory door. The dapper lawyer, Renny and Johnny, grabbed hold of the contacts to the queer, battery-appearing machines.

Motors hummed.

Monk suddenly squealed, came running back. "Out of bombs," he bellowed, "and one of those mugs almost touched me!"

Doc nodded. "It is time to go," he said.

And it was time to go.

Yardoff and Hoskins had discovered that although the glass bombs made a terrific roar, they were practically harmless. The cherry-red men were so inflamed they did not think of danger at all.

Doc ran toward the maddened convicts. His men followed.

A small, runty killer was in the lead of the pack. He was bleeding from a score of wounds, but his bloodstained hands bore mute witness that he had slain his share of victims.

The bronze man halted directly before him. The runty killer raised his knife.

Long Tom's breath came in sharply. Doc no longer was cherry-red; the electricity that had been in his body was gone. If the killer even touched him, that touch would be fatal!

One of Doc's hands shot out. It was sheathed in a rubber glove. It caught the killer's wrist, threw him back.

"Wait!" the bronze man said.

The average man could not have done it. It is doubtful that even Ham, with all his power of oratory, with all his knowledge of how to grip attention, could have done it.

But Doc Savage did. The horde stopped.

The bronze man's flake-gold eyes swept over them. There was something hypnotic in his eyes.

"Look at me," he said. "Look at me carefully. A few moments ago, I was cherry-red, even as you are. I, too, was doomed to death. I am not now."

A gasp of awe went up from the killers. The bronze man had seized the only thing, had said the only thing that would have halted their rush for long, that would have brought the light of sanity back to their eyes.

"My friends and I have solved the secret of how to get rid of the living fire," Doc said.

Behind him, Yardoff and Hoskins had reached the door of the laboratory. They paused for a moment, fearing a trick. But it could only be seconds before they smashed through. The bronze man paid no attention, spoke as if he had hours for the task.

"You will find three machines in the laboratory," he went on. "Three at a time, grab hold of the control handles that are attached to them. You will become normal, will no longer be walking dead men."

A scream of excited jubilation came from one of the killers. That was all that was necessary.

The next instant they were sweeping past Doc and his men, the thought of killing them forgotten.

Knives flashed again as they fought to be the first at the machines that would mean life if they could ever escape.

When Yardoff and Hoskins thrust open the laboratory door, Doc and his men had vanished.

JOHNNY tried to take the lead. He thought he knew the path that led to the submarine.

"If we get away now," Long Tom argued, "we can come back later, save what men are still alive. If we delay, we'll be dead and no one will survive."

Doc Savage nodded his agreement.

"You figured it out, Doc, you know what it is all about?" Monk asked pridefully.

"Of course he did, stupid, or we wouldn't have any chance at all!" Ham gibed.

Doc and his aides raced into a maze of tunnelways. Some of them were so low they could hardly pass through them. Others were high, and winding. Sounds of shooting and shouting became dim.

There was only the steady, monotonous roar.

"I'm completely nonplussed," Johnny confessed.

"If you mean lost, I am, too," Long Tom said.

Doc moved in the lead. He turned in a direction that seemed directly opposite the right one to Johnny, but the geologist gulped and said nothing.

The six slid forward on silent feet. The noise of shooting grew more loud. Now and then a shriek could be heard plainly. Tommy guns roared. Occasionally there was the blast of a grenade.

Tension grew. For the first time in their careers, Doc and his men were completely without weapons. Cherry-red men might jump from any of the side passageways they passed. If they did, Doc and his aides would be helpless.

A face appeared ahead of them. It was the face of one of Stinger Salvatore's thugs.

The killer yelled gleefully; he yanked up his gun to fire.

Doc's hand shot out. A rock sped through the air with unerring accuracy. It caught the killer on the nose. Blood spurted, blinded him.

Howling vengefully, the thug opened fire. But he could not see. His shots went wild.

"Come," said Doc.

If the six had moved fast before, now they fairly flew. Doc did not seem to hesitate. Without a second's pause he moved from one corridor to the others.

The bronze man had not been to the submarine, but that appeared to make no difference. And it didn't. From the slant of the passageways and the geological structure of the walls, Doc figured out the only direction in which the underground stream would lie.

And if his men had felt tense before, now they felt doubly so. Not only were Petrod Yardoff and Hoskins after them, not only would they most likely die if they encountered the cherry-red convicts, but they knew Stinger Salvatore would realize that he could not let them escape alive, that he would go to any length to stop them.

A sigh of relief was wrenched suddenly from Long Tom. A heavy door had loomed ahead.

Monk squealed happily. Before Doc could stop him, he raced in the lead, grabbed at the lock on the door.

There was a sudden flash. Monk was hurled through the air, to land sprawling.

HAM raced to the hairy chemist's side. "Monk! Monk!" he pleaded. "Speak to me! Speak to me!"

"Why should I, you overripe specimen of a razor-back pig?" Monk's words came weakly— but he could speak.

Ham leaped to his feet. He was as nearly flustered as it was possible for an astute lawyer to be. It always embarrassed him when Monk caught him showing emotion of any kind.

"You—you. I'll slit your gullet when I get my sword cane back!" he raged.

"The machines did not take all the electricity from our bodies," Doc explained. "I was afraid that they would not, since we did not have time to do a thorough job."

The bronze man took a small glass bottle from his breechcloth. It was one Long Tom had watched him fill while he was in the laboratory.

Quickly, Doc poured out liquid. He ran it from the tip of one finger, up his arm, across his shoulders and down the other arm.

Without hesitation he stepped toward the door. He placed one hand on the ground. With the other he touched the metal.

There was a streak of flame. It followed exactly the path of the liquid. Doc was unhurt. He opened the door without difficulty.

"Juice will seek the easiest conductor," Long Tom explained to Renny. "What juice there was left in Doc shot out along the line of liquid metal, without hurting him."

The second door was also opened easily. In front of them lay the submarine, deck awash in the huge, subterranean stream.

Sounds of fighting came clearer behind them. Their pursuers, battling among themselves, but each eager to grab Doc and his men, were growing closer.

"Safe!" Johnny shouted. He raced along the tiny wharf to the sub.

Doc delayed a moment, a faint frown creasing his bronze forehead.

There was no sign of life about the submarine.

Johnny threw up the hatch, dropped down inside. The others followed.

As Doc landed, men seemed to pour out onto them from all sides.

They were the sailors who handled the sub. Some held deadly guns. Others were armed with heavy wrenches.

## Chapter XIX
### THE SUB AFIRE

SOMEWHERE nearby a girl screamed. It was the voice of Virginia Hoskins.

"Help! Help!" she cried.

A gun was pointing directly at Monk. The gun went off when the hairy chemist jumped at the man behind it.

Ordinarily Monk respected a gun. He knew how quickly one could end the life of even the strongest man. But the pure terror in Virginia

Hoskins' voice had made him forget all ordinary caution.

His very recklessness saved him. The sailor shot at the place where Monk had been. Monk was no longer there.

His long, apelike arms swinging, animal noises coming unconsciously from him, the hairy chemist went into battle. He knocked the sailor out with one punch, turned hungrily for more.

Ham was jabbing with the scientific accuracy of the trained boxer. He missed his sword cane, but he could fight just as well as the average-trained ring man.

Renny's huge arms were working pistonlike. His bony monstrosities of fists crunched jaws or skulls with equal facility.

Johnny was probably the poorest fighter of all Doc's aides, but he was far better than average. And he was giving an excellent account of himself.

The geologist was frankly angry, not so much at the attack, as at what that attack might mean.

Johnny wanted to come back to the underground caverns when he could work uninterrupted, when he could have time to study the queer geological strata, prepare papers on it that would confound his scientific associates.

He did not approve of being trapped at the last moment, of losing out when all seemed won. He was expressing that disapproval with straight rights and lefts, interspersed with a few well-aimed kicks at shins.

Doc alone seemed to be taking no very active part in the mêlée. And that was strange. For ordinarily the bronze man was in the front rank, leading even causes that appeared hopeless.

The bronze man's eyes swept the room of struggling figures. The room was small, the fighters were constantly getting into each other's way. Knuckles aimed for one jaw quite often smacked the jaw of another.

And creeping toward them, hard faces set in sardonic lines, were two men carrying submachine guns!

The fighters were between Doc and the approaching killers. He could not get at them. Soon those weapons would swing into action.

And from the look on the faces of the men carrying the guns, they wouldn't care if a few of their own men got killed, as long as Doc and his crew were wiped out.

"Cease fighting! Drop to the floor!" Doc roared.

Monk groaned; Renny seemed to want to argue. But none hesitated.

Doc's aides did not know what it was all about, but they trusted the bronze man implicitly.

Without hesitation they dropped.

*Br-r-r-r-r-r-r!*

A Tommy gun spoke. Slugs tore over the heads of Doc's aides. It was aimed directly at the bronze man.

He was no longer there. He had dived through a hatchway behind him.

SOME sailors tore frantically in pursuit. Others paused to tie up the five men who had dropped to the floor.

Renny's face was a study. He did not need to be told why Doc had acted as he had, but he liked a fight almost as much as Monk did, despite his disapproving features.

Doc had seen the killers approach, his men realized, had known some of them might be killed, even if they could overcome all their foes in the end.

And the bronze man would try any strategy rather than permit one of his aides to be killed.

His strategy was now plain. He had drawn all attention to himself, was willing to play a lone hand against the dozen or more men who were on the boat.

A man with a short, black beard—the one who had first conducted Long Tom and Johnny before Yardoff—issued crisp instructions, his beard bobbing energetically.

"The bronze devil cannot get off this boat," he said in his queerly accented voice. "He is the one Yardoff most wished. Try to get him alive if possible, but if not—kill him. He is dangerous."

Ham was forced to grin. "Black-beard" evidently hadn't heard all the fighting in the big caverns, did not know that possibly by this time Yardoff had no interest except in his own safety.

But it was understandable that the sailors did not know. The doors leading into the caverns were thick and heavy. Noise could not be heard through them.

The searchers went to work swiftly but cautiously. They knew their boat, knew every possible hiding place, and hiding places are not so many on pigboats where every inch of space must have its use.

One by one, those searchers disappeared. At first their absence was not noted.

They would drift toward the battery room, enter—then all sign of them would cease. Each of them was armed. It seemed unlikely that even if the bronze man were hiding there that he could overcome them all without at least one being able to fire a warning shot.

The black-bearded leader returned to the control room. His eyes were puzzled as he noticed how few men he had left. He called. There was no answer.

The puzzled look was replaced by one of slight alarm. He sniffed the air.

"Gas!" he rapped suddenly. "The bronze devil has gotten to the chemicals in the battery room, has made a gas!"

The black-bearded man raced toward the battery room. His remaining sailors were at his back.

"Be careful," he warned, "Savage is tricky. He may have figured out a way to save himself."

He thrust open the door, stood at one side, gun ready. His mouth dropped open.

Inside the battery room, the floor was covered with sprawled figures. In the center of those figures was the big form of Doc Savage.

"S-strange," the black-bearded man muttered.

A peculiar expression crossed his face. He turned, tried to flee. His legs would not carry him. He slumped, went down. Behind him, sailors crumpled to the floor.

Above, Doc's five aides were bound and tied so that they could not move. The gas from the battery room spread toward them.

NOR were things going well for those in the caverns.

The big, bluish-lighted rooms held mute evidence of the carnage that raged. Of the more than one hundred convicts who had been alive less than an hour before, fewer than two score remained.

Stinger was practically without aid. That puzzled him.

Weapons that his men had carried had suddenly turned into death agencies for their owners. Flame had spurted, the killers had died.

Stinger did not know that the bodies of his men had become filled with electricity, that the metal of the guns had caused death-dealing shocks. But he had been smart enough to throw his gun away when he saw electrical sparks play along the weapons of others.

He found a glass pistol, went on. The humming noise of the caverns, the wild screams of the maddened convicts, acted on the flashily dressed gangster's nerves, also, but he did not know it.

He thought he was sane, that everyone else was crazy.

A group of cherry-red men plunged into view. In front of them, running for his life, was the barrel-shaped figure of Clement Hoskins.

Stinger Salvatore's lips were back, his unblinking, steely eyes filled with desperate purpose. He pulled the trigger. Hoskins staggered. The bullet had caught him high up, near a shoulder.

A smaller man would have gone down. Hoskins did not. He proved that his big body was not fat, but the powerful, solid muscle he had bragged about.

A deadly grin wreathed his moon face. He brought his own gun up carefully. As Stinger fired a second time, Hoskins pulled the trigger.

Lead from Stinger's gun plucked Hoskins' sleeve. Hoskins scarcely noticed it. A third eye appeared in Stinger's forehead. This eye was unblinking, also. But it was not steely, it was black that rapidly changed to crimson. He was dead.

Yardoff was running down the corridor that led to the submarine. He was pursued by several of the cherry-red men. Their flashing knives foretold his fate if he was caught.

Clement Hoskins lumbered after then. He ran slowly. He could not run fast. His strength was seeping from the bullet wound in his shoulder.

A queer, misshapen figure slid into the corridor almost at his back. The man had an almost flat head, with little, deep-sunken red eyes.

"Hoskins!" called Professor Torgle.

Hoskins turned with a snarl. It was then Torgle leaped, plunged his knife deep into the barrel-shaped man's heart.

CLEMENT HOSKINS was dead, but he did not know it. One of his hands reached out, caught Torgle by the wrist, held him fast. The other encircled the misshapen man's throat. Slowly that fist tightened. Torgle scratched and kicked, he clawed and fought.

Hoskins went down. Torgle went with him; strange, strangling noises came from his throat.

After a while they both lay still.

Petrod Yardoff was more clever. He tricked his pursuers by dodging off, taking a winding passageway. But he made one mistake, too. He did not take time to close the doors when he passed them.

Panting, he came through the second door, saw the submarine resting peacefully on the subterranean stream.

He paused, looked behind him for a moment, took off a rubber glove to wipe his forehead.

It was at that moment that Doc's big figure rose from the group of sprawled men in the battery room. An oxygen tablet in his mouth had saved the bronze man from being overcome, while the others had dropped.

Swiftly he turned on blower fans. The gas he had concocted with chemicals in the battery room brought quick unconsciousness, but its effects would not linger long.

Then the bronze man raced to the control room, freed his men.

"Tie up the sailors," Doc said calmly. "Then get to your posts. We are ready to leave."

As his aides rushed to obey, Doc looked out the conning hatch.

It was then Petrod Yardoff saw him.

The scarecrow man realized Doc and his crew had seized the submarine, that all his own plans to escape had been blocked. He knew then that he was lost.

But he knew something else, too, knew one final trick that would carry those who had blocked him to death.

An almost insane shriek came from his lips. He leaped to a switch beside the lead door. He shoved the switch home.

Instantly, water began to boil about the submarine. A wire carrying a tremendous load of electricity had been hooked to the pigboat. In a moment its plates became red-hot.

It was a flaming submarine of death!

## Chapter XX
### JOURNEY'S END

DOC had only an instant of warning. He saw the switch as Petrod Yardoff lunged toward it.

"Stand on rubber!" the bronze man shouted. His voice penetrated every part of the submarine. His men heard. They obeyed.

Several of the unconscious sailors were touching metal. It was unfortunate, but there was no hope for them. They were electrocuted instantly, dying as if they had gone to the electric chair for murders they had committed.

The submarine was rapidly becoming unbearably hot due to the tremendous current that was running through the metal, and the strong resistance of that metal.

Something had to be done, and done fast, or motors inside the pigboat would become worthless.

A terrible leer was on Petrod Yardoff's face.

Doc went into action. A diving suit was in one corner of the control room. Evidently one of the crew had been inspecting the bottom of the mysterious stream.

With dazzling speed, the bronze man donned the suit. He grabbed a pair of wire-cutting pliers. The handles were taped, but that seemed slight protection against the enormous flow of electricity that must be coming into the submarine.

The wire was fastened near the nose of the sub.

Doc took a long breath, popped out of the conning hatch. The next moment and he was running down the top of the sub, had slipped into the water.

The water surrounding the pigboat was so hot the diving suit immediately became a turkish bath. Steam clouded the glass.

Working blind, the bronze man fumbled for the wire.

Frantic cries were coming from inside the submarine. It was becoming unbearably hot there. And Doc's aides did not know what was happening, did not know whether the bronze man had escaped or not.

The pliers encountered the wire. Sparks flew.

With steady hand, Doc slipped the cutters over the wire, applied pressure.

Despite the tape on the handle of the pliers, despite the rubber gloves of the diving suit, a sudden surge of electricity went through the bronze man's body.

He was thrown in the air, tossed about by the mighty, invisible force.

Doc's lips came together hard, his flake-gold eyes almost closed. With the last ounce of his strength, he pressed the pliers home.

The wire parted.

IT was seconds before the bronze man recovered enough to scramble back on the boat. Yardoff stood as a man amazed. His last hole-card had failed.

Once more he wiped perspiration from his forehead. He took a step toward the boat—and halted.

Monk and Renny appeared out of the conning tower. Renny's face was grim and merciless. Monk gave a sigh of relief as he saw that Doc was uninjured.

It was then that the surviving cherry-red men appeared.

They came running through the lead door noiselessly, running as a wolf pack runs when the kill is near. A terrible sound came from their throats as they saw Yardoff.

The scarecrow man screamed—once.

As far as he could see there was death behind him and death in front of him, for he could not understand that others might be more merciful than he, that Doc might save him.

"Back to your posts, prepare to dive," Doc Savage ordered his aides.

There was an unusual note of urgency in his voice. Monk looked wonderingly. He could not see what could cause the bronze man to speak so when all seemed won.

Then he saw what Doc had seen seconds earlier, and for once he lost his color. He was almost trembling as he raced into the submarine. And Renny was right behind him.

"Come on, Yardoff! Come now!" Doc shouted.

Petrod Yardoff hesitated. He looked behind him. The pack of cherry-red men were almost upon him. Their weapons were raised.

Certainly there was no mercy there. There might be some hope with Doc. Yardoff made up his mind. He raced forward, out on the tiny dock toward the submarine.

Had he looked behind him, he would have seen a strange thing then. The cherry-red convicts had halted. They tried frantically to yell. Their voices seemed paralyzed.

With one accord, they turned, raced back in the direction from which they had come.

But Yardoff did not see. He stretched out one hand, grabbed a rail to lift him up.

There was a sudden sheet of fire. Flame played over the scarecrow body of the man who was playing for millions.

The odor of burned flesh came into the air. Petrod Yardoff died as others had died from the living flame. He died from a trap of his own devising, only he had made it for others.

He had forgotten to replace his rubber glove after he had wiped his face.

Doc glanced once more at the shore. The long, electricity-charged wire he had cut was still dancing. Sparks were flying from it. Those sparks had already done their work well—too well.

A fuse was flaming slowly. It was leading under the leaden door where buried explosive lay waiting.

"Crash dive!" ordered Doc.

THE submarine shuddered. It smashed downward, under the water, as its tanks were thrown wide open to fill at once.

"Full speed ahead!"

Doc gave the order before the submarine could reach the bottom of the subterranean stream. He knew he must do so.

And barely in time.

There was a muffled roar, a noise that did not echo loud inside the submarine, now underwater and nosing toward the outlet that led to the sea.

But if the noise was not loud, the results of that noise more than made up for any lack of sound.

There was a rush of water. The submarine was lifted up, hurled backward as if by a gigantic hand. Its propellers raced; its motors labored.

The explosive under the leaden door evidently had been buried deeply enough so that water from the stream was released into the underground cavern.

Possibly the blast opened up a new passageway into the lower depths of the land of living fire.

Only the fact that the submarine was in the big stream saved it. Had it been caught in a narrow passageway, even its strong hull would have been crushed under the beating it would have taken.

As it was it was almost an hour before the surge of waters passed, before the battle for safety finally ended.

Then Doc headed toward the open sea.

VIRGINIA HOSKINS was still pale. She had passed through much. But her cheeks became a faint pink when she saw the admiring gaze Monk could not keep from his face. The girl had escaped being electrocuted by standing on a rubber mat after hearing Doc's warning.

Doc turned over the controls to Renny, let the big engineer show his stuff as he piloted the way through the twisting tunnel, fought against the surge of the tide.

The bronze man with the others relaxed in the ward room, relaxed for the first time in hours.

"Now will you tell me what it was all about?" Monk demanded.

Doc nodded. "As nearly as possible," he said. "To begin with, I think Yardoff and Hoskins first discovered the wealth of native mineral in the upper passageways of the cavern. A majority of those minerals, particularly pyrites, are vital to the munitions industry.

"Many nations are arming. Some wish to hide that fact. If they bought in the open market, they could not keep it secret. Yardoff was once an agent for an international munitions firm. His reputation was shady. Hoskins contacted him. Together they smuggled out the minerals they had found."

"Bootlegged it by submarine," Ham said with satisfaction.

"Then they discovered the lower cavern, the cavern with the living fire. The ore there, as we all know, was highly charged with electricity. It operated the furnaces of the glass factory; the very ore itself provided light.

"But they needed men to work there, men who would not talk. Hence the prison breaks which they engineered with the Stinger's help. That is where Z-2 came in. As an F.B.I. man, he was investigating a Federal prison break. He tried to get away, and knew something of the peril he faced, but even then he died."

"But," objected Long Tom, "where did Hoskins and Yardoff hope to profit? They could have used the ore for power, that would have brought them a fortune, and legitimately."

"Yes," Doc agreed. "They could. But did you not notice how hard and how heavy that ore was? If they could have learned how to smelt it, how to work it, so that it would have been used, they would have had an impenetrable armor plate, something worth many millions."

"So that's why they wanted us!" Johnny gasped.

The bronze man nodded. "Without doubt, that is why."

Virginia Hoskins shuddered. "But I still don't see where the horrible living-fire death came in."

"The ore has strange electrical qualities," Doc explained gently. "The longer the human body was exposed to it, the more electricity it absorbed, until the convicts were walking dynamos. If they touched anything that grounded them, they died. If they touched a person not affected as they were, that person died. That was apparent from the first. Z-2 touched an oil barrel with his bare hand. The man at the office had the sole of one shoe eaten away by quick-acting acid. Hoskins and Yardoff, however, evidently had a battery arrangement much as we used to de-electrize ourselves."

Johnny wet his lips. "A-and what was the ore, Doc?" he mumbled at last.

"You are a geologist, Johnny. Don't you know?"

"I think I do. I am almost afraid to say."

"But you are right, you must be right," Doc said. "We were privileged to be among the first to see the ore that comprises the core of the earth. There was a bulge there, one that brought that core comparatively close to the surface.

"No one else has ever seen it, although scientific tests prove it must be of the hardness and density that we found. It could have changed the history of the world—made into armor plate. The nation that owned it would be unbeatable."

"I—I'm going to take a vacation!" Monk blurted suddenly. His eyes were on the beautiful face of Virginia Hoskins. "When we get out, I'm going to visit Palm Springs, that is—" He gulped, became as vivid a red as he had appeared in the cavern.

"He means," Ham explained maliciously, "that he is going to visit there if you are anywhere near, Miss Hoskins."

"I am going there, also," Johnny said. "The phenomenon must be investigated. I wish to probe further the strange workings of the labyrinth."

But Johnny and Monk were mistaken. Johnny lost all interest in Sandrit and the desert when he read the first newspaper he saw as they returned to civilization.

The newspaper told of a strange eruption that had occurred on the desert.

Citizens of Sandrit were quoted as telling of a strange gun fight that had preceded the eruption, but authorities were inclined to doubt that.

But a glass factory owned by Clement Hoskins, who was missing, had suddenly been swallowed by the earth. In its place was a huge, bubbling stream, heated by some strange, subterranean force. And queerly, the water was salty.

The sea had hidden nature's secret.

THE END

---

## Coming in DOC SAVAGE Volume #9:

# THE MAJII

He had all the power of mystic India; power over people and things. To change glass into precious jewels was as nothing—and, Doc Savage learned, crime was not unknown. See Doc overcome intrigue and mysticism with courage and science!

Then, the Man of Bronze encounters …

# THE GOLDEN MAN

Was he supernatural or charlatan? How could he know all the past, and all the future, too? It's a job for Doc Savage—and one that gives him the most exciting experience of his unusual career.

Don't miss these two action-packed novels in *DOC SAVAGE Volume #9!* Ask your bookseller to reserve your copies today!

# HAROLD DAVIS, PULP INVENTOR

Writer Frank Gruber once said of Lester Dent, "He was the best gimmick and gadget creator who ever lived. He would have been terrific on the present-day tricks-and-gadget spy stories."

While he was ghosting Doc Savage, newspaperman Harold A. Davis ran a close second. In addition to Doc's emergency belt kit—an adaptation of the U.S. Army cartridge belt—Davis conceived numerous new devices for the Man of Bronze to use in his exciting adventures.

One of these was introduced in 1939. Doc Savage captures from a spy ring an ingenious communications device worn as a wristwatch, adopting it for his own use. Thereafter he and his aides communicate secretly with one another via this method.

Microwave radio transmissions trigger silent infra-red heat pulses in the watch casing, which are then felt on the skin. Some models were merely receivers. Others transmitted in code as well. They first appear as standard Doc Savage equipment in *The Crimson Serpent.*

After that, not a single subsequent Davis Doc failed to feature them.

When Davis stopped writing Doc Savage in 1940, the watches vanished from the series, never to return.

These devices harken back to the "telewatches" Lester Dent had earlier introduced in 1933's *Pirate of the Pacific*, which received closed-circuit television transmissions only. What influence any of these handy gadgets had on Dick Tracy's creator Chester Gould is unknown. Tracy's famous two-way wrist radio first appeared in January 1946.

Special protective suits, designed for different needs, litter Davis' novels. A transparent garment resembling an insulated asbestos suit debuted in *The Land of Fear* in 1937. Other such outfits were later employed to protect Doc from specific threats, often used in conjunction with the bronze man's oxygen tablets—chemical pills that provided the body with necessary oxygen without the need for respiration. A version of the suit seen in *The Mountain Monster*, augmented by a fire-quenching chemical foam bubble system, was used to escape a crashed plane.

A more elaborate coverall suit, fitted with a transparent hood, was designed to function like a portable chemical refrigerator. It saves the lives of Doc and Long Tom when they are trapped in a blazing building in another novel. When they emerge, they resemble walking snowmen, thanks to cold-producing coils filled with ammonia and other cooling chemicals circulating within the garment.

There is also a variation used as a diving suit which doesn't require oxygen tanks, thanks to Doc's chemical pills. It saw service in *Devils of the Deep,* Davis' final pre-war Doc.

It's not too much of a stretch to imagine that Batman's assorted special costumes were inspired by Harold Davis ideas. The Dark Knight kept a battery of alternate outfits designed for unusual situations, such as extreme or hostile environments.

Doc Savage seldom carried offensive weapons. But Davis came up with unusual defensive devices such as a trick pocketknife rigged to fire a single-shot mercy bullet. His version of the Savage supermachine pistol differs from Dent's in that the ammo drum is mounted atop the breech, and when in operation revolves like a World War I-era Lewis gun. Presumably this is a variant model.

Some of the Colorado-born writer's concepts were decidedly over-the-top, like the atomic cannon Doc Savage employed in *The Golden Peril* to defend the Valley of the Vanished.

Davis loved trotting out Doc's personal dirigible. Just as much, he enjoyed spectacularly blowing them apart. But this was a plot device he learned from Dent. Davis attached rocket tubes to it in one adventure, turning it into a crude rocket ship. In Davis' *The Mountain Monster,* one of Doc's big transport planes was also fitted with auxiliary rocket engines designed for emergency evasive maneuvers, making it a prototype rocket plane.

The final adventure of the *Helldiver,* Doc's unique submarine, was *Devils of the Deep.* For this last voyage, Davis equipped the aging sub with new scientific devices, including the sonar-like "propelcheck," which enabled the U-boat's crew to identify any lurking vessel from the sound of her propellers.

Harold A. Davis was also the father of Chemistry, Ham Brooks' South American pet ape. It was perhaps his most infamous creation. Introduced in *Dust of Death,* Chemistry was a tiny monkey who closely resembled a miniature Monk Mayfair. But Davis often forgot that fact. In several of his yarns, Chemistry was the size of a full-grown gorilla!

Harold Davis often wrote his Doc novels while working the telegraph desk of the *New York Daily News.* No doubt some of his ideas came to him while reading Associated Press stories as they moved over the wire. Many Davis Docs reflected the warclouds sweeping over Europe in the late 1930s.

—Will Murray

*Richard Henry Savage*
*Senior Major U.S.V. Engineer Brigade*
*War with Spain 1898*

# HIS NAME WAS SAVAGE by Will Murray

The three greatest superheroes ever produced by the Street & Smith fiction factory in the 1930s were The Shadow, Doc Savage, and Richard Henry Benson, better known as The Avenger.

Although written by three different writers, these pulp greats were all brainstormed by the team of S&S business manager Henry William Ralston and editor John L. Nanovic.

The Shadow, Doc and The Avenger had another common connection, too. They were all inspired, to varying degrees, by the life of one man!

As John Nanovic explained, "Doc was Bill Ralston's idea. When he talked to me the first time, he had 70% or 80% of everything worked out. He suggested we ought to have a character with science adventures.... He mentioned that he knew a person named Savage and began to describe him. Of course, he could have been describing himself because Ralston was a big powerful man."

Richard Henry Savage is today so obscure the world has virtually forgotten him. But in his day he was one of the most colorful figures of the late 19th century. To call him a soldier of fortune might be accurate, but that doesn't do justice to the true breadth of his short but remarkable life.

Dick Savage was an amazing American. Born in Utica, New York on June 12, 1846, he grew up in San Francisco during California's wild Gold-rush era where his father, Richard Savage, Senior, was Collector of Internal Revenue. Appointed to this office by President Lincoln, Savage Senior was at the forefront of squelching Rebel attempts to align California with the South at the outbreak of the Civil War during the winter of 1860-61.

Although only 15, Savage Junior meanwhile ran off to join the California Legion for service in Virginia. His upset father found him, and wrangled a discharge for his underage son, sparing him from the horrors of war and probably a premature end.

Evidently, this bitter disappointment didn't cool the younger Savage's military aspirations, for in 1864 his father used his influence to get him appointed to West Point. Young Savage made the dangerous journey on a Pacific Mail liner, which had to dodge the gold-hunting privateers of the Confederacy.

It was at West Point that Richard Henry Savage flowered into the unusual individual that he was destined to be. "He was at this time a youth of most striking appearance," wrote a classmate, Eugene Oscar Fechet, "very tall and very thin, solemn of countenance, a sharp angular face, piercing black eyes, aquiline nose and heavy overhanging eyebrows; his courteous address and readiness of speech quickly caught and held the attention."

This is almost a word for word description of the unmasked face of The Shadow! But in other ways, Savage most resembled the chief character he later inspired, his namesake Doc Savage.

"Gifted with a clear, logical and analytic mind, joined to a rich and glowing imagination, and the faculty of clothing his thoughts in concise and appropriate language, and with a most tenacious and marvelous memory, Savage was equally at home in the intricacies of the higher Mathematics as in studies like Law and Ethics," recalled Fechet.

Savage graduated from West Point in 1868 as a Brevet Second Lieutenant, Corps of Engineers, the sixth in a class of 55, by most measures the most brilliant Cadet of his time there.

Assigned to Company "D" Engineer Batallion, he was stationed at Yerba Buena Island in San Francisco harbor, but did survey work throughout California and Arizona. As engineer officer and personal aide-de-camp to General George H. Thomas, his fearless discharge of dangerous duties on the Frontier captured official attention.

Despite the prospects of a promising career, Lieutenant Savage resigned from the Army in 1870 and spent two years in Europe, ostensibly to travel prior to settling down to a career in business.

This may have been a pretext, because soon after President Grant conferred on Savage several diplomatic appointments. He served as U.S. vice-consul in Marseilles and Rome in 1872, the next year marrying Madame Anna Josephine Schuble of Berlin in the German Consulate in Washington, D.C. Her father was the court chamberlain to the Emperor of Germany. They had one daughter, who later became Mme. Anatole de Cat Carriere, wife to a chamberlain to the Emperor of Russia.

Within three years, Savage was attached to the Egyptian Army with the rank of major, as staff engineer and confidential military secretary to General Charles P. Stone. Clearly, he was pursuing no ordinary career.

Returning to the States in 1874, Savage was appointed as a joint commissioner on the Texas-Mexican frontier, then served as chief engineer of the Corpus Christi and Rio Grand Railroad Company in Texas. He also constructed various architectural ironworks in San Francisco in partnership with his father and his brother, John. There, he became embroiled in the problem of the Kearney-Sand Lot Riots in 1877 as Chief Military Executive Officer of the Committee of Safety, a Citizen's Vigilance organization. At this time, Savage was a colonel in the 2nd Cavalry, National Guard.

"During this carnival of unrest and agitation," wrote Eugene Fechet, "when demagogues were poisoning the public mind, and when it was a common occurrence for mobs to hoot at, shout down and hurl missiles at any speaker bold enough to oppose the popular side, Col. Savage at a public meeting held in San Francisco, was the only prominent citizen of the Law and Order side that was allowed to speak, and he not only fearlessly exposed the dangerous fallacies that were leading to social and civic anarchy, but was allowed to state the whole case of Law and Order in its entirety. Old residents of San Francisco when recalling those stormy days, have tesified that Savage's eloquent, daring and convincing speech was the turning point that marked the high-water mark of riot and misrule. He was presented with handsome testimonial by the citizens of San Francisco for his services in behalf of good government."

For a time, Savage practiced law in this city with his brother, Lincoln. Then either restlessness or duty called him to foreign lands. Between 1884-91 he traveled extensively through the Orient, visiting Turkey, Japan, Korea, China, Asia Minor and Honduras. His position—if official—is unclear, but his political connections indicate State Department work of a highly secretive type. Savage was also supposed to be an accomplished linguist. Lighthouses on the Red Sea were erected under his supervision.

"Colonel Savage is matched in social and personal experience by few men," the *Chicago Herald* reported in 1893. "His range has been from Siberia to the Red Sea, from the wilds of Central America and the plains to the Greek Sea and the Winter Palace.

"Tall, energetic and animated, his conversation teems with memories of many lands and grades. It is hard to realize that Cortina the raider, William Walker, Lola Montes, and Billy Florence are companion negatives with Pius IX, General Grant, Ismail Pasha and Denis Kearney in one man's mind. From the frontier camp-fire to the Coliseum, from the Sand Lot to a palace ball, the traveler has threaded the mazes of a strange life."

Updated to 20th century terms, those lines could have been used to describe globe-trotter Lamont Cranston, Clark Savage, Junior, or Richard Henry Benson, AKA The Avenger.

Savage was admitted to the New York bar in 1890, but a distaste for criminal law and political chicanery made him revert to an earlier interest in letters. He had been contributing articles and poetry to a forgotten periodical called *Golden Era* as early as 1861. Savage turned to writing while convalescing from a combination of jungle fever and exposure incurred during a trip to Honduras. Former West Point classmate David Stewart Denison housed Savage in his Lake George, New York country home during the protracted recovery.

"While slowly convalescing," wrote Eugene Fechet, "Denison, recalling the old days at the 'Point' when Dick Savage's brilliant and witty skits were the life of the Corps, suggested to him that he kill the weary hours of inactivity by writing up his experiences. The result was *My Official Wife*. This dashing story was first a mere sketch of five chapters but was received with such marked favor by his friends to whom he read it that he was inspired to rewrite and extend it into a novel."

*My Official Wife* is the exciting tale of Major Arthur Bainbridge Lenox who, while crossing the Russian frontier by train, is guiled into allowing a mysterious young woman claiming to be the wife of Lenox's former West Point classmate into posing as his wife. In reality, Helene Marie is a Nihilist determined to convey a secret cipher to her anti-Czarist cell. The novel is complicated by the fact that Major Lenox's daughter has married into the Czar's court. If the imposture is unmasked, both face Siberia—or worse.

"The story is said to be literally true up to the arrival at St. Petersburg," claimed Fechet. "Savage had left Madame Savage at Saint Heliers, Isle of Jersey for a run to St. Petersburg where they had friends. It was in the fall of 1884, just after the killing of the Czar and the police were in an ugly mood. The heroine of the story was a daring conspirator; she was later captured at Wilna, Russia, and Col. Savage believed she was quietly strangled and buried, as she was never heard of again."

Clearly autobiographical, the novel is packed with tantalizing hints about Dick Savage's amazing life. A self-described veteran of many armies, Major Lenox talks about his adventures with Don Carlos in Spain and recalls fighting under Chinese Gordon in the Sudan. One wonders if the author, too, was known to the Carlists under the *nom de guerre,* "To-the-knife" Savage, or hailed by the British Army in Egypt as "Bull-dog" Savage.

*My Official Wife* was published by the Home Publishing Company in 1891, and later appeared in dozens of foreign-language editions and was adapted for the stage. Its huge success launched Dick Savage on a long career as a popular novelist. Most of his novels were published in America by Home, which produced forerunners of the modern trade paperback. Their star writer was one Archibald Clavering Gunter, forgotten now, but extremely popular in his day. His humorous novel of an American tourist in Europe *Mr. Barnes of New York* was an early bestseller, and Home kept Gunter busy turning out similar works. Public demand for more adventures of sturdy Americans getting the best of snobbish Europeans prompted the Home editors to impress Richard Henry Savage into full-time production. He produced some forty novels and story collections, emulating Gunter in theme and style so well it was for years rumored that Richard Henry Savage was merely a *nom de plume* of Gunter's.

Savage's books were typical Mauve Decade romantic fiction. Titles like *The Masked Venus, A Modern Corsair, In the Shadow of the Pyramids*, and *The Spider of Truxillo* made good use of Savage's extensive travels and experiences. One interesting book, *The Passing Show,* collected true tales of Savage's exploits from California to Korea. He also dabbled in poetry, but was no dilettante despite his membership in the Société des Auteurs, Paris. He referred to his fiction as "my slush," composing most of it on coarse yellow paper while sitting at a plain deal table. In the manner of pulp writers of all eras, Savage never revised, but confidently submitted first-draft manuscripts. It was said he recorded his story ideas as they came to him on a mirror with soap instead of with pencil and paper. This was a habit he picked up at West Point, where writing materials were forbidden in cadets' rooms. It may possibly have inspired Doc Savage's use of "invisible" chalk for writing secret messages.

Savage's Herculean literary career was interrupted by the Spanish-American War of 1898. Down in Cuba, revolutionists José Marti, Maximo Gomez and Antonio Maceo—nicknamed the Bronze Titan—were faring poorly. When Marti was killed, the U.S. contemplated picking up his fallen flag and going at the oppressive Spaniards. The mysterious sinking of the *USS Maine* in Havana Harbor provided the pretext for war, thanks in part to the machinations of newspaper publisher William Randolph Hearst. Reenlisting, Savage was appointed Senior Major of the Second U.S. Volunteer Engineer Brigade.

The heroic exploits of future President Teddy Roosevelt and his Rough Riders ensured a U.S. victory in short order.

On November 21, 1898, Major Savage's command landed in Cuba and he personally hoisted the first American flag to fly over Havana Province after more than 400 years of Spanish rule, improvising the mast of an abandoned yacht for a flagpole. The Spanish had surrendered, but the peace treaty was not set to go into effect for another month. The armistice hung on his ability to pacify the area. It was Savage's duty to hold the restive Havana Province until the Seventh Corps could reinforce him. Setting up camp on Marianao Hill, his force of nine officers and 233 men surrounded by 28,000 still-armed Spanish troops and Cuban irregulars, Major Savage personally stood guard that first night, sword in hand. When a Spanish officer approached to warn him that he could not restrain his men from coming up the hill, Savage replied, "I can, for we will pile up a wall of your Spanish dead around us! And my country will send a hundred thousand men to find our bodies!"

The Spanish wisely declined to attack Savage's command, which was known as the Butcher Brigade. The city of Marianao soon surrendered. On January 1, 1899, Havana itself was handed over. The war in Cuba was over.

Still weakened by his earlier bout with jungle fever, Savage contracted Yellow Fever in Cuba and was forced to return to the States to recover. But the call to duty proved too strong. He requested service in the Philippines—the other theatre of war—and was commissioned as Senior Captain of the 27th U.S. Volunteer Infantry, then set about readying his company for duty. The effort nearly broke the 53-year-old Savage, and he was honorably discharged for health reasons, while his men sailed without him.

Returning to New York City, Savage took up residence in the Hotel Gerard on West 44th Street and resumed writing. His literary popularity continued to grow. His best work was considered *Prince Schamyl's Wooing, The Little Lady of the Lagunitas* and of course *My Official Wife*, which served as the basis for several early silent films. A collection of short stories, *Our Mysterious Passenger and Other Stories,* was published in hardcover by Street & Smith, replete with a photo of the then-major, showing a stern, mustached countenance that might been the face of Doc Savage's explorer father.

Once again invoking The Shadow, and to a lesser degree Doc Savage, the colonel's home was described as his "sanctum." A veritable museum, it was filled with trophies and other memorabilia of his life and travels, including a treasured silver bowl presented by the Committee of Public Safety in San Francisco for his help in suppressing the Kearny riots of 1877.

Savage's torrent of popular novels continued. They sold well, but like most authors who wrote for the general public, he was sometimes accused of failing to write a book worthy of his potential. To this, Savage replied that if he had two years to do it in, he would pen such a book.

Richard Henry Savage never found those two golden years.

In October 1903, Savage's colorful life came to an ignominious end. While crossing busy Sixth Avenue under the Sixth Avenue elevated trestle on the 3rd, he found himself in a tangle of cars and horse-drawn carriages. Trying to get out of the way of a southbound trolley, the colonel stepped into the path of a Featherbone & Company delivery wagon which knocked him down. The front wheel passed over him before 18-year-old driver George Doyle could pull up his horse, resulting in serious head contusions and five broken ribs.

Savage was taken to Roosevelt Hospital in serious condition, while the hapless Doyle was hauled off to the 47th Street Jail. The next day the *New York Tribune* reported, "Colonel Savage was in no danger, and would undoubtedly recover." But he took a turn for the worse, dying on the night of October 11th, just days before publication of his final novel, *A Monte Cristo in Khaki.* He was 57.

In what must be some sort of cosmic coincidence, exactly a year and a day later, Lester Dent would be born.

On October 12th, Colonel Savage was posthumously elected Commander in Chief, National Spanish-American War Veterans. He was interred at West Point with full military honors. After his death, the *New York Herald* said of him:

"There was no more picturesque figure among American fiction writers of this generation than Richard Henry Savage. The union of the qualities of soldier, traveller, engineer, poet and novelist was produced by a romantic career."

*The New York Times* added: "Colonel Savage had a wide reputation for personal prowess. He was a superb rider and a splendid shot, and had always been an ardent sportsman. He was of athletic build and of a physique which enabled him to endure the most severe privations in his

adventures in all parts of the world, except India and Australia."

The circumstances under which Henry William Ralston met Colonel Savage are not known. Ralston went to work for Street & Smith in 1898, just before the firm published Savage's *Our Mysterious Passenger and Other Stories,* so it's reasonable to assume they came into contact at the original Street & Smith building at 238 William Street. The acquaintance must have been casual; Ralston was still young when Savage died, but he left a vivid impression. Years later, while explaining his ideas about a new adventure hero to John Nanovic, Ralston spoke of a tall and impressive man with hawkish features and a clear, steely gaze. A man who had played many roles in life—soldier, lawyer, diplomat, engineer and author—and who traveled to strange climes. A soldier of fortune. The perfect model for their new character, whom Ralston decided would be a "supreme adventurer." Even his name fit. It was a strong, dashing name. It would do for the new character. Dick Savage would become Doc Savage. Doc, to symbolize his scientific skill, while Savage would suggest a civilized Tarzan. (They borrowed Doc's Christian name from popular actor, Clark Gable.) Like Richard Henry Savage, Clark Savage, Junior would have a namesake father.

Little known or suspected is the fact that over a year before Ralston and Nanovic were preparing Doc Savage for publication, some of Richard Henry Savage's blood was transfused into The Shadow. This occurred in the fourth Shadow tale, *The Red Menace,* where it was first revealed that The Shadow had been a member of the Seventh Star, a Russian secret society in service to the Czar. In this story, when The Shadow unhinges his fire opal ring, the sign of the Seventh Star is revealed engraved on the base. Perhaps Ralston suggested to writer Walter B. Gibson that he graft some of Richard Henry Savage's colorful background (if not hawklike looks) onto the still-developing character. In later years, after The Shadow got rolling, Gibson quietly ignored the outdated Russian backstory for one with an Oriental flavor. This explains why in later novels, when The Shadow pops open the stone, it exposes the sign of the Chow Lee instead.

Both Doc Savage and The Shadow proved enormously successful for Street & Smith. Whenever readers wrote, asking whether Doc had been based on a true-life person, Ralston patiently cited the life of Richard Henry Savage, already half-forgotten by then. Later S&S heroes not inspired by Savage, like The Skipper and The Whisperer, did not fare as well.

So it was no surprise that in 1939, when Ralston and Nanovic were preparing The Avenger for publication, they once again looked to Richard Henry Savage, this time basing retired adventurer Richard Henry Benson on Savage's later life, and making the character a successful amalgam of The Shadow and Doc Savage. Like Dick Savage, Benson had a wife and daughter, and had enjoyed a long career roaming around the globe, working in different exotic professions. But then tragedy struck, turning Benson into the cold-eyed man of steel known as The Avenger.

Neither Lester Dent nor Henry William Ralston ever spoke publicly on the seminal influence Richard Henry Savage had on Doc Savage. For Dent's part, this was something foisted on him. He had his own influences and liked to say, "Doc seems to be an unconscious composite of the physical qualities of Tarzan of the Apes, the detective ability of Sherlock Holmes, the scientific sleuthing mastery of scientific dick Craig Kennedy, and the morals of Jesus Christ."

As for Ralston, he would sometimes answer reader mail with the true story of the original supreme adventurer, but otherwise kept the secret of Dick Savage to himself. But he might have been hinting at the original Savage and his final novel *A Monte Cristo in Khaki* when, on the eve of *Doc Savage*'s cancellation in 1949, he was quoted as saying, "We grabbed him right out of thin air. We made him a surgeon and scientist, because we wanted him to know chemistry, philosophy, and all that stuff. We also made him immensely wealthy—he'd inherited a huge fortune from his father. You might say he was a poor man's Monte Cristo."

*Will Murray is the literary agent for the Estate of Lester Dent, and collaborated posthumously with the Man of Bronze's principal writer on eight* Doc Savage *novels, beginning with* Python Isle.

# THE MEN BEHIND DOC SAVAGE

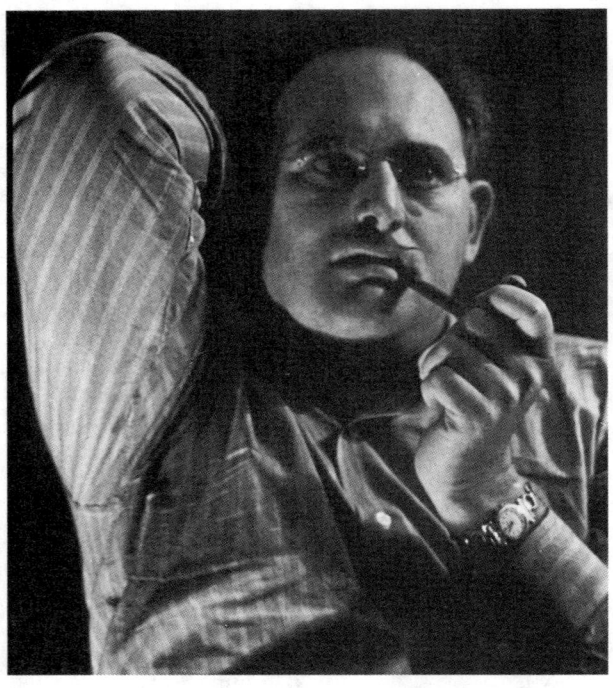

**Lester Dent** (1904-59) could be called the father of the superhero. Writing under the house name "Kenneth Robeson," Dent was the principal writer of *Doc Savage,* producing more than 150 of the Man of Bronze's thrilling pulp adventures.

A lonely childhood as a rancher's son paved the way for his future success as a professional storyteller. "I had no playmates," Dent recalled. "I lived a completely distorted youth. My only playmate was my imagination, and that period of intense imaginative creation which kids generally get over at the age of five or six, I carried till I was twelve or thirteen. My imaginary voyages and accomplishments were extremely real."

Dent began his professional writing career while working as an Associated Press telegrapher in Tulsa, Oklahoma. Learning that one of his coworkers had sold a story to the pulps, Dent decided to try his hand at similarly lucrative moonlighting. He pounded out thirteen unsold stories during the slow night shift before making his first sale to Street & Smith's *Top-Notch* in 1929. The following year, he received a telegram from the Dell Publishing Company offering him moving expenses and a $500-a-month drawing account if he'd relocate to New York and write exclusively for the publishing house.

Dent soon left Dell to pursue a freelance career, and in 1932 was hired to write the lead novels in Street & Smith's new *Doc Savage Magazine.* From 1933-1949, Dent produced Doc Savage thrillers while continuing his busy freelance writing career and eventually adding an aerial photography business.

Dent was also a significant contributor to the legendary *Black Mask* during its golden age, for which he created Miami waterfront detective Oscar Sail. A real-life adventurer, world traveler and member of the Explorers Club, Dent wrote in a variety of genres for magazines ranging from pulps like *Argosy, Adventure* and *Ten Detective Aces* to prestigious slick magazines including *The Saturday Evening Post* and *Collier's*. His mystery novels include *Dead at the Take-off* and *Lady Afraid.* In the pioneering days of radio drama, Dent scripted *Scotland Yard* and the 1934 *Doc Savage* series.

**Harold A. Davis** (1902-55) worked alongside AP telegrapher Lester Dent at the *Tulsa World* before joining the staff of the *New York News American* in 1932. While serving as the *New York Daily News'* assistant telegraph editor from 1935-40, Davis wrote most of his pulp fiction including his Doc Savage novels, some Skipper short stories and his Duke Grant and Bill Wheeler series. He also wrote westerns for *Pete Rice Magazine* and *Wild West Weekly.* Davis pounded out his final Doc Savage novel in April 1940. The following month, he became the first managing editor of Alicia Patterson's *Newsday,* hiring and organizing the newspaper's editorial staff. Davis resigned his *Newsday* position in January 1944, and was replaced by his friend (and fellow Doc Savage ghost) Alan Hathway. He later returned to the *New York Daily News* where he served as a foreign correspondent in Moscow, before relocating to become telegraph editor for the *Los Angeles Daily News.*

Davis ghosted twelve fast-paced Doc Savage novels beginning with *The King Maker* and concluding with *The Exploding Lake* in 1946, including *The Golden Peril* (the classic sequel to *The Man of Bronze*).